Allen Steele was born in Nashville, Tennessee, and received his BA in Communications from New England College and a Masters Degree in Journalism from the University of Missour[illegible]n, he worked as a staff w[illegible]e, Missouri, and Massach[illegible]C. He is a two-time winn[illegible]la category. He lives w[illegible]y, Massachusetts.

Find out more about Allen Steele and other Orbit authors by registering for the free monthly newsletter at www.orbitbooks.net

By Allen Steele

COYOTE
COYOTE RISING
COYOTE FRONTIER
SPINDRIFT

ALLEN STEELE

SPINDRIFT

www.orbitbooks.net

ORBIT

First published in the United States in 2007 by
The Berkley Publishing Group, Penguin Group (USA) Inc.
First published in Great Britain in 2007 by Orbit

is available from the British Library.

ISBN 978-1-84149-600-9

Papers used by Orbit are natural, recyclable products made from
wood grown in sustainable forests and certified in accordance with
the rules of the Forest Stewardship Council.

Typeset in Caslon 540 by Palimpsest Book Production Limited,
Grangemouth, Stirlingshire

Printed and bound in Great Britain by Mackays of Chatham, Chatham, Kent
Paper supplied by Hellefoss AS, Norway

Orbit
An imprint of
Little, Brown Book Group
Brettenham House
Lancaster Place
London WC2E 7EN

A Member of the Hachette Livre Group of Companies

www.orbitbooks.net

In memory of all astronauts, from all nations,
who have given their lives for the exploration of space.

CONTENTS

Main engine
Radiation shield
Fusion reactor
Main fuel tank
Maneuvering thrusters (4)
Probe "Larry"
Probe "Jerry"
Primary airlocks (4)
Docking cradle (2)
Shuttle *Maria Celesta*
SPE generator
Emergency airlock (2)
Hab module
Deflector array
Diametric drive torus (deployed)

Prologue

FEBRUARY 1, 2344 – HIGHGATE

A leviathan from the ocean of space, the CFSS *Robert E. Lee* slowly entered the vast sphere of Alpha Dock. Spotlights reflected off its sleek hull as the massive starship glided toward its skeletal berth; when it was close enough, the podlike tugboats that had rendezvoused with the vessel five kilometers from Highgate detached their lines and peeled away, to be replaced by a squad of dockworkers. Tiny figures in hardsuits, they hauled behind them carbon-nanotube mooring cables as thick as their arms. One by one, the workers attached grapples to recessed ports along the hull, then moved away while the vessel was gradually pulled the rest of the way into dry dock.

From the window of an observation cupola, John Shillinglaw watched the *Lee* return to its home port. Correction – what used to be its home port. It had been over a year and a half since the European Alliance and the Coyote Federation signed the treaty that, among other things, had conferred ownership of the ship – formerly christened the EASS *Francis Drake* – to Coyote. No one in the European Space Agency had liked losing the *Drake*; it was a steep price to pay for continued use of the starbridge it had established in the 47 Ursae Majoris system. Yet the colonials had made it clear that they were willing to destroy that same starbridge in order to preserve their independence, and the ounce of flesh they'd exacted from the European Alliance was an armed starship capable of defending their world.

Damn these people, he thought, observing the dock rats as they pulled umbilical lines to the ship and clamped them in place. *You'd think they'd be grateful* . . . He had to remind himself that Coyote's history was one of political struggle, and that the colonists had good reason to distrust the governments of Earth. Even so, he couldn't help but grimace as a worker's headlamp briefly illuminated the flag of the Coyote Federation – the Ursae Majoris constellation against horizontal bars of red, white, and blue – on the forward port side just below the hump of the command center, where the flag of the European Alliance had once been.

'Sir? Are you all right?' The aide who'd been assigned to him floated a little closer, his hands reaching up to grasp the rail running across the low ceiling just above their heads. 'Is there anything I can get you?'

'No. I'm fine, thank you.' Shillinglaw kept his temper in check. The young man meant well, yet Shillinglaw disliked this sort of deferential treatment. It came with the position of Director General of the European Space Agency, but Shillinglaw didn't enjoy being reminded of his age. He might be in his late nineties, yet gene therapy had kept his years in check; there was grey in his hair and beard, but regular exercise on a treadmill had tightened his stomach and strengthened his heart. Whenever he came up to Highgate, though, he was treated like a doddering old coot; those who'd been born and raised on the orbital colonies seemed to believe that anyone from Earth was a fragile doll, ready to break at any minute.

No matter. He had more important issues to worry about. Through the window, he could see the gangway telescoping into place against the portside crew hatch. A dockworker made sure that its collar was firmly in place, then raised a hand. 'How long until I can see them?' he asked.

'I don't know. Let me ask.' The aide, whose name Shillinglaw had already forgotten, turned aside as he cupped a hand around his headset mike. As he waited for a reply, Shillinglaw leaned closer to the window, stretching his ankles against the floor-level bar of the foot restraint as he sought to get a better view of the ship. For an instant, he caught a glimpse of someone behind the porthole beside the hatch, yet he couldn't see who it was.

You can't be this anxious, he thought, self-consciously backing away from the window. *Get hold of yourself*. And yet, the thing he wanted most just then was to see the three passengers aboard the ship.

Theodore Harker. Emily Collins. Jared Ramirez. The last time he'd laid eyes on them was fifty-six years ago. Shillinglaw remembered the date well. June 1, 2288: that was when the EASS *Galileo* had departed from Earth, never to be seen again. History long since presumed it to be lost with all hands. Over the years, the disappearance of the first ESA starship had become the source of legend and mystery.

And now, all of a sudden, these three had reappeared. Yet not aboard the *Galileo*, and not on Earth. There were those on Coyote who knew the whole truth; of that, Shillinglaw had little doubt. But the Coyote Federation didn't share its secrets with the European Alliance; indeed, it was another mystery why the three had even been allowed to return in the first place.

'They're still aboard ship, sir.' The aide turned back to him. 'Next stop is the quarantine facility. Once they complete sterilization procedures and undergo the usual postflight physical, you'll be allowed to . . .'

'Oh, for the love of . . .' Shillinglaw glared at the young man. 'I thought I issued a waiver.' Quarantine was required for the crews and passengers of all ships inbound from Coyote. The procedure could take hours, though, and Shillinglaw didn't have the luxury of time. Not if he wanted to interview Harker and his people before his counterpart from the Union Astronautica got to them. 'Never mind. Tell someone to keep them aboard. I'm on my way over.'

Before the aide could object, Shillinglaw pulled his feet from the restraint bar. Grabbing hold of the ceiling rail, he pulled himself toward the nearby floor hatch. The younger man was still stammering into his headset as Shillinglaw pushed himself down the manhole to the deck below.

A short passageway brought him to the gangway leading to the ship. As Shillinglaw reached the hatch, a security officer moved to stop him. He'd barely raised his hand before he apparently heard something in his headset. Clasping a hand against his ear, the sentry listened for a moment; he took a closer look at the ID badge clipped to Shillinglaw's breast pocket, then reluctantly moved aside.

'Thank you,' Shillinglaw murmured. Behind him, his aide had just emerged from the manhole. 'Don't let him through,' he added. 'In fact, don't let anyone through without my authorization. Understood?'

The guard nodded, then twisted the hatch lockwheel.

A brief rush of escaping pressure as he pushed it open; Shillinglaw ducked his head and entered the gangway. He waited until the guard sealed the hatch behind him before making his way down the tunnel.

He was halfway to the ship when he heard the klaxon of the gravity alert. Now that the *Lee* was safely berthed, a localized Millis-Clement field was being reactivated on this section of Alpha Dock. Grasping the handrails on either side of the gangway, Shillinglaw swung his feet down until they almost touched the floor. A minute passed, then weight gradually returned to him. Releasing the handrails, he let his feet drop to the deck; he took a second to straighten his cravat, then continued the rest of the way down the gangway.

Lee's outer hatch was already open, but the woman waiting for him in the airlock wasn't about to let him pass. 'Should've known it would be you,' she murmured, obviously displeased to see him.

'Welcome back, Commodore,' he replied, giving her a tight smile. 'I trust you've had a good flight.'

Shillinglaw wasn't happy to see Anastasia Tereshkova either. Only eighteen months before, he'd recommended to the ESA directorate that the *Lee*'s commanding officer, along with its senior crew members, be bound for courts-martial *in absentia* for their role in the *Drake* mutiny. Yet his colleagues had backed down, if only reluctantly; no one wanted to do anything that might harm diplomatic relations with the Coyote Federation. Nonetheless, Tereshkova was still a turncoat so far as he was concerned. The fact that her tunic was the same one she'd worn as an ESA officer, save for the different insignia and shoulder braid, only served to remind him of that.

Commodore, indeed, he thought, trying not to smirk. *You're still no more than a captain, so far as I'm concerned.*

'As always.' Tereshkova didn't bother to return the smile. 'You understand, of course, that you're now on Coyote territory . . . and you've violated quarantine protocol. There's no reason why I should let you aboard.'

'I understand perfectly.' Shillinglaw stared back at her. 'Just as I hope you realize that, if you throw me off, I'll only go back the way I came, then issue orders that'll make your stay quite unpleasant.'

Tereshkova's eyes narrowed ever so slightly. She knew exactly what he meant. Indefinite isolation for her crew and passengers, along with endless rounds of medical examinations, would be only the least of it; her cargo could also be impounded, hauled to the station's storage deck and left to collect dust while customs inspectors sent fiche upon fiche to the Coyote Federation consulate. Their ambassador would complain, of course, but the European Alliance wielded great influence on the Highgate bureaucracy. By the time everything was cleared up, there'd be enough red tape to stretch from here to 47 Ursae Majoris.

'*Da*. Perfectly.' Tereshkova still refused to budge. 'You're taking quite a chance coming over here . . . you didn't even put on isolation gear.'

'Not really. I've been arguing that we should ease the quarantine procedures. If there's any contagious diseases over there that your people haven't been able to inoculate themselves against, we would've known about it by now.'

A brief nod. She knew that scare tactics wouldn't work on him. There may be no love lost between them, but the fact remained that they still had to work together. 'So what is it you want?'

'You know.' Shillinglaw stepped a little closer. 'Take me to them.'

Her gaze flickered. 'And why should I?'

'I need to speak with them before anyone else does. And don't tell me I don't have that right . . . Harker and Collins are still ESA officers.' Once again, he locked eyes with her. 'Don't fight me on this one, Ana. I guarantee that you'll lose.'

Tereshkova remained silent for a moment, as if weighing her options. Shillinglaw heard boots scuffle on the deck past the half-open hatch behind her; he didn't need to look that way to know that there were probably Federation Militia soldiers standing less than eight feet away, carbines in hand. The Coyote Federation might have signed UN-sanctioned treaties, but it would be a long time before the governments of Earth would be trusted again.

'All right,' she said, letting out her breath as if in resignation. 'You get ten minutes . . . but only ten. Then I'm personally escorting them to quarantine, and after that you wait your turn along with everyone else.'

Meaning representatives from the Western Hemisphere Union, the Pacific Coalition, the unaligned nonspacefaring nations, the press corps, and anyone else who had an interest in speaking with the survivors of the *Galileo* expedition. Which was exactly why Shillinglaw had jumped a shuttle to Highgate as soon as he learned that the *Lee* was bringing them back to Earth; he had to get their story before anyone else did.

'I'd rather have fifteen, but' – he gestured toward the hatch – 'your call. Lead the way.'

Without another word, Tereshkova turned away. As he

followed her from the airlock, Shillinglaw did his best to ignore the soldiers standing just outside the hatch. One remained in position while the other fell in behind them. The captain was taking no chances.

They moved aft through the ship, making their way down narrow corridors just wide enough for two crewmen to squeeze past one another. They passed crew compartments, fire equipment lockers, and ladders leading to upper decks until they reached another airlock. The lamp above it was green; Tereshkova turned its lockwheel and pushed open the candy-striped hatch. Shillinglaw followed her inside and waited until she shoved the second hatch open. She stepped aside and motioned for him to go through.

The shuttle bay was as cavernous as the rest of the ship was cramped, its ceiling nearly sixty feet above their heads, the deck long enough to serve as a basketball court. Two skiffs were parked wing to wing on the other side of the bay, their tricycle landing gear chocked and tied down, and a repair pod rested within its cradle nearby. Yet it was the spacecraft in the center of the bay that caught Shillinglaw's attention.

The EAS *Maria Celeste* was an older shuttle, a model retired from active service nearly a generation ago. Downswept wings on either side of a broad aft section connected to a sleek forward crew module that vaguely resembled a cobra head; an access ramp had been lowered from beneath the hull. There was one much like it on display at the ESA museum at Elysium Centre, complete with stairs leading to the cockpit so that kids could climb inside and play with the controls of the craft that had once been the workhorse of the Mars colonies. Very sturdy, very reliable, and very obsolete.

This one might have just rolled off the assembly line, though, were it not for blackened carbon scores along the underside of its hull and the leading edge of its wings. Yet the wear and tear of atmospheric entry wasn't what made it unusual. In the stern section, where there had once been the twin bulges of its gas-core nuclear engines, were now a pair of oblong pods, fat and seamless, with no discernible features save for darkened plates along their sides. The old engines were missing; these contraptions were now in their place.

Shillinglaw stared at the shuttle with disbelief. The *Maria Celeste* had returned, all right . . . yet it wasn't the craft that had been mated with the *Galileo* when it left Earth nearly sixty years ago. Something had gotten to it, changed it . . .

'Like my ship?' A woman's voice, from his left side. 'You should . . . it got us home.'

Shillinglaw looked around, saw a woman in a long white robe strolling toward him. She reached up to pull back its hood, and that was when he recognized Emily Collins.

Despite all his best efforts, Shillinglaw was an old man. There was no way this could be denied: telomerase manipulation could give the illusion of youth, but nothing could change the subtle expression of age that lurked within one's eyes. Yet one look at Collins, and Shillinglaw saw she hadn't changed since he'd last seen her. She had the same svelte figure, same short-cropped blond hair, same attractive face . . . but, most importantly, her eyes were still young.

She had not aged. She was still the same woman he'd last seen fifty-six years ago. Gene therapy couldn't accomplish this feat any more than cosmetics could transform a crone into a virgin. Trying not to stare at her face, Shillinglaw looked down. The outfit she wore wasn't an ESA jumpsuit: a floor-length cloak, made of some soft, off-white material threaded with an intricate pattern of whorls and angles and odd, arabesque designs.

'I remember you.' Collins gazed at him with almost as much curiosity as he regarded her. 'Shillinglaw, isn't it . . . John Shillinglaw? Associate director for the agency?'

'Director General now.' He couldn't help but stare at her. 'I'm surprised you remember me.'

She raised an eyebrow. As she did, the patterns of her robe seemed to change every so slightly, becoming reddish orange. 'You made an impression on us,' she murmured. 'Or perhaps you don't remember?' He shook his head, and for a moment her eyes rolled upward. 'Yes, well . . . it has been some time, hasn't it?' She glanced at Tereshkova. 'He's the only one? No one else . . . not even Beck?'

Not recognizing the name of Shillinglaw's predecessor, Tereshkova's face expressed ignorance. 'Rudolph Beck passed away about fifteen . . . no, twenty years ago,' Shillinglaw replied. 'I'm sure he would have wanted to be here now.'

'Oh. So sorry to hear that.' Collins shook her head in dismay; the patterns of her cloak assumed a purple hue. She turned away from him, looking toward the shuttle. 'All right, you can come down now. I guess we're going to have to deal with him.'

A moment passed, then Theodore Harker emerged from the shuttle. *Galileo*'s first officer was followed by Jared Ramirez, the astrobiologist from the Western Hemisphere Union who'd belonged to the mission's science team. As they walked down the belly ramp, Shillinglaw saw that, like Collins, the two men had remained ageless. Although Harker's hair was long enough now to be pulled back in a ponytail, and Ramirez had cultivated a beard, neither of them were any older than when they'd left Earth. And like Collins, both wore robes identical to her own, with the same complex patterns.

'Sorry about that, sir,' Harker said, grinning sheepishly. 'We just wanted to be sure who we were dealing with.' Noticing Shillinglaw's curious gaze, he pinched a fold of fabric upon his left arm. 'Gifts from our friends in Rho Coronae Borealis . . . *sha*, they call them. Sacred robes.'

'Of course . . . sure.' Still trying to catch his breath, Shillinglaw sought to remember details of the classified memo that had been transmitted via hyperlink from the EA ambassador on Coyote. 'The *hjadd*, you mean . . . the alien race you contacted.'

'That's them, yes.' Harker stepped forward to extend his hand. 'Don't know if you remember me, sir. Theodore Harker, first officer . . . former first officer, rather . . . of the *Galileo*.'

'Certainly.' Shillinglaw shook his hand, once again marveling at the younger man's apparent immortality. Tall, broad-faced, hair just as dark as it had been almost six decades ago. Shillinglaw glanced again at the shuttle. 'Are they . . . ?'

'The *hjadd* emissary? No.' Ramirez stood to one side, as if reluctant to join the other two. 'Heshe chose to remain on Coyote, or at least until we've satisfied himher that our mission is successful.'

Like the others, Jared Ramirez remained unaged; tall and thin, with bushy grey hair and a trim beard, he was still several years older than Harker and Collins, just as he'd been when he joined the expedition – or rather, was drafted. Shillinglaw regarded the scientist with as much distrust as the first time he'd laid eyes on him. The man had once been a traitor; there was no reason for Shillinglaw to think that he had changed.

Instead of looking away, though, as he'd done so often in the past, Ramirez calmly gazed back at him. Only the subtle violet shading of his cloak's patterns gave any hint to his emotions. 'In time, the *hjadd* may come here,' he went on. 'For now, though, they're waiting to learn what our response . . . humankind's response . . . will be to the news of their existence.'

Shillinglaw had seen the images transmitted via hyperlink from Coyote: a bipedal form, vaguely human-shaped but definitely not human, hisher features rendered indistinct by the silver visor of the environmental suit heshe wore when heshe had come down *Maria Celeste*'s ramp. Despite repeated requests from various government leaders, though, the *hjadd* Prime Emissary had declined to reveal anything about himherself, aside from hisher long and elaborate name: Mahamatasja Jas Sa-Fhadda.

No one knew anything about himher. No one, at least, except these three.

'Anyone here going to tell me what happened?' Shillinglaw let out his breath. 'You launched from here, successfully went through KX-1, made a quick survey of Eris, then set out to intercept Spindrift . . . and that was it. Last transmission from the *Galileo* was received June 4, 2288.'

'That pretty well summarizes it, yes,' Harker said dryly.

'It does?' Shillinglaw regarded him with skepticism.

'Thirteen days ago, you came through the Coyote starbridge, claiming that the *Galileo* had been destroyed, the three of you were the only survivors, you'd been to a planet fifty-four light-years away . . .'

'Fifty light-years.' Collins shyly raised a hand. 'Pardon me, sir, but it's fifty-four-point-four l.y.s from Earth, but only fifty light-years from 47 Uma.' She hesitated, then added, 'In another direction, that is.'

Obviously trying to hide his amusement, Harker coughed into his fist. 'Excuse me . . . she's right, yes. Fifty light-years.' Then he smiled. 'Landed during the wedding reception for the president's daughter. Afraid we caused something of a commotion.'

'She wasn't too pleased.' Ramirez fought to keep from laughing and wasn't quite succeeding. 'But, hey, if we'd known, we would've baked a . . .'

'I don't care.' Impatient with the way this was going, Shillinglaw turned toward Harker. 'Commander, I'm glad you're home, but . . . damn it, do you realize that you're supposed to be dead? We wrote you off almost sixty years ago. And now you turn up, in' – he gestured in the general direction of the shuttle – 'in this thing, which doesn't even look like . . .'

'Right, yes.' Harker raised a placating hand. As he did, the patterns of his robe became a warm yellow; Shillinglaw found himself wondering why it did that. 'I'm sorry, sir. It's just that . . . we've been gone a long time, and everything takes getting used to.' He reached over to take Collins's hand. She smiled, and casually rested her head against his shoulder. 'But you're correct,' he went on. 'There's a story to be told here. A rather long one . . .'

'I can only imagine.' Shillinglaw nodded. 'Frankly, I'm envious. I wish I could have been there . . .'

'No, you don't. Remember, we're the only survivors. If you had been aboard the *Galileo*, you'd be dead by now.' Harker glanced at the others, and Shillinglaw saw that their expressions had become solemn. 'Which is one of the reasons why we've come back, in fact. To deliver a message . . . and to give you something.'

'Oh? And what might that be?'

Harker reached into his robe, withdrew a small object: a data fiche. 'It's all here,' he said, holding it up for Shillinglaw to see. 'Our final reports, along with logbooks, flight recorder transcripts, scientific data . . . the works.' Shillinglaw started to reach for it, but Harker pulled it back. 'Don't be so eager. You may not like what you'll find.'

'Let me be the judge of that.' Shillinglaw held out his hand insistently. Harker hesitated, then extended the disk to him. 'And the message?'

Harker nodded toward the disk. 'Read this first. Then we'll talk.'

Part One

Transit of Centauri

One

April 10, 2288 – Dolland Centre, the Moon

The lunar bus that met him at the prison landing field was driven by a pair of hard-faced Union Guard soldiers who didn't speak to Shillinglaw any more than was necessary. As soon as he entered the vehicle via an accordion ramp that mated with the transport's passenger hatch, they subjected him to a thorough inspection that began with a shoulders-to-shins pat-down and wand sweep and ended with his briefcase being opened and searched. His pen, wallet, pocket change, and watch were confiscated, as was his datapad, despite his protests. It wasn't until the guards were satisfied that he was harmless that one of them went forward to the cab, partitioned by a wire-mesh screen, while the other sat on a bench across from Shillinglaw, gun in hand, saying nothing yet never letting his eyes wander from him.

Shillinglaw distracted himself by gazing out the window. The ride took only a few minutes, but it gave him a chance to take a quick look at the prison. At first glance, Dolland Centre Penal Colony resembled the ordinary lunar settlement that it had once been: lunox processing and wastewater treatment facilities, long banks of black photovoltaic cells, six-wheeled vehicles trundling across graded roads, with the low hills of the Descartes highlands rising in the background. It wasn't until he noticed the fifteen-foot security fence with particle-beam lasers positioned every thirty feet that he was reminded that this place was a medium-to-maximum security prison. The European Alliance had one very much like it, near Mare Crisium, but somehow the Western Hemisphere Union's version looked much more menacing. On the other hand, since Shillinglaw had never visited so much as a small-town jail, he didn't know quite what to expect.

The bus approached Dolland crater itself, a grey wall of rock looming against the pitch-black sky, light seeping from thin slits along its sloping flanks. The driver slowed down to a crawl; the vehicle's inflated wheels bumped slightly as they moved onto a mooncrete ramp, then the bus began rolling downward toward a pair of double doors. The bus entered the subsurface airlock and came to a halt. The doors shut, and there was a rush of grey silt around the windows as electrostatic scrubbers rinsed moon dust from the vehicle, then a loud roar while the chamber was pressurized. Another pause, during which Shillinglaw presumed the bus was being scanned, then a second pair of doors rumbled open and the transporter was permitted to go the rest of the way inside.

A short, slender gentleman dressed in a collarless business suit was waiting for Shillinglaw in the underground garage. 'Welcome to Dolland,' he said, stepping forward to introduce himself as Shillinglaw came down the ladder. 'I'm Rubin Torres, the warden. And you're Mr Shillinglaw, I presume?'

'John, please. Call me John.' Shillinglaw grasped the other man's hand. 'I assume, of course, my government has already been in touch with yours.'

'Of course. Otherwise, you couldn't be here.' Not

wouldn't, but *couldn't*; Shillinglaw noticed the subtle way Torres shaded his choice of words. Indeed, the warden seemed faintly amused by Shillinglaw's belaboring the obvious. 'We don't welcome casual visitors,' he went on, a whisper of a smile touching the corners of his mouth, 'and Inmate 7668 is someone to whom we pay very close attention.'

'I'm sure you do.' *And you damn well should*, he added silently. Shillinglaw turned to glance at the soldiers who'd driven him there. 'Not to make a point of it, but . . . the man on the right has taken away my pad. I understand this is a normal precaution, but . . .'

'No, you can't. Not until you leave.' Torres looked down at his briefcase. 'And I'd appreciate it if you'd leave that with us. You'll have everything back before you go, but we insist that we hold your belongings while you're here.'

Shillinglaw's first impulse was to argue, but common sense told him to restrain himself. It had taken an extraordinary amount of negotiation, at the top levels of government, before the Union had reluctantly consented to allowing the associate director of the European Space Agency to pay a visit to one of its most infamous convicts. Now that he was so close to seeing him, Shillinglaw couldn't afford to screw things up by refusing to abide by security procedures. Nonetheless, there were things he carried with him that were vital to this meeting.

'You can have the briefcase,' he said, 'but I need the papers inside.' He hesitated. 'That's not too much to ask, if it? Especially since you insist on keeping my pad as well.'

Torres said nothing for a moment, yet Shillinglaw could tell that wheels were turning in his mind. 'May I examine the papers, please?'

'With all due respect . . . no, sir, you may not.' Torres's eyes narrowed with suspicion as Shillinglaw went on. 'As you yourself observed, this isn't a casual visit. I'm here on business urgent to both our governments, and the material I'm carrying has been classified. If you need to consult with higher authorities . . .'

'That I will.'

'If you must . . . but I'll warn you that you're just asking for trouble. And if you so much as look at my papers . . .'

'He won't,' a voice said from behind them.

Unnoticed by either of them, another person had quietly emerged from a nearby elevator, a heavyset man in his midfifties, with a receding hairline above a ruddy, pockmarked face. Shillinglaw didn't know him, but Torres obviously did, for he stiffened and quickly stepped back.

'Mr Sinclair . . . I thought you were still in my office.' Torres's demeanor instantly changed. 'Allow me to introduce you to John Shillinglaw, associate director for . . .'

'I already know who he is.' Sinclair sauntered over to them, hands clasped behind his back. 'Thanks for the drink, Warden Torres, but as Mr Shillinglaw says, we're on urgent business.' He extended a hand to Shillinglaw. 'Donald Sinclair. Senior representative for the Council of Patriarchs.'

Oh, bloody hell, Shillinglaw thought as he grasped his hand. He spotted the small enamel pin fastened to Sinclair's lapel: the two overlapping circles of social collectivism. *This guy's a political officer*. 'Pleased to meet you, *señor*.'

'Likewise.' Sinclair favored him with the briefest of smiles, then he returned his attention to Torres. 'Mr Torres, I expect you to respect our guest's privacy. Please return his property to him, and allow him to retain his papers. I'll personally take responsibility.'

Anger burned in Torres's eyes, and for a moment he seemed to bite his lower lip, yet he reluctantly nodded. 'As you wish, Mr Sinclair.' He looked at Shillinglaw. 'Remove your papers, please, and give the briefcase to me.' Then he glanced at the soldiers. 'Which of you has his pad? Give it back to him.'

The Guardsman who'd confiscated Shillinglaw's belongings stepped forward, producing the pad from a thigh pocket of his uniform. Shillinglaw put it in his jacket pocket, then pressed a forefinger against his briefcase's verification plate and opened it. 'My apologies,' Torres said as Shillinglaw removed a manila folder from the case and shut it again, 'but we have to exercise certain precautions. Anything that might conceivably be used to carry in a weapon . . .'

'I understand perfectly.' He almost felt sorry for Torres. Any other time, he might be lord of this particular domain, yet in the presence of a political officer he'd been reduced to little more than a mere turnkey. 'All I want to do is cooperate.'

'As do we all.' Sinclair gave Torres a look that seemed to shrink the poor man even more. 'Now that we're finished here, may we see the prisoner, please?'

'Of course. This way, gentlemen . . .' Torres signaled for the two Guardsmen to accompany them. With one quickly stepping forward to lead the way and the other bringing up the rear, they marched toward a vaultlike metal door watched by two sentries behind a louvered glass partition. A brisk wave of a hand, and the door buzzed and parted in its center, revealing a mooncrete corridor whose floor sloped gently upward.

Shillinglaw waited until the door shut behind them, then he slid in beside Sinclair. 'Thanks for coming to the rescue,' he murmured.

'Think nothing of it.' Sinclair didn't bother to lower his voice. 'I'm just sorry we had to meet this way. Some of our officials have an unfortunate tendency to put their noses where they shouldn't.' If Torres overheard them, he pretended otherwise; he kept his back toward his two guests as they walked up the corridor. 'Where's the prisoner now?' Sinclair added, speaking as if Torres had heard everything they'd said. 'In an interrogation room?'

'No . . . no, sir, he's not.' Torres tried to keep his voice steady, but Shillinglaw detected a nervous stammer. 'He's on the farm just now . . .'

'On the farm?' Sinclair's voice raised just slightly. 'Why wasn't he taken to . . . ?'

'I didn't . . . I'm sorry, *señor*, but I didn't understand your earlier message. I didn't think you yourself wanted to participate in this meeting, so I . . .'

'Never mind. Just take us to him.' Sinclair briefly closed his eyes in exasperation, then gave Shillinglaw a sidelong glance: *Bureaucrats . . . never can get anything right.*

Yet Shillinglaw wasn't so certain that Torres had screwed up. Something about the entire arrangement raised his suspicions, yet he couldn't quite put his finger on it. 'Pardon me, Mr Torres,' he asked, 'but I thought he was confined to maximum security. Isn't the farm . . . ?'

'We transferred him to the medium security wing three years ago.' The warden glanced back at him. 'His conduct had been very good for the previous six years, and so when he formally requested the transfer, the board decided to let him take a job on the farm . . . on probation, of course. So far, he's behaved quite well.'

'And the other inmates?' Sinclair's tone was skeptical. 'They've accepted him?'

'Pretty much so, yes. Only a handful are aware of the nature of his crimes, and they either avoid him or else decided to look the other way. For the rest, he's just another convict. And he's volunteered to lead a couple of activities. Teaching astronomy classes, organizing a chess club . . .'

'Trying to earn points toward parole, I take it.' Shillinglaw didn't mean to sound cynical, but nonetheless it came out that way. By then, they'd reached the end of the corridor. Another vault door confronted them, with two more Guardsmen watching them from behind an armored window.

'I don't think you understand.' Torres stopped to let the soldiers open the door. 'He'll never get out, and he knows that. Even if he lives to be five hundred, he's here for the rest of his life.'

I wouldn't be so sure of that, Shillinglaw thought. He kept his mouth shut, yet from the corner of his eye, he saw a knowing smile flicker across Sinclair's face.

The prison reeked of marijuana.

The floor of Dolland crater was a little more than four miles in diameter, and nearly every square foot of it had been cultivated with hemp. Acre upon acre of dark green weed, ranging from tiny sprouts nurtured in hydroponics tanks until they reached maturity and could be transplanted to beds of rich brown soil, to mighty giants twice the height of a man, their serrated leaves reaching for the sunlight streaming through the polarized panes of the airtight dome that covered the crater from rim to rim.

The prison farm grew cannabis for the Union's lunar colonies. Once the plants were harvested, they were processed for all variety of industrial uses: paper, rope, machine oil, ink, pharmaceuticals, paint, clothing, shoes, anything that could be made from the hardy, easily grown weed. The fact that the female plants had once enjoyed a heyday as a vice was almost forgotten; the underground now had dope half as easy to produce and twice as potent. Of course, those caught manufacturing or distributing these things were often sentenced to Dolland, where they'd find themselves growing hemp until they were sick of seeing it.

The medium-security inmates lived in cells excavated within the crater wall; every morning they rose to look out upon a vast jungle of weed, and their days and nights were spent with its dank, cloying odor in their noses and mouths. Still, it was preferable to the fate suffered by the maximum-security prisoners; isolated within lava tubes beneath the crater, they saw neither sunlight nor the faces of anyone else save their guards, and spent their time pacing their cells and quietly going mad.

Shillinglaw found Inmate 7668 on his hands and knees beside a half-grown cannabis bush, carefully pruning vestigial leaves from its underside. He didn't look up from his work until one of the guards ordered him to stand, and even then he took his time getting to his feet. He put down his blunt-nosed plastic clippers, then slowly rose, casually brushing away the dirt from the knees of his bright orange coveralls. It wasn't until he turned around that Shillinglaw recognized him.

Jared Ramirez had changed considerably in the years since his face had been on every netcast and newspage.

His wiry frame had thickened slightly in the middle, a testament to a diet of carbohydrate-rich prison food, and his hair, once jet-black and artfully groomed, had become a raggedy grey mop. Yet his eyes remained as sharp as ever, his gaze direct and inquisitive as he regarded his visitors with sullen curiosity.

'You've got visitors, convict,' the closer of the two guards said, his voice formal and yet not unkind. 'You can take a break now. Warden says it'll count toward your work quota, so take your time.'

'Thanks. Tell Mr Torres I appreciate it.' Ramirez ignored Shillinglaw and Sinclair as he pulled off his work gloves. 'I can speak to them, can't I?'

'Sure. Just watch what you say.' The guard stepped back a couple of feet, the butt of his rifle resting upon his hip, while his companion moved past them and took up a similar position on the gravel pathway leading between the rows of plants.

Once again, Shillinglaw nervously looked around. Even with two armed guards as escorts, he didn't like where he'd found himself. The farm surrounded them like a primeval forest, its warm air humidified by the fine spray of water from the gridlike network of irrigation pipes high above their heads. Here and there among the cannabis, he spotted other inmates, some spreading mulch and trimming leaves while others cut full-grown plants and loaded them into wheelbarrows. Gazing at the nearby crater wall, he saw a couple of prisoners lounging against the railing of one of the lower-level cell tiers; they stared back at him, their expressions implacable until one of them raised his fingers to his lips and blew him a kiss.

Shillinglaw hastily looked away. No wonder Torres had

left him and Sinclair at the crater entrance. Even with armed guards at his side, he felt vulnerable. He suddenly realized Torres's intentions: instead of letting him talk to Ramirez in the privacy of an interrogation room, he'd made sure the meeting took place where his unwanted visitor would be intimidated. But with Sinclair in the picture, that idea had backfired, and now the warden wanted to distance himself as much as possible.

'So . . . let's hear what you have to say.' Ramirez shoved his gloves in his back pocket. 'Better not be another psych profile, though. I'm done with them.'

'I'm sure you are.' Sinclair regarded him with undisguised contempt. 'Anyone ever find out what's wrong with you? I mean, besides the fact that you hate the human race?'

'Not the entire human race, no . . . just certain members.' Ramirez bent forward to peer at Sinclair's lapel pin. 'We've never met, but I have little doubt that you're among them.'

Sinclair smirked, a retort hovering on his lips. Shillinglaw cleared his throat. 'Perhaps we should introduce ourselves,' he said before the conversation could degenerate further. 'I'm John Shillinglaw, associate director of the European Space Agency. My collegue . . . um, companion . . . is Donald Sinclair, from the . . .'

'I know where he's from, thank you.' Ramirez turned his attention to him. 'ESA, you say? How interesting . . . which department?'

'Extrasolar Exploration. It's . . .'

'New, isn't it? Have you made any progress? Toward building your own starship, I mean.' He absently glanced up toward the pressure dome high above. 'We don't get much news here. Or at least *I* don't . . . the warden restricts my net access. Just sports and the occasional fic.'

From the corner of his eye, Shillinglaw saw that Sinclair was listening with great interest. 'We've made some progress,' he replied, and quickly changed the subject. 'I've come here to discuss an important matter with you . . . something you may be able to help us understand.'

'I hope it's not about the Savants again.' Ramirez looked down at the ground. 'Look, it was a mistake. I've lost everything because of what they did . . . and if I'd known what they were planning, I would've never helped them in the first place. So if you're trying to find out more about their plans, believe me when I tell you that I've already . . .'

Sinclair made a flatulent sound with his mouth. Shillinglaw chose to ignore him. 'It's not about the Savant genocide,' he said. Mindful of the nearby guards, he lowered his voice. 'It's about Raziel. It's received a signal.'

Ramirez's eyes snapped toward him. For a moment he seemed to shake, like a man who'd just received a cold chill. Then he stepped closer to Shillinglaw, closing the distance between them. 'Artificial?' he whispered, and Shillinglaw nodded. 'Confirmed?' Shillinglaw nodded again. 'When? How?'

'Ten days ago . . . and no, this is not an April Fool's joke, although that possibility crossed a few people's minds. Two radio telescopes on Earth unpinned their dishes and used them to confirm what showed up on Raziel's multichannel analyzer.' Shillinglaw paused, then added, 'It's real. It's as real as it can get.'

'Oh, dear God.' For the first time, Ramirez noticed the folder Shillinglaw carried in his left hand. 'Is that the data? Let me see it . . .'

Impatient, he started to reach for the folder, as if to snatch it away from Shillinglaw. The suddenness of his action drew the attention of the closer of the soldiers; before either of them could react, the Guardsman grabbed Ramirez's arm and roughly hauled him back, while the other one brought up his gun to cover his partner.

'It's all right!' Raising his hands, Shillinglaw moved between Ramirez and the second Guardsman, blocking his shot. 'It's okay! I'm fine! No problem!' In the background, he could hear whistles and catcalls from the other inmates; somewhere above them, one of the prisoners who'd been watching them pounded on the railing, apparently signaling to the others that a fight was about to break out. Shillinglaw tried to put it out of his mind. 'He just got excited, that's all,' he said quickly. 'Leave him alone, please.'

The soldiers seemed unconvinced until Sinclair walked over to the one holding the rifle and murmured something in his ear. Shillinglaw couldn't hear what he said, but it was enough to make the Guardsman lower his weapon. A brief nod to his collegue, and the other soldier released Ramirez, albeit reluctantly, and stepped back. More whistles, this time mixed with a few boos, then the inmates gradually quieted down.

'Sorry.' Ramirez gently massaged his arm where the guard had grabbed him. 'Just a little overstimulated.' A wan smile. 'Nine years in this place, and now this . . . I hope you understand.'

'Sure. I would be, too.' Shillinglaw was surprised to see that Ramirez's face had gone pale; there was a sheen of perspiration on his forehead. 'Besides, if there was any trouble, your friends would've helped you out.'

Ramirez's smile faded. 'No, I'm afraid not,' he said

quietly. 'They were probably hoping that the guards would beat the crap out of me.' He glanced at the folder again. 'If I may . . . ?'

Shillinglaw held out the file. Careful not to take it from him too quickly, Ramirez accepted the folder with quivering hands. Half-turning away from him, he opened it and began to study the technical printouts. Some pages he flipped quickly past, while others he examined more thoroughly, his lips moving as he whispered to himself.

As Shillinglaw watched him, he found himself torn between long-standing disgust for the man and a certain grudging respect. Nine years ago, no one outside the scientific community had ever heard of Jared Ramirez. An American astrobiologist working within the confines of the Western Hemisphere Union, his principal line of research had been the search for extraterrestrial intelligence . . . a field that had gone out of vogue in recent years, despite the Union Astronautica's development of the diametric drive, due to lack of evidence that intelligent life existed beyond Earth. Indeed, it'd even been argued that, because humankind had discovered the means to go to the stars, only to find no one waiting for them, this was proof that *Homo sapiens* occupied the pinnacle of creation.

Yet although the strong anthropic principle had become the philosophical basis for Dominion Christianity, Ramirez's research had earned just enough support within the Proletariat – particularly among the Council of Savants – that he was able to acquire funding for a SETI project based at Mare Muscoviense on the lunar farside. It made sense that the Savants remained interested in finding other forms of intelligent life, for they were no longer quite human themselves. Scholars, philosophers, and dreamers who, for one reason or another, had decided that the normal human life span was a death sentence they couldn't tolerate, they'd taken advantage of radical advances in cybernetics to have their cerebral patterns scanned and downloaded into quantum comps contained within mechanical bodies, thereby giving birth to posthuman life.

For a time, it appeared as if the Savants would peacefully coexist with baseline humans. Their enhanced ability to process new information, coupled with near immortality, seemed to make them the intellectual vanguard. Although they were still viewed with suspicion by the European Alliance and the Pacific Coalition, the Savants took advantage of the Western Hemisphere Union's doctrine of social collectivism to have their representatives elected to the Proletariat, where they formed a third council that worked alongside the Patriarchs and Matriarchs. There they wielded considerable influence; it was upon their advice that the Union decided to build a fleet of five starships that would journey to 47 Ursae Majoris in order to wrest control of Coyote from the handful of colonists who'd arrived there only a few years earlier.

Yet no one knew that the Savants had their own agenda. Least of all Jared Ramirez, who'd become a collaborator in their plan to obliterate nearly one-third of Earth's population. Unwittingly, or so he claimed . . .

'This is . . . this is absolutely incredible.' Still staring at the papers in his hands, Ramirez turned toward Shillinglaw. 'And it happened by accident?'

'Pretty much so, yes.' Walking over to Ramirez's side, Shillinglaw reached past his shoulder to turn back a couple of pages. 'There, you see?' he said, pointing to the first column of figures. 'The object was spotted when Raziel aimed itself at Proxima Centauri. It wasn't engaged in a search pattern at the time, just using that star to recalibrate itself . . .'

'As it's programmed to do, yes.' Ramirez shook his head in amazement. 'I picked Proxima because it's an M-class dwarf close enough for Raziel to locate without any trouble.' He chuckled to himself. 'Of all the stars I'd least expect . . .'

'It's not in orbit around Proxima. See?' Shillinglaw flipped to the next page, indicated another set of figures with the tip of his finger. 'Once Raziel locked on to the object, it continued to track it while it occultated Alpha Centauri A and B, and later HR6416. So that means it's . . .'

'A transient, right.' Shutting his eyes, Ramirez lifted his left hand from the page, almost as if he was visualizing a star map indelibly etched in his mind's eye. 'Coming from the general direction of the outer Orion Arm. Heading toward the galactic center, slightly below the solar plane of ecliptic. And how far away did you say it was?'

'When it was first spotted about four and a half years ago . . .'

'Four and a half years ago? Why didn't you . . . ?' He stopped himself, and a wry smile appeared. 'Oh, right. I was still in solitary. Makes consultation a bit difficult.'

'It was approximately two-point-one light-years from Earth. We estimate it as being approximately one thousand two hundred kilometers in diameter, spherical in shape . . .'

'Only one thousand two hundred kilometers?' He

sighed and shook his head in dismay, then thrust the folder at Shillinglaw's chest. 'A rogue asteroid,' he muttered. 'Space junk. Don't waste my time. Nice to meet you, but I'm not . . .'

'Since then the distance has decreased to approximately two-point-oh-five l.y.s, and it's on a trajectory perpendicular to our solar system.' Shillinglaw didn't take the file from him. 'With that sort of velocity, does it still sound like a rogue? And before you answer that, let me show you one more thing.'

Reaching into his pocket, he pulled out his pad. 'Raziel is one hell of a system,' he continued as he opened its cover and entered a code number. 'When it spotted something that looked like a possible candidate, it did what it was supposed to do . . .'

'It would've transmitted a signal. But it wouldn't have done that unless . . .' Ramirez's voice trailed off as a three-dimensional image materialized a couple of inches above the pad's holoscreen: a dark, featureless sphere, like a small moon or a large asteroid, save for lack of surface textures. Yet it wasn't that which attracted his attention, but the tiny object that circled around it like a miniature satellite.

'When the transient occultated Proxima Centauri,' Shillinglaw went on, pointing to the orbiting blip, 'it spotted this thing. So, as you say, its recognition program kicked in, and it transmitted a signal.'

He paused. 'Two days ago, we received a response.'

Ramirez's jaw dropped. His shoulders sagged, and his knees buckled. For a moment, Shillinglaw thought the man was about to faint; he started to reach forward to steady him, but Ramirez recovered himself. Putting a hand to his mouth, he stared at the holo with such fascination that tears began to form at the corners of his eyes. A nervous giggle, almost like a little girl's self-conscious laughter, escaped from his throat; he made an effort to choke it back, but it came forth again, no less hysterical than before.

'We received a signal,' he whispered, almost breathless. 'My God . . . oh, my God . . . we received a signal.'

'Yes, we did.' Until then, Sinclair had remained in the background, quietly observing the conversation. Now he came forward, hands clasped behind his back. 'And you see why we need your help. Obviously, this is something that needs to be investigated, the sooner the better . . .'

'Yes . . . yes, of course.' Ramirez took a deep breath; Shillinglaw could tell that he was trying to calm down. 'I need . . . I need a comp. Or at least a pad. And as much access to current data as you'll allow me.' He looked again at Shillinglaw, his eyes pleading. 'If you could speak with the warden, perhaps ask him to let me . . .'

'Actually, I think we think we can do better than that.' Shillinglaw glanced at Sinclair, received a curt nod in response. 'A high-level conference has been scheduled to discuss the matter. It'll be held in England, about a week from now. We'd appreciate it if you'd agree to attend . . . if you don't mind, that is.'

Jared Ramirez, traitor to the human race, stared at him in shock. For an instant, it seemed as if all color was suddenly bled from his face. He blinked rapidly as his mouth opened and shut several times.

'Yes,' he whispered, his voice choked with emotion. 'Yes, I'd like to do that, very much.'

Two

April 16, 2288 – Wilton Park, England

The Daimler hovercoupe glided up the narrow country road that wound its way through rolling meadows, passing ancient oaks where magpies fluttered from limb to limb. Once the fields had been filled with vast flocks of sheep placidly grazing upon emerald grass; when the global climate began to change, though, sheep were among the livestock in the United Kingdom to succumb to disease and longer winters. Although the West Sussex countryside was one of the few places in England that remained relatively unspoiled, even the small, white-shouldered birds had become an endangered species, and it was nothing short of a miracle that a semblance of springtime had come to the downs.

The coupe slowed down as it approached a security gate. Its scanner recognized the vehicle, and the gate swung open. The Daimler moved up the serpentine driveway, heading toward the grey manor house that sprawled across the crest of the hill, until it finally came to a halt within a courtyard in front of the main entrance.

Jared Ramirez waited until the Daimler's skirts deflated and the coupe came to rest. Even then, though, he was not at liberty to leave the vehicle by himself; he had to be patient until a pair of Special Air Service officers – or at least that was what he assumed they were, even though they were dressed in civilian clothes – came out from beneath the archway and opened the back door for him. Seated beside him, John Shillinglaw prompted him with an unnecessary nudge to the elbow. Ramirez ignored him, and instead glanced toward the driver.

'Thanks for the lift, David,' he said. 'See you on the way back?' The driver, who'd picked them up at the shuttle landing field at the nearby RAF base and doubtless was another SAS man, favored him with a brief nod and a smile. Picking up his cane, Ramirez swung his right leg out of the vehicle, ducked his head and, with his wrists still bound together by magnetic handcuffs, allowed the two security guards to extract him carefully from the car.

'Welcome to Wilton House,' one of them said, as if he were an honored guest instead of a prisoner. 'May I take your bag for you?'

'Certainly. Thank you.' Leaning heavily on his cane, Ramirez watched as his escort opened the coupe's boot and removed the nylon duffel bag that contained everything he owned, not counting his prison jumpsuit and the handful of trinkets he'd left behind on the Moon. Almost everything else he'd brought with him, including the suit he wore, supplied courtesy of ESA along with the cane that he used to help himself cope with Earth's gravity. If all else failed, at least he'd return to Dolland with a few items he might use for barter with his fellow inmates.

But you're not going back there, are you? he thought. *You got off the Moon. And one way or another, you're getting out of here, too.*

Ramirez gazed up at the weather-beaten Tudor walls and mullioned windows of Wilton House. During the short ride over from Wilton Field, David had obliged his curiosity by giving him a brief history of the place. Established on a private estate that dated back to the eleventh century, the manor had been erected in the 1500s, with additional wings, along with an adjacent chapel and carriage house, built during the eighteenth century. Although parts of the original edifice had been demolished during the nineteenth century by an overenthusiastic architect, Wilton House remained largely unchanged through the mid-twentieth century, when the family that owned the manor put it under long-term lease to the British government. Since then, Wilton Park had served as a site for high-level conferences. The manor's interior might have been remodeled many times to suit contemporary requirements, yet its purpose was still the same: a dignified and comfortable place where diplomats, scholars, defense officials, and scientists could discuss the pressing issues of the day.

This wasn't the first conference Ramirez had been invited to attend, but it was the first one where he'd arrived wearing manacles. As one of the SAS men carried their bags through the front entrance, he turned to Shillinglaw. 'Think you could have these removed?' he asked. 'They're rather unnecessary . . . not to mention humiliating.'

Shillinglaw hesitated, yet before he could respond, someone else answered for him. 'I don't think that's an inappropriate request. If you're willing to trust us, then we should be willing to trust you.'

A tall, young-looking man with thinning blond hair sauntered toward them from the door. 'Rudolph Beck,' he said, his voice thickened by an Austrian accent. 'Director General, European Space Agency.' He glanced at Shillinglaw. 'Good to see you again, John' – Shillinglaw briefly nodded – 'and you must be the famous Dr Jared Ramirez. Delighted to meet you at long last.'

'The pleasure is all mine.' For the first time since this all began, Ramirez found himself taken off guard. 'Are you sure you don't mean the *infamous* Dr Jared Ramirez? I believe that's who you're expecting.'

'Only if he's still in the car and hasn't gotten out yet.' Beck made a show of glancing past him at the coupe. 'No? Well, then, I suppose we'll just have to make do with you.' He looked at their driver. 'David, would you please . . . ?'

Without a trace of reluctance, David produced a remote unit from his pocket, aimed it at Ramirez's wrists. A brief buzz, and Ramirez felt the cuffs loosen as his hands parted from each other. 'There's an interesting legend about this place,' Beck went on, while David removed the manacles. 'The first conference was held here shortly after World War II. The subject was the rebuilding of Germany, and the participants included a number of high-ranking former Nazi officials. One of the conference organizers asked whether they should take special precautions to make sure that none of the POWs escaped, to which another is said to have replied, "Then we'll have to make sure that they don't *want* to escape."'

The Director General pointed to the long driveway leading down the hill. 'As you see, there are no guards, no watchtowers. Nothing but the gate, and you can walk around it easily enough. So there's nothing to prevent you from leaving anytime you choose to do so.'

'Honor system?' Ramirez tried not to smirk, but he couldn't help himself. 'I appreciate your . . . um, candor, but unless you haven't heard, I'm the man who sold out the human race. I've just spent the last nine years of my life in a place where people barter sex for an extra roll of toilet paper. And when I'm done here . . .'

'You're going back. Or at least so you assume.' Beck turned to lead them toward the iron-strapped front door; Ramirez noticed that the SAS men remained behind. 'Dr Ramirez . . . Jared, if I may? . . . if you don't wish to participate in this conference, that's your choice. Your manacles have been removed, and as I said, you're free to go as you will . . . although I doubt you'll get very far. There are quite a few people who won't want you running loose.'

Passing through a small foyer, they strolled through the manor's great hall. Ramirez paused to marvel at the hammer-beam rafters of the high ceiling, rising sixty feet above a Renaissance dining room lined with oak tables and high-backed chairs. At the far side of the room was an ornate fireplace, its white-marble mantel carved with a family crest. Midmorning sunlight streamed in through tall windows; from the kitchen door, he caught the mixed aroma of broiled salmon, steamed asparagus, fresh-baked bread. A team of waiters quietly moved through the room, setting the tables for the luncheon soon to come, while Mozart gently filtered from speakers concealed within the minstrel gallery.

'But if you choose to work with us,' Beck continued, oblivious to the luxury through which they casually passed, 'we may find a way to ease your sentence. Make it possible for you to reenter society in your former capacity.'

Distracted, Ramirez almost missed this part. He stopped, turned around. 'What are you saying? Are you telling me . . . ?'

'Not now,' Beck said quietly, raising a hand to shush him. By then they'd reached a hallway running lengthwise across the manor's ground floor. To their left, past a mahogany staircase leading to the second floor, was an open door leading to what appeared to be a parlor. Ramirez spotted several men and women standing around, drinking coffee and chatting among themselves. Other conference members, taking a break between sessions.

'You've missed the keynote,' the Director General said quietly, 'but you have a few minutes before we begin your presentation.' He pointed to the nearby stairs. 'Your bag has already been taken to your room. Perhaps you'd like to go up there, freshen up a bit . . .'

'Thanks, but that's not necessary.' During the long trip from the Moon, he had spent the last two days preparing his notes and mentally rehearsing what he'd have to say. Although he was tired and his clothes felt rumpled, he was ready for what lay ahead. To the right, he saw another door at the other end of the corridor. 'That's the conference room?'

'Yes, it is.' Beck turned to escort him that way. 'Come. We'll get you set up.' Then he smiled, and gently grasped his elbow in what was meant to be a comradely gesture. 'Relax. This is supposed to be informal. And besides, you're among friends.'

I doubt that, Ramirez thought, although he didn't say so aloud.

The Wilton Park conference room was long and broad, with tall windows that looked out across the downs and a fireplace topped with a gilded antique mirror. An oak-top table shaped like an elliptical ring dominated the room, with a decorative floral arrangement set up in its center and high-backed leather chairs evenly spaced around the ring's outer rim. The table was equipped with built-in data screens and microphones; bottles of spring-water and crystal jars of hard candy had been set out, refreshments intended to keep the attendees comfortable during the long hours they spent in session.

As the principal speaker for this session, Ramirez was seated in front of the fireplace, with the conference chairman to his right. He turned out to be someone Ramirez had encountered many years ago: Sir Peter Cole, the Royal Society professor of physics at Cambridge, who, only a little while ago, had been appointed Britain's Astronomer Royal. Tall and slender, with longish grey hair and an air of studied affability, he greeted Ramirez with a firm handshake and a pleasant smile, as if they were old colleagues who'd simply been too involved with their own careers to drop each other a line now and then. Yet Ramirez hadn't forgotten that Sir Peter once published a blistering critique of his work in the *Astrophysical Journal*; perhaps he was no longer a foe, but he certainly wasn't a friend either.

His left knee involuntarily twitching beneath the desk, Ramirez watched the other conference members as they filtered into the room to resume their places at the table. Besides Cole, Beck, and Shillinglaw, the only person he recognized was Donald Sinclair. The political officer gave him a cursory nod, then opened his screen and began to review his notes from the previous session. The rest were strangers, identified only by last-name placards arranged along the table. Most looked like tenured academics or government officials of one stripe or another; they regarded him with guarded curiosity, as if he were a rare beast, reasonably domesticated yet nonetheless dangerous, that had been temporarily released from his cage and trotted out on a leash.

Once Cole rang a small silver bell to bring the meeting to order, he began the meeting by reminding everyone that the proceedings were officially classified Top Secret, and that the nondisclosure agreements they'd signed forbade them from any public discussion or publication of what they learned during the conference. Knowing nods from around the table, yet once again Ramirez was puzzled by Sinclair's presence. Why had a WHU political officer – along with a contingent of Union scientists, no doubt – been invited to attend a high-level scientific conference sponsored by the European Alliance? Had the rivalry between the two superpowers eased that much while he was in Dolland? He doubted it, yet nonetheless there they were, just the same.

Sir Peter then briefly introduced Ramirez. He pointedly didn't mention where he'd been the last nine years, or the crimes for which he'd been convicted – everyone there knew those things already. Instead he stated that Ramirez was an astrobiologist associated with the Union Astronautica and, in his capacity as a SETI researcher, the creator of Raziel. Then Cole turned the session over to Ramirez.

Ramirez didn't rise to speak, but instead remained in his seat. Although he made use of his screen's interactive features, for the most part he consulted the handwritten notes he'd made during his trip from the Moon. Much of his material was already well-known, of course. Christened after the ancient Hebrew angel of mysteries, Raziel was a lunar-based optical interferometer: twenty-seven twenty-meter reflector telescopes configured along a Y-shaped axis, with each arm six kilometers in length and the entire array having a baseline of ten kilometers. Located within Mare Muscoviense on the far side of the Moon, a few kilometers from the Union Astronautica's long-baseline radio telescope to which it was linked and operated, Raziel was designed to work independently for years at a time, conducting full-sky sweeps of the galaxy in cycles that would take up to two years to complete before they'd begin again.

In the beginning, Raziel hadn't been intended for SETI research. Its primary mission had been the discovery of habitable worlds – or at least terrestrial-size planets – in orbit around distant stars. But that mission had been largely fulfilled by 2278 with the discovery of a little over a hundred terrestrial planets within a seventy-light-year radius of Earth; fewer than ten were considered be habitable, and none was closer than Coyote, forty-six light-years from Earth. Furthermore, none of these worlds displayed any signs of intelligent life.

Yet even as the public had embraced the anthropic principle – the idea that natural selection favored the emergence of humankind as the heirs of the galaxy, to the point that it seemed like divine will – Ramirez dissented by reintroducing an old theory. Although a highly advanced alien race might try to transmit radio messages, as generations of scientists had assumed they would, it was also possible that they might instead resort to visual means of announcing their existence.

To this end, he proposed that Raziel be retasked from searching for terrestrial planets to a search for intelligent life. It was Ramirez's theory that, given sufficiently advanced technology, aliens might build very large rotating structures – triangles, for instance, or even louvered rectangles – that couldn't be mistaken for planets, which in turn would be established in heliocentric orbits around their native stars. When these structures passed in transit across the faces of those stars, the resultant light curve could be recognized even across the distance of many light-years by high-power telescopes.

Raziel's new mission was to visually search those cataloged stars within seventy l.y.s of Earth believed to have habitable zones, to see if such macrocosmic structures might exist. The array was reprogrammed to disregard already identified planets that might briefly occultate those same stars; it would take two or more transits for Raziel's AI to log a newfound object as a possible target. From there it would proceed to the next step, which entailed instructing the nearby deep-space network to transmit a recognition signal – a digitalized series of prime numbers – toward the suspect.

For nearly ten years, Raziel had conducted its lonely vigil, its telescopes moving from one star system to the next, observing it for a while before moving on. Yet none of these systems showed signs of being inhabited, and although there had been the occasional tiny object that, if only for one-thousandth of a second, occultated a distant sun in a way that suggested it might be artificial in nature, there was no repetition of their light-curve patterns.

After each sweep, Raziel was programmed to reposition its telescopes toward Proxima Centauri, a routine procedure that allowed the telescopes to recalibrate themselves. Ramirez compared it to a reader relieving eyestrain by focusing upon a random object across the room. Although only 4.2 light-years from Earth, Proxima Centauri was a red dwarf that had been long since determined not to support any terrestrial planets.

And that was when, against all odds, Raziel produced its first positive contact.

'At first, Raziel thought it might only be an undiscovered Kuiper Belt object that just happened to cross its focal plane,' Ramirez said. 'But when it locked on the target and began tracking it, a different sort of light-curve signature was produced.'

He reached forward to tap a command into his screen. Above the floral arrangement, a holographic image appeared: a tiny black dot silhouetted against the ruddy orb of Proxima Centauri. 'When our people saw this initial image, they believed at first that the system had made a mistake. When they magnified it further, though . . .'

Ramirez entered another command; the holo expanded, and the dot became a small, featureless sphere. At that magnification, they could see a small speck hovering close to the object. 'That's what drew Raziel's attention,' he went on, pointing to the speck. 'It might have only been a natural satellite . . . a small captive asteroid, perhaps . . . but the primary's mass was too small and the second object's orbit around it was too narrow. So Raziel gave it a closer look, and as you can see . . .'

He magnified the holo to twice its previous size, this time adding wire-frame lines of latitude and longitude. Ramirez then tapped in a sequence of time-lapse images; although the primary object didn't gain any additional detail, it became apparent that its companion was moving in orbit around its equator. 'Again, it could have been a natural phenomenon,' he continued, 'but then Raziel captured this one particular image . . .'

He waited until the speck had almost completed its transit of the object, then froze the image and magnified it to its highest resolution. Only the western limb of the primary could be seen, but that wasn't what drew everyone's attention. For the speck was no longer a speck but instead a tiny ellipse, with Proxima sunlight gleaming through the cavity at its center.

'Clearly, this is an artificial construct.' Even though Ramirez had studied this particular frame dozens of times in the past few days, he still felt a shiver run down his back. 'Not only that, but subsequent examination of the primary confirmed it was a little more than two-point-oh-five light-years away. In other words, the primary, along with its companion, wasn't in orbit around Proxima, but instead passing in transit between the Centauri system and our own.'

Murmurs from around the table as conference members studied the image. While some were awestruck, others were plainly skeptical. Ignoring them, Ramirez went on. 'Although Raziel spotted it only for a moment – one-ten-thousandth of a second, to be exact – it was sufficient to trigger its recognition mode. Even as it relayed a priority message to Muscoviense Centre, it proceeded to the next stage.'

He touched his screen again, relaying a graphic image to everyone else's screens. 'In the event of something like this, Raziel was programmed to transmit a sequence of short-burst microwave signals representing prime numbers . . . three, five, seven, eleven, and so forth . . . on a frequency of fourteen hundred twenty megahertz, or twenty-one centimeters wavelength. This has been long considered the frequency most likely to be noticed by an intelligent observer . . . or, at least, one possessing the proper equipment . . . that wouldn't be mistaken for cosmic background radiation.'

Ramirez waited a moment, letting his words sink in. 'That was about four years and a half years ago. On April 1, Mare Muscoviense's long-baseline array intercepted a signal, this one transmitted at the exact same frequency. At first we . . . I mean, our people . . . thought it might only be an echo of some sort, because the signal commenced with an identical string of prime numbers. But then the sequence became much more complex, lasting thirty-four seconds until it began to repeat itself.'

He touched another key, and a new image appeared on the attendees' screens: rows of digits, beginning with 1, 3, 5, and 7 and continuing into five-place prime numbers, before breaking pattern and becoming a complicated string of numbers that had no obvious pattern. 'We have no idea what this means, of course,' Ramirez went on, 'but there's no doubt that it's the product of extraterrestrial intelligence. Nor is there any doubt that it came from the . . . um, object.'

'Spindrift,' Cole murmured.

Ramirez looked at him. 'Pardon me?'

'Spindrift. The code name ESA and the Union Astronautica have agreed upon for this phenomenon.' Cole sat up a little straighter, touched his mike to activate it. 'Thank you very much for the background on this discovery, Dr Ramirez. I think I speak for everyone when I say that I'm very pleased that you agreed to participate in this conference and that your creation has fruit at long last.'

'Yes, but . . .'

'We'll now open the floor to comments.' Cole gave him

an admonishing glance, silently telling him to shut up. Then he pointed to a stuffy-looking academic who'd picked up his placard and placed it end up on the table, indicating his desire to speak. 'Dr Waterstone . . .'

Many hours later, Ramirez found himself alone in his room, gazing through the window and, once again, wondering why he was there.

His quarters were located on the second floor of the southwest wing, a cozy but comfortable suite with a private bath, a modest luxury that he'd almost forgotten after nine years in Dolland. The window overlooked the small graveyard of the adjacent chapel; floodlights along the manor's roof eaves illuminated rows of eroded slate tombstones, each marking the final resting place of a member of one of the families that had possessed Wilton House since the mideighteenth century. The last mellow glow of twilight had fallen over the distant hills; he'd cracked open a window to get some air, and now he could hear the crickets commencing their evening concerto.

The conference had dragged on through the rest of the morning and late into the afternoon, interrupted only by lunch in the main hall and teatime in the library. He'd spoken little since his presentation, save to answer the occasional question from another attendee. Indeed, no one except Shillinglaw, Cole, or Sinclair seemed willing to acknowledge his presence, even though it soon became obvious that, even after having been absent from the scientific community for nearly a decade, he was still the person in the room most knowledgeable about extraterrestrial intelligence.

That was to be expected. Even before his conviction, the field had shrunk until it'd largely consisted of little more than a dozen specialists, all of whom had been struggling for recognition. Humankind had finally gone to the stars, true enough, but when no alien races had been found out there, the view that *Homo sapiens* was alone in the cosmos had gradually gained widespread acceptance. In its wake had come Dominion Christianity, with a belief system based upon a misreading of the anthropic principle; it wasn't natural selection that favored the human race as the inheritors of the galaxy, but the will of God. The fact that, so far, only one habitable world had been discovered was enough to bolster this particular article of faith; if the Western Hemisphere Union hadn't nearly bankrupted itself by building a small fleet of starships that it had already dispatched to the 47 Ursae Majoris system, then subsequent vessels would've doubtless contained legions of Dominion missionaries.

Even if none of the conference members were Dominionists – and Ramirez suspected that one or two might be – enough remained skeptical of Raziel's findings that, for the rest of the day, the sessions had bogged down in endless debate over fine points of data. At first, Ramirez tried to defend his findings, but after a while he realized that few seemed willing to listen to him. It wasn't because of what he'd said, but because of who he was. The message had been accepted, but the messenger was to be ignored. So finally he'd gone silent, sucking on hard candies and absently playing with the wrappers, while scientists who'd earned their credentials while he was doing hard time in Dolland split hairs over the mathematical permutations of the Spindrift signal that even a postgrad physics student could have correctly interpreted.

So why was he there? He didn't know. All things considered, though, he might as well be somewhere else.

There was no chain-link fence around Wilton Park, and no one had put him back in manacles after dinner. Leaning upon his cane, Ramirez had stood at the window for nearly a half hour now, and still he hadn't spotted any security guards. All he had to do was open the window a little more, then slip his legs over the sill. No more than an eight-foot drop lay between him and the ground below; if he did it right, he might be able to land without breaking a leg. He had little more than the clothes on his back, and it wouldn't be long before a police alert was put out for him, but nonetheless there was a small chance that he might be able to escape.

Do it, man, he thought, staring at the half-open window. *Now or never. Wait until the conference is over, and they'll just pack you off to Dolland, and you'll spend the rest of your life in that hellhole. Go. Get out of here . . .*

All of a sudden, there was a knock at the door.

Startled, Ramirez looked around. He started to reach over to shut the window, then resigned himself to his fate. Cursing beneath his breath, he hobbled across the room to the door. No doubt the window was rigged with sensors. And this would be one of the SAS men, politely wondering if he was all right, if there was anything he might need . . .

Instead, he found Shillinglaw waiting for him, hands clasped behind his back.

'Ah, Jared . . . good to see you're still up and about.' Shillinglaw beamed at him, and Ramirez nodded. 'Would you be so kind as to join us for a drink downstairs? We'd like to have a chat with you.'

The library was on the ground floor, a spacious and comfortably furnished room whose oak-paneled walls were lined with shelves stuffed with books and academic journals. Mahogany sculptures of Zeus and Athena stood on either side of a marble hearth in which a holographic fire burned; concealed heaters warmed the men seated in leather armchairs in front of it.

Sinclair was there, and so was Beck; they smiled as Shillinglaw escorted Ramirez into the room. The third man seated in front of the fireplace, though, he didn't know; in his midthirties, he guessed, although he somehow seemed younger, with a trim build and an unlined face. He hadn't been in attendance at the meetings that day, or otherwise Ramirez would've recognized him.

'Jared! Please, come in. Have a seat.' Beck waved him toward an empty chair. 'Can we get you something? Wine, perhaps?' Ramirez had never been much of a drinker, but everyone else either had wine stems in their hands or had parked them on the coffee table between them. He nodded, and Beck made a silent gesture to the waiter hovering nearby. 'I hope we haven't disturbed you, but . . .'

'Quite all right. I was just . . . meditating.' Whatever conversation the men had been having had ceased the moment he walked into the room. Unnerved by the sudden attention, Ramirez sat down in the offered seat. 'I understand there's something you wished to discuss with me?'

'Well, yes, but . . .' Beck smiled. 'Relax. You've had a long day. And that was quite a presentation you gave this morning. At the very least, it gave everyone much to think about.'

Shillinglaw chuckled. With all the chairs taken, he leaned against a bookcase beside the hearth. Sinclair's mouth briefly ticked upward, yet they continued to regard Ramirez as if he was a bug someone had neglected to crush. The young man, though, gazed at him with unabashed curiosity, like a university student coming face-to-face with a notorious figure whom he'd studied in one class or another, but never dreamed of meeting in real life.

'Glad to hear it,' Ramirez said dryly, 'but I wasn't under the impression that "thinking about it" was the prime concern of this conference.' The waiter reappeared, bearing a tray with a glass of wine. 'In fact, I've begun to wonder why I'm here in the first place,' he added, as the waiter handed his drink to him. 'Not that I haven't enjoyed the change of scenery' – even Sinclair smiled at this – 'but anyone knowledgeable about Raziel could have delivered that talk.'

'Yes, quite.' Beck folded his arms together. 'You're absolutely correct . . . although your presence added a certain *gravitas* that might otherwise have been lacking. But that's beside the point, really. As I said, we have something more important we'd like to discuss with you.'

Shillinglaw cleared his throat. 'Perhaps I should introduce our friend here.' He gestured to the young man seated across from them. 'Commander Theodore Harker, first officer of the EASS *Galileo*.'

'Which ship?' Ramirez shook his head. 'Sorry, but I haven't heard of the *Galileo*. Is that a new Mars cycler?'

'No, sir.' Harker's voice held a slight Welsh accent,

watered down by years of refinement. 'We completed our shakedown cruise to Mars just six weeks ago, but interplanetary service is not our principal mission.' He paused. 'The *Galileo* is a starship.'

Ramirez blinked. It took a moment for this to sink in. 'A starship,' he murmured at last. 'I'll be damned . . .' He looked at Shillinglaw. 'You *have* made progress while I've been away, haven't you?'

'Don't feel bad. You haven't been that far out of the loop.' Shillinglaw stepped away from the bookcase. 'Most of *Galileo*'s development was classified, strictly on a need-to-know basis. We didn't go public with the project until we actually began construction four years ago . . .'

'And by then, of course, your intelligence operatives had achieved their goal.' Sinclair glowered at both him and Beck. 'I have to hand it to you . . . they were very good at unearthing the details of our diametric drive. My government didn't even know they'd been stolen until . . .'

'Oh, Donald, please.' Beck closed his eyes, shook his head. 'ESA didn't steal the diametric drive, and you know it. Our people developed it independently. Otherwise, why would the configuration of the drive torus be so different?'

'Because you . . .'

'Look,' Ramirez interrupted, 'I'm really not interested in hearing this.' Then a new thought occurred to him. 'Or maybe I am. The last starship the Union Astronautica built . . . um, the *Spirit* . . .'

'The *Spirit of Social Collectivism Carried to the Stars*,' Sinclair said, reciting the ship's cumbersome but politically correct full name. 'The last of the five colony ships sent to 47 Ursae Majoris.'

'After the *Alabama*, of course.' Sinclair's face reddened as Ramirez said this. Good social collectivists – particularly political officers – didn't like to be reminded that it was the old, right-wing United Republic of America that built and launched humankind's first starship, long before the Western Hemisphere Union rose from the wreckage of the former government. He started to sputter something, but Ramirez ignored him. 'But the Union Astronautica exhausted their resources building that fleet,' he went on, 'and . . . at least so far as I know . . . haven't built any since.'

'Sometimes, there's a certain advantage to being the tortoise,' Shillinglaw said quietly. 'Especially when it's obvious that the hare will soon take a nap.'

Sinclair glared at him, while Beck covered his bemused expression with his hand. 'That's one way of putting it,' Harker said, making an attempt to be diplomatic. 'The fact remains that, at this moment, the EA has the only operational starship.' He smiled, and Ramirez couldn't help but notice a certain twinkle in his eye. 'Among other resources,' he added, as a mischievous grin crept across his face.

'I think you can see where this is going.' Beck leaned forward to place his empty wineglass on the table. 'We mean to send the *Galileo* to Spindrift, with the intent of investigating the origin of these signals.' He nodded toward Sinclair. 'This will be a bilateral mission. After all, it was the Union Astronautica that discovered Spindrift . . .

'And ESA has the means to get there.' Ramirez toyed with the untasted drink in his hand. 'Not a bad idea, if you have a ship capable of reaching the object . . . Spindrift, I mean . . . when it makes its closest approach.' He searched his memory. 'Just short of two light-years, about two and a half years from now. You're going to be cutting it close, even with diametric drive.'

'We have a certain . . . well, edge . . . that gives us confidence that we can make it,' Harker said. 'In order for us to achieve our launch window, we're looking at a departure date of June 1.'

Ramirez raised an eyebrow. 'So soon? That's only six weeks away.'

'We believe that it can be accomplished.' Beck settled back in his chair, steepled his fingers together. 'We already have a good crew, with Captain Lawrence in command . . . sorry he can't be here, but he's attending to other matters just now.' Harker made a face, but said nothing. 'And we're presently assembling our science team, with representatives from both the Union Astronautica and the European Space Agency.' He paused. 'Which is why we've asked you to be here, Dr Ramirez. We'd like to have you aboard.'

The glass slipped from Ramirez's hand, spilling wine across the dark green carpet. He barely noticed the waiter as he rushed forward to sop up the mess with a terry-cloth towel. His heart skipped a beat; for a moment, it was hard for him to breathe. No one in the room spoke; Ramirez waited for someone to grin, laugh, tell him it was just a gag – *oh, no, we're not serious . . . you're staying behind, to act as a consultant* – but everyone simply gazed at him, waiting for a response.

'Sure,' he said at last. 'I'd love to.'

'Splendid,' Shillinglaw said. 'We were hoping you'd say

that.' He grasped Ramirez's shoulder as he gazed at Harker. 'You've got your astrobiologist, Commander . . . the best in the business.'

Harker gave him a tight smile, then nodded to Ramirez. Sinclair let out his breath and shook his head, while Beck asked the waiter to fetch a round of champagne so that they could make a toast to the mission. None of them noticed Shillinglaw as, still holding Ramirez's shoulder, he leaned forward to whisper in his ear.

'There, you see?' he said softly. 'You didn't really want to jump out that window, now did you?'

Three

MAY 29, 2288 – TSIOLKOVSKY STATION, NEW GUINEA SPACE ELEVATOR

Like a silver caterpillar ascending an impossibly long strand of silk, the tram from New Guinea climbed the last hundred yards toward its berth within the station's outer hull. As it approached the terminus, the vehicle began to decelerate, the conical fairing of its nose bisecting to reveal the flanges of its docking module. The tram almost seemed to coast the rest of the way home; it slowly entered the sleevelike berth, then there was a slight jar as it came to a halt.

A recorded voice came through speakers within the passenger lounge, announcing the tram's arrival. First-time travelers, impatient to board the elevator for its descent, unbuckled themselves from their seats. Clutching the straps of their carry-on bags, they began to waddle toward the hatch leading to the boarding gate, careful not to let the soles of their stickshoes leave the floor's densely fibered carpet. The gate agent didn't hurry to collect their tickets as it would take a while for the outbound passengers to disembark. After that the stewards had to clean the cabin and restock its galley. The more seasoned passengers knew this; they remained in their seats, reading their pads or watching netcasts, or gazed out the lounge window at the impressive sight of the space elevator, a massive and seemingly infinite cylinder that fell away from them, gradually diminishing in width but never in length, until it became a mere wire that pierced Earth's upper atmosphere almost 22,300 miles away.

Harker lingered at the window until he heard the hatch open, then he turned away to saunter across the lounge. The first few people to disembark were all civilians; some looked distinctly pallid, and it wasn't hard to tell which ones would soon be rushing for the nearest toilet to become spacesick. And, as always, there were the kids who seemed to bounce everywhere at once, drunk with their first taste of microgravity. None of them would be here very long; they'd soon board ferries that would transport them to orbital colonies, lunar shuttles or, in a few instances, one of the giant Mars cycleships parked elsewhere in geosynchronous orbit.

Harker almost envied them. Not because of where they were going – he'd spent most of his adult life on the Moon, and two trips to Mars was enough for him – but with whom they'd be traveling. It didn't bother him so much that it would be nearly five years before he set foot on Earth again. What he wasn't looking forward to was the company he'd keep.

Please, change your mind, he thought, even though he knew that this was a futile hope. *Please let there be a death in the family, or some unforeseen illness, or anything else that might lead you to think that this is something you just can't do. Even an attack of common sense, unlikely as that may be. But please . . .*

'Mr Harker!'

No such luck. Ian Lawrence emerged from the gate, pushing past a couple of vacationers who'd come off the tram just in front of him. Harker forced a smile, even though his face felt as if it was made of lead. 'Welcome back, Captain,' he said, as pleasantly as he could. 'Have a good trip?'

'Splendid, just splendid.' Lawrence had an overstuffed duffel bag in one hand and an attaché case in the other. Without bothering to ask, he held out the bag for Harker to take. 'Thanks for coming to meet me. Nice to see a familiar face.'

Captain Ian Lawrence, commanding officer of the EASS *Galileo*, apparently hadn't received the memo requesting crew members using the space elevator to travel incognito. Either that or, more likely, he'd decided to disregard it. Whatever the reason, his dress uniform attracted attention; from the corner of his eye, Harker saw other passengers taking note of his service beret and the gilded braid and epaulets of his tunic. Perhaps that was why Lawrence insisted on wearing them; besides a handlebar mustache cultivated to mate with a pair of muttonchop sideburns, there was nothing about the *Galileo*'s captain – short, slightly overweight, with a weak chin and mercurial temperament – that commanded more than a moment's notice.

'Of course, sir. Not a problem.' *Unless you count the fact that you should've been here five days ago, along with the rest of us.* Harker took the bag from his captain, then turned toward the lift. 'If you'll follow me, sir . . .'

'Just a moment. We've got one more person.' Lawrence looked around, then raised his hand. 'Over here, John!'

Looking back, Harker felt his heart sink even further. John Shillinglaw, the ESA associate director whom he'd met at Wilton Park a few weeks earlier. Shillinglaw had impressed him as little more than a bureaucrat who'd found his way into his position by being in the right place at the right time. It only figured that he'd make friends with Lawrence; they both belonged to the same social class. The only difference was that, in Shillinglaw's case, he actually showed some aptitude for his job.

Cut it out. Harker bit the inside of his lip as he watched Shillinglaw make his way through the crowd. *You've got to work with these guys ... especially Ian ... even if you don't respect them.*

'Sorry. Got hung up back there.' As Shillinglaw joined them, his gaze fell to the V-neck sweater and baggy trousers Harker wore. 'A little out of uniform, aren't we, Commander?'

'Sorry. Wasn't aware that this was a formal occasion.' Praying that Shillinglaw's presence didn't portend another unexpected crew addition – they'd had one of those already – Harker began to escort them to the lift. 'We weren't expecting you. I take it this is ... ah, official business?'

'Of course.' Shillinglaw smiled. 'Don't worry, I won't be here long. I've just come up to observe the final mission briefing before you go into quarantine.'

Oh, thank God. 'In that case, glad to have you aboard.' Harker caught the sour expression that crossed his face. 'That is,' he quickly added as he pushed the button that opened the lift doors, 'I hope your visit is ...'

'John was my guest at my family estate this last week.' Lawrence's voice was cool as they entered the lift. 'We spent some time discussing the mission in a more comfortable environment.' He cast a sideways look at Harker. 'You were welcome to join us, of course ...'

'Thank you, sir, but I had my duties.' Harker stared

straight ahead as the lift began to ascend. *All the things you couldn't be bothered to take care of yourself*, he thought. *But, after all, one last weekend loitering around the Yorkshire manor was more important, wasn't it?* 'The rest of the crew is already aboard. They've completed training, and we'll commence final preparations tomorrow.'

'Very good. If you could deliver an update by 1900, I'd appreciate it.' Lawrence turned to Shillinglaw. 'See? I told you Ted was efficient. That's why I personally requested for him to be my first officer.'

That, Harker thought, *or you knew you'd get someone who'd cover your ass. Just as you always have . . .*

The lift came to a stop, and the doors slid open to reveal a circular corridor. Harker stepped aside to let the other two men through, then followed them into the passageway. At least Lawrence knew where he was going; making small talk with Shillinglaw, he led them around the bend to a round hatch on the outer wall marked SEC. 2 – AUTHORIZED PERSONNEL ONLY. A quick scan of his thumbprint and a typed-in password on the keypad were enough to open the hatch. On the other side was a cramped sphere, just large enough for four persons, with padded seats arranged around its interior. Ducking their heads, they climbed inside and sat down. Harker took a moment to secure the captain's baggage within nets beneath the seats, then they grasped rungs positioned at shoulder level and inserted their feet beneath the floor bar. Once they were settled in, Harker pushed a button to seal the hatch.

'So we've got everyone?' Lawrence asked as the cab began to descend down the axial spoke leading to the station ring. 'Flight crew, science team . . .'

'Yes, sir. All present and accounted for.' The cab rotated

ninety degrees, and Harker briefly closed his eyes, feeling his body gain weight as the cab crossed the gravity gradient. 'Dr Ramirez came up last week. He's handled the training quite well . . . better than I expected, in fact.'

'I'm not . . .' Shillinglaw belched; his face went pale, and for a moment Harker was afraid that he might get sick. 'Surprised,' he finished, his voice little more than a gasp. 'He's very . . .'

'Adaptable, yes.' Lawrence looked away, tactfully sparing his guest a moment of embarrassment. 'Good, very good. And the crew . . . ?'

'No problems so far.' *Except that you decided to take a holiday while the rest of us were busting our chops.*

The cab eased to a halt, and the doors automatically opened. They climbed out to find themselves in another circular passageway, this one with a wider arc than the one within the station hub. Once again, Lawrence left it to Harker to carry his bag. As they walked toward a frosted-glass door at the end of the corridor, a new thought seemed to occur to him. 'Ted, have you been letting people visit the rest of the station?'

'Of course, sir.' This section of the ring was already off-limits to anyone who didn't have ESA clearance. By the next day it would be under full quarantine as well, with access denied to anyone who wasn't going aboard the *Galileo*, and no one allowed to leave either. 'When they've finished training, they've generally gone up to the hub. There are a couple of good restaurants there, and a rather good pub . . .'

'Well . . .' Lawrence frowned as he pressed his thumb against the identification plate. 'Afraid there'll be enough of that. Don't want to risk any loose talk in public about this mission. From here on out, everyone is confined to this section.'

'Sir . . .'

'That's an order, Mr Harker. I expect you to carry it out.' The door slid open with a faint hiss. Lawrence reached over to take his bag from Harker, then stepped through the door with barely a glance behind him. 'One more thing . . . I want the crew and the science team assembled in the conference room in one hour. It's time to go through our final briefing.'

Harker was glad that Lawrence had taken the bag from him; otherwise, he might have been tempted to drop it on his foot. He watched as the captain marched down the corridor, Shillinglaw following him like a puppy.

'Insufferable bastard,' he muttered.

Like the rest of Tsiolkovsky Station's deep-space training section, the conference room was spartan and antiseptic, with plastic chairs surrounding an oval table fashioned to look like bird's-eye maple. The only relief was a broad window. Standing before it and looking straight down, one could see Earth revolving at the end of a long silver string like a giant blue-green yo-yo, an optical illusion produced by the ring's axial rotation.

There weren't enough seats to accommodate everyone, so a few expedition members had to stand against the window and the walls. Even so, Harker reflected, the *Galileo* party was remarkably small: fifteen in all, divided between nine crewmen and six passengers, with Shillinglaw as an observer who, along with a handful of ESA physicians, would be among the last few to see them before they left Earth. No one was happy about Captain

Lawrence's abrupt edict against further visits to the hub, but Harker had little doubt that some of them would attempt to sneak up there anyway. Well, then, so be it. Unless Lawrence specifically ordered him to do otherwise, he intended to forget about locking down the spoke cab until 0800, and look the other way if anyone came back before then reeking of ale.

Sitting at one end of the table, Harker let his gaze travel across the room. Of everyone gathered here, he was most familiar with the ship's flight crew. Antonia Vincenza, the executive officer, her brow furrowed as she studied the datapad in her lap. Martin Cohen and Werner Gelb, the chief engineer and life-support engineer respectively, involved in some technical discussion. Arkady Rusic, the communications officer, and Simone Monet, the helmsman, sharing some private conversation in hushed tones. Nick Jones, the ship's doctor, dozing in his chair, arms folded together and head tilted forward against his chest.

Seated at the opposite end of the table was the shuttle pilot, Emily Collins. As always, they were careful not to acknowledge each other's presence. Nonetheless, when she briefly looked up from the pad she was reading, there was a moment when they caught each other's eye. The most secretive of smiles, then she returned her attention to her pad. No more covert rendezvous in the station pub, Harker reflected. From here on out, they'd have to find other ways of spending time with each other.

He knew the science team less well. Tobias Rauchle was a German astrophysicist who'd been picked to lead the team; he sat on the opposite side of the table, arms folded across his chest, staring straight ahead with a perpetual frown upon his face. Standing behind him was his former student, Robert Kaufmann, also from ESA's extrasolar exploration directorate; the two of them were never far apart, with Kaufmann almost always seconding Rauchle's opinion, but at least the younger man was a little easier to take than his mentor. On the other hand, there was Jorge Cruz, the astrogeologist from the University of Havana who'd been sent by the Union Astronautica. Judging from their previous conversations, Harker had come to realize that Cruz, while apparently less than a bred-in-the-bone social collectivist, was only too happy to disagree whenever possible with his European colleagues.

Harker doubted that he'd get a chance to be influenced by counterrevolutionary ideology. Donald Sinclair stood beside Cruz, quietly observing everything that was going on. The Proletariat had apparently decided that it was more important to send one of its own on the mission than another scientist; if the Union Astronautica had objected, Harker hadn't heard of it. Which certainly wasn't the case when the ESA decided that it needed to put aboard its own political representative as well; Sir Peter Cole might be a Cambridge fellow and England's Astronomer Royal, but it was clear to everyone that he was intended to be Sinclair's counterpart. In any case, neither government wanted to risk being left out when the *Galileo* discovered . . . well, whatever it was that the expedition would discover when they reached Spindrift.

Which left Jared Ramirez. Once again, Harker found his eyes drawn to the astrobiologist. He sat quietly midway down the table, not participating in any of the conversations around him. Throughout this last month, when the crew and science team had undergone intensive training – first in Geneva, then on the ship and the station – Ramirez had been largely left alone by the others. He'd demonstrated a willingness to cooperate with the rest of the science team, even a wry sense of humor at times. Yet the fact remained that everyone knew who he was. Perhaps he'd once been a respected scientist in his field, but no one was willing to forget his role in the Savant genocide, or that his actions had led to the deaths of over thirty-five thousand people.

Why did you do it? Harker studied Ramirez from across the room. *You said that you didn't know what the Council of Savants was planning when you supplied it data about disease vectors within third-world populations . . . but when people in those regions started dying from viruses that had been obliterated years ago, you didn't tell anyone that the pattern mimicked possible scenarios you'd mapped out for the Savants. Were you really just a pawn? Or did you believe as they did, that the planet could only be saved if there were three billion fewer people living on it?*

He glanced again at Emily, and wasn't surprised to see that she was quietly watching Ramirez as well. Once more, she met his gaze, only this time she didn't smile. Like it or not, Jared Ramirez was the foremost expert in extraterrestrial intelligence. If Spindrift was, indeed, an alien artifact of some sort, his knowledge would be invaluable.

But could they trust him? Harker didn't know.

The door slid open just then, and Captain Lawrence strode into the room. 'Don't get up, please,' he said, although no one made an effort to rise from their seats, as he walked past them to take his place at the head of the table. 'I'll try to make this as brief as possible, so you can return to work.'

'Thank you, sir.' Arkady's face remained stoical. 'There's much that remains to be done.'

Some knowing smiles from around the table, and a couple of coughs. The fact of the matter was that there was little for anyone to do in the forty hours that remained before they left the station, save for preflight physicals and last-minute teleconference calls with family and friends back on Earth. Yet the irony was lost on the captain; Lawrence nodded, then opened his pad and placed it on the table.

'This will be our last mission briefing before we commence final countdown,' he said, tapping in commands that slaved his pad to the conference room comp. 'If there's anyone who has any objections' – a glance at Arkady – 'substantive objections, that is, now is the time to voice them.'

No one spoke up, although Cohen, noticing that Jones was still asleep, nudged him with his elbow. The doctor's eyes opened; he blinked a few times, then sat up straight in his chair. *Should've let him sleep*, Harker thought. *Nothing here he hasn't heard before.*

'Our profile calls for us to board *Galileo* at 0900 GMT on June 1.' The wallscreen behind Lawrence lit to display the schedule. 'Both the flight crew and the science team will disembark from this station at 0800, aboard OTVs piloted by Commander Harker and Lieutenant Collins. They will dock with *Galileo* at ports two and four . . .'

Harker slid down into his chair. Everyone here knew this already; he could see their eyes beginning to glaze over. Lawrence was trying to assert his authority. Once again, he found himself pondering the twists of fate that brought this buffoon to the command of the *Galileo* instead of . . .

No. Let's not go there again. Harker forced himself to concentrate on the briefing, even though everything Lawrence said was already committed to memory. Prelaunch checkout of all major systems, followed by AI tests and rundown of the checklist, the entire procedure lasting six hours. At T minus thirty seconds, full activation of onboard power systems. At T minus zero, primary ignition and departure from dry dock . . .

'Mission clock begins at 1500.' Lawrence tapped another command into his keypad, and a holo shimmered into existence above the table: Earth, with Tsiolkovsky Station connected to it by a slender thread and a wireframe model of *Galileo* parked in geosynchronous orbit nearby. As they watched, *Galileo* departed from orbit and, leaving a dotted line in its wake, began to move away from Earth. 'At this point, we'll turn over command and control to the gatehouse, and its AI will interface with our own during rendezvous maneuvers with the starbridge.' The holo expanded to show *Galileo* heading for a small silver ring positioned in Lagrangian orbit near the Moon, a space station hovering nearby. 'It'll be a hands-off approach, of course,' he added, giving Simone a meaningful glance. 'The comps will take care of hyperspace insertion.'

Simone nodded, but didn't say anything. Harker had no doubt that she didn't much like the idea of surrendering the helm to *Galileo*'s AI, but it couldn't be helped; the timing was too critical to be trusted to human reflexes. And since this would be the first time a manned vessel would go through the starbridge, no one was willing to take any chances.

As if we're not taking enough already, he thought.

'If all goes well,' Lawrence said, 'we'll achieve hyperspace insertion at exactly 2100.' As he spoke, the holo expanded again, this time to show *Galileo* entering the starbridge's event horizon, depicted as a funnel-shaped grid, with the gatehouse floating beyond its gravitational reach. 'We shouldn't feel any major effects beyond some minor turbulence, but even then, we've been cautioned to have our harnesses securely fastened . . .'

'And our heads firmly positioned beneath our legs,' Arkady murmured. Everyone laughed out loud save for Lawrence, who glared at him. 'Sorry, sir,' he added, unable to keep the smile off his face. 'Small joke.'

'I hope it's your last.' Lawrence looked away again, giving the others a chance to roll their eyes and shake their heads. Harker quietly sighed. Not a good sign.

Galileo entered the ring and disappeared. Lawrence tapped his pad again, and the starbridge, along with Earth and the Moon, suddenly diminished in size, vanishing into near nothingness as, in their place, there appeared a schematic diagram of the solar system as seen from a ninety-degree angle. The orbits of the major planets were traced by a series of concentric circles, with the inner planets all but disappearing within a tight halo close to the Sun and the outer planets of Jupiter, Saturn, Uranus, and Neptune positioned at various places along its nether regions.

Far beyond the orbit of Neptune, there appeared a vast elliptical loop, skewed at a forty-four-degree angle above and below the plane of ecliptic and, at its farthest point, extending deep into extrasolar space. A tiny black spot was located almost midway to the apogee of this orbital track, below the plane of ecliptic. Lawrence manipulated the holo, and it zoomed to reveal a small, off-white sphere, with another ring-shaped starbridge orbiting nearby.

'The jump shouldn't take more than a second,' he went on, as the tiny replica of *Galileo* exited the second starbridge, 'but once we're through, we'll be in orbit near Eris. At this point, we'll be approximately forty-two-point-seven AUs from Earth . . .' He suddenly stopped, pointed across the room. 'You have a question?'

'If I may.' Donald Sinclair had raised his hand. 'Granted, this is an efficient use of KX-1' – he referred to the second starbridge by its official designation – 'but, as I understand it, forty-two AUs is less than one percent of the distance we need to travel in order to intercept Spindrift. If that's the case, why not engage the diametric drive earlier? After all, if we'll eventually be traveling at ninety-five percent light-speed, we could cross the same distance in only a matter of hours.' He paused, allowing a fatuous smile to creep across his face. 'Our ships didn't do that.'

For a moment, Lawrence's expression was one of bafflement. His mouth opened, but nothing came out. *Oh, for the love of Christ*, Harker thought. *The poor dumb bastard doesn't know the answer to this.*

'That would be true,' Harker said, sitting up in his seat, 'if we could achieve relativistic velocity from a standstill. But it'll take *Galileo* three months to accelerate to one gee, using its fusion engine, before its diametric drive can reach full efficiency, and even then it'd have to work hard to escape the Sun's gravitational pull. That's something your ships had to deal with. But since we'll be using KX-1, we can instantly put ourselves beyond the Sun's gravity well so that it's no longer much of a consideration. And since Spindrift's course puts it beneath the solar plane of ecliptic, it'll also give us something of a head start.'

'Exactly, yes.' Lawrence recovered his poise. 'Thank you, Mr Harker.' He pointed to the miniature *Galileo*, circling the minor planet. 'We'll spend a couple of days in orbit around Eris, deploying the drive torus and making a final check of all systems, before we ignite the main engine and depart for our rendezvous with Spindrift.'

Again, he touched his pad. The solar system shrank until only the orbit of Eris was apparent; far away, a dotted line traced Spindrift's estimated trajectory. A blue line appeared between the two, showing *Galileo*'s flight path. 'We'll enter into biostasis shortly after that,' the captain went on, 'and remain that way until we reach Spindrift at its closest approach, two light-years . . .'

'One-point-nine-nine l.y.s.' This from Ramirez, who had been quiet until that point.

'Yes, right. By that time, we'll have spent two years and one month in biostasis . . .'

'Seven and a half months,' Jones said. 'Shiptime, that is, taking into consideration time dilation at relativistic . . .'

'Right. Yes, of course.' Lawrence was becoming visibly flustered. 'But the ship's comps will be preset to disregard this . . . um, effect . . . so when we reach Spindrift, the date will be January 7, 2291, counting three months for acceleration and three more for braking. Or at least so we estimate . . .'

'If all goes well,' Ramirez muttered.

'No doubt it will.' Lawrence touched his pad again, and the holo dissolved. 'I believe that's all for now,' he said, bending down to fold his pad. 'If anyone has any further questions or concerns, I'll take them in my quarters. Until then . . .'

He paused, looked around. It was almost as if he was taking into regard a roomful of strangers, none of whom he knew well enough to consider his friends, let alone teammates. 'Thank you,' he said, then picked up his pad and, without a glance behind him, hurried from the room.

So much for the final mission briefing. Sinking back in his chair, Harker rubbed at his eyelids with the tips of his fingers. Around him, he could hear crewmen murmuring to each other. Someone made a remark that he didn't catch – probably Arkady – that caused others to laugh. If he'd been in any other mood, he might have asked what it was. Yet just now, the mission itself seemed like some sort of practical joke.

Good grief, he thought, *the man is such a fool.*

A soft hand touched the back of his neck. He opened his eyes and looked up to see Emily standing behind him. 'Hey, sailor,' she said quietly. 'Buy you a drink?'

'Love one.' Then he frowned. 'We're going to have to wait a while, though. Can't let him see us sneaking off to . . .'

'Don't worry. I know the best place in town.' She looked around, making sure no one was listening to them, then leaned closer. 'My quarters. Half an hour.'

A quick tap upon his shoulder, then she was gone. Harker watched as she left the conference room, admiring the graceful movement of her hips within her jumpsuit.

Ah, well, he mused. *At least I won't be lacking for company these next few years.*

Even if most of them would be spent asleep.

Four

June 1, 2288 – EASS *Galileo*

From the distance, the *Galileo* was almost invisible; only the gunmetal-grey bell of its main engine could be seen within the latticework of its dry dock. As the orbital transfer vehicle drew closer, though, the vessel gradually took on form, becoming an elongated spindle illuminated by flood-light arrays. Even so, the spacecraft remained toylike, its true dimensions not readily apparent until the OTV was only a hundred meters away.

'*Galileo* command, Charlie Victor two-ten.' Emily Collins kept her hands upon the yoke, moving it ever so slightly to fire maneuvering thrusters. 'Requesting clearance for final approach and docking.'

A moment passed, then she heard Arkady's voice in her headset: '*We copy, Charlie Victor. We have you acquired. Proceed to docking at port four.*' She was about to reply when she felt a gentle nudge at her left elbow. Not taking her eyes from the wedge-shaped window, Collins stole a sidelong glance at Jared Ramirez, sitting beside her in the copilot seat.

'Yes?' she said, tapping the lobe of her headset to mute the wand-mike.

'Sorry to bother you, but . . .' Ramirez hesitated. 'Do you think it's possible that we might have a last look before we go aboard? After all, we're going to be cooped up in her . . . it, whatever . . . for quite some time.'

'Yes, please.' This from Cole, seated along with the rest of the science team in the rear. 'Of course, if the schedule is too tight . . .'

Collins checked the chronometer above her head. The countdown stood at T minus five hours, nine minutes. The flight crew had arrived a little more than forty-five minutes ago; although they were preparing *Galileo* for launch, there wasn't much for the science team to do between now and then except find their way to their quarters, stow their belongings, and wait for launch. And although they'd toured the ship during training, this would be the last time any of them would see the outside of the vessel for many months.

'I'll see what I can do.' Collins tapped her mike again. '*Galileo*, Charlie Victor two-ten. The passengers have asked for visual inspection of the vehicle. Requesting permission for flyby.'

Another pause, this time a little longer. Collins imagined Arkady turning to Captain Lawrence, repeating her request to him. She half expected it to be denied because . . . well, simply because . . . but then his voice returned. '*Roger that, Charlie Victor. You have permission for a brief flyby, with the captain's compliments.*'

With the captain's compliments. Oh, how grand! Collins could only picture the look on Arkady's face as he relayed this; if he was smart, he'd turned his back to Lawrence. 'Thank you, *Galileo*. Charlie Victor two-ten over.'

She muted the mike again, then inched the yoke slightly to the left, delicately negotiating a starboard turn that put the OTV on a parallel heading with the dry dock. 'You got your flyby, Dr Ramirez,' she said. 'Better look sharp, because we're only doing this once.'

'M'lady, you're a princess.' Ramirez favored her with a dashing smile, then lowered his voice. 'Captain's something of a . . . well, y'know . . .'

'No, I wouldn't,' she said tightly, even though she could think of a dozen apt descriptions that would fit the diplomatic pause in his last comment. 'And it's my pleasure,' she added, even though she probably would've ignored his suggestion if Cole hadn't seconded it.

The OTV was traveling alongside *Galileo*, moving from the stern toward the bow. One hundred thirty meters long, the vessel was a collection of cylinders of various sizes, with the propulsion module taking up nearly half of its length. Through the dry dock's cradlelike trusswork, they could see ropelike umbilical lines running to ports along the sides of the enormous main fuel tank, containing deuterium and helium-3, just aft of the fusion engine. Like the rest of the ship, they were enclosed by plates faintly resembling hand-woven blankets: nine-millimeter beryllium shields, the first line of defense against interstellar dust, a nuisance barely worth noticing most of the time but potentially lethal at relativistic velocities.

'Not that I have anything against Captain Lawrence,' Ramirez said quietly. 'It's just that . . . well, I can't help but noticing a certain difference between him and Mr Harker.'

'Is that so?' Collins kept an eye on the radar, carefully maintaining a safe distance between the OTV and the dry dock. 'I hadn't noticed.'

By then they were passing the service module. Forward of the reaction-control thrusters, two probes were mounted on either side of the hull: Larry, the lozenge-shaped vehicle meant for atmospheric entry, and its larger brother Jerry, a spherical robot designed for orbital reconnaissance. She had no idea why they'd been given these names, other than that they held some literary significance for their designers. Past the service module was the four-port docking module, the most narrow part of the ship. Her own craft, the *Maria Celeste*, rested belly-up within its cradle, her dorsal hatch mated with the airlock. She noted that the OTV that had transferred the flight crew from Tsiolkovsky Station had already departed, flown back by a harbor pilot who'd been waiting aboard ship for the crew's arrival.

'You haven't?' A dry chuckle. 'I certainly have. Mr Harker is . . . well, forgive me for saying so, but he's obviously the more capable officer. Or at least that's how it seems to me.'

'Not my place to say.' *Although I completely agree*, she silently added. By all rights, Ted should have been given command of the *Galileo*. He'd graduated at the top of his class from the ESA training center in Geneva, and his grasp of astronautics far exceeded Lawrence's, who'd struggled through the four-year officer training program and was barely qualified to hold command-level rank in the astronaut corps. Yet lan Lawrence was the scion of landed gentry, his father a peer in the House of Lords, while Ted Harker came from a working-class family in Wales. Since the UK had been the primary financial backer of the *Galileo*'s construction, though, Lord Lawrence was able to pull strings to make sure that his son was named as its commanding officer, despite the objections of those in the ESA who knew that Theodore Harker was far more suitable for the job.

Bloody class system, she thought. *This ought to be Ted's ship. Ian's just a rich laird looking for something to add to the family crest.*

She distracted herself by inspecting the concentric bulge that protruded from the hull just forward of the telemetry platform. The housing for the diametric drive, stowed until *Galileo* reached the Kuiper Belt. Ramirez stretched forward against his seat harness to admire it. 'Very efficient engineering,' he murmured. 'Have to admit, it's an elegant solution to a problem . . . how to make the drive torus small enough to pass through the starbridge.' He looked back at her again. 'You haven't answered my question.'

'That's because you haven't asked one.' Before he could reply, Collins nodded toward the window. 'There's our home for the next four years.'

Galileo's hab module was the foremost section of the ship: a drum-shaped cylinder, little more than forty meters long, with portholes and emergency hatches spaced along its four decks. At the end of its blunt bow was its deflector array, six conical pods arranged along a ring-shaped structure; it was designed with redundancy in mind, so that even if two more deflectors failed, the rest would continue to operate. Likewise, the module was connected to the rest of the ship by a slender neck; in the event of an emergency, the module could be detached, to survive on backup power and life-support systems until – at least in theory – the crew could be rescued by another ship.

Yet rescue was almost a moot point. Although plans were being made for the eventual construction of a sister ship, the *Columbus*, the fact of the matter was that if the *Galileo* met with disaster, a rescue mission was almost out of the question. Although the ESA had a small fleet of interplanetary spacecraft, none were designed to pass through KX-1. Indeed, *Galileo*'s first mission had originally been intended to be nothing more than a survey of the Kuiper Belt, with a flight to 47 Ursae Majoris being contemplated if that was successful. No one thought that its maiden voyage beyond the solar system would be to investigate an anomaly like Spindrift.

As they reached the end of the dry dock, Ramirez said something else, but Collins ignored him. Twisting the yoke hard to the right, she assayed a tight starboard turn that brought the OTV around in a 180-degree arc. *Galileo* lay dead ahead, the silver coating of its deflector pods catching the spotlights of her craft. She fired forward thrusters to decelerate, then gently coaxed the OTV forward.

'As I was saying . . .' Ramirez began.

'Not now, please.' She prodded her mike. '*Galileo* command, Charlie Victor two-ten. Flyby completed, resuming docking maneuvers.'

'*Copy that, Charlie Victor.*' Arkady again. '*Clear for docking at port four. Wave as you go by.*'

She grinned despite her nervousness. Maneuvering the OTV within the confines of the dry dock would be a tight squeeze; Arkady knew that her hands would never leave the yoke. 'Wilco,' she replied. 'Watch for my lights.'

The OTV slipped into the dry dock with scarcely twenty meters on either side to spare. Emily chewed her lower lip as she let forward momentum do most of the work, firing aft thrusters only when necessary. From the corner of her eye, she caught a glimpse of a figure floating within one of the broad oval windows on Deck A; Arkady, watching her from the command center as she passed by.

She stole a second to flip a toggle switch twice, causing her formation lights to blink a couple of times, then she put both hands on the yoke again.

Once she guided the craft past the forward mooring cables, she was home free. Emily rolled the OTV forty-five degrees to starboard, then pitched the bow ninety degrees to port. Charlie Victor was flying perpendicular to *Galileo*. When the docking module drifted into view, she fired another burst to brake her momentum. The designated docking port lay directly below her; a quick fire of the aft thrusters, and she moved toward it. Ten meters . . . seven meters . . . five . . . three . . .

A hollow rasp as the OTV's docking probe slid into the collar, then its flanges engaged and there was a sudden thump as the OTV mated with the ship. Emily let out her breath as she reached forward to flip switches that would withdraw the probe and begin pressurization. '*Galileo*, Charlie Victor, we are home.'

'*Confirm that, Charlie Victor.*' Only this time it was Ted's voice, not Arkady's. '*Nice flying there. You've always been good at this sort of thing.*'

Ted, you bastard . . . Emily felt her face grow warm and prayed that no one noticed the innuendo. 'Roger that,' she replied, trying not to smile. She waited a second, studying the gauges to make sure that the seal was tight and there were no air leaks, then turned her head to look back at the passengers. 'All right, now, I'm popping the forward hatch. Might be a slight pressure difference, so I suggest you swallow a couple of times. But don't touch the hatch . . . someone aboard will let you through.'

The science team murmured; they were already unclasping their harnesses and reaching down to pull their baggage from the nets beneath their seats. Collins reset the comp and put the engines on standby mode; since she'd be the last person to exit the craft, it was her duty to make sure that the harbor pilot had a safe craft to fly home.

'Nice work,' Ramirez said. 'You've got a real feel for this sort of thing.'

She'd almost forgotten about him. 'Yes, well . . . it's a small job, but it's mine.'

'And you do it well.' Apparently at ease with where he was, he patiently awaited his turn to leave the ferry. 'Not like other individuals, at least . . .'

Collins cast him a hard look. 'Let them do their work,' she said, 'and see to your own.' She paused, then lowered her voice. 'Sorry, but there're no Savants aboard. You're just going to have to make do with us normal humans.'

He scowled and looked away, and Collins left him alone. She didn't know whom she distrusted more: him or the captain.

With six extra passengers aboard, Deck C was more crowded than usual. Emily carefully made her way through the circular passageway surrounding the hab module's central core, trying to avoid collision with scientists searching for their assigned quarters while, at the same time, adjusting to microgravity. The Millis-Clement field wouldn't be activated until the diametric drive torus was deployed; until then, everyone aboard would have to maneuver around each other in free fall. This didn't pose a problem when *Galileo*'s complement consisted of nine seasoned spacers. Add six eggheads who'd only recently completed deep-space training, and the potential for chaos was magnified a hundredfold.

Fortunately, Ted was on hand to get the mess under control. Emily found him directing the members of the science team to their compartments while trying to deal with their individual problems. At the moment, it appeared to be Tobias Rauchle's turn to lodge a complaint.

'I'm sorry, Dr Rauchle, but we don't have any rooms with connecting doors.' Holding on to the ceiling rail, Harker spoke to the team leader as if he was a hotel concierge handling an irate guest. 'Dr Kaufmann is in the next compartment, though, so . . .'

'No, that's not satisfactory.' Rauchle glared at him in a way that might have been intimidating if the physicist hadn't been upside down; as it was, Rauchle was making his demands to Harker's knees. 'Robert and I are research collaborators. We have important discussions that we need to do in private . . .'

'Then you'll just have to go to his quarters, or him to yours. Or you can talk in the lounge on Deck D when no one else is . . .'

'Toby, it's all right.' Kaufmann hovered behind the senior scientist, his arms laden with their duffel bags. Although he didn't have hold of the handrail, at least his head was in the direction of the ceiling. 'We can work this out.'

'No. That simply will not do.' Trying to reposition himself upright, Rauchle spread out his hands and, touching the narrow walls of the passageway, attempted to perform a cartwheel. Right idea, wrong technique; all he succeeded in doing was bumping his head and nearly kicking Kaufmann in the face. 'If you can't give us connecting compartments, then you could at least reassign one of us to a larger . . .'

'No one aboard has larger quarters,' Emily said. 'Except the captain, but I wouldn't try talking him out of it.' Then she slipped her hand around Ted's waist, letting her fingertips brush his rear. 'Besides,' she added, smiling at both men, 'I'm sure the two of you can work something out. We always have.'

Rauchle's face became scarlet, while a smile briefly flickered across Kaufmann's. Jorge Cruz chose that moment to flounder through their midst, muttering apologies to everyone as he clumsily hauled his bag behind him. Rauchle waited until the astrogeologist was out of earshot. 'Yes, of course,' he muttered. 'My apologies, Commander. I suppose you're right.'

'Sorry we can't be more accommodating.' Harker leaned past him to push the button that caused the pocket door of Rauchle's compartment to slide open. 'If you have any other concerns . . .'

'*Nein. Danke.*' Still upside down, Rauchle pushed himself headfirst through the door. Kaufmann gave them an embarrassed smile, then followed the older man inside. Harker waited until they were both inside, then touched the button again, shutting the door behind them.

'How did you figure that out?' he murmured. 'I mean, I thought this was only . . . y'know, a professional . . .'

'C'mon. You think they only want to compare notes?' She couldn't blame them for wanting to be discreet; one of the unfortunate consequences of the recent religious revival had been the return of intolerance. 'I just let them know it's all right, so long as they keep it to themselves.'

'Yeah. Right.' Releasing his grip on the ceiling rail, Harker pushed himself down the corridor. All of a sudden, it seemed as if the corridor had emptied out. Everyone had found their quarters, save for Cruz, who tugged against the recessed handle of his compartment door. Harker took a moment to show him how to use the door button and explain that the handle was only there for power-loss emergencies, and Cruz entered his quarters with a grateful smile. 'You realize, of course, that could come back to bite us,' he continued once they were alone again.

'What do you mean?' Emily couldn't help herself; with a saucy grin, she grabbed Ted's ass. 'Oh, you mean this . . . ?'

'Yes, I mean that.' He swatted her hand away, then glanced back to see if anyone was watching. 'Emcee . . .'

'Oh, come now. They're not going to tell.' Collins gently pushed him aside as she found her own compartment. 'Besides, it's not like the rest of the crew doesn't know . . .'

'Ian doesn't.'

Collins pushed the door button, waited until it opened, then pulled herself inside. What Harker had told Rauchle was the truth; all the crew and passenger quarters aboard *Galileo*, with the sole exception of the captain's, were exactly alike, at least in terms of size and furniture. A wedge-shaped room, narrow at the entrance and wide at the outer wall, with a fold-down bunk, a collapsible desk and chair beneath a book-shelf, a comp with an intercom phone, and a tiny closet with hanger space above three drawers. Its most valuable luxury was a privy that, once its sink and commode were folded against the bulkheads, could double as a shower stall. But only when the Millis-Clement field was in operation; until then, they'd use sponges for baths and plastic bags for answering the call of nature.

Small, functional, and barely comfortable. Yet, like the rest of the crew, she'd managed to personalize her quarters a bit during *Galileo*'s shakedown cruise. A few favorite paper books on the shelf. Pictures of her mother and two brothers, the former long since deceased and the latter whom she barely knew anymore, taped to the wall above the comp. A Martian tapestry with an abstract reddish-gold design, both enigmatic and sensuous, that lent the room a touch of mystery. A toy spaceship, resembling a fighter craft from a twenty-first-century fantasy fic, that her flight instructor had given her several years ago.

'If we're careful, he'll never know.' Sliding open the closet, she pushed her bag inside, then shut the door before it could float out again. 'No connecting doors here, either, but since you've managed to assign yourself to the next compartment over . . .'

'Don't count on seeing too much of me. Discretion is the better part of . . .'

'Oh, shut up and give me a kiss.' Grabbing hold of a hand rung above her bunk, Emily pulled him closer. Ted grinned, then put his arms around her. The kiss was sweet, but like all things stolen, it was furtive and all too brief. 'Enough of that,' she said softly, pushing him away before temptation could get the better of either of them. 'You've got things to do upstairs.'

'Yeah. Like making sure we get out of dry dock without crashing into something.' Harker sighed as he gazed past her. Through the porthole, they could see a cargo pod maneuvering into docking position, carrying more supplies they'd need for the voyage. 'What do you think?' he asked. 'Can we get there and back without Ian killing us all?'

At first she thought he was joking, but one look at his

face told her that he was serious. 'Don't have any confidence in him, do you?' Raising his right hand, Ted closed his thumb and index finger an inch apart from each other. Emily shook her head. 'Give him a chance. Maybe he'll surprise us.'

'Remember the botch he made of the rendezvous maneuver with Deimos Station? If Simone hadn't corrected his orders . . .'

'I'm sure he's learned something from that.' She smiled. 'Besides, you said it yourself . . . there are seven other people aboard who know their jobs, yourself included . . .'

'Only seven?' Harker raised an eyebrow. 'You don't count yourself?'

'I'm just the shuttle driver. My job doesn't begin until we reach Spindrift.' She shrugged. 'Even then, chances are it's only a lump of rock with some . . . I don't know, something floating around it. If that's the case, I'm just along for the ride.'

'Yes, well . . .' Harker glanced at his watch, then backed toward the door. 'Look, I'd better go. Come upstairs when you're done here, all right?'

'Wouldn't miss it for the world. Ta.' She waved her fingertips, and he gave her a wink before pushing himself out into the corridor. Collins closed the door behind him, then reopened the closet and, pulling out her bag, began to unpack her things.

She hoped she was right, that their mission would be uneventful, save for a practical demonstration of the starbridge's hyperspace capability and perhaps the establishment of a cooperative relationship between the European Alliance and the Western Hemisphere Union. Yet it was hard to ignore the fluttering sensation in the pit of her stomach, or the sense of unease she had when glancing through the porthole to see an Earth that she might never lay eyes on again.

'T minus thirty seconds and counting.' Simone Monet's slender hands ran across the board of the helm station, tripping a set of toggle switches. 'Disconnecting from external power sources.'

Green lights blinked along the panel above the engineering station. 'Confirm that,' Martin Cohen said. '*Galileo* now on internal power. Stand by for main engine ignition in twenty-nine seconds.'

'All stations, sound off.' Ian Lawrence turned his head to gaze at the members of the flight crew, seated around him in the horseshoe-shaped compartment of *Galileo*'s command center. The view of the dry dock through its wraparound windows was all but ignored; everyone's attention was focused upon the screens above their consoles.

'Life support, go.' This from Werner Gelb, seated next to Martin.

'Telemetry, green for go.' Arkady had his left hand clasped against his headset, listening to last-minute communiqués from the dry dock.

'Helm is go.' Although Simone was moments away from ceding her responsibilities to the ship's AI, she wasn't about to surrender without a fight.

'Engineering is go.' Martin was the most nervous person in the room; his eyes didn't move from the screens displaying the condition of *Galileo*'s fusion reactor.

'Logistics, go.' As executive officer, Antonia Vincenza's primary task at that point was making sure that the ship's AI and computer subsystems were fully functional. An almost redundant task, since those systems would have long since alerted the crew to any anomalies. Indeed, the case could be made that *Galileo* itself was the smartest member of the flight team.

'Medical, standing by.' Nick Jones sat in his chair, arms folded and legs crossed together, observing everything with calm detachment. No one would need his services unless everything went to hell, at which point he'd become the most important member of the crew.

Next it was Emily's turn. 'Shuttle on standby,' she said. Like Nick, her job was redundant unless there was a dire emergency. Then she'd be responsible for packing everyone aboard the *Maria Celeste* and flying them to safety. *Unless we're so far away*, she thought, *that it's a useless gesture*. She didn't want to think about that. Instead, she sat alone in a chair at one end of the command center, watching the rest of the crew as they went through the countdown procedure.

'All stations affirmative.' Ted sat next to Lawrence, his eyes on the lapboard he'd unfolded from the left arm of his chair. 'Mooring lines detached. *Galileo* floating free.'

'T minus ten seconds.' Simone turned a key on her board, then flipped open a tiger-striped safety cover to expose a single toggle switch. 'Main-engine ignition in nine seconds. Eight . . . seven . . .'

'Hey, guys,' Arkady said aloud, 'I think I left something behind.' No one laughed, and the grin vanished from his face. 'Sorry. Bad joke.'

'Four . . . three . . . two . . . one.' Simone clicked the switch. 'Ignition. Main engine start.'

From somewhere behind them, a low rumble, steadily rising in volume. A subtle tremor passed through the hull.

Emily felt it through the seat of her chair and the soles of her shoes, and she grasped her armrests as weight descended upon her, just enough to push her back into her chair. Through the windows, she could see the scaffolding of the dry dock slowly move away from either side of the ship until only the black abyss of space lay before them.

'Away from dry dock.' Arkady listened intently to his headset; he was all business now. 'Trafco reports our attitude looks good. We're clear to proceed to rendezvous with starbridge.'

'Copy that.' Antonia tapped a command into her console. 'Mission recorder started. Helm, stand by for starbridge AI interface.' She glanced at Lawrence. 'On your mark, Captain.'

'Thank you, XO.' Lawrence stared straight ahead. 'Com?'

'Receiving uplink from gatehouse.' Arkady typed in a couple of commands, then glanced over at Antonia. 'Ready when you are, Captain.'

'Thank you, XO . . . mark.'

'Copy that.' The executive officer entered the code prefix that would slave *Galileo*'s AI to the one aboard the starbridge control station. She studied her screens for a moment, then nodded with satisfaction. 'Interface complete. Helm, stand down.'

'Yes, ma'am. Helm standing down.' Simone clicked one more switch, relinquishing control of her station to the comps, then let out her breath and folded her hands together in her lap. Until *Galileo* completed its hyperspace jump, there was little for her to do other than sit and watch. Emily felt pity for her; no pilots like to feel as if they have no control over their craft.

The initial vibration subsided, the roar of main engine ignition lapsing into a background rumble. Although there was sufficient gravity for the flight crew to stand up and move around, none left their seats. Emily hoped that the science team had obeyed Ted's instructions to remain on Deck C; they didn't need any visitors just then. Through the windows, they caught a brief, final glimpse of Earth – three-quarters full, its daylight terminator somewhere above the Pacific – before lateral thrusters fired to correct their trajectory and put them on a correct heading for rendezvous with the starbridge. Then their world slowly swam away, to be replaced by the distant crescent of the Moon.

On the overhead screens, they could make out the starbridge, a tiny silver ring that grew in size with each passing minute. Until ESA began its construction two years earlier – along with its prototype companion, KX-1, robotically built in orbit around Eris – the hyperspace program had been one of the European Alliance's most closely guarded secrets. Although the Western Hemisphere Union loudly proclaimed that its development, along with that of a second-generation diametric drive, was the result of espionage, the EA dismissed this as propaganda, insisting that its own scientists had come up with it on their own.

Yet perhaps there was some truth to the charge. Although the facts were still classified, Emily had heard the rumors: that a former United Republic of America physicist, one who'd been involved in the construction of the URSS *Alabama* and long since assumed to be dead, had been discovered in biostasis, reportedly in a former URA lunar research station that had been lost after the collapse of the Republic. No one knew who he was, but the story had it that he'd carried with him not only his own knowledge of hyperspace physics but also a disk containing his research notes for the development of wormhole travel, and that it was only lucky happenstance that caused him to be found by the Alliance instead of the Union.

Well, that was only hearsay. Reality was something else entirely. Emily let out her breath, loosened her seat harness, and stretched herself. She caught Ted's eye, gave him a nervous smile. He responded with a sly wink. They were on their way.

At constant thrust, it took *Galileo* less than six hours to reach the Lagrange point where the starbridge was suspended between the gravitational pulls of Earth and the Moon. What had once been a tiny ring had expanded to a torus, forty meters in diameter, its blue and green navigational lights flashing along its outer surface. One hundred kilometers away, a small cylindrical station was positioned in close orbit, the gatehouse that controlled access to the starbridge.

'Gatehouse confirms final approach, Captain.' Arkady looked up from his console. 'All vectors nominal, and starbridge powering up for hyperspace insertion.'

'Thank you, Mr Rusic. Give them our regards.' Lawrence paused, then added: 'Status of KX-1?'

'All systems clear, sir.' Arkady's tone was matter-of-fact, as if he'd never thought his commanding officer would ever ask. 'Status nominal.'

Emily glanced at Ted, saw him briefly raise an eyebrow. Nice of the captain to double-check. Unless the twin starbridges were properly synchronized, the wormhole wouldn't be formed and *Galileo* would vanish into a singularity. In which case, their last thoughts, just before their bodies were crushed into streams of subatomic particles, would be the confirmation of their suspicions that their captain was an idiot.

'Thank you.' Lawrence looked up at the mission chronometer, then cinched his seat harness a little tighter. 'T minus seventy-two seconds. Mr Cohen, status of main engine?'

'MECO in eleven seconds.' Almost as soon as Martin spoke, an alarm went off, signaling main engine cutoff. Emily had just enough time to tighten her harness before the engine ceased its rumble and microgravity returned. Cohen silenced the alarm. 'MECO complete, sir. Main engine in standby mode.'

'Thank you.' Lawrence took hold of his armrests. 'All stations, report in.'

Once again, just as they'd done a few hours earlier, the flight crew reported affirmative. It was almost an unnecessary procedure; *Galileo* was now fully under control of its AI, which would presumably alert them to any system malfunctions. Yet Emily was glad for the distraction; it helped take her mind off the fact that the ship was entering the wormhole's event horizon.

Relax, she told herself. *The probes have done this before. The first two failed, but the next five came back. Everything's going to be fine.* From behind her, though, she could hear Nick muttering the Lord's Prayer; Ted shot a look at him, and the doctor lowered his voice to a whisper.

As the starbridge filled the screens, Simone's voice became a nervous cadence. 'T minus ten . . . T minus eight . . . T minus five . . . four . . .'

'Everyone, hang on!' Ted yelled. 'Shut your eyes!'

'Three . . . two . . . one . . .'

Through the windows, a white-hot flash. Emily squeezed her eyes shut, but not before her retinas were dazzled by its negative afterimage. She gasped as she felt herself slammed against her seat. From somewhere behind her, hull plates creaked in protest.

A sensation of falling into a bottomless pit . . .

Part Two

Beyond the Heliopause

Five

JUNE 1, 2288 – EASS *GALILEO*

One moment, the starbridge was inert and still, a giant ring floating in the outermost reaches of the solar system. The next, a silent flash of defocused light, then the *Galileo* hurtled from hyperspace.

Opening his eyes, Harker took a slow, deep breath. The palms of his hands were slick where they clutched his seat's armrests; wincing from a cramp in his neck, he carefully turned his head to gaze about the command center. The rest of the flight crew didn't look much better; a lot of pale and sweat-soaked faces, along with a few groans and murmured curses. At least no one had lost consciousness.

A retching sound to his right. Harker glanced around to see Lawrence suddenly clamp a hand against his mouth, a tendril of vomit slipping from between his fingers. Congealing as a constellation of bilious green orbs, it drifted upward, captured by the air currents as it floated in the direction of the ceiling exhaust vent. Trying to control his nausea, Lawrence doubled over in his seat, fumbling with his free hand to unclasp his harness.

'Nick?' Harker turned toward Jones, who was rubbing his eyes. 'Hey, Doc, we got a problem here. Can you . . . ?'

'I'm on it.' Nick unsnapped his harness, then unsteadily pushed himself out of his seat. Using the ceiling rails to pull himself hand over hand across the compartment, he unbuckled Lawrence's harness, then gently prized the captain from his chair. Lawrence continued to hold his hand against his mouth, yet he was clearly in danger of choking on his own vomit. The doctor whispered something in his ear, and when the captain shook his head, he grabbed Lawrence's hand and yanked it away from his mouth.

Lawrence loudly and explosively puked, and the constellation became a nebula. That was enough; Harker shook off the rest of his grogginess and unclasped his own harness. 'Get him out of here,' he snapped, pushing himself out of his chair before the mess could reach him. An apologetic glance, then Nick wrapped an arm around Lawrence's shoulder and hauled him toward the access shaft.

'Will someone please take care of this?' Disgusted, Harker shied away from the vomit cloud. 'Werner . . . ?'

'No problem.' Recognizing the threat it posed to the compartment's air-circulation system, Gelb opened a maintenance locker and pulled out a handheld vacuum cleaner normally used to clear dust from the consoles. Switching it on, the life-support chief went about the revolting but necessary chore.

'Thank you.' Despite the absurdity of the moment, Harker realized that he'd just become the senior officer on the bridge. Yet he had no time and less inclination to savor the moment. There were more important things to think about just now. 'Simone, how are we doing?'

'We're in good shape, sir.' The helmsman had shaken off her torpor; her hands moved across her console, snapping switches as she studied her console's comp screens. 'We were in a lateral spin, but . . .' Simone paused, let out her breath. 'Yes. RCS firing to compensate. Bringing her back into trim, sir.'

'Excellent.' Harker pulled himself over to Simone's station, peered over her shoulder. As she said, *Galileo*'s attitude was beginning to stabilize; the screen to her left showed its profile coming back to its proper orientation on its x-, y-, and z-axes, while the one to the right displayed its position relative to both the starbridge and Eris. 'Nice work,' he said. 'Rather have you in the driver's seat than the AI.'

'Thank you, sir.' Simone smiled. 'Sorry for the rough ride.'

'We're through, safe and sound. That's what matters.' Raising his gaze to the windows, Harker looked out at Eris: a whitish-grey crescent, little larger than a soccer ball, dully reflecting the radiance of a distant star. It took him a moment to realize that the star was the Sun, and that he was seeing it from a perspective that few other humans had ever experienced. So large and bright back home, but out here in the Kuiper Belt he could have covered it with a raised thumb.

'Find me an orbit. Can you do that?' Simone nodded, and he turned away. 'Toni? Ship status?'

'Nothing to worry about. All systems green.' The XO paused, studying the screens above her station. 'All the same, I'd like to inspect the engine module. There may have been some stress on the portside radiation shield, section three.'

'Can it wait? I'd like to engage the field first. Might make things a little easier.' Antonia nodded, and he looked over at the chief engineer. 'Martin, you think we're ready for that?'

The chief engineer looked a little green, but he nodded. 'One-minute warning on your mark, sir.'

'Mark.' Grasping the ceiling rail, Harker hurried back to his seat. He'd barely settled back into it when the klaxon whooped three times, signaling all hands that the Millis-Clement field would be activated in sixty seconds. When it fell silent, Harker glanced over at the com station. 'Arkady . . . ?'

'Already done it, Captain . . . I mean, sir.' An apologetic grin. 'Transmitted a message back home via hyperlink, informing them that we've safely . . .' Arkady held up a hand as he listened to his headset. 'Receiving signal from the gatehouse, confirming our arrival,' he added. 'They're ready to close the bridge.'

'Well done. Tell 'em we copy, and we'll be in touch.' This would be the last exchange between *Galileo* and Starbridge Earth; the hyperlink was capable of sending and receiving radio messages only so long as the wormhole remained open, and the gatehouse couldn't keep it that way indefinitely. 'Raise the LCP and begin calibration with Mare Muscoviense. Soon as you've got a lock, transmit a test message.'

Arkady nodded as he turned back to his console. From there on, all contact with home would be achieved by means of a 250-kilowatt laser communication platform located on the service module, which would transmit messages to the Union Astronautica's deep-space tracking station on the lunar farside. The laser wouldn't move any faster than x-band radio, but it would allow for more information to be sent with less interference from interstellar matter.

Behind him, Martin recited a countdown: 'MCI in five

. . . four . . . three . . . two . . . one . . .' Harker felt his body settle into his seat as gravity returned to *Galileo*. Doing this so soon would cause a small spike to the zero-point energy generator, but it shouldn't affect the deployment of the diametric drive torus. He looked again at the chief engineer; Martin carefully studied his screens, then silently gave him a thumbs-up. The ZPE generator was copacetic.

What next? Harker let out his breath. Not much, at least for the time being. The ship appeared to be in good shape. Everyone had recovered from the stress of the hyperspace jump and was going about their business. He supposed that he should go down to Deck C and check on the passengers, yet until Captain Lawrence returned to duty . . .

'Nice going there, Mr Harker.' Feeling a hand touch his elbow, he turned to find that Emily had come up behind him. Her face was flushed, her hair matted with sweat, yet there was an encouraging smile that gave him reason to relax a little more.

'Thank you.' He raised a hand to gently brush back the hair from her eyes. 'Simulator didn't quite prepare us for that, did it?'

'Prepared us enough, I think.' A wry glance at the access hatch. 'More than Ian, I think,' she added, lowering her voice. 'Maybe that'll teach him to skip training.'

'Yeah, well . . .' He shook his head. 'Not that any of this will be entered in the log.'

'Of course not.' Emily glanced about the command center. 'But you know what the main difference is between you and him? He treats everyone here like subordinates. He barks orders and expects everyone to obey him . . .'

'That's what a captain's supposed to do.'

'Uh-uh. A captain's supposed to be a leader, not a boss.' Another smile. 'You treat these people with respect. They're your friends, and you trust them . . . and they know that. Half of them were ready to puke their guts out, just like he did . . . but they sucked it in and did their jobs before you had to ask. You think they would've done that for him?' Before Harker could respond, she took his hand. 'C'mon, now. They're just fine. Let them do what they're supposed to do. You, on the other hand . . .'

'I should go below. Check on the science team.'

'Sure. That comes first. And then . . .' Emily tugged at his hand, pulling him from his chair. 'You need to take a lady out to see the stars.'

A glance at Antonia. She looked back at him, gave him a stoical nod; she'd take care of things on the bridge. With an inward sigh, Harker let Emily escort him from the command center.

The science team had handled the jaunt better than he expected, at least for the most part. When Harker stopped by Rauchle's quarters, he found the team leader collapsed on his bunk, waxen-faced and in a foul mood. He'd become violently ill, leaving Kaufmann to clean up the mess with a handful of paper towels he'd hastily snatched from the privy. Harker made his exit before Rauchle could vent his temper in his direction. He was getting fed up with Rauchle's tantrums; sooner or later, he'd have a chat with the physicist, but not just yet.

Cruz, on the other hand, had accepted the chaos that erupted in his cabin with grace and good humor. The astrogeologist had brought with him a small library of disks, paper books, and loose-leaf binders; all well and good, except that he'd neglected to secure them to the shelves with the safety straps provided. They'd scattered in midair all over the place, then come crashing down once the field was engaged; when Emily came to visit him, she found Cruz picking up books and loose pages. Yet even though he'd suffered a bump on the forehead from *The Proceedings of the Planetary Geography Society, Vol. VXXI*, Cruz's only protest came as a rueful grin. Harker left her to help Cruz gather his belongings, then pushed himself down the corridor.

The door to Ramirez's quarters was shut, yet as Harker approached it, his nose caught a faint odor that he couldn't identify: somewhat like burning leaves, only more pungent. When he rapped his knuckles against the door, he heard Ramirez's voice, yet it was muffled and indistinct, and the astrobiologist didn't open it. Becoming suspicious, Harker decided that his prerogatives outweighed the scientist's privacy and touched the door button.

The cabin was filled with smoke, pale and intoxicating. Ramirez was sitting at his desk, the palm of his left hand cupped around something in his right hand. When Harker demanded to know what he was trying to hide, Ramirez sheepishly held up a small, hand-carved wooden pipe.

'Many apologies, Commander,' Ramirez murmured, a beatific smile upon his face. 'A small indulgence on my part . . . one I cultivated at Dolland.' He offered the pipe to him, the ember in its bowl still smoldering. 'Care to join me? Does wonders for the nerves.'

'No, thank you.' Harker had heard that cannabis could be smoked, but until then he'd never met anyone who would ever indulge in such an archaic vice. As it was, his eyes were already beginning to water. 'That's rather dangerous. I'm surprised you didn't trip the fire alarm.'

'That?' Ramirez pointed to a dislodged service panel in the ceiling. 'Sorry. Deactivated.' A sleepy grin. 'Little trick I learned in prison. Made life there a bit more bearable.'

'Yes, well . . . be that as it may, that's one trick you'll have to do without.' He extended his hand. 'If you'll please . . . ?'

'Mr Harker . . .'

'Dr Ramirez, this isn't Dolland. This is my ship, and its safety is more important than your nerves.' He snapped his fingers. 'Hand it over . . . or I'll ask Ms Vincenza to come down here and help me search your quarters. And believe me, you won't like that very much.'

The smile vanished from Ramirez's face. He hesitated, then surrendered the pipe. Harker carefully laid his thumb upon the bowl to snuff out the ember, then put it in his breast pocket and held out his hand again. Ramirez glared at him, then reached beneath his left thigh and pulled out a small pill container.

'This isn't very fair, you know,' he said, tossing the container to Harker. 'Perhaps you should ask Dr Rauchle for the liter of schnapps he has in his bag.'

'If you want, we can have a shot of Irish whiskey together. I brought a bottle with me. That's not the issue.' Harker juggled the container in his hand. 'Tell you what, chum,' he said, reaching over to a wall panel to activate the exhaust fan that Ramirez had failed to notice. 'You do your job, and I may find a way to let you use one of the emergency air locks for your indulgence. Think you can do that?'

The smile reappeared. 'Sure. So long as you show me how to use it so that I don't space myself.'

'That's your problem,' Harker replied, and Ramirez's smile became an irate glare. 'Whenever you're ready, you know where to find me.'

Harker backed out of the cabin, closing the door behind him. He turned to discover Emily waiting for him in the corridor. 'I heard,' she said quietly. 'I never would've believed it.'

'Weird, huh?' Harker uncapped the container, peered inside: a couple of grams of cured and crumbled cannabis leaves, light brown and resinous. 'Thought this sort of thing went out with rock and roll.' She gave him a confused look, not understanding the historical reference, and he shook his head. 'Never mind. Who's next?'

'Haven't seen Cole or Sinclair. Guess we'd better check on them, too.' She turned to head down the corridor, and Harker followed her. They made their way around the bend until, just past the captain's quarters, they reached Cole's cabin.

The door was shut; Harker knocked on it and waited a moment. Receiving no answer, he pushed the button. 'Sir Peter?' he asked as the door slid open. 'Pardon me, sir, but . . .'

'What do you want?' Lawrence demanded.

Startled, Harker stepped back. The captain's back was turned to the door; he looked over his shoulder to glare at him. Past him, Harker spotted Cole, seated on the edge of his bunk. The Astronomer Royal seemed more surprised than angry, yet it was clear that he didn't welcome the interruption either.

'My apologies, Captain,' Harker said. 'I only meant to check on . . .'

'We're doing fine,' Lawrence snapped. 'Now get out.'

'Yes, sir . . . sorry, sir.' Harker hastily backed away. Lawrence was still glowering at him as he pushed the button; the door slid shut, and he let out his breath. 'Damn,' he murmured. 'Wasn't expecting that.'

'Why should you? If he's not in sickbay, then he ought to be on Deck A.' Emily regarded the cabin with suspicion. 'What's he doing here, anyway?'

'Damned if I know, but it's none of my business.' Harker turned away to continue down the corridor. 'We'd better get lost. Right now, he's angry enough to . . .'

Realizing that she was no longer with him, Harker looked back around. Emily had quietly moved close enough to the door that she could place an ear against it. Shocked by what she was doing, he started to say something – *are you insane? get away from there!* – but she held a finger to her lips, then urgently gestured for him to come closer.

Eavesdropping on the captain. Beneath the proper conduct of a first officer. Yet curiosity got the better of him; Harker quietly moved back toward Cole's cabin and, lightly grasping Emily's shoulder, laid his left ear against the door.

'. . . *nothing of this*.' Lawrence's voice, just barely intelligible. '*He hasn't been briefed, nor shall he, unless there's an emergency*.'

Cole said something. Exactly what, Harker couldn't tell; his voice came to him as little more than a murmur.

'*If it comes to that, certainly.*' Lawrence again. '*But I'd just as soon that he not be aware of its existence. Or anyone else, to tell the truth, other than my crewman. It was installed just before we left, and only we have the activation codes. If we need to . . .*'

Cole interrupted him to say something. This time, Harker made out a single, midsentence word: '. . . *Spindrift* . . .'

'*Then the responsibility will be mine,*' Lawrence replied. '*But the risk is more than acceptable, I think, even if . . .*'

Emily glanced past him just then; her eyes widened, and she suddenly pulled herself from the door. Harker turned to see Sinclair only five meters away. Apparently he'd just come around the bend in the passageway; now he stood nearby, quietly observing them.

Mortified, Harker backed away from the cabin. No point in denying what they'd been doing; the political officer had seen everything. To make matters worse, the hatch leading to the access shaft was a few meters down the corridor past him; they would have to go around Sinclair in order to leave Deck C.

Harker touched Emily's shoulder, a mute signal for her to follow him, then he walked toward the hatch. His face burned as he approached Sinclair; for a moment, he thought the other man might say something to him, but instead Sinclair quietly moved aside, making room for them to pass. They'd almost reached the shaft when Sinclair spoke up.

'Commander . . . ?'

Harker stopped, looked back at him. 'Yes, Mr Sinclair?'

'If there's something you think I should know, I hope you'll give me the benefit of the doubt and tell me.'

Sinclair's expression was stoical, his voice quiet, yet there was no doubting the sincerity of his words.

Harker nodded. 'I'll keep that in mind, sir,' he said softly.

'Please do.' He hesitated. 'And Mr Harker? Please keep in mind that I leave my door cracked open. That way, I always know when someone' – a pause, followed by a wry smile – 'wants to drop in for a visit.'

Harker swallowed. 'I'll try to remember that.'

Galileo's wardroom was located on D Deck, one level down. Although the adjacent library was intended to serve as the lounge, the ship's architects had apparently realized that crew and passengers needed a place in which they could simply sit and gaze out at the stars. The ship, after all, had been designed with long-term scientific exploration in mind. So the wardroom doubled as an observation area; a pair of floor-to-ceiling windows, larger than even those in the command center, had been installed in the hull, its multiple-pane glass equipped with a virtual telescope capable of zooming in upon anything that could be seen with the naked eye and identifying it upon the windows themselves.

The wardroom was dark when Harker and Collins entered, its chairs still strapped in place beneath long faux-oak dining tables. Harker started to turn on the lights, but Emily stopped him; instead, she moved across the room, guided by the amber glow of the emergency lamps, until she reached the windows. She pressed a button, and the outside louvers rolled upward to reveal the ghost-grey orb of Eris, its tiny satellite Dysnomia just coming into view beyond its limb.

Harker could have activated the virtual telescope, but instead he took a moment to let himself identify the planets and constellations by memory. Above the bright star that was the Sun, he made out Perseus, with Jupiter a bright orange orb just to the left of Algol. Saturn lay between Triangulum and Ares. And there, rising beyond Eris, the lower legs of Andromeda. Or at least he thought it was Andromeda; from this perspective, it was hard to be sure. A beautiful sight, one that might have inspired a poet to compose a sonnet. If Emily had romance in mind when she'd suggested that they go to the wardroom, though, that notion soon vanished.

'What do you think he meant?' she asked, once they were sure they were alone.

'I think he meant for us to stay the hell away from his cabin.' Still practicing astronomy, Harker slowly let out his breath. 'Christ, I've never been so embarrassed . . .'

'Not Sinclair . . . Ian.' She glanced at him sharply. 'What, you didn't hear what he said?'

'I heard as much as you did . . . not much.' He frowned, trying to recall the one-sided snatch of conversation. 'Something was installed aboard ship just before we left without my knowledge. Whatever it is, Ian has access to it. Or at least that's what I assume he meant when he said that he was the one person who had the codes . . .'

'No.' Emily shook her head. 'That's not what he said. He referred to someone as "my crewman," then he said that only "we" have the codes.' She hesitated. 'If there's something you're keeping from me . . .'

'No.' He took her hand. 'I swear to you, I have no idea what's going on. And I have no idea who Ian was referring to, either.'

'I didn't think you would.' Her hand absently traveled up his arm to his elbow. 'Let that be for now. If activation relies on a code sequence, then it must be computer-controlled. All right, then, that's easy enough. All we have to do is search the AI . . .'

'Emcee, do you have any idea . . . ?' Harker shook his head. 'What's the size of the main AI memory? Seven-hundred-point-seven terabytes. How many major subsystems does it control? Twenty-eight. How many comps are in that network? Sixty-five, not counting twenty-four backups. Even if you knew what you were looking for . . . and we don't . . . it could take days, even weeks, to find it. And we're scheduled to go into biostasis in . . .'

'Two days.' She hissed between her teeth. 'Damn. You're right.' Then her eyes narrowed. 'But look . . . if it's that important, then something like this couldn't have been installed without someone else knowing. That must be what Lawrence meant. Toni, perhaps, or Arkady . . .'

'Oh, c'mon . . .' Irritated, he shook off her hand. 'We know those guys. We've been working with them for nearly a year now. I can't believe either of them would allow that to happen without letting me know.' Harker gazed out the window. 'No, this must have been something that was put in place while *Galileo* was still in dry dock. Perhaps at the last minute, after we'd come aboard but before we launched.' He glanced at her again. 'When you did your flyby, did you see anything unusual?'

'No. Nothing.' She shrugged. 'But we were in dry dock for five hours after that, and cargo was being loaded right up until T minus one hour. Anything could have been slipped aboard during that time.'

'Well, I could check the cargo hold, but I doubt it's going to be there. The word Ian used was *installed*, remember?' Another thought occurred to him just then. 'What if it's not inside the ship, but outside? Attached to the hull, I mean.'

'Possible.' Emily slowly nodded. 'The auxiliary ports along the service module are meant for that sort of thing. Two were used for Larry and Jerry, but there's room for one more. If it's there . . .'

'Then we might be able to find it.' Harker didn't respond for a moment. 'Whatever it may be, that is,' he added. 'That's what bothers me. Ian said he'd only tell me about it in case of an emergency. What sort of emergency, do you reckon?'

'Enough of one that he considered having this thing aboard to be an acceptable risk.' She frowned. 'Or a precaution, rather. And of sufficient magnitude that Sir Peter knows about it, yet not tell . . .'

From behind them, the sound of the door sliding open. They looked around to see a pair of figures captured in silhouette within the doorway. For an instant, he thought they were Lawrence and Cole. Then the ceiling lights flickered to life. Dazzled by the abrupt glare, Harker raised a hand to his eyes. 'Who . . . ?'

'Oh, no . . . not you two again.' Arkady stepped into the compartment, a lecherous grin on his face. Simone was right behind him, looking vaguely amused. 'C'mon, you kids, find a room. Some of us would like to eat.'

'Like food was all you had in mind.' Emily quickly slipped her hand into Harker's. 'Or are you really that eager to sample the freeze-dried lasagna?'

Arkady's eyes rolled upward, and Simone blushed; it

was no secret that the two of them were carrying on an affair of their own. 'We won't tell if you won't.'

'Fine with me.' Harker glanced at Emily. 'I think we all have something to hide.'

Six

JUNE 2, 2288 – EASS *GALILEO*

Whatever Ramirez expected the ship's library to be like, that wasn't what he found when he got there.

He stood in the doorway, staring at a drawing room that wouldn't have been out of place within a Victorian manor of the nineteenth century. Brass-caged bookshelves containing dozens of leather-bound volumes lined mahogany-paneled walls, their moldings carved to resemble oak leaves and acorn clusters. A vaulted ceiling rose above him, its bowstring beams forming a star pattern from which a crystal chandelier was suspended. The floor was covered with a thick Persian carpet woven with a rose motif; the furniture consisted of brown-leather armchairs and love seats upholstered with soft purple velvet, separated by round study tables draped with braided silk cloths. A gilded pendulum clock, ticking ever so quietly, stood near a marble fireplace in which a couple of logs slowly burned. An oil portrait of a woman, buxom and yet demure, hung within a gilded frame above the mantel, upon which rested a pewter miniature of the *Galileo*.

This can't be real, Ramirez thought. *It must be a hologram*. Yet when he stepped closer to one of the walls and touched it, his fingertips felt only polished wood, right down to subtle imperfections in the grain. The carpet was soft beneath the soles of his shoes; exploring it with his left toe, he noted that the fibers moved as he prodded them. The fire burning within the hearth, of course, wasn't really there, yet it was only after he stared at it for a while that he noticed a slight, nonrandom repetition of the flames and the smoke. That part was an illusion, at least, but the rest . . .

'Spared no expense, did they?' Sir Peter asked. 'Personally, I think they should have included a billiards table, but I suppose you can't have everything.'

It took a moment for Ramirez to locate Cole. He was seated in an armchair within a cozy little alcove near the fireplace, a book in his lap and his feet crossed together on an ottoman. The country squire at home and hearth; all he needed to make the scene complete was a pipe, a glass of brandy, and a terrier curled up by his side.

'Perhaps, but they might have also . . .' Ramirez stopped as he caught sight of the casement window behind Cole. Through thick mullioned panes, he saw what looked like a small English town, the gothic spire of an old church rising among the rooftops, the afternoon sun casting shadows upon the distant hills. A pigeon alighted upon the windowsill; it nervously glanced through the window, cocked its head, then fluttered away.

'Arundel, England. In case you're wondering.' Sir Peter followed Ramirez's gaze through the window. 'The view from the library of Arundel Castle, although the actual room is considerably larger. Of course, if you'd like to be reminded where you really are . . .'

Turning away from Ramirez, he leaned over to push a button on a small panel half-hidden beneath the window. The town vanished, suddenly replaced by the endless night of space, with Eris floating in the distance. The bottom quarter of the view was eclipsed by a long, outward-curving structure; the torus of *Galileo*'s diametric drive, deployed from its housing a few hours earlier and rapidly gaining size as millions of microassemblers worked tirelessly to erect it into its doughnut-shaped cruise configuration.

'I like the other view a bit more, don't you?' Sir Peter touched the panel again. Deep space disappeared, and Arundel returned. The pigeon came back; again it peeped through the window, nodded in satisfaction, and flew away. Illusion destroyed.

'Nice trick.' Ramirez nodded toward the book in Cole's lap. 'Anything good?'

'This?' Cole lifted the volume. 'Shakespeare. *The Tempest.* Seemed appropriate. But it can be anything you'd like.' He offered the book to Ramirez. 'Here. See for yourself . . . just ask. Operates by voice command, of course.'

'Of course.' Ramirez took the book from him, opened it to a random page. Sure enough, he found it to be a folio of Shakespeare's plays. He closed the cover, thought for a moment. 'Alexandre Dumas, *The Count of Monte Cristo*,' he said, then opened it to the first page: *On February 24, 1815, the watchtower at Marseilles signaled the arrival of the three-master* Pharon, *coming from Smyrna, Trieste, and Naples . . .*

'They're all like that.' Cole pointed to the shelves surrounding them. 'Remote links to the library subsystem. Open any volume at random, you'll find only this.' Taking the book back from Ramirez, he closed the cover and said, 'Neutral.' He opened it again. Blank pages. 'But request something in particular, such as . . . oh, say, H. G. Wells, *The War of the Worlds*.' He drummed his fingertips upon the cover, as if performing a magic trick, then opened the book once more. 'See?'

'Impressive.' Ramirez didn't bother to look. 'But I prefer Dumas.'

'Hmm . . . I suppose you would.' Looking down at the book, Cole began to read aloud. '"No one would have believed in the last years of the nineteenth century that this world was being watched keenly and closely by intelligences greater than man's . . ."'

'Thank you, but I've never much enjoyed fantasy.'

'Oh?' Cole seemed mildly disappointed. 'And I'd have sworn that would be one of your favorites. Perhaps something that you'd read as a boy, thereby inspiring you to search for Martians.'

'No. Only a belief that the galaxy is too vast for only one intelligent race.' Taking a seat across from Sir Peter, he reached over to touch the panel beneath the window. The quaint English town vanished again, and once more they looked out at the stars. 'Reality is much more interesting.'

'Yes, well . . . that's why I requested this meeting. Thought we'd have a chat about that very thing.' Cole closed the book and put it aside, then settled back in his chair, steepling his fingers together. 'What do you think Spindrift is?'

'I told you what I thought at Wilton Park. You sat next to me, remember?'

'Yes, yes, of course, but . . .' A cunning smile. 'What do you *really* think it is? Or don't you have any theories?'

'Oh, I have dozens of theories.' Ramirez toyed with a braided tassel at the end of the armrest's embroidered coverlet. 'But until we have more evidence, they're nothing more than idle conjecture.' He paused. 'Nothing I'd deem worth the attention of the Astronomer Royal.'

Sir Peter said nothing for a moment. Instead, he regarded Ramirez with languid eyes, like a tenured professor sizing up a promising yet insolent student. 'You still resent me,' he said at last. 'After all these years, still you're jealous.'

'No . . . and no.' Ramirez stared back at him. 'Whatever was once between us is long in the past. Prison tends to help put things like that in their proper perspective. As for jealousy . . .' He shrugged. 'So far as I'm concerned, you got what you deserved.'

Cole's eyelids fluttered, and Ramirez suppressed a grin. Some things, at least, never changed: Peter had always done that when he was irritated but trying not to show it. 'I don't know whether I should feel complimented or insulted.'

'You tell me.' Ramirez crossed his legs. 'Why did you volunteer for this expedition? Your chair at Cambridge getting a little too soft for you? Or did you think there might be a book out of this?'

The smile disappeared. Cole sat up a little straighter, laying his hands upon the armrests. 'I took a leave of absence because my government requested me to do so,' he said evenly, 'and I'll thank you not to speculate otherwise.' Realizing that his temper threatened to get the better of him, he forced himself to relax. 'Look, I didn't mean to get off on the wrong track here . . .'

'Naturally. Just banter among old friends, that's all.'

'Quite.' A tentative nod. 'What I'm trying to get at, really, is . . . if this is an alien artifact of some sort, do you think it could be hostile?'

Ramirez looked at him sharply. Something in Cole's face told him that this was the true focus of this conversation. Sir Peter was worried but trying not to show it. 'Anything's possible,' he said tentatively, 'although I couldn't say for sure either way. Why do you ask?'

Again, Cole didn't say anything for a moment. Instead, he leaned forward, cupping his hands between his knees. When he spoke again, his voice was low. 'I had a conversation with Captain Lawrence yesterday, and he expressed certain . . . reservations, shall we say? . . . about the potential for a dangerous encounter.'

'Did he now? I'm surprised he has that much imagination.'

Cole raised an eyebrow. 'I take it that your opinion of the captain is less than favorable.'

'My opinion is that he's a fine example of how far wealth and power can take you even when you're a moron.' Cole's brow furrowed; he started to say something, but Ramirez didn't let him interrupt. 'I stand by what I said before, but I'll also add that I think the possibility of meeting up with hostile aliens is rather remote.'

'Why not?'

'The correct question is "why?"' He nodded toward the book. 'That's why stories like that have never appealed to me. It assumes that aliens would think as we do . . . that they'd be just as bloodthirsty as humanity.'

'You have a low opinion of your own kind.' Cole peered at him. 'Perhaps that's why you ended up in Dolland, hmm?'

Ramirez felt his face grow warm. He let his gaze shift toward the window. 'Think what you will,' he said quietly, contemplating the stars. 'I just prefer to believe that, somewhere in the galaxy, there must be a race better than our own.' He glanced back at Cole. 'You can tell the captain that if you think it'll calm his nerves.'

'If he asks again, I shall.' Cole shook his head. 'But your philosophy isn't the issue. What I'm trying to ask you is . . . if they're indeed hostile, then how do we know?'

Ramirez searched Cole's face, looking for signs of subterfuge. It was an honest question, to be sure, perhaps even an obvious one . . . and yet, he couldn't help but feel that Sir Peter was holding something back from him. Something that worried the Astronomer Royal so much that he'd taken a colleague whom he disliked as much as Ramirez into his confidence. Perhaps he had his own doubts about Lawrence's competence.

'I couldn't say,' he said warily. 'I suppose we'll just have to cross that bridge when we get there.'

'Hmm . . .' Cole slowly nodded. 'I expect you're right. We'll probably just have to play this by ear, no matter what happens.' Then he inched a little closer, lowering his voice even more. 'However, when the time comes,' he said softly, 'I'd like for you to be with me in the command center, as close at hand as possible. So that I can consult with you as quickly as possible.'

'Not in the OC?' The other half of Deck A, adjacent to the command center, served as the ship's observation center. That was where the science team would monitor *Galileo*'s encounter with Spindrift.

'No. I'd like to have you on the bridge as much as possible. Until we're sure there's nothing to worry about, at least.' Cole hesitated. 'The captain needs to be reassured that he doesn't have to take . . . well, certain emergency measures . . . if there's no reason for him to do so. Do you understand?'

'Perfectly.' *Like hell!*

'Excellent.' Sir Peter patted his knee. 'Thanks, Jared. Glad you decided to come around. Always knew you'd be an asset to this mission.'

'Thank you, Peter. Appreciate your confidence . . .'

'And you'll say nothing of this to anyone, will you?' Again, Cole's eyelids fluttered. 'I can trust you to keep your mouth shut? To keep this strictly between you and me?'

'Of course.' And that, too, was a lie.

Ramirez located Collins on Deck C just as she was about to enter the access shaft. She looked around when he called her name, and waited as he jogged toward her. 'Lieutenant Collins . . . just the person I want to see,' he said, coming to a breathless halt. 'May I have a few minutes of your time?'

'I'm rather busy.' For some reason, she wore a fleece-lined jacket over her jumpsuit; various tools and instruments swung from a utility belt. 'Can this wait till later?'

'It's rather important, actually.' He glanced back and forth to see if anyone else was in the corridor. A door shut somewhere around the bend; he heard footsteps, going the other way. 'If we could speak in private,' he added, softening his voice, 'I think it would be for the best.'

Collins was visibly reluctant. That didn't surprise him; he'd become used to the suspicion in her eyes. Ever since he'd joined the expedition, no one aboard *Galileo* had been willing to trust him . . . save perhaps Cole, and clearly he had his own agenda. Yet among the members of the flight crew, Collins was the only person willing to talk to him. She might only be the shuttle pilot, but she had Harker's ear, and Harker was not only second-in-command, but obviously no friend of the captain. If he could persuade her to listen . . .

'Well . . . c'mon then,' she said, with no small reticence. 'I'm going down below to check out *Maria*.' She paused, looking him over. 'It's going to be cold down there. I'd put something on, if I were you.'

'I'll be fine.' Although his cabin was only a few meters away, Ramirez didn't want to give her an excuse to leave him behind. 'After you.'

Collins nodded, then pressed the button on the bulkhead that opened the access shaft. Ramirez waited until she'd climbed through the hatch, then followed her. Once again, he tried not look down as he placed hands and feet upon the ladder rungs protruding from the shaft's burnished-steel walls. Ever since the Millis-Clement field had been activated, this part of *Galileo* made him nervous; the shaft yawned below him like an empty well, leading straight down through the core of the ship until it reached the sealed hatch leading through the ZPE generator module. It wasn't so bad from there; it was when he had to climb all the way up to Deck A, twenty meters above, that he had to fight vertigo.

They didn't speak as they descended the ladder, their footfalls ringing faintly upon its rungs, until they reached the bottom hatch. Collins stopped to enter a security code into a keypad mounted on the bulkhead; Ramirez tried not to notice how she shielded the pad with her left hand to prevent him from observing the sequence. The hatch buzzed, and she bent down to twist the lockwheel counterclockwise. Lifting it open to reveal darkness, Collins reached farther down to push a button just inside the hatch. Lightstrips glimmered to life, and she climbed down through the hatchway.

'Close it behind you,' she said. Then she looked back up at him. 'Coming?'

Ramirez hesitated. He'd been this way before, of course; the first time during training, the second when the science team had been ferried over from Tsiolkovsky Station. Then the shaft had been a horizontal tunnel, no more threatening than a crawl space. Now it was a pit even deeper than the one within the hab module, its bottom nearly sixty meters below them. The ever-present hum of the engines was louder now that they'd left behind the soundproofed warrens of the hab module, as though they were entering the ventricle of an immense heart.

'Yeah . . . sure. Right behind you.' Carefully lowering his feet over the edge, he slowly climbed through the hatchway, the palms of his hands moist as they grasped the ladder rungs. He somehow managed to reach up and shut the hatch behind him. Collins patiently waited for him, and he earned a brief smile and a nod from her once that task was complete. Then they began to make the final descent.

Don't look down, he told himself. *Don't look down*. Ramirez stared straight ahead, concentrating on placing his hands and feet on the rungs one at a time, not releasing his grip until he was sure that he had a solid foothold on the one below. It wasn't until they finally reached the bottom of the shaft that he noticed how much colder the air had become, the sweat on his back and beneath his arms suddenly turning to ice water.

'You're right,' he murmured. 'I should've worn a jacket.'

'Told you so.' Standing above the hatch to the docking module, Collins again entered a code number into a keypad, then crouched to twist another lockwheel. 'Last bit of the way,' she said, glancing up at him. 'Think you can make it?'

'Sure.' He tilted his head back to peer back up the shaft; it rose above them like the chimney of a factory smokestack. 'Might even stay a while, if you don't mind.'

'You wanted to talk privately. Can't get more private than this.' Collins raised the hatch, then reached down again to switch on the lights. 'All right, let's go.'

Below them lay the primary airlock: a spherical compartment with round, vaultlike hatches on four sides, its bulkheads cramped with suit lockers and storage bins. Collins peered through the small, round window of the Dock 1 hatch, then reached to the panel beside it to flip switches that would initiate the pressurization sequence. 'So,' she said, turning to him, 'what do you want to discuss?'

'I had a chat with Sir Peter just a little while ago, and he said something . . . well, I'm not sure what to make of it. He seems concerned that Spindrift may be hostile.'

'You're the alien expert. You tell me.'

Ramirez smiled at this. 'You know what they used to call astrobiology? Science without a subject. Oh, we've found microfossils on Mars and extremophiles on Europa and Titan, but aliens? No one's an expert, because . . .'

'We haven't found any. Right.' She checked the pressure gauge. 'So I take it you don't know either.'

'That's what I told him. And he seemed to accept that. But . . .' He hesitated. 'Apparently he's not the only one who's concerned. The captain is, too.'

'Why shouldn't he be? This is his ship.' The gauge reached the green line; she flipped another switch, then reached up to grasp the lockwheel. It was more resistant than the others; she grunted as she hauled at it, and swore under her breath when it refused to budge.

'Allow me.' Ramirez took hold of the lockwheel and put his arms to work. Three years of hard labor in the prison farm hadn't been for nothing; the wheel squeaked, then turned counterclockwise. 'There we go,' he murmured, as the hatch wheezed with escaping air. 'Must have frozen.'

'Thanks. I'll have Marty look at it.' Collins pulled the hatch open, revealing the low, narrow tunnel of the airlock sleeve. 'You were saying?'

'Well, certainly it's his business, but there was something else . . .'

Collins no longer seemed to be paying attention. Ducking her head and shoulders, she began crawling on hands and knees down the tunnel, the tools on her belt clinking together as they dangled from her waist. Watching her, Ramirez found himself thinking about how long it'd been since the last time he had been with a woman. He'd shut down that part of himself a long time ago; although there had been female prisoners in Dolland, sexual relations had been forbidden among inmates, and rape was punishable by spacing: a one-way trip out the airlock. He looked away, took a deep breath. It was not the time . . .

'Go on. I'm listening.' Collins glanced back at him. 'We can talk in the shuttle.'

Lowering his head, Ramirez followed her down the tunnel. Collins stopped to use a power screwdriver to open a cover on the shuttle's fuselage. She pressed a couple of buttons; another hiss, and the hatch popped open. Again, he saw only darkness. Collins crawled through the hatch; squatting at its edge, she turned herself around, then carefully descended within the craft, as if climbing down a ladder. Her head disappeared from sight; a moment passed, then interior lights flickered to life.

'Everything all right?' he asked.

'Sure.' Her voice came to him from the other side of the hatch. 'Just be careful. Everything's sort of upsy-daisy in here.'

Ramirez crawled to the hatch, put his head and shoulders through it, and looked down. Below him, he saw what appeared to be a narrow manhole leading down to the shuttle's cockpit; recessed rungs within what was usually the floor of the central aisle made descent possible within a cabin that, under normal circumstances, would be in a horizontal position.

Collins had already made her way down to the cockpit, passing four seats arranged on each side of the aisle. Clinging to the ladder with one hand, she pulled a pair of elastic straps from her belt and, using her other hand, hooked them to floor rings on either side of the center aisle. Once she secured their other ends to her belt, she was able to move freely, like a mountaineer rappelling down a vertical slope.

'Come on down, if you want,' she said, craning her neck to look up at him. 'Just be careful not to fall on me.'

'No thanks. Think I'll remain here. Let the pro take care of this.' He gazed down at the wraparound control panels of the cockpit, arrayed below and above a set of teardrop-shaped windows. 'What are you doing down there, anyway?'

'Tucking *Maria* away for the night.' Planting her feet against the floor, Collins leaned over backward to switch on the instruments. 'I could do this from Deck A, of course, but I never trust the comps. Besides, I also need to do this . . .' She unsnapped a pocket on her left thigh and withdrew a data disc. As Harker watched, she arched her spine even more to insert the disc within its slot in the main computer. 'Backup flight recorder,' she explained, gasping slightly with the effort. 'From here on out, everything that happens aboard *Galileo* gets relayed here via comlink. Log entries, scientific data, voice and video communications, the works. That way, if we had to abandon ship . . .'

'You'd have a record of what happened,' Ramirez said. 'Wise precaution.' It was hard to ignore the inherent sexuality of her position. In a conscious effort to get her off his mind, he gazed upward. Another compartment lay on the other side of the passageway: suit lockers and equipment racks, for the most part, along with what looked like the hatch of a belly airlock, yet something else caught his attention: four large cylinders, each two meters in height, arranged on either side of the aft compartment. He immediately recognized them for what they were.

'Lieutenant?' he asked. 'Why are there biostasis cells aboard?'

'Same general idea . . . just in case there's an emergency. God help us if we ever have to use them.' Without looking up from her work, Collins continued to use the main comp to run diagnostic tests of the shuttle's primary systems. '*Maria*'s designed for long-term sorties, but her air and water supplies are limited to only a few days. Five at most. If something were to happen to her . . . say, she had to crash-land somewhere . . . then the idea is that we'd activate the homing beacon, go into biostasis, and wait for someone to rescue us.'

'Yes, but . . .'

'How would they rescue us if we've only got one shuttle? Yeah, I know.' Collins tapped another command into the keyboard, watched as the screen above it changed. 'We had problems with the *Arcangela* during the shakedown cruise . . . the airframe wasn't quite stable . . . so it was taken off for a complete refit. If *Galileo* hadn't launched so quickly, we might have had a second shuttle as well. But since our launch window was so narrow, we've had to leave without it.' She glanced up at him. 'That's why I say we better hope that . . .'

She suddenly stopped. Looking down at her again, Ramirez saw that she'd been distracted by something she'd spotted through the starboard cockpit window. 'Well, well,' she murmured. 'Isn't that interesting?'

'What? See something?'

'You might say that, yes.' Twisting herself upright, Collins grabbed hold of the ladder and unsnapped her harness. 'Come down and look for yourself,' she added. 'Just be careful where you put your hands and feet.'

Ramirez turned himself around within the sleeve so that he was feet-first to the hatch. Grasping the handrails, he carefully lowered his legs through the hatch. After a few seconds of blindly searching for a foothold, he finally managed to locate one of the recessed floor rungs. Slipping out of the airlock, he eased his way down to Collins. Clinging to the ladder with one hand and bracing the soles of her shoes against the edge of the console, the shuttle pilot moved aside to make room for him.

'There,' she said, pointing through the window below the copilot's seat. 'See?'

Ramirez peered in the direction she indicated. They were looking toward the ship's stern; he could see the bulge of the main fuel tank and, beyond it, the gold-plated shield surrounding the fusion engine. In the foreground, less than fifteen meters away, lay the service module. He could see Larry and Jerry, *Galileo*'s two probes, resting within their respective ports, and between them . . .

'What's that?' he asked. 'I didn't notice this when you showed us the ship.'

A cylindrical object, tapered at one end and broad at the other, with small fins running along its sides. No more than six or seven meters long, it was enclosed by a small cradle attached to the hull, with bundled cables leading from it to a nearby port.

'That's because it wasn't there when we came aboard.' Collins's voice was low. 'But I know a torpedo when I see it.'

Ramirez felt cold, yet the chill didn't only come from the trapped air within the shuttle. 'That's what I've been trying to tell you,' he said softly. 'Sir Peter told me that, if it turned out Spindrift was hostile, the captain was prepared to take emergency measures. I didn't know what he meant by that, but . . .'

'I think we do now.' Collins's voice was an angry murmur. 'Those goddamn idiots . . .'

'You can't tell anyone we found this.' Ramirez darted a look at her. 'If Cole finds out I told you . . .'

'Quiet.' Reaching into her breast pocket, she pulled out her headset. Putting it on, she tapped at its wand. 'Harker. Private channel.'

'Commander, please . . .'

'Hush.' Collins cast him a warning glance, then glanced away. 'Ted? Emcee. Meet me in my quarters in fifteen. Urgent.' She paused. 'Yeah, I found it. I'll meet you there. Go.'

She tapped the wand again, then pulled the headset around her neck. 'Go back to the airlock and wait for me,' she said to Ramirez. 'I'll finish up here, then take you back upstairs.'

'Sure.' Ramirez started to climb back up the ladder. Then he stopped and looked at her. 'You and Ted . . . Commander Harker, I mean . . .'

'I think he'd let you call him Ted.' She favored him with a brief smile. 'I'm Emily.'

'Thank you, Emily . . . and please, call me Jared.' He paused. 'You two know what's going on, don't you?'

'We didn't until now.' Again, the smile, more warm than before. 'Thank you, Jared.'

'You're welcome.' Despite the danger, he felt a surge of relief. 'Nice to know I have friends.' Collins gave him an uncertain look, and he felt like saying something else. Yet words failed him, so he continued to scale the ladder back to the hatch.

Seven

June 3, 2288 – EASS *Galileo*

Climbing the last rungs of the ladder, Emily pushed open the Deck A hatch and stepped into the command center. For the first time since *Galileo* came through the starbridge, all the flight officers were at their stations; the only exceptions were Nick and Werner, who were down in Deck B getting the biostasis cells ready. Hands quietly tapped at keyboards as comps beeped and purred, but otherwise there was little sound save for the occasional murmured comment. At T minus 00:49:39 to main engine ignition, the crew was busy preparing the ship for departure from Eris. Once *Galileo* was under way, only the most dire emergency would cause them to abort the mission.

At the center of the horseshoe, Captain Lawrence was seated in the command chair. Legs casually crossed, he studied status reports on his lapboard, looking up only when Arkady or Simone or Martin said something to him. To all outward appearances, he seemed calm, yet Emily couldn't help but notice that his right foot, propped up on his left knee, twitched like the fretful swish of a cat's tail. As if feeling her eyes on his back, Lawrence peered over his shoulder at her. She said nothing, only gave him a nod, and the captain looked forward again. Yet his ankle stopped jiggling as he self-consciously uncrossed his legs and placed both feet flat upon the floor.

Nervous, Captain? Worried about the countdown? Or perhaps it's just your guilty conscience? Emily smiled to herself. She'd find out soon enough.

On the other side of the compartment, Ted stood next to Antonia, hunched over her console as he quietly discussed some matter with the XO. Looking up, he caught Emily's eye. A brief nod, then he finished talking to Toni and moved away, slowly walking toward Lawrence. Emily felt her heart flutter. Time for the mice to put the bell around the cat's neck . . . and suddenly, it was as if her own tail had begun to twitch.

Go on, girl. Get this over and done. She and Harker had spent the last evening weighing their options: first in her quarters, then in the library where they'd accessed technical information from *Galileo*'s data banks, and finally in Ted's cabin, where they'd sought solace in each other's arms. It wasn't until this morning, though, that they'd finally agreed upon a course of action. And now . . .

'Captain?' Harker stopped next to Lawrence's chair. 'May I have a word with you, please?'

Lawrence raised his eyes from the lapboard. 'Yes, Mr Harker?'

'I have something . . .' Harker paused, waiting for Emily to join him. She stepped closer, approaching Lawrence from the other side of his chair. 'A matter has come to our attention that we'd like to discuss with you . . . sir.'

Surprised to see her coming at him from the opposite direction, Lawrence's expression became wary. 'What . . . well, yes, of course.' He looked at Harker again. 'What do you have on your mind?'

Simone half turned in her seat at the helm to gaze back

at them. From the corner of her eye, Emily could see Arkady and Martin watching with curiosity. 'I think it would be best if we discussed this in private, sir,' Harker replied. 'Perhaps in your office?'

The adam's apple in Lawrence's throat bobbed up and down. He knew the protocol; if two members of the flight crew, one of whom was either the first officer or the executive officer, formally requested a private hearing, he couldn't refuse their request. 'As you wish,' he said, then he folded the lapboard and stood up. 'Commander Vincenza, please take the conn until I return. Proceed with the countdown.'

'Yes, sir.' Antonia stood up, waiting for Lawrence to leave his station before she assumed command. Emily noticed that the XO didn't seem surprised by this sudden turn of events. Ted must have warned her that something was going down. The others looked away, assuming the polite pretense that nothing unusual was happening.

The captain's office was a small compartment located adjacent to the command center. A fold-down couch took up room where a bunk might have been; above a small desk was a shelf crammed with operations manuals and loose-leaf binders containing printouts of the ship's log. The only touches of personality were a few framed photos on the walls; among the pictures of Lawrence's family, there was one Emily had seen before in Ted's quarters, a group photo from the ESA astronaut training program. Both Harker and Lawrence stood on the second row, separated from one another by several other cadet-trainees.

'Well, then,' Lawrence said once he shut the door behind them, 'what do you want to see me about?' He stepped around behind his desk, motioning to the couch. 'Take a seat.'

Harker remained standing, his hands clasped together behind his back. 'Sir, it's come to our attention that a torpedo has been attached to *Galileo*'s outer hull. We suspect that it's a weapon of undetermined—'

'Oh, hell!' Lawrence snapped, suddenly angry. 'Who told you this?'

'No one told us, sir.' Slipping from behind Ted, Emily took an identical stance beside him. 'I discovered it when I went below to check out the shuttle. I determined that it was my duty to inform the first officer.'

'I see.' Lawrence calmed down, if only slightly. 'And what leads you to believe that it's a torpedo?' he added, sitting down behind the desk.

'There's nothing else it could be, sir.' Harker continued to stand at attention. 'There's mention in our manifest of a new probe being added at the last minute . . .'

'Ah . . . and what makes you think it was? Added at the last minute, I mean?'

'Because I didn't spot it when I flew past the ship while we were in dry dock,' Emily responded. 'I saw the service module clearly at that time, and there was nothing attached to it other than the probes we were already carrying. Of that, I'm quite positive, sir.'

'Are you really?' Lawrence meant his tone to be scornful, yet it only came off as childish annoyance, like a kid who'd been caught lying and was now trying to wiggle out of it by splitting hairs. 'Are you sure you haven't mistaken it for . . . ?'

'Yes, sir, we are.' Harker refused to be led off track. 'Sir, we have strong reason to believe that this object is a torpedo, possibly containing a nuclear warhead. If that is the case, we respectfully request to know its purpose, and why it was placed aboard *Galileo* without the crew's being informed.'

Lawrence silently regarded them for a moment, as if trying to decide what to do next. Then he turned around in his chair, unhooked the receiver of the intercom phone, and murmured something into it. Another moment passed, then he returned the phone to its hook and turned back to them. 'Who else have you spoken to about this?'

'No one, sir,' Harker replied. He and Emily had already promised Ramirez that they'd keep him out of this. There was no reason why he should become involved any more than he already was, and he could face dire consequences if his role were to become known.

'Very good. A wise decision on your part.' Lawrence rocked back in his seat, turning his head to gaze out the porthole beside him. For a few moments he didn't speak; it was as if he was waiting for something and knew that time was on his side. 'You know, Mr Harker,' he said at last, his voice assuming a reflective tone, 'I've always believed that, if things had been just different, you would've been in command and not me. Has that ever occurred to you?'

'No, sir, it hasn't.'

'Don't lie to me, Ted. I'm sure it has . . . and we both know the reasons. That's why I've allowed you a certain amount of leeway, such as ignoring your little dalliance with Lieutenant Collins here.' A sardonic smirk played across his mouth. 'Don't believe for a second I haven't noticed what's been going on between you two.'

Emily's face became warm; she quickly looked down at the floor. 'But that's the nature of secrets, I suppose,' Lawrence went on. 'You've chanced upon something you weren't supposed to know. In hindsight, I suppose it was inevitable. All the same, we're going to have to deal with it. What do you think . . . ?'

A knock on the door. 'Come in,' Lawrence said loudly, and Emily looked around to see Cole enter. She felt a chill, even though Ted had warned her this was possible. 'Sir Peter. Thank you for joining us. Everything going well in the OC, I take it?' Without waiting for an answer, the captain nodded toward her and Ted. 'Mr Harker and Ms Collins appear to have tumbled to . . .'

'Right.' Cole shut the door behind him. 'Now you know.' Pushing his way between them, he took a seat upon the couch. 'So . . . where do we go from here?'

For a second, Harker was at a loss for words, while Cole crossed his legs as if this were little more than a polite meeting between friends. 'Let's cut to the quick, shall we?' Cole went on, not waiting for a response. 'You've become aware that a nuclear torpedo has been placed aboard ship. You want to know why it's here, and why you haven't been advised. Well, then, here it is . . .' Lifting his right hand, he raised a finger. 'First, there's little doubt that Spindrift is an alien artifact of some sort . . .'

'Although I'm not entirely convinced that's the case.' Lawrence's voice was low. 'The possibility of extraterrestrial intelligence seems . . . well, rather far-fetched.'

Emily glanced at Harker, saw his eyes widen in surprise. 'If I didn't know better, sir,' he murmured, 'I'd say that you sound like a Dominionist.'

Lawrence's face colored; he glared at his first officer. Before he could speak, though, Cole shook his head. 'I'd just as soon not get into a religious debate just now, if you don't mind.' He shot the captain a look, and Lawrence kept his mouth shut. Cole raised another finger. 'Second, if we accept that as a given, then there's a possibility, however remote, that it may be hostile . . .'

'We can't assume that,' Ted said.

'Of course not. But the possibility remains nonetheless.' Cole raised a third finger. 'Third, if Spindrift is indeed hostile, then we have to protect not only ourselves but also Earth itself. We have no idea what we may be facing out there.'

'Exactly . . . we don't know.' Harker stood his ground. 'Sir Peter, if this is a first-contact situation, don't you see the risk of charging in there with guns blazing?'

'Mr Harker, no one is suggesting that we shoot first and ask questions later . . .'

'Nonetheless, the mere fact that we're carrying a nuclear weapon could jeopardize any chance of establishing peaceful contact. Not to mention the risk just having this thing aboard carries for the ship and . . .'

'Mr Harker, you're out of line,' Lawrence said, his voice terse. 'Stand down.'

'Captain, you can't . . .'

'Stand down, mister!' Lawrence half rose from his chair. 'Or you're relieved!'

Emily practically felt Ted tremble with outrage. She alone noticed that his right hand curled into a fist. For a moment, she thought he was going to take a swing at his former classmate. She started to raise a hand to his shoulder, but before she could, Ted slowly let out his breath.

'My apologies, sir,' he muttered. 'And to you, Sir Peter.'

The tension eased, if only to a degree. Still glaring at his first officer, Lawrence settled back into his chair, while Cole shifted uneasily on the couch. 'I understand your concerns. Mr Harker,' Sir Peter said quietly. 'You're thinking of you ship and its crew, and that's commendable. To a certain extent, I share those concerns as well.' He paused, letting his words sink in. 'But it's the opinion of our government and the ESA senior directors that we take . . . well, certain precautions . . . in the event that this encounter proves to be less peaceful than we might desire.'

'I see.' Harker straightened his shoulders. 'So this comes from the top?'

'From the very top, yes, that's correct.' Cole glanced at Lawrence. 'If it makes any difference, your captain wasn't informed of this decision until shortly before launch, when he met privately with the associate director.'

Now it all fell together. Emily pursed her lips, trying to remain calm. This was why Lawrence had taken a leave of absence during training to return to Earth. It wasn't just to have a holiday in England, but rather to be briefed by Shillinglaw.

'Naturally, this aspect of the mission remains classified,' Sir Peter continued. 'We'd rather hoped that you'd remain in blissful ignorance, but . . .' An offhand shrug, as if all this were merely a minor nuisance. 'Well, I trust that the two of you will keep this to yourselves and not tell anyone else what you've learned.'

'Consider that an order,' Lawrence added, his voice low and menacing.

'Aye, sir.' To Emily's surprise, there was no trace of reluctance in Ted's reply. He glanced at her, and the look in his eyes was as clear as words: *We're beaten. Do as he says.*

'Yes, sir,' she said, feeling a tightness in her voice.

'Very good.' Lawrence appeared to be satisfied. He looked over at Cole, and Sir Peter nodded. 'Right, then . . . resume your duties. Dismissed.'

Without another word, Harker turned to open the door. Emily followed him. The command center was very quiet. The rest of the flight crew had heard the raised voices of an argument, yet no one looked away from their consoles; this was none of their affair.

Emily watched Ted as he strode across the compartment to his station. Taking his seat, he pulled up his lapboard, punched up a status report. The countdown stood at 00:27:14. In less than a half hour, *Galileo* would fire its main engine and depart from the solar system. Into the abyss, and whatever awaited them.

A peaceful scientific mission, she thought. *God help us.*

The diametric drive made no sound. Despite the immense power generated by its zero-point energy generator, it operated in total silence, the torus creating an invisible bubble that wrapped itself around the *Galileo*. Within the ship, the only noise was the steady hum of the main engine, slowly but inexorably thrusting the vessel toward cruise velocity, at which point the fusion reactor would automatically shut down and allow *Galileo* to glide across the fabric of space-time like a surfer riding the crest of a wave that would never break.

Emily finished making up her bunk. Satisfied that

the bedspread and pillows were neatly in place, she reached down to pick up the bunk by its bottom and lift it into its slot within the bulkhead. Stepping back, she took a last survey of her cabin; all her belongings had been put away, nothing had been left out that might fall over and break during retrofire and turnaround maneuvers.

Seeing that she'd taken care of everything, she unzipped her jumpsuit and hung it within the closet, then pulled out a hempcloth robe that she put on over her tank top and panties. She slipped her feet into a pair of paper moccasins, then, with one last look behind her, she opened the door and stepped out into the corridor. Even though she didn't need to do so, she turned off the lights before she slid the door shut.

The passageway was deserted, as quiet as the rest of the ship. From behind the closed doors of the cabins around her, there were no voices, no clicking of keyboards. Deck C was already getting colder; obeying its programmed schedule, the AI had lowered the thermostat to 18.3°C to conserve energy. Emily padded down the corridor, her arms folded around herself, until she reached the access shaft. As she opened the hatch, she looked back to see that the AI, registering the departure of the last crew member, was dimming the ceiling lights to a thin twilight glow.

Deck B was the section of *Galileo*'s hab module that was the least visited, yet it was also the part of the ship that would be occupied for the longest period of the voyage. Windowless and heavily shielded, it contained the hibernation compartment in which crew and passengers would spend most of the journey. Until then, it hadn't been used at all; the shakedown run to Mars had lasted little more than six months, and *Galileo*'s life-support systems were sufficient to keep the crew alive for such a relatively short time. But this mission would last considerably longer than that, so biostasis was necessary to conserve air, water, and food, not to mention preserve the sanity of all aboard.

When Emily arrived, she found most of the flight crew already there. Shivering in their robes, they impatiently waited for Nick to put them into the biostasis cells. 'Ah, there she is! Fashionably late as usual.' Arkady gallantly swept open his left arm as he assayed a formal bow. 'Right this way, m'lady. Table for one or two?'

'One, please.' Emily looked around the compartment. Tables, indeed. All she saw were rows of boxlike cells, beige-white and sterile, faintly resembling old-fashioned refrigerators save for their thick windows and readout panels. Yet she knew that, if she laid her hand upon one whose lid was already shut, she'd feel not cold but warmth. No clumsy cryogenics here, but instead the more benign technology of DNA reconstruction; she'd awaken literally feeling like a new person, her dead cells replaced by nanites that, over the course of weeks and months, would select, discard and substitute them with new material cloned *in situ* according to the patterns of her individual genome, while drugs shut down her mind and kept her brain functioning only at those levels necessary for survival.

Immortality, of a kind . . . and yet, she couldn't help but regard hibernation as a short-lived form of death, with the biostasis cells little more than temporary coffins. Like the others, her training had included a twenty-four-hour term in suspended animation, and despite the predictable jokes – *you don't look a day older than when I last saw you* – she couldn't help but regard the whole process with a certain suppressed horror. Like it or not, she was about to enter a dreamless sleep that was as close to a coma as she could get without her condition becoming terminal.

Turning away from the others, she found Ted leaning against a cell, hands shoved in the pockets of his robe. Walking over to him, she expected no more than a polite nod; to her surprise, he pulled his hands from his pockets and reached out to her. She hesitated, then let him pull her body against his, an embrace that was both comforting and sexual.

'Hey, that's a change,' she murmured, sliding her arms around him. 'Not afraid the captain's going to see this?'

'Relax. He and Martin are upstairs, closing down Deck A. They'll be the last ones to go down.' Ted patted the side of the cell. 'This one's mine,' he added, giving her a lascivious grin. 'You're welcome to share, of course. I'll even let you get on top . . . as always.'

'Hush!' From behind her, she heard Arkady laugh out loud. Feigning irritation, she started to shove him away. Harker resisted, though, and instead pulled her closer, affectionately burying his face in her hair.

'Something's going on,' he whispered in her ear. 'Nick tells me the captain gave him instructions to change the revival schedule . . .'

'The *what*?' She tried to keep her voice low. 'I don't . . .'

'The order in which we're supposed to be revived.' Ted gently stroked her back, keeping up the pretense of giving her a farewell hug. 'Lawrence told him to bring us up last, even after the science team. He didn't say why, just told him to do so.'

Emily frowned. 'I don't get it. Why would he . . . ?'

'I don't know . . . but I've got my suspicions.' Ted released her, but took her hands to keep her close. 'Nick's on our side. He's going to revive us first, right after himself, and leave the captain for last. Or at least before he brings up the science team.'

She glanced over her shoulder. At the far end of the compartment, she saw a row of six cells, their lids sealed. The science team had already been put to sleep. 'He can do that?' she murmured.

'He's the doc. He can do anything he wants.' The smile reappeared. 'He'll tell Lawrence that he noticed readings on our cells that led him to believe that our conditions were unstable, so he brought us up first as a precaution.'

'Nice.' Emily cocked her head to one side. 'You talked him into this, didn't you?'

'Sure. I just had to promise that I'd let you sleep with him.' He winced as she swatted his arm, then his expression became more serious. 'Really, though . . . he knows something's going on. Everyone does. That little quarrel we had with Lawrence didn't exactly go unnoticed . . . and even if they don't know the details, they're on our side.' He hesitated. 'Most of them, at least.'

'You think someone else . . . ?' Her eyes widened. 'Martin?'

'That would make sense, wouldn't it? Who else is in a better position to assist him?' He shook his head before she could interrupt. 'Like I said, the others are with us . . . but if this is going to work, we're going to have to go down first. You and me both.'

She stared at him. 'Why?'

'Nick's programmed our cells to display the revival sequence Lawrence wants. We're counting on him checking our readouts to be sure. But once the captain himself goes down, Nick will reprogram the cells so that we're revived before he is. That way, Doc's got his alibi, and we get a few minutes to see . . . well, to see whatever he's up to.'

'Right.' Still holding Ted's hands, Emily looked around the compartment. The other members of the flight team were quietly chatting among themselves, yet from the way Antonia, Werner, Simone, and Arkady occasionally glanced their way, it was clear that they knew something was amiss. Ted had earned their respect a long time ago, while Lawrence had been nothing but trouble. And so far from home, they were willing to trust one man more than the other, rank notwithstanding.

'All right, now . . . who's first?' Nick had been inspecting the cell next to Harker's; he turned to glance around the room. 'Got a nice warm place for a little nap. Who's up for it?' Then he looked directly at her. 'Emily, my dear . . . how about you?'

Knowing that she wasn't really being given a choice, she reluctantly nodded. Yet Ted held on to her for a moment longer. Pulling her close again, he gave her a last kiss. 'See you on the other side,' he murmured. 'Love you.'

'Love you, too,' she whispered. Then she pried herself away from him and walked over to her cell.

Nick drew a privacy curtain around the cell, then asked her to strip. Despite Ted's earlier joke, though, he didn't stare at her as she took off her robe and removed her underwear, and treated her no more or less than if she was another patient under his care. The doctor had already told everyone that shaving their scalps wasn't necessary for short-term biostasis – if their hair grew longer than they felt comfortable, he'd play barber after they woke up – yet for the sake of hygiene he used an electric razor to remove her pubic hair. She'd endured the procedure before, but it didn't make it any easier; she closed her eyes and hummed an old country music song her mother had once taught her. The half dozen injections Nick administered to her arms and the buttocks were the worst part of the ordeal; her worst moment of humiliation was the suppository he let her insert by herself, and during that he gallantly turned his back.

Finally, she was allowed to climb into the cell. Lying down upon a soft pad, Emily clenched her teeth while she watched Nick gently insert an intravenous feeding tube into the soft flesh of her left elbow. The breathing mask came next; lifting her head, he carefully fitted it around her nose and mouth, tugging on it to make sure that it had an airtight fit.

'Ready?' he asked. She nodded. 'All right now . . . sweet dreams.'

She closed her eyes. Another spark of pain as he inserted another tube into her right elbow. A pair of small plastic caps were placed over her eyes, but by then she wasn't feeling very much of anything save for a certain euphoria, sensuous and almost erotic, as liquid gel began to flow around her body.

Suspended within a warm blue cloud, she allowed herself to be carried upward into darkness. Her last conscious thought was that sleep should always be like this. Without anxiety, without pain, without bad dreams. A lovely cruise to oblivion, with a starless night as her destination.

Eight

JANUARY 7, 2291 – EASS *GALILEO*

Harker sat on the edge of his biostasis cell, watching as blue gel dripped from his body to form a pool at his bare feet. Nick had given him a plastic cup filled with a yellow liquid that smelled vaguely of citrus and tasted like lemonade mixed with rubbing alcohol; he did his best to drink it, but his stomach roiled at the odor and it was all he could do to keep from throwing up. His mind felt sluggish and stupid, and were it not for the fact that the doctor had already extracted the tubes from his elbows and drained the cell, he would just as soon have gone back to sleep until *Galileo* returned to Earth.

Hearing a harsh, phlegm-filled cough from behind him, Harker slowly turned his head to see Emily come back to life. Nick stood beside the open hatch of her cell; he'd removed her air mask and eye protectors and was helping her sit up, holding her shoulders as she fought to breathe normally for the first time in over thirteen months. Like himself, her naked body was covered with a blue film that matted her hair against her head; Harker duly noted that it had grown a few inches since he'd last seen her and almost reached her shoulders. The doctor lowered the left wall of her cell, then carefully turned her around until her legs swung over the side. Emily doubled over and coughed a few more times, then raised a listless hand to rub her eyes. She looked like a little girl who'd just been rudely awakened, and Harker could only empathize; a few minutes ago, he'd been in the same condition.

Nick murmured something else to her, then hurried away, no doubt to fetch another cup of the vile medicine he'd given Harker. As he passed his cell, the doctor paused to look at him. 'Doing all right there?' he asked. 'Not getting sick, are you?'

'No . . . fine.' His voice came as a dry rasp. Truth was, he felt like hell, but he didn't want to distract Nick from looking after Emily. 'Just . . . wanna get cleaned up . . . s'all . . .'

'Hang on. Be right back.' Nick went to a nearby bench to pour some more of the liquid into another cup. He returned to Emily and handed it to her, and waited until he was sure that she drank at least half of it before he strolled back over to Harker. 'Can you stand up? Let's see if you can, hmm?'

Lazarus, come forth . . . Harker inched forward a little more until he was sure that his feet were firmly planted on the wet floor, then he carefully rose from the crypt. His legs felt rubbery, and he felt a joint in his left knee crack, yet it was easier than he expected. More blue goo slid down his body; more than anything else, he wanted to get the obscene stuff off him. 'Okay . . . I'm okay . . .'

'You sure?' Nick offered a hand to steady him, and Harker nodded. 'I see you've enjoyed my little refreshment.' Harker scowled as Nick took the cup from him. 'Head's over here,' he added, taking Harker by the arm to guide him toward a frosted-glass door on the other side of the compartment. 'Don't take too long . . . we're going to have more people wanting to use it soon enough.'

Through the dense fog that shrouded his mind, Harker

caught Nick's meaning. It wouldn't be long before the rest of the flight crew were revived. He needed to get up to the command center before Lawrence if he was going to find out what the captain had done before they'd gone into biostasis. 'Bring up Arkady next,' he mumbled. 'Simone, too. I'm going to need them.'

'I'll do what I can.' Nick stepped over to a cabinet, pulled out a plastic pouch containing a fresh change of clothes. 'Get cleaned up,' he said, handing it to him. 'Your girlfriend's going to be waiting for you. And Ted . . . ?' Harker stopped to look back at him. 'Remember that promise you made me?'

It took Harker a second to recall what Nick was talking about. 'Sorry, Doc,' he said, forcing a grin. 'Don't think I do.'

'Good.' Nick grinned. 'Just checking.'

The toilet had a commode and a sink at one end and a shower stall at the other. His bladder was empty and his bowels were void, though, so there was nothing else for him to do but stagger to the shower and pass his hand across the temperature plate. As he waited for the water to heat up, he caught sight of himself in the mirror above the sink. A Neanderthal stared back at him. He needed a shave and a haircut, but those would have to wait. First things first . . .

Harker stepped into the stall. He gasped as hot water hit him; planting his hands against the tile wall, he let it sluice the suspension gel from his body. How long had it been since the last time he'd had a bath? He didn't want to think about it, but it forced his mind to get back to work. Seven and a half months at cruise velocity, shiptime, plus six more months for acceleration and braking . . . how long would that be back on Earth? About twenty-five months. Two years. More than two years. Christ . . .

So what secret task did Lawrence perform before the crew went into biostasis? Harker didn't have time to investigate before he and the others had gone to sleep. Indeed, it was pure luck that Doc tipped him off at the last minute. Highly probable – no, more than that; very likely – it had something to do with the nuke *Galileo* was carrying. The fact that he'd confronted the captain about its presence might have forced Lawrence to take action of some sort.

What would Lawrence have done? No reason why he would've jettisoned the torpedo, however sensible that action might be. So far as the captain knew, only four persons aboard were aware of the nuke's presence. Five if Harker counted Martin, who'd helped him close down the command center and thus might be part of the conspiracy. Six if he also included Ramirez, who'd been sworn to secrecy; Harker still wasn't sure on whose side he was playing. Yet even so, what could Lawrence have accomplished in the command deck that would have made any difference when they were so far from . . . ?

The sound of the stall door sliding open, a sudden rush of cold air. Harker looked around to see Emily stepping into the shower. 'Move over,' she murmured. 'I feel utterly nasty.'

'You couldn't be nasty if you tried.' Harker moved aside, allowing her to get the benefit of the hot water. 'Blue does a lot for you, y'know,' he added, reaching up to gently wipe some gel from her face. 'Brings out your eyes . . .'

'Behave yourself.' Emily slapped away his hand as she slipped beneath the spray. Sighing with relief, she let the water sluice away the suspension fluid. 'Damn. Time goes fast when you're having fun, right?'

'Thinking just the same thing myself.' This was the wrong time and place to let himself get aroused; leaving the shower, he found a locker containing a stack of folded towels. 'Soon as you're done here, I'd like you to go below and check the torpedo . . . if you're up for it, that is.'

'If it means avoiding any more of that wretched stuff Nick made us drink, I'll go EVA if I have to.' Emily paused. 'You know, that's not a bad idea. Might find a way to get rid of the damned thing . . .'

'Don't even think about it.' He didn't want to do anything that might constitute mutiny. Or at least not until he had a better sense of what Lawrence had in mind. 'Just give it a visual inspection and report back to me. I'll be on Deck A.'

Her response was lost beneath the water cascading down around her head. Harker finished drying himself off, then ripped open the pouch Nick had given him. A two-piece outfit of drawstring trousers and a loose tunic, along with underwear and a pair of monkey boots. Not as warm as his uniform jumpsuit, but at least he wouldn't be prowling the ship in a bathrobe.

'Oh, and one more thing . . .' Emily cracked open the stall door to peer out at him. 'Lose the beard but keep the hair. Looks good on you.'

'I'll take that under advisement.' Harker dressed quickly, then left the toilet before she could offer any more grooming tips.

Arkady was awake. Sitting on the side of his cell, his shoulders slumped and his hands clasped together around a cup, he stared at Harker like a drunk coming off a three-day bender. Behind him, Nick was helping Simone sit up in her cell. 'You doing okay there?' Harker asked, and Arkady gave him a groggy nod. 'Drink that, then take a shower and get dressed. I need you upstairs as soon as possible. Tell Simone, too.'

The com officer looked at him as if he'd just suggested that he run a three-minute mile, but he yawned and nodded again. Harker gave him a slap on the knee, then headed for the access shaft.

The shaft was a dark and bottomless pit, its metal walls echoing with the distant throb of the main engine. Harker found the switch that turned on the lights, then began to climb upward. The fact that he could hear the engine indicated that the AI had automatically initiated the braking maneuver, rotating *Galileo*'s stern in the direction of flight and firing the fusion engine for the braking sequence. With any luck, the ship would be on course for rendezvous with Spindrift.

The command center was cold and dark. The temperature on Deck A still hadn't risen to a comfortable level, and the only illumination came from comp screens above the workstations. Harker briefly considered going below to get some warmer clothes from his quarters but decided against it; that would take too long, and he'd need every spare minute. So instead he switched on the ceiling lights, then temporarily adjusted the thermostat to 23.8°C in an effort to get more heat into the compartment.

At Antonia's station, he located the controls that raised the shutters from the windows. As they slowly glided upward, he walked over to the center window to gaze out into space. He wouldn't be able to see Spindrift, of course

– *Galileo* was still oriented stern first toward their destination – but he might be able to see the Sun. It took a few seconds, but he was finally able to discern a white-yellow star slightly more luminous than the ones surrounding it.

Despite his hurry, Harker found himself staring at it. From a distance of almost two light-years, Sol was little more than a bright point of light among many, its planetary system invisible to the naked eye. Everything he knew, everyone whom he'd ever met, indeed all of human history . . . reduced to insignificance, just another world somewhere in the cosmos.

No time for this sort of contemplation. Harker sat down in his chair and pulled the lapboard across his legs. Typing in a series of commands, he pulled up a status display. He absently rubbed his fingers through his whiskers as he went down the menu, one item at a time.

The diametric drive had been powered down, and the main engine was operating at rated capacity. With fuel reserves standing at 64 percent, the consumption rate was more than he would've preferred, but the tanks still held enough helium-3 and deuterium to allow *Galileo* to make rendezvous and orbital maneuvers with Spindrift, then get them home with fuel to spare. Life-support systems were satisfactory: the oxygen-water regeneration plant was nominal, with atmospheric carbon dioxide and nitrogen at tolerable levels and no apparent air leaks. Internal temperature was still low, as he'd already discovered, but now that the AI had sensed human movement within the hab module, it was raising the thermostat and switching on internal lights. Electrical systems were okay; same for all computer networks.

In short, everything seemed fine. *Galileo* had operated like a precision machine, its dozens of subsystems working together in harmony, while its crew and passengers slept in biostasis, dreaming of . . . well, nothing really, or at least not anything that Harker's conscious mind cared to remember. If there were any nightmares, they were of his own creation.

He closed his eyes, rubbed the bridge of his nose between thumb and forefinger. *Is that it? Am I just getting paranoid?* He let out his breath. Perhaps he was wrong. It could well be that Lawrence had done nothing more than make sure that his ship was safely closed down. There wasn't a plot of any sort, aside from the fact that the ESA had put aboard a nuclear torpedo as a precaution. He was jumping at shadows, seeing things that weren't there . . .

'Goddamn it,' he muttered. 'I'm such a fool.'

'Pardon me, sir? Did you say something?'

Startled, Harker looked around. He hadn't noticed that Arkady had entered the command center. The com officer's hair was still wet, his beard flecked with blue gel that he hadn't quite rinsed away. 'Sorry. Just thinking aloud.' Harker managed a wan smile. 'Apologies for getting you up so early. Maybe I should've let you sleep a while longer.'

'Well . . . so be it.' A shrug of surrender to the inevitable. 'I'm here, and Simone's on her way. Might as well go to work, *nyet*?'

'*Da. Spacibo*. You can start by transmitting a message home. Tell them we've arrived safely.' He paused. 'Then keep the signal open. I have something private to add to it.'

'Sure. Whatever.' Arkady shuffled over to the com

station, pulled back his chair, and slumped down into it. Stifling a yawn, he tapped at the keyboard; a menu appeared on one of his screens and he moused it to open a page. Harker smiled as he watched him go to work. Even if Arkady was half-asleep, he needed him just now.

Turning back to his lapboard, Harker typed in a command to open a text file. The next order of business was to send a coded priority message back to ESA headquarters in Geneva, care of Director General Beck and Associate Director Shillinglaw. Harker intended to issue a formal protest in regards to their covert decision to place a nuclear torpedo aboard *Galileo*. He didn't know how much good this would do, but at least it would put his opinion on the record, just in case there was an official inquiry somewhere down the line.

'Damn.' Arkady peered closer at his screen. 'Just a moment, chief. Having a little trouble here.' His fingers ran across his keyboard, typing in another set of commands. 'Hmm . . . now this is odd . . .'

'For God's sake,' Simone said as she came through the hatch, 'don't you know how to use that thing yet?'

She didn't appear much more awake than Arkady; her hair was tousled and there were dark rings beneath her eyes. One look at her, and Harker realized that it wasn't a good morning to annoy *Galileo*'s helmsman. 'Reporting for duty, sir,' she added, barely giving Harker more than a passing glance as she headed for her station. 'Any coffee?'

'Sorry. Didn't think to make any.' Harker kicked himself for neglecting to do this. He'd rushed these people out of Deck B before they were fully awake; the least he could have done was make their jobs a little easier. 'Give us a fix on our position and heading and prepare for turnaround, and I'll see what I can do.'

Simone sighed as she settled behind her console, but went to work without any more complaints. Pushing aside his lapboard, Harker stood up, intending to head for the alcove where the coffeemaker was located. An irritated grunt from Arkady brought him up short. 'Having a problem?' he asked.

Arkady responded with a string of Russian obscenities. 'Sorry, sir, but this . . . this makes no sense.' He waved an impatient hand at his screen. 'According to this, we've lost downlink with Mare Muscoviense.'

Harker froze. 'What are you . . . ?'

'Just as I said, sir.' Arkady gestured at his screen. 'According to the log, the last transmission we sent home was June 3, 2288, at 1335 GMT . . .'

'Just before we went into biostasis.' Harker quickly walked over to the com station. 'What was sent?'

'Routine status report. See?' Arkady moved the cursor to an icon at the bottom of the screen and clicked it. Several pages of data expanded to fill a window; Harker saw nothing unusual, only technical information that the ship's AI sent back as part of its normal telemetry. 'And that's it . . . nothing since.'

'Oh, for the love of . . .' Harker checked the sudden impulse to push Arkady out of the way and take over the station himself. His communications officer knew his job; if Arkady said something was wrong, Harker had to trust his judgment. 'And we haven't received anything?' he asked, even though he knew this was a pointless question.

Arkady shook his head. Of course not; once *Galileo* went

to cruise mode, any return messages transmitted via laser from the lunar farside would still be on their way. 'So why can't we send . . . ?'

'That's just it.' Turning around in his chair, Arkady punched in another command, then pointed at his screen. 'See? The LCP is out of alignment. We've lost track of Mare Muscoviense. I can transmit, of course, but . . .'

'They won't receive.' From behind them, Simone quickly worked her board. '*Galileo*'s on correct trajectory, just as programmed, but I'm finding the same thing Arkady has. The LCP no longer has a lock on the Moon.'

Harker felt the blood drain from his face. He clutched the back of Arkady's chair, trying to steady himself. The laser communications platform depended upon the AI maintaining a precise fix upon the Moon's stellar location; if that lock was disturbed by even a few degrees, then no telemetry could be transmitted. To all intents and purposes, at least for those back home, *Galileo* was lost.

'I don't know how this could have happened.' There was a high-pitched note of desperation in Arkady's voice as he continued to type instructions into his comp. 'Solar wind might have thrown the platform out of alignment. Perhaps bow shock when we passed through the heliopause . . .'

'No. The LCP is designed to compensate for those factors.' Harker clenched his fists as he stood upright. Something else caused the com system to go down. He had more than a suspicion as to what it was. He took a deep breath, slowly released it. 'All right, then, we're just going to have to deal with it. Simone, set us up for the turnaround maneuver. Once we're on course for rendezvous with Spindrift, relay our new bearings to

Arkady.' He tapped the com officer on the shoulder. 'Soon as you get the data from her, do your best to reestablish a fix . . .'

'Do you realize how hard that's going to be?' There was hopelessness in Arkady's eyes as he looked up at him. 'I mean, this isn't like trying to find Earth through a telescope. If I can't achieve an exact . . .'

'Just do it.' Harker was done with patience and understanding; time to play the role of first officer. 'I don't care how long it takes. Get it done.' He let out his breath. 'You know your jobs. Now go to work. I'll make coffee.'

Arkady and Simone seemed to share a look between them. Then, without another word, they turned back to their consoles. No longer were they tired and wrung out; the success or failure of the expedition hung in the balance. Harker watched them for another moment, then fulfilled his side of the bargain. He went off to make coffee.

Now we know what Ian did before we went to sleep, he thought. *And I think I know why.*

'Main engine cutoff in five seconds, on my mark.' Lawrence studied the status panel on his lapboard. 'Mark.'

'Aye, sir.' Flipping open the cover of the engine ignition switch, Simone turned the key to STANDBY. A quick look at her console to confirm that everything was as it should be, then she gripped the handle of the thrust control bar. 'MECO in five . . . four . . . three . . . two . . . one . . .'

She slowly pulled down the bar, and the omnipresent rumble of the fusion drive gradually faded away, followed by an eerie silence that hadn't been heard since the *Galileo* departed from the Kuiper Belt. For an instant, Harker felt himself rise slightly from his seat before the AI automatically adjusted the Millis-Clement field to compensate for the lack of thrust. He watched as Simone switched the key to the SAFE position, then toggled a couple of switches on her board.

'Main engine down and safed,' she reported, not looking back at the captain. 'Ready to initiate turnaround sequence, on your mark.'

'Thank you, Lieutenant Monet.' Once again, Lawrence checked his screen. It seemed to Harker that he was almost reluctant to issue the next order, as obvious as it might be. He glanced nervously at his first officer, as if seeking confirmation. Harker was tempted to pretend ignorance, but instead he nodded in agreement. Lawrence looked away again. 'Mark.'

'On a ten-second count,' Harker quietly added. 'Sound general quarters.'

'Aye, sir. Mark on ten seconds.' Simone pushed a button that caused a bell to ring four times, then she typed a set of commands into her keyboard before settling back into her seat and hitching her harness around herself. 'Ten . . . nine . . . eight . . .'

Harker looked around the command center, making sure that the rest of the flight crew had secured themselves. Through the open hatch leading to the observation center, he could hear Rauchle yelling for everyone to strap down. Harker smiled to himself. Turnaround wasn't that big a deal, really, unless you'd never done it before.

'Three . . . two . . . one . . .' Simone touched a button on her board. 'Commencing turnaround maneuver.'

A faint vibration as the RCS fired, then the deck seemed

to tilt upward beneath their feet. Through the windows, Harker saw the stars slowly slide away as *Galileo* commenced a 180-degree yaw that would realign its bow with its direction of flight. With the Millis-Clement field active, there was no perceptible change in the ship's artificial gravity; nonetheless, for everyone aboard, there was a sensation that they were aboard an enormous centrifuge. Gripping his armrests, Harker pretended that this was just a carnival ride.

Another shudder passed through the hull as the RCS fired again. 'Turnaround maneuver complete,' Simone said. '*Galileo* maintaining course.'

'Thank you, Lieutenant Monet,' Lawrence said. 'Well done.' A compliment that, while not unearned, wasn't without some irony; like hyperspace insertion, the turnaround had been computer-controlled, its logistics too precise to be left to fallible human reflexes. The captain wiped sweat from his forehead with the back of his hand, then unclasped his harness. 'Well done, all of you,' he said, rising from his chair. 'I'll be in my quarters if you need to see me.'

From the corner of his eye, Harker saw puzzled looks pass across the faces of the flight crew. *Galileo* was just over a hundred thousand kilometers from Spindrift; although they couldn't see it yet, nonetheless their destination was close enough that the science team should soon be able to commence its initial survey. Hell of a time for the commanding officer to take a nap.

'Actually, sir, there's another matter that needs to be attended to.' Harker turned around in his seat. 'The loss of signal with Mare Muscoviense . . .'

'I'm aware of that, Mr Harker.' Lawrence's response

came as an impatient snap. 'Unfortunate, but something we'll just have to work around.' He looked at Arkady. 'Mr Rusic, now that we're on course for rendezvous, please begin recalibrating the LCP. Report to me once this is done.'

'Yes, Captain. At once.' There was no mistaking the insolent tone of Arkady's voice. Unlike Simone's job, his task couldn't be accomplished with a preprogrammed command. Recalibration of the laser communication platform was something that would take several days to perform, and only then if he got lucky and managed to get a precise fix on the Moon's position. With less than half a degree of error to spare, Arkady had his work cut out for him.

'Be that as it may, sir,' Harker went on, 'I'd like to discuss the circumstances of . . .'

'You have the conn, Mr Harker. Call me if there are any problems.' Lawrence barely looked at him as he headed for the access shaft. 'Carry on.'

The captain shut the hatch behind him, leaving behind a command center that had gone quiet. His abrupt departure hadn't gone unnoticed; no one was paying attention to their consoles but instead stared after him in astonishment.

'Like losing contact with Earth isn't a problem,' Arkady murmured.

Right now, Arkady's droll sense of humor was the last thing Harker needed. He shot the com officer a harsh glance, then touched his headset. 'Emily, you copy?' he asked, shielding the mike wand with his hand and keeping his voice low. 'What did you find down there?'

A moment passed, then he heard her voice: '*Same as*

before. Nuke's still in place, nothing about it seems different. Did you have a chat with the captain?'

'Tried to. Claimed it was an accident, then left the deck like he had to take a dump.' Harker rubbed the back of his neck. 'C'mon back up then. We'll talk about this later.' He clicked off, then unfastened his harness and rose from his chair. 'I'm going over to the OC to see what the brain trust has found,' he said to no one in particular. 'Toni . . . ?'

'I'll handle things here.' She was already getting up from her station.

'Thanks.' He turned and headed for the hatch leading to the observation center.

As he expected, the science team was already on the job. Kaufmann had taken the middle seat at the center console in the semicircular compartment, with Rauchle to his right and Cruz to his left; they'd raised the telescope and lidar arrays from the service module and were using them to acquire Spindrift. Cole stood behind them, watching over their shoulders as they worked, while Sinclair leaned against a nearby bulkhead, nursing a cup of coffee as he silently observed everything being said and done. Which didn't seem like very much; the scientists quietly murmured among themselves, their hands busy at the keyboards as their eyes swept across the screens.

The only person who didn't appear to be occupied was Ramirez. Sitting by himself at the far end of the compartment, he gazed out the window beside him, listening to everything that was going on yet removed from it just the same. Harker hadn't felt much empathy for him when he'd joined the expedition, and the incident in his cabin hadn't done much to raise his opinion of the man. Yet

Emily had apparently come to respect Ramirez a bit more – after all, he'd confided in her when he didn't have to – and if Emcee was willing to trust him, Harker supposed that he had to as well. Or at least relax his suspicions somewhat.

Ramirez apparently caught Harker's reflection in the window, because he looked around as he walked over to him. 'Ted . . . good to see you again. Sleep well?'

'Like a baby. It's waking up that's murder.' Harker cocked his head toward the rest of the team. 'Decided not to join the party?'

'Toby thinks I'm the type who'd dance around with a lampshade on his head.' Ramirez shrugged. 'Or something like that. In any case, he's made it clear to me that my input isn't necessary unless . . . well, necessary.'

Harker felt a surge of anger. Looking over his shoulder, he caught Rauchle's eye as the team leader glanced up from his console. A cold stare in response, then Rauchle returned his attention to the screen before him. 'He shouldn't do that,' Harker said quietly. 'You're the astrobiologist. You should be . . .'

'Quite right. I should . . . but I'm not, and that's all there is to it, yes?' A dejected smile. 'Still have my pipe? I could use a smoke just now.'

'Maybe later.' Harker sat down in the chair next to him. 'I didn't get a chance to say so before,' he said, dropping his voice to a near whisper, 'but . . . well, thanks. Thanks for coming clean with Emily.'

'Sure.' Once again, Ramirez gazed out the window, only this time he seemed more nervous. Raising a hand to his mouth, he absently gnawed at his fingernails. 'She's your lady, isn't she? I mean, you two are an item, right?'

Something in the way he asked stirred the hair on the back of Harker's neck. 'Yes, she is. And I'd prefer if you didn't . . .'

'Oh, no. No, no, no.' Ramirez looked straight at him. 'Sorry. Didn't mean to get your back up like that. It's just . . .' His face turned red, and he hastily looked away. 'You're a lucky man. If you don't know that already, then you should.'

Oh, hell, Harker thought. *Does he have a crush on . . . ?*

'Got it!' Kaufmann yelled. 'We've got it!'

The rest of the team let out a collective cheer and began pounding each other on the back. Ramirez sprang to his feet, rushed over to the console; Harker followed him as he pushed his way past Cole and Sinclair to squeeze in behind Rauchle. Sinclair started to object, but stopped when Harker blocked him with his arm and quietly shook his head. The astrobiologist had more right to be there than the political officer.

Peering over Cruz's shoulder, Harker examined the console's center screen. Displayed upon it was a thin crescent that dimly reflected the wan light of the distant sun. For a moment, Harker thought he was looking at Eris again, yet the crosshatches overlaid upon the image made it clear that the object was much smaller than that minor planet, its albedo considerably lower.

'Distance, 95,867 kilometers,' Kaufmann said, once everyone quieted down. 'Just about where we thought it would be.' He glanced up at Harker and smiled. 'My compliments to your navigator. She put us almost exactly where . . .'

'Never mind that now,' Rauchle grumbled. 'Get us a better resolution.'

'Patience, Toby, patience.' Grasping the joystick of the optical telescope's remote manipulator, Kaufmann carefully centered the bull's-eye upon Spindrift, then turned a knob to zoom in. The image grew larger, then refocused. They could see that it was iron grey, the color of an old bridge girder, its surface wrinkled with rills and small ridges, pockmarked by countless craters both large and small.

'Thank you.' Cruz was already tapping at his keyboard. 'Initiating spectrographic analysis now.' On his screen, columns of figures appeared, began to scroll upward; bending closer, the astrogeologist carefully studied the readout. 'Iron . . . magnesium . . . carbon and carbon silicates . . . oxidized iron . . . surface traces of frozen carbon dioxide . . .'

'No sign of the secondary object,' Ramirez said. 'Where is it?'

'Haven't spotted it yet.' Kaufmann gently moved the telescope to the left, bringing the curvature of Spindrift's visible horizon into view. 'Perhaps it's orbiting on the far side, but . . .'

'A planetary transient.' Rauchle's expression was sour with disgust. 'A rogue, nothing more.' He glared at Harker. 'Thank you for the exciting ride, first officer, but there's little here that we couldn't have seen if we'd stayed in the Kuiper—'

'Robert, look here.' Ignoring Rauchle, Cruz tapped Kaufmann on the shoulder, drawing the physicist's attention to his screen. 'See that percentage of carbon dioxide? Don't you think it's rather high for a metallic body?'

Kaufmann studied the screen for a moment, slowly nodded. 'The ratio is high, yes. Frozen-out atmosphere?'

'I thought so, too, but see here . . .' Cruz typed another

command into his keyboard; his screen changed to display bar-graphs of different elements and compounds. 'Look at that spike,' he continued, pointing to an orange bar that rose a little higher than most. 'Not evenly spread out, like it would be if it was atmospheric in orgin, but instead concentrated in certain places.'

'Vented from the interior?' Rauchle's brow furrowed. 'Seismic activity, perhaps . . .'

'From a rogue?' Cruz glanced at Rauchle. The team leader folded his arms together but otherwise remained silent. 'I doubt it. Can you give us an infrared image?'

Without a word, Kaufmann entered a prompt into the telescope command. The visual image of Spindrift disappeared, to be replaced by a false-color IR display. Now it appeared as a complete sphere, brown, with splotches of red, blue, silver . . .

Harker heard Ramirez gasp. Looking around, he saw that the astrobiologist was staring at the screen. Everyone else had gone silent as well; no one said anything as they, too, noticed the pattern of orange circles that described a semicircular line across Spindrift's surface. An almost perfect arc of longitude, stretching from pole to pole.

'That can't be natural,' Ramirez murmured. 'That's not something that . . .'

'Hold it. Wait a second.' Kaufmann held up a hand. 'Getting something else.'

Without bothering to explain, he pushed the IR image to one corner of the screen. Cruz and Rauchle angrily protested as the visible-light image of Spindrift reappeared, but Kaufmann paid no attention to them; using the joystick, he pulled back from the close-up until Spindrift resumed the same appearance as it had before.

Harker saw what had drawn Kaufmann's attention: a small circular object, coming into view just beyond the limb of the rogue. Ramirez pointed to it, but Kaufmann was already tracking it with the telescope. He centered the crosshairs upon the satellite, then zoomed in. It took a moment for the telescope to focus, but when it did, Harker felt his heart skip a beat.

'My God.' Ramirez's voice came as a whisper. 'Oh, my God . . .'

Although the ring wasn't perfectly identical to the one they'd left behind in the Kuiper Belt, no one had any doubt what they were seeing.

A starbridge.

Part Three

Dark Star

Nine

JANUARY 8, 2291 – EASS *GALILEO*

Spindrift lay before them like a hole in space, a circular patch of darkness where no stars shone. As *Galileo* swung around its nightside from an orbital altitude of eight hundred kilometers, it looked less like an asteroid than some vast, dark form that seemed to absorb all light around it. Ramirez reminded himself that this was because of its low albedo; according to Cruz, the high ferrocarbon content of the regolith rendered its surface even less reflective than the average transient body. Nonetheless, he couldn't help but think of it as a dark star, cold and mysterious. A wildly inaccurate description, to be sure, yet he could find no other words to describe his impression of this world.

Sitting in a leather armchair in the library, mug of hot chocolate nestled in his hands, he gazed out at the rogue through the alcove window. As mysterious as Spindrift was, it was the unexpected presence of the alien star-bridge that immediately captured everyone's attention. There was no question of what it was; although larger than KX-1 – sixty meters in diameter, as opposed to forty meters for its human-made replica – *Galileo*'s instruments nonetheless registered a field of low-level radiation identical to that emitted by a zero-point energy generator in standby mode. And its close vicinity to Spindrift left no doubt that it had been deliberately positioned in orbit above the asteroid.

But by whom, and for what purpose? Ramirez could only frown as he took a sip from the mug. If he had answers to those questions, he'd be assured a seat of honor at the next Nobel prize ceremony in Stockholm. Or at least the return of his fellowship in the International Astronomical Union. For the time being, though, he'd have to content himself with the fact that his stock had lately risen among the expedition's science team.

His newfound value manifested itself shortly after the captain hurried back to the command center. Lawrence listened to the report given to him by Rauchle – predictably, the pompous ass tried to take full credit for the discovery – while doing his best to ignore Harker, who listened quietly from his station. Then Lawrence did the unexpected; he turned to Ramirez and asked his opinion.

'Captain Lawrence,' he said, consciously assuming a formal tone, 'I strongly recommend that we divide our efforts equally between Spindrift and the artifact. That is, instead of concentrating upon one or the other, we treat them as two parts of the same puzzle and conduct our investigation on that basis.'

'That should be obvious,' Rauchle grumbled. Arms folded across his chest, the team leader was nonplussed to find himself no longer the center of attention.

'It should be, yes . . . but frankly, it hasn't been.' Ramirez pointed to a screen displaying the respective positions of Spindrift, the starbridge, and *Galileo*. 'Since we've discovered the ring, it's been our main focus . . . and no wonder, because whatever else we expected to find out here, that isn't it. But I think it'd be a mistake to regard the ring as if it's something that just happened to be here.'

'I wasn't suggesting anything of the sort.' Rauchle's voice rose in irritation. 'I only think that we should prioritize our efforts. Granted, Spindrift exhibits some intriguing qualities, but the ring . . .'

'Yes, of course. Because the ring is clearly artificial in origin, it's probably the source of the signal that got our attention in the first place.' Ramirez pointed to a close-up of Spindrift on another screen. 'Nonetheless, there must be a reason why it's here. Jorge, show him what else we've found.'

So Cruz reiterated the results of radiometric and ultraviolet spectrometer surveys, wisely simplifying complex data into layman's terms so that the captain could understand them; by then, it had become clear that Lawrence was uninterested in the finer points of astrophysics. At first glance, Spindrift appeared to be little more than a transient body – a rogue asteroid, perhaps even a moon that once orbited some faraway planet until some cataclysmic event sent it careening into interstellar space – yet there were surface anomalies that defied natural explanation. The deposits of frozen carbon dioxide, doubtless the result of interior outgassing, stretched from north pole to south pole; eight in all, each circular in shape, they were separated by almost exactly 150 kilometers from one another, and lay upon an almost exact line of longitude. Natural vents wouldn't be so symmetrically aligned.

And then there was the massive crater, nearly 100 kilometers in diameter, that lay precisely at Spindrift's equator. At first, they thought it was the result of a meteor impact, yet closer examination revealed no visible floor, nor any ejecta rays surrounding its perimeter. The lack of a raised caldera, on the other hand, ruled out the alternate explanation that it might be a volcano, extinct or otherwise. It was simply a bottomless pit, its interior walls forming an enormous funnel that plunged deep within the asteroid's crust, perhaps to its outer mantle.

But the real surprise came from the results of the mass-spectrometer survey. Cruz guarded his words carefully, often resorting to raw numbers as if the data could save him, but the facts were unarguable. Judging from perturbations in its rotation, coupled with spectral analysis of its surface, it was evident Spindrift lacked the necessary mass for an asteroid its size. Indeed, despite the amounts of carbon and ferrous compounds in its crust, the lack of a magnetic field indicated that Spindrift lacked an iron core, strange for a transient body that otherwise showed all indications of being a class-M asteroid. In short, although Spindrift appeared to be solid, at least from the outside, there were strong indications that vast, hollow pockets lay within its interior.

I know what you are. Ramirez stared at Spindrift through the library window, its terminator line becoming visible as a slender curve catching the dim radiance of faraway Sol. *They wouldn't believe me even if I told them, but it doesn't matter. Soon enough, you'll reveal yourself to me . . .*

'Enjoying the view?'

Startled, Ramirez looked around to find Donald Sinclair standing just outside the alcove. He hadn't spoken with Sinclair since they'd emerged from biostasis; as neither a scientist nor a member of the flight crew, the political officer tended to fade into the background, seen but not heard. Which was probably Sinclair's intent; the less noticed he was, the more he'd be able to observe.

'I was, yes . . . good place to get away from everyone.'

He hoped that Sinclair would take the hint and leave him alone.

'I'm sure it is. But I think we need to have a chat.' Sinclair sauntered over to the couch. 'You should remember that, if it wasn't for me, you wouldn't be here at all.'

'Come again?' Ramirez raised an eyebrow as Sinclair sat down. 'As I recall, the ESA asked me to . . .'

'But if I hadn't made my recommendation to the Proletariat, you'd still be cutting cannabis in Dolland.' A smile, callous and without humor. 'A stroke of the pen, and you'll be back there again as soon as we're home.'

Ramirez stiffened. 'You wouldn't dare. Once we make our final report . . .'

'Need I remind you that you're still a convicted criminal? Your opportunities for defection are rather limited . . . and believe me, the European Alliance won't risk a political incident on your behalf.' Sinclair crossed his legs. 'But if you cooperate . . .'

'What do you want?' Ramirez's voice was cold.

'Information.' Sinclair folded his arms together. 'There's something going on aboard ship. Something between you and Harker, and also between Harker and the captain . . .'

'I have no idea what you're talking about.'

Sinclair stared at him long and hard. 'Don't lie to me, Jared,' he said at last. 'If you know something, and I find out about it . . .'

'All right, then.' Ramirez shrugged. At this point, there was no sense in hiding anything. 'There's a nuke aboard . . . a nuclear-tipped torpedo, to be precise. It's to be used in case we run into anything hostile. Bug-eyed monsters from another galaxy, if you go in for that sort of thing.'

'Jared . . .'

'You wanted truth. So here it is. The ESA placed the nuke on ship without anyone's knowing about it except Lawrence and Cole, but then Collins and I stumbled upon it, and now Harker is pissed off about the whole thing.' Glancing up at the ceiling, he snapped his fingers. 'Oh, yes . . . and we've lost contact with Earth, if you haven't heard. My guess is that this is the captain's misguided way of covering his ass, but I could be wrong. I have a hard time understanding stupid people.' He paused, relishing the look on Sinclair's face. 'Any more questions? Or would you like for me to repeat what I just said, slowly?'

Sinclair blinked several times, as if trying to digest everything Ramirez had just told him, obviously indecisive about whether it was the straight truth. 'About the bomb . . . the nuke, I mean . . . is it? . . . that is, do you know if . . . ?'

'Sorry, can't help you there. You know as much as I do . . . which isn't much.' Ramirez picked up his mug of hot chocolate. Finding that it had gone cold, he put it back down, then checked his watch. ''Fraid that's all the time I have for this. Need to go upstairs, see to the launch of the probes. We should be in proper position about now.' Standing up, he stepped past Sinclair. 'You'll keep this under your hat, won't you? After all, it wouldn't do for the captain to know that you know all this. Right?'

'Of course. Whatever you say . . .' Sinclair struggled to recover his earlier poise. 'You've done the right thing, Dr Ramirez. Your government appreciates your cooperation.'

That remark stopped Ramirez. Halfway to the library door, he paused to gaze at the fake fire burning in the hearth. 'Mr Sinclair,' he said quietly, not looking at him, 'the last time I thought I was doing the right thing, my government . . . *your* government . . . sent me to prison for the rest of my life. Do you really think I'm doing this for them?'

'No. I don't suppose you are.' Sinclair hesitated. 'But tell me . . . when you go to bed, do thirty-five thousand ghosts keep you awake?'

Ramirez had an answer for this, but not one that he was willing to share with anyone. Stiff-legged, he marched out of the library. Even after the hatch shut behind him, he felt the political officer's eyes upon his back.

'I know all about the dead,' he whispered. 'When I get to Hell, I'm sure they'll be waiting for me.'

As it turned out, Larry and Jerry raised more questions than they answered.

Jerry went first. Once *Galileo* was maneuvered within sixteen hundred kilometers of the starbridge, the probe – faintly resembling an oversize bowling ball with a high-impulse ion engine mounted at its aft end – was launched from the service module. While Simone maintained safe distance from the alien construct, Antonia controlled Jerry via telepresence. Wearing a head-mounted display, her face covered by an opaque visor upon which a stereoscopic view was assimilated from images sent by the probe's twin cameras, she pantomimed a pilot flying a small craft, her gloved hands gliding back and forth in midair, while the science team monitored the flatscreen displays within the observation center.

Yet Jerry revealed little they hadn't already known. As the probe approached the starbridge, no one was surprised to find that it wasn't completely identical to KX-1.

Although it was also ring-shaped, closer inspection showed that it was comprised of a series of inward-curved segments, triangular in cross-section, that were joined together at regular intervals. This led Kaufmann to speculate that the starbridge had been brought here in sections by a relativistic-speed craft, much the same way KX-1 had been assembled. Yet the surfaces of each segment were seamlessly smooth, with no visible plates or junctures. Indeed, the entire structure had an almost biomemetic appearance, more organic than mechanical. The product of advanced nanotech? Again, the team could only speculate.

At Ramirez's suggestion, Antonia maneuvered Jerry to a parking position only a hundred meters from the center of the starbridge. Once the probe was looking straight down the ring's bull's-eye, Ramirez asked Arkady to retransmit the recognition signal sent by Raziel, again at a frequency of 1,420 megahertz. For five seconds, nothing happened . . . then Jerry received the very same response received by Mare Muscoviense. As before, the science team had no way to interpret the numerical sequence that appeared on their screens; a second attempt to communicate yielded the same results, It was as if the starbridge were some sort of lighthouse, programmed to respond automatically the exact same way time and again.

Frustrated, Lawrence ordered Antonia to fly Jerry through the ring, even though Ramirez cautioned him against this. Although the starbridge seemed inert, the fact that it reacted to radio transmissions clearly showed that it wasn't a derelict. Yet the captain was impatient; damn the torpedoes, full steam ahead. So Jerry flew through the starbridge, and came out the other side as if it were nothing more than a trained dog who'd jumped through a hoop. Red-faced, Lawrence instructed Antonia to return Jerry to its previous position, then issued the order for Larry to be launched.

Larry was designed for atmospheric entry, so its aeroshell was unnecessary. Once the probe was three hundred meters above the ground, it jettisoned its curvilinear outer casing and parachute pack and continued the descent upon liquid-fuel thrusters that brought its payload module to a featherlight touchdown. Once its petal-shaped flanges unfolded, and with Antonia once again guiding the probe via telepresence, Larry crawled out onto Spindrift's dusty surface, an arachnid robot whose antenna-mounted lights prowled the coal-black terrain.

Since Larry was incapable of returning to *Galileo* and had a maximum range of only twenty kilometers, its landing site had been selected only after long argument among the members of the science team. In the end, the majority voted in favor of Ramirez's proposal that they investigate one of the CO_2 'cold spots' surrounding Spindrift's central meridian. Although the massive equatorial crater was just as intriguing, the fact that the meridian features were so equidistant aroused their curiosity. As Cruz had pointed out, it wasn't Spindrift's exterior that was interesting so much as its interior, and the cold spots had greater potential to answer their questions.

In the end, though, Larry told them no more than Jerry had. After scuttling across rough, dusty ground pockmarked by countless micrometeorite strikes, the probe finally made its way to a small crater about thirty meters in diameter. Standing at the edge of its rim, Larry peered down upon an expanse of frozen carbon dioxide that scintillated beneath the probe's lights, eerily resembling a snow-covered pasture on a moonless night.

The infrared sensor picked up a heat source from the center of the crater, so Antonia carefully maneuvered Larry down its slope and sent it in that direction. Yet the dry-ice layer turned out to be deeper than expected; Larry got no farther than seven meters before its six legs disappeared within the fine white powder, and it was all Antonia could do just to keep it from being immobilized. Ignoring Rauchle's protests, she backed the probe out of the crater and returned Larry to its earlier position at the top of the rim.

The trip wasn't a total loss, though. Larry's ultraviolet imaging spectrometer picked up a plume of gaseous CO_2 rising from the heat source at the crater's center, almost as if it was a natural geyser. As the team watched, the carbon-dioxide emission immediately froze out, descending to the ground as a haze of snowlike crystals. No question about it: something deep within Spindrift was venting gas, apparently at regular intervals. And there were at least seven other sites just like this one, equidistantly spaced along Spindrift's central meridian.

Antonia returned Larry to its lander and put it in recharge mode; just as when she'd parked Jerry in orbit near the starbridge, she kept its transponder active so that the probe's cameras and sensor package could be accessed at any time. Then, at Kaufmann's suggestion, the science team went down to the library to discuss their next move. Lawrence showed up as well; so did Harker, although Ramirez wasn't surprised that he kept his distance from the captain. *Galileo*'s commander and his first officer had apparently reached an impasse; Ramirez wondered if they'd be able to work together for the rest of the mission.

'We should reposition Larry,' Rauchle began, once everyone had coffee and had found seats near the fireplace. 'If we can send it to another vent, we might be able to get it closer so that . . .'

'That won't work.' Harker leaned against the mantel, studying the pewter miniature of the *Galileo*. 'Larry's designed for only short-range excursions, and the next vent is too far away. Sure, it might be able to get there, but the cold will kill the batteries. It'll make it to the crater and' – he snapped his fingers – 'out go the lights. Dead 'bot.'

'Besides, there's no guarantee that the same thing won't happen again.' Kaufmann nibbled on a slice of dried apple from the snack plate Emily had put together in the galley before returning to the command center. 'The snowpack was at least a half meter thick when the probe bogged down the first time . . . and that was eight meters or so from the vent. No telling how deep it is closer in.'

'But if . . .' Rauchle began.

'I think we're dodging the main issue here.' Cruz gazed out the window as if quietly contemplating the dark world that lay below them. 'We've tried using probes, but they've only given us limited results. Like it or not, we're going to have to get our feet dirty. We need to go down there.'

No one said anything for a moment. Everyone glanced at each other, wary of what Cruz was suggesting. Ramirez knew what was going through their minds. Rauchle, Kaufmann, Cole . . . they'd spent their careers in labs and lecture halls, analyzing data others had gathered for them, then telling students and colleagues what they'd found. It had been a long time since any of them had done serious fieldwork, and that was when they were quite a few years younger, and even then in the relatively benign conditions of the Moon or Mars. None relished the idea of leaving *Galileo*'s safe and warm confines to set foot upon a place where the slightest mistake could be fatal.

'Look,' Kaufmann said, 'we're here just to study and report, right? That being the case, I see no reason why we can't continue to survey the rogue from orbit . . .'

'It's not just a rogue,' Ramirez said, breaking his accustomed silence. 'I believe something else is going on down there.'

All eyes turned toward him. 'Yes?' Rauchle asked, his sardonic smirk making another appearance. 'Do tell, Dr Ramirez. What do you believe it is?'

He took a deep breath. 'I believe . . . that is, I think . . . Spindrift may be a starship.'

For a moment, no one spoke. The rest of the science team stared at him as if he'd just suggested that Spindrift was inhabited by elves who rode flying dragons. Sir Peter coughed in his hand. 'That's an interesting theory, Jared, but . . .'

'Look at the evidence. The presence of vents at regular intervals . . . that suggests some large-scale organic process beneath the surface that would necessitate the discharge of gaseous carbon dioxide. The huge equatorial crater . . . hasn't that reminded anyone else of the exhaust funnel of a large engine? And the fact that it's on a trajectory that puts it in a direction leading out from the center of the galaxy . . .'

'An asteroid transformed into a starship?' Rauchle was

openly skeptical. 'Tell me, Dr Ramirez . . . during your sabbatical, did you develop a taste for twentieth-century science fiction?'

A couple of ill-concealed chuckles from around the table. Ramirez chose to ignore them. 'The concept predates science fiction. The British physicist J. D. Bernal came up with the idea in a monograph published in 1929. He . . .'

'I'm familiar with Bernal's work,' Sir Peter said. '*The World, the Flesh & the Devil.* Quite interesting, really . . . but as I recall, he imagined such "globes," as he called them, carrying their inhabitants on voyages that would last hundreds of years. Even if that were the case here, why would that be necessary, if the builders had the ability to construct faster-than-light starbridges?'

'I don't know,' Ramirez replied. 'I'm just as puzzled as you are about this. Nonetheless, the presence of one factor doesn't necessarily rule out the existence of another, does it?'

Cruz and Kaufmann glanced at each other as Rauchle allowed his eyes to roll upward. Before anyone could object, though, Harker cleared his throat. 'He has a point. We shouldn't rule out any possibilities, no matter how far-fetched they may seem . . . and relying on probes hasn't gotten us very far.'

Lawrence glared at him. 'Mr Harker, I don't recall that you're a member of the science team.'

'No, sir, I'm not.' Harker stared back at the captain with ill-disguised contempt. 'Nonetheless, our job is to enable the team to conduct their investigation, is it not?' Lawrence looked away, and Harker continued as if he hadn't been interrupted. 'I think we should send a party down to Spindrift, have them take a closer look. After all, we have the *Maria Celeste* . . .'

'And that would distract us from examining the star-bridge.' Rauchle shook his head. 'No. We shouldn't divide our efforts.'

'Why not? We have more than enough people aboard to do both at once.' Harker turned back to Lawrence. 'I'm willing to lead the ground survey, sir. I'm sure Emily is capable of making a successful landing. If Dr Ramirez would care to join us . . .'

'So would I,' Cruz said abruptly. 'After all, this is my area.' He looked at the others and shrugged. 'He has a point, you know . . . since we're here, we might as well cover all the bases.'

Ramirez was faintly surprised to see Cruz so eager to volunteer. On the other hand, Jorge wasn't as narrow-minded as either Rauchle or Cole; nor, unlike Kaufmann, was he committed to being Rauchle's protégé. He seemed to have a spirit of genuine scientific curiosity. Or perhaps he just wanted to get off the ship for a little while.

'That would leave everyone else free to study the star-bridge,' Harker went on. 'A ground survey shouldn't take more than twenty, maybe twenty-four hours to complete . . . thirty-six at most, if we decide to investigate more than one site. And since the shuttle is equipped for sorties of that . . .'

'All right, yes. Of course. You've made your point.' Lawrence closed his eyes. 'If you really think it's that important, then please do so, by all means.' He let out his breath as if in annoyance. 'Mr Harker, if neither Dr Ramirez or Dr Cruz has any objections' – both Ramirez and Cruz shook their heads – 'then consider them your landing party . . . along with Lieutenant Collins, providing that she's willing to do this.'

'I'm sure she is, sir.'

'Of course.' Absently running his fingers through his mustache, Lawrence studied the datapad in his lap for a moment. 'Let's go for launch in . . . oh, 0800 tomorrow, shall we? That should give you adequate time to prepare your team, plus enough time to catch up on your sleep. I daresay you'll not have much rest once you get there.'

'That'll be fine, sir. Thank you.' Harker pushed back his chair. 'If I may be excused . . . ?'

Lawrence distantly nodded, his eyes still on his pad. Ramirez glanced at Rauchle; he was in whispered conference with Cole, with Kaufmann and Cruz leaning over to listen in. No one paid much attention to him as he quietly followed Harker from the library.

'Mr Harker . . . ?'

'Ted.' Harker stopped in the corridor to look back at him. 'We're going to be together for a while. Might as well dispense with formalities, right?'

'Yes, we should . . . thank you.' Ramirez relaxed a little. 'Thanks for coming to my aid back there. I was getting a bit overwhelmed.'

'Yes, well . . .' Harker shrugged. 'I'm just as curious as you are. And I'm sure Emily wouldn't mind having something to do.'

'Of course.' At a loss for what else to say, Ramirez fell silent. Harker gave him a querying look, then started to head for the access hatch. 'Just one more thing . . . do you believe I'm right about all this?'

Harker paused at the hatch. For a moment, he said nothing, then he looked back at him. 'The only difference between me and the captain is that I'm willing to listen.'

'The only difference?' Ramirez felt a trace of amusement. 'I think not.'

'Show me the evidence, then I'll believe you.' Harker hesitated, then dropped his voice. 'Meet me in the main storage compartment . . . B4, two decks up . . . in an hour. We'll talk more then.'

Then he disappeared through the hatch, leaving Ramirez in the corridor.

The ship's stores were located on Deck B, on the opposite side of the access shaft from the hibernation compartment. The room was narrow, its grey walls lined with lockers and cabinets. When Ramirez arrived, he found Harker waiting for him, yet they weren't alone. Much to his surprise, he found Emily with him as well.

'Shut the hatch, will you?' Harker asked Ramirez as he entered the compartment. 'No sense in letting in a draft.' Ramirez couldn't tell if he was joking or not, but he turned to shut the hatch anyway. 'Thanks. Did you tell anyone where you were going?'

'Oh, Ted . . .' Emily shook her head, a wry expression on her face. 'We've a perfectly sound reason to be here . . . you said it yourself. We need to collect the EVA equipment.'

'And that we do.' Harker raised the pad in his right hand. 'Have the list right here. But it's also the one place aboard, besides the shuttle, where I can guarantee that we won't be overheard.'

Emily's smile disappeared. 'You don't trust our cabins anymore?'

'Not after that little scene with the captain, no.' Turning away from them, Harker slowly walked down the line of cabinets, one eye on his pad's screen. 'He knows now that he can't trust either of us . . . and since Jared here suggested this trip, he probably doesn't trust him very much either.' He glanced at Ramirez. 'No offense.'

'None taken. I've become used to it.' Ramirez glanced at the hatch behind him. 'But if we're supposed to be gathering equipment, shouldn't Jorge be here, too?'

'I've put Dr Cruz on a different task. He's working with Marty to devise some means of clearing away all that frozen CO_2 from the crater vent. That should keep both of them occupied for quite some time. And we've got reasons why we shouldn't trust Marty . . . ah, here we are.'

Tucking his pad beneath his armpit, Harker pulled open a storage locker. Within it hung several coils of nylon rope. 'Stack everything over there,' he said, nodding toward a nearby bench as he unloaded the coils and began handing them to Emily. 'The rest of the climbing gear should be . . .'

'Next compartment. I checked the inventory, too.' Emily looked at Ramirez askance. 'Always thinks he knows everything and no one else does.' She carried the ropes over to the bench. 'So what is it you think we need to talk about, love? Or don't we already know.'

'Just a sec . . .' Harker consulted the pad again, then bent to open the drawer Emily had indicated. 'Yes, here we are,' he said, pulling out a large stainless-steel case. 'Tool kit. Just what the doctor ordered.' He handed the case to Ramirez. 'Take it over there. I'll inspect it later.'

'You haven't answered my question,' Emily said. 'What do you . . . ?'

'Doesn't it seem strange that the captain went along so easily with your suggestion that we dispatch a survey team?' Harker wasn't talking to her, but rather to Ramirez. 'After all, Rauchle all but ruled out the possibility that there's anything down there of any interest. They're completely obsessed with the starbridge.'

'I thought Jorge and I made our case rather well . . .'

'And so you did.' Harker shut the drawer, then stood erect and continued to move down the row, studying his pad once more. 'But Rauchle is the man in charge, after all, and Sir Peter . . .'

'Peter Cole is a horse's ass.' Ramirez couldn't keep the edge from his voice. 'He hasn't had an original thought in his head in twenty years. And Rauchle likely built his rep on Kaufmann's work, if I read him correctly.'

'You probably have. And I agree with you about Cole. He and Lawrence got to where they are now because of social class and little else. But the two of them are working together, and since Rauchle is on their side . . .'

'So what are you getting at?' Emily pointed to another cabinet. 'Expedition rations, in here.'

'I know, I know.' Harker regarded the pad with puzzlement, as if trying to understand something he'd found there. 'I just think it's rather . . . well, convenient . . . for Lawrence to find a way to get three troublemakers off the ship.'

Emily peered at him. 'You're not suggesting . . . ?'

'What do you think this means?' Harker held out the pad for her to examine. 'This line here, see? 'B4-128C – LRC.' Never seen that before.'

'Makes sense to me,' Ramirez said. 'I mean, there's no love lost between Tobias and me, that's for certain. If he wants to . . .'

'That's the long-range com platform.' Emily ignored Ramirez as she stepped closer to Harker to peer over his shoulder at the pad. 'Thoughtful of someone to send one with us. It'll help us establish a direct link between you and the ship once you're on the surface.' Turning away from them, she began to walk down the row of cabinets, reading aloud the serial numbers from each drawer, 'B4-127A . . . B4-127B . . . B4-127C . . . here it is.'

She stopped in front of a cabinet, slid it open. Within it was another equipment case. 'Heavy sucker,' Harker murmured, grunting with the effort as he pulled it out and placed it on the floor. Opening it, they found a large instrument, its antenna neatly collapsed and folded against its top surface. 'Never used one of these before,' he added. 'Guess I'll have to study the specs before we . . .'

Emily snapped her fingers as if in sudden inspiration. 'You know, this gives me an idea. We're going to be in contact with *Galileo*, of course, but not continually.'

'No?' Ramirez looked at her. 'Why not?'

'Because its orbit will periodically take it around the other side of Spindrift,' she said. 'Which means that they'll have to reestablish contact with us every few hours.' She glanced at Harker. 'When that happens, maybe we can tap into another com channel without Lawrence knowing what we're doing.'

'So we can monitor what's going on up here while we're on the ground?' Harker nodded. 'Nice idea . . . but that means we'll have to get someone here to cooperate with us.'

'Arkady will do it.' Emily smiled. 'He doesn't have any particular love for Ian. After all, the whole bollocks with the LCP breakdown will fall on his head once we get back to Earth. If I can get Arkady to piggyback an active signal to the downlink for the backup flight recorder . . .'

'Tell me the details later.' Harker closed the LRC case, picked it up, and moved it aside. 'Just get it done. If we can have that particular ace up our sleeve, the better I'll feel about all this.

Surprised, Ramirez turned to gaze at him. 'Not having any reservations, I hope.'

'I've been having reservations about this mission before we even left Earth,' he said quietly. 'Now I'm just trying to shave the odds a little more in our favor.'

Ten

JANUARY 8, 2291 – EAS *MARIA CELESTE*

'Everyone strapped down? Suits zipped up?' Although she turned her head to look back, her helmet's faceplate prevented Emily from seeing the passengers seated behind her. Both Ramirez and Cruz answered in the affirmative, though, and she didn't need to ask Ted if he'd secured his harness or sealed his flight suit, so she touched the MIC switch on the com panel above her head. '*Galileo*, this is *Maria Celeste*. Requesting permission to depart.'

'*We copy*, Maria.' Arkady's voice came through her earphones. '*Permission granted. Ready to disengage on your mark.*'

'Roger that, *Galileo*. Mark in T minus thirty.' Emily switched over to internal power, then initiated the primary ignition sequence for the main engines. A quick glance at the idiot lights on the environmental control panel told her that all hatches were secure and cabin air pressure was nominal. Flipping the switch that would retract the docking collar, she heard a hollow thump above and behind her. She reset the comps and loaded the new programs. All safety and rescue systems were on standby; with luck, none of them would be needed.

Emily glanced at the chronometer. Ten seconds left. Time enough for one last detail. Briefly raising her faceplate, she kissed the fingertips of her glove, then gently touched the small medal of St Christopher she'd attached to a discreet place just above her control yoke. She'd given up on Catholicism a long time ago – or at least it'd been many years since she had last attended Mass – but this was one small ritual she'd maintained ever since her first solo. From the corner of her eye, she saw Ted quietly observing her. He'd seen her do this before; as always he said nothing, instead maintaining a respectful silence. She flexed her fingers within her gloves, took a deep breath, then grasped the yoke.

'Maria to *Galileo*,' she said. 'Mark. Disengage.'

Another thump, a little harder this time, as the docking cradle opened on either side of the shuttle, allowing the spacecraft to float free. '*Disengagement complete*, Maria,' Arkady said. '*You're on your own.*'

'We copy, *Galileo*.' Through the forward cockpit window, Emily watched the service module as it slowly drifted away, surrounded by a thin halo of frozen oxygen that had broken away from the docking collar. She pulled back on the yoke, and the RCS fired, lifting the shuttle away from the starship. Now she could see *Galileo* in all its immensity, a giant spindle shoved one-fifth of the way through an enormous torus. Its hull was illuminated by red and green formation lights, and mellow radiance came from the windows of the hab module, but otherwise the ship was cloaked by the shadows of interstellar night.

A brief, almost undetectable shudder as the shuttle passed through the periphery of the Millis-Clement field. She felt herself rise slightly within the confines of her seat. 'We're in the clear, *Galileo*,' she murmured. 'Go for deorbit burn.'

'*Roger that*, Maria. *Got you on our scope*.'

Emily twisted the yoke to the left, firing thrusters to execute a barrel roll. Like a dancer performing a deft pirouette, the *Maria Celeste* twisted around on its axis, realigning itself within its new sphere of orientation. Through the cockpit windows, *Galileo* veered sharply away, the starship disappearing beneath the belly of the shuttle until it was replaced by the vast dark curvature of Spindrift.

'Firing mains on the count of three,' Emily murmured as she laid her right hand upon the thrust bars. 'One . . . two . . . three . . .' She eased the bars upward; a faint rumble from behind them, then she was gradually pushed back in her seat as the shuttle's twin nuclear engines ignited. Spindrift seemed to move closer, gradually but inexorably. She counted silently to ten, then pulled the bars back three-quarters. 'Deorbit burn complete. We're on our way.'

'*We copy*.' Arkady's voice had become scratchy with static; in a few minutes, *Galileo* would be out of direct line of sight with the shuttle. '*Have a good flight. We'll be in touch again soon*. Galileo *over*.'

'Thank you, *Galileo*. *Maria Celeste* over.' Until they reached the ground and *Galileo*'s orbit brought it over the local horizon, this would be their last radio contact with the ship until after they landed.

'Nice job, Emcee.' Harker gave her a brief smile, then loosened his harness and turned to look back at Ramirez and Cruz. 'How're you two holding up?'

'Fine. Just fine.' Cruz's voice was tight, as if he was holding his breath.

'Couldn't be better.' By contrast, Ramirez sounded no more concerned than if he was enjoying a rickshaw ride through Tranquility Centre. 'Just glad I took your advice about skipping breakfast.'

'Helps prevent motion sickness,' Harker said. 'Besides, until we get back, we're on a liquid diet. You don't want to be pinching a loaf when you're on EVA for eight hours.'

'Thank you for that image.' Ramirez sighed. 'Just what I need to take with me where no man has gone before.'

'No pun intended, of course,' Emily murmured.

'An obscure cultural allusion, my dear.' Turning back around, Harker typed a command into the comp. Side-looking radar painted a wire-frame image of Spindrift across the screen; midway up the northern half of the central meridian, a tiny red spot blinked amid a maze of hills, craters, and crevices. 'There's Larry. Want me to lock on?'

'Be my guest.' Emily engaged the autopilot, then reached between her knees to withdraw a squeeze bottle from its sling. Pulling out its straw, she had a sip of water. A double beep from her console told her that *Maria*'s navigation subsystem was locked on to the probe's transponder. If she cared to do so, she could program the shuttle to land on its own, without any manual guidance on her part. Not that she'd ever do that, of course. What fun was it to be a pilot if you left everything to the comp?

'How long till we get there?' Cruz asked.

'About an hour, more or less.' Emily recapped the bottle, placed it back within the sling. She hesitated, wondering whether she should reiterate what had already been said during the mission briefing. A little repetition couldn't hurt. 'I know you've heard this before, but let's go at it again. This is my ship, so while we're in the air, I'm in charge. Once we're on the ground, though, and the three of you have gone EVA, it's Ted's mission. That means you listen to everything he says. If he tells you to do something . . .'

'Then we do it.' Ramirez's voice affected a tone of boredom. 'Got it. Understood.'

'Jared . . .' Emily loosened her harness, then half turned in her seat so that she could look him in the eye. 'Look, you've received . . . what, ten hours of suit training at Tycho Centre? If you got in a fix back there, there were a dozen people to come to the rescue.'

'None of us had any mishaps during training.' Cruz became defensive. 'And may I remind you that I've been EVA before? Twenty-six hours logged on Mars . . .'

'This is different. As Ramirez said, we're going where no one has gone before. If you run into any problems, you won't have anyone to count on but each other.'

'Except you, of course,' Ramirez added.

'Wrong,' Harker said. 'Her job is to stay put in the shuttle. Under no circumstance is she to leave the ship. Even in the most dire emergency.' He reached over to pat her arm. 'Emily here is our lifeline. Without her, none of us go home.'

'Which means that, once you set foot on Spindrift, you're under Ted's supervision.' Emily looked at Cruz. 'Don't assume that this is like Mars, because it isn't.' Then she glanced at Ramirez. 'And, as I told you, we don't have the luxury of having a second shuttle able to come to our rescue. Once we're on the ground . . .'

'We're on our own.' Sobered, Ramirez nodded. 'All right, I understand.'

'Yeah, sure . . . same here.' Cruz paused. 'But, look . . . if there's nothing down there, then why . . . ?'

'C'mon, Jorge.' Ramirez shook his head. 'If you really think that, then why are you with us?'

Cruz didn't respond. Emily turned back around in her seat. A glance at the comp screen told her that her first chance to touch down at the landing site was coming up in less than a minute. 'Right,' she murmured. 'Glad we got that settled.' Tightening her harness again, she reached forward to switch off the autopilot. 'Fasten your seat belts, gentlemen. We're going in.'

Landing on Spindrift presented its own special challenges With no atmosphere and an escape velocity of only .6 kilometers per second, it was much like landing on the Moon only in a slightly higher gravity. Emily locked down the wing ailerons, useless in the airless environment, and made the final approach relying almost entirely upon the RCS and the vertical landing thrusters.

What precious little light the asteroid received from the Sun was no help to her. Even after she switched on the floodlights, all she could see was a dark, rock-strewn landscape, with little sense of height or dimension Keeping a sharp eye on the eight ball, she had Harker call out altimeter readings and didn't lower the landing gear until they were only sixty meters above the ground when she was sure that she wouldn't have to abort the descent.

'Fifteen meters,' Harker said. 'Ten meters . . . eight . . seven . . .'

The thrusters kicked up a cloud of fine grey powder that swirled within the floodlights and clung to the panes of the cockpit windows. Emily gently inched back the thruster bars; a bead of sweat rolled down her forehead and stung her left eye, but she didn't dare take her hands from the controls. *C'mon*, Marie . . . *we can do it, baby* . . .

'Six . . . five . . . four . . . three . . .'

She pulled the bars to horizontal position, then grasped the yoke with both hands and, with one last nudge, hauled it to neutral. A half-second sensation of falling, then a gentle bump beneath her feet as the skids made contact with hard surface.

'Goal,' Harker said. 'And the crowd goes wild at Wembley.'

'Score one for the English team.' Emily killed the engines, then quickly checked the cabin instruments. No loss of internal pressure, no indications of fire or short circuits. 'All safe and secure. We're down, gents.'

'Nice. Very nice.' Behind them, Ramirez slowly let out his breath. 'I had only one cardiac event . . . well, no, make that two . . .'

'Cynic. I'll have you know that you've just met the best pilot in the European Space Agency.' Harker grinned, then formally offered his hand. 'Congratulations. This may have established some sort of record.'

'Call Guinness when we get home.' Emily let out her breath, then shook his hand. 'At least it'll give the lads at the pub something new to argue about.'

Now that they'd landed in one piece, she didn't have to worry about regulations; she grasped her helmet with both hands, moved it counterclockwise until it snapped loose from the collar ring of her flight suit, then dragged it off her head. Despite the warmth supplied by the cabin heaters, she felt cool air touch her forehead and the nape of her neck. She pushed a strand of damp hair away from her face as she looked at Harker. 'Well?'

'Well what?'

'What do you mean, what?' She nodded toward the cockpit windows. 'We're here, aren't we? I got you where you wanted to go. What did you think we were going to do, have a picnic?'

'She can't be serious.' Cruz was about to remove his own helmet; he stopped short of unlocking it.

'She's serious.' Harker unsnapped his harness and stood up, ducking his head to avoid the instrument panel. 'Our itinerary calls for sixteen hours EVA, max, in two walk-outs. That may sound like a lot of time, but it isn't. Don't count on taking any naps.'

'I wasn't, but . . .' Ramirez fumbled with the clasp of his harness. 'Pardon me, but do you have any idea where we're going?'

Emily reached down to the keyboard, punched in a couple of commands. A lidar map of the landing site appeared on the screen, with two red markers distanced about two centimeters from each other. 'There's Larry,' she said, pointing to the one at the top, 'and here's us. All you have to do is find Larry, then follow his tracks to the vent. I'll feed the coordinates to your suits' direction finders once you've put 'em on.'

'See? Piece of cake.' Stepping between Cruz and Ramirez, Harker made his way toward the aft deck. 'Time to put on the long johns. Gentlemen, if you please . . . ?'

Ramirez pushed himself up from his seat. 'And the *Galileo* . . . ?'

Emily dropped her helmet in Harker's seat, then reached down to pull out her water bottle. 'When it comes over the horizon, I'll let them know we've arrived. Believe me, they're just as worried about us as you are.'

'Who said I was worried?' Ramirez asked. 'Like the man said . . . I'm in the hands of the best the ESA has to offer.'

Emily had no idea whether he was being sarcastic or not, so she simply nodded and watched as he headed aft, Cruz behind him. Gazing out the windows at the barren landscape just beyond the range of the lights, a chill ran down her back.

She'd brought them to Spindrift. And now, for reasons she couldn't explain, she felt like a little girl being left alone in a cold and dark house.

The suit-up procedure took little more than an hour. For the sake of their modesty, she didn't go aft to watch the men get ready for EVA, although she knew the process by heart. Strip off the flight suit, meant only to protect the wearer in the event of cabin decompression, and put on underwear that resembled a thong save for a unisex groin cup, which in turn was attached to a urine collection tube that dangled between the legs like an absurd penis. Next came the skinsuit, an elastic one-piece outfit that faintly resembled a wet suit except that it was made of multi-layer polymers embedded with whisker-thin wires that would conduct heat to all parts of the body while pulling away perspiration and distributing it, along with urine, to the suit's closed-loop life-support system, where waste fluids would be broken down to oxygen, nitrogen, and coolant water. The suit also contained integrated electronics that monitored and automatically adjusted its internal temperature; once gloves, boots, and helmet were donned, and the chest yoke and rebreather pack were in place, the suit was virtually a one-man spacecraft, capable of keeping its wearer alive for eight hours at a stretch. All that was needed was the overgarment that would provide protection against dust and radiation, and the wearer was ready to enter the airlock.

Harker, Ramirez, and Cruz left the shuttle through the belly hatch, making their way down a narrow ramp lowered from the aft airlock. Although Emily heard every word they spoke through the comlink, she couldn't see the three men until they emerged from beneath the forward hull. With their skinsuits covered by the bulky white overgarments, they were indistinguishable from one another save for the colored stripes running across the tops of their ovoid helmets: gold for Harker, blue for Ramirez, red for Cruz. Caught within the bright circle cast by the spotlights, they trudged out from under the shuttle, each carrying two stainless-steel equipment cases, their boots kicking up dusty regolith that clung to their legs like dirty talcum powder.

Once they were within sight of the cockpit, Harker stopped and turned around to look up at her. '*Com check*,' he said. '*You're reading me, right?*'

Emily touched the wand of her headset. 'Loud and clear. Got the fix on Larry?'

'*On my heads-up*.' He pointed to the right, northwest from the shuttle. '*About a half klick from where we are now, correct?*'

She looked up at a screen above the windows. Just as he said, the lander was located only 570 meters from their touchdown point. From there, it would be a simple matter of following Larry's tracks to the vent previously explored by the probe. 'You got it. Set up the LRC once you've reached the vent.'

Within one of the equipment cases was a portable long-range communications system designed to amplify transmissions from their suit radios. The same hardware would allow them to communicate directly with *Galileo* once she linked the com channel from the shuttle. '*Roger that*,' Harker said. '*Not that it's necessary, really. We're only going a couple of kilometers.*'

'Do it anyway, please.' Emily became persistent. 'You don't know what kind of mascon interference we may get down here.'

'*Ball and chain.*' Ramirez's voice came through her headset as a murmured aside, followed by a sound that might have been Cruz chuckling with amusement.

Emily reached up to the com panel and switched off his comlink. She waited a couple of seconds, enough time to cause Ramirez to turn around and look up at the shuttle. 'Sorry about that,' she added, switching him back on again. 'Loss of signal there. Want to repeat that last transmission, please?'

'*Ahh . . . negative on that.*' Ramirez's tone became contrite. '*Like you said . . . only some local interference.*'

'*Hope we don't have any more accidents like that.*' Irritation in Ted's voice.

'You won't.' Emily couldn't help but smile. 'Just a small glitch in the system, that's all.'

'*Hey, how about making some coffee for when we get back?*' Harker said, as if to mitigate the situation. '*I don't care if these suits are supposed to keep us warm . . . it's cold out here.*'

Now that he mentioned it, that wasn't such a bad idea. The shuttle's galley was little more than a closet-size larder, but it did contain a coffeemaker with its own water tank, along with foam cups to be used when the craft was in a gravity environment. Someone at ESA had realized how important such small amenities would be during long sorties.

'Wilco.' Suddenly, Emily realized there was nothing more to be said. 'Be careful out there,' she added, trying not to sound concerned. 'Keep the channel on, all right?'

'*Will do.*' Ted raised his right arm as far as he could, to shoulder height, and bent his elbow in a clumsy salute.

She waved back to him, then watched as he and the others turned around and began to walk away. Their helmet lamps switched on before they left the field of illumination, but it wasn't long before they became three small blobs of light, gradually receding into the darkness.

Emily stood within the cockpit for a long time, watching them go. It wouldn't be long before she'd be able to regain contact with *Galileo*. A glance at the comp screen told her that the ship would soon reappear above the western horizon. For the time being, though, she was left to mind the home fires, so to speak.

Except for the crosstalk on the com channel, the shuttle was quiet. Too quiet for her nerves. And a little too warm, besides; might as well make herself more comfortable. Unzipping her flight suit, she peeled down to the drawstring trousers and T-shirt she wore underneath and opened a cabinet to retrieve the pair of felt moccasins she had stowed away. Then she bent down to the comp and punched up a music program she'd loaded into the system for just such an occasion. Some late-twentieth classical jazz, perhaps: Dexter Gordon, *Our Man In Paris*. She put it over the speakers; as a saxophone's mellow chords drifted through the cockpit, she went aft to open the galley. She'd need coffee; it would be a few hours before the guys returned.

She'd just loaded a cartridge labeled MOCHA JAVA into the filter slot when Arkady's voice came through her headset: 'Galileo *to* Maria Celeste, *do you copy? Please respond.*'

About time. She touched the lobe of her headset. 'This is *Maria Celeste*,' she said as she placed the ceramic carafe on the hot plate between the valve and pushed the BREW button. 'Read you loud and clear, *Galileo*.'

'*Nice to hear you again*, Maria. *How's tricks?*'

Emily smiled as she headed forward to the cockpit. 'We're down and safe, *Galileo*. Touchdown point about six hundred meters south of Larry, approximately two kilometers southeast from the crater. Survey team has left the craft, proceeding on foot to the primary target. You should be receiving the LRC signal once they've arrived.'

As she spoke, she bent low to peer upward through the cockpit windows. For a moment, she didn't see anything save for a black sky sprinkled with stars. Then she spotted a bright point of light, vaguely cruciform in shape, rising above the western horizon. The *Galileo*, following its equatorial orbit around Spindrift.

'*We copy*, Maria. *Looking good*.' A pause. Emily held her breath, waiting for more. '*Think you can send us a postcard? We'd love to get some pictures*.'

There it was: the code phrase she'd worked out with Arkady. 'We'll try to do that, *Galileo*,' she said, hastily resuming her seat and reaching up to the com panel. 'You'll need to send me your address, though. You're a long way from here.'

'*Oh, you know . . . the usual one will do*.' Arkady's voice was breezy, casual. Just a little chitchat among shipmates, so far as anyone else was concerned. As he spoke, though,

Emily switched over to the secondary frequency normally used for backup telemetry. She patched the signal to a comp screen, then bent to peer more closely at it.

A concave view of *Galileo*'s command center, as seen by a small video camera mounted within the com station. In the foreground, she could see the top of Arkady's head; behind him, a wraparound image of the flight deck, distorted by the camera's fish-eye lens. In mid-distance, she saw Lawrence, seated in his chair with his legs crossed, looking straight ahead. In front of him, she spotted Simone at the helm. Antonia was nowhere in sight . . . no, wait, there she was, walking past Arkady, heading from one side of the bridge to the other.

The camera was meant to be used for real-time video transmissions between *Galileo* and Earth, but hadn't been utilized since the shakedown cruise. With any luck, Captain Lawrence would've forgotten that it even existed. But Ted hadn't, and neither had Emily or Arkady; the com officer had surreptitiously activated the camera and slaved it to the secondary channel, allowing Emily to monitor what was going on within *Galileo*'s command center while the shuttle was on Spindrift.

'I'll send you that card,' Emily said, and Arkady briefly raised his face to the camera to give her a wink. 'Anything else you'd like?'

'A perfect red rose . . .'

Her eyes widened as she realized what he was saying – *stand by* – but before she could react, Lawrence glanced over his shoulder at Arkady. He said something Emily couldn't quite make out, but Arkady turned his head to look at him. '*Yes, sir*,' he said, then leaned forward.

An instant later, Lawrence's voice came over her

headset: '*Ms Collins, do I understand that Mr Harker and his party have already left the ship?*'

It felt odd to be speaking with the captain while watching him from behind. 'Yes, sir, he has. They're proceeding to Larry, and I expect . . .'

'*Very well. When you make contact with them again, please advise Mr Harker that we're changing orbit with the intent of rendezvousing with the starbridge.*'

Stunned, Emily stared at the screen. 'Do I understand you correctly, sir? You're planning to change the orbital parameters?'

'*You understand correctly.*' Lawrence uncrossed his legs, then turned his head to the right and made a small gesture to someone off-screen. '*I expect we'll be approaching our target within the next three orbits. Do you copy?*'

'I . . . yes, sir, we copy.'

'*Very good, Ms Collins. Make sure Mr Harker gets this message.*' As if she were little more than a London taxi driver, waiting at the curb while her passengers went shopping at Harrods. '*Good luck with your mission.* Galileo *over.*'

His voice cut off, yet his image remained on the screen. Arkady looked up at the camera again; a discreet nod, then he briefly raised two fingers. The secondary com signal would remain active so long as *Galileo* was above them.

A perfect red rose, indeed . . . complete with thorns.

Eleven

JANUARY 8, 2291 – SPINDRIFT

The world was a cold and lightless plain, its horizon discernible only as a jagged line where the stars rose from the darkness. Caught within the beams of their helmet lamps, Larry's tracks ran straight ahead of the three men as a pair of shallow furrows through charcoal-black dust, swerving every now and then to avoid a boulder too large for the probe to climb over. Shoulders bowed by the weight of the equipment cases, their boots scuffing up tufts of regolith, they followed the tracks through a land of perpetual night.

'*I don't care what my suit tells me,*' Ramirez grumbled. '*My feet are freezing. If I don't get warm pretty soon, I'm going to come down with frostbite.*' He hesitated. '*Maybe I've got a suit leak.*'

'Your suit's rated for –240° Celsius.' Harker didn't look back at him as they trudged along. 'If there was a leak, you'd have worse problems than cold feet. It's all in your head.'

'*You sound like the prison shrink,*' Ramirez replied, and that evinced a dry chuckle from Cruz. '*Don't laugh until you've been there,*' he added. '*Five years of psychotherapy is no fun.*'

'Tell us about it another time.' As curious as he was about Ramirez, Harker didn't want to get distracted then. Most EVA accidents occurred when guys forgot where they were and what they were supposed to be doing. 'Right now, I just want to reach the crater.'

Although he couldn't see it yet, a glance at the pedometer and the translucent map displayed on his visor's heads-up told him that the crater should be less than a hundred meters away. Once again, he paused to turn around and look back the way they had come. A couple of kilometers away, he could make out the lights of the *Maria Celeste*; it should have been a comforting sight, but for some reason it only added to a growing sense of foreboding. That lonesome shuttle was all that kept him and the others from being marooned on this rock for the rest of their lives. Which would be very short indeed, once their suit batteries went down and the rebreather units failed . . .

Stop scaring yourself, he thought. *You've got Ramirez to do that for you*. 'Onward and forward,' he said, forcing himself to be cheerful as he turned around again. '"Half a league, half a league, half a league onward . . ."'

His voice trailed off as he remembered the rest of the verse. Much too grim to be repeated, under the circumstances. But Ramirez had apparently read Tennyson as well. '"*All in the valley of Death rode the six hundred*,"' he finished.

'*Thanks for those happy thoughts*,' Cruz said. '*Last time I go for a hike with you guys*.' Of the three of them, the geologist was the most upbeat. His curiosity insatiable, he'd already stopped a couple of times to collect rock samples, and when they'd located Larry he had taken a couple of minutes to download the probe's memory directly into his suit comp. So far as Jorge was concerned, everything about Spindrift was a source of wonder; if the relentless cold and dark of this castaway world dispirited him at all, he didn't show it.

'Sorry 'bout that,' Harker said. 'I'll try not to . . .'

A double beep in his headset, then he heard Emily's voice: 'Maria Celeste *to EVA team, you copy?*'

'Right here, Sister Maria,' Harker replied. 'What's up?'

'You should be close to the crater by now. Seen anything yet?'

Harker had been caught up in the conversation, he'd failed to notice anything more than the rover tracks. Looking up, he caught sight of a moundlike bulge only a few dozen meters away. 'Got it. Very close now . . .'

'*Whoa!*' Cruz stopped, tilted back his head so that his helmet faced upward. '*Switch to IR . . . you gotta see this!*'

Putting down the equipment cases, Harker raised his left hand to the side of his helmet and found the recessed stud that activated the visor's infrared filter. Immediately, the landscape became more visible, albeit tinged pale green; the mound was obviously the outer wall of a small crater, gently sloping upward about ten meters above the ground. Yet that wasn't what caught his attention, but rather a shaft of light, pale yellow and rippling like a desert mirage, that rose above the crater's center.

'*That's heat,*' Cruz said. '*Coming from the same place as the carbon dioxide emissions.*'

'Volcanic?' Harker stared at it in puzzlement.

'*I don't think so.*' Setting down his own equipment cases, Cruz opened one of them, pulled out a portable UV spectrometer. Aiming the gun-shaped instrument at the crater, he raised his visor so that he could study its luminescent readout. '*No. Not hot enogh. Only sixteen-point-two degrees Celsius. Practically room temperature.*'

'Wonder why Larry didn't pick this up,' Harker murmured.

'*Perhaps because it wasn't there yesterday.*' Ramirez's voice was low. '*If it's some sort of radiator, it may open only periodically. To keep the interior from overheating.*'

That fit with Ramirez's theory, yet Harker still wasn't convinced. 'Right,' he said dryly. 'You getting all this, Emcee?'

'*Loud and clear.*' A brief pause. '*Ted, may I have a chat with you, please?*'

'Yes, of course.' Through Cruz's faceplate, he caught a glimpse of a wry grin before the geologist looked away; Ramirez said nothing. Harker raised his right hand, touched a stud on the suit's wrist control unit that switched the comlink to a private channel. 'I'm here. Do you read?'

'*Copy.*' Emily's voice sounded distraught. '*Ted, I've made contact with* Galileo. *They're changing orbit.*'

'What the hell?' Harker was astonished. 'Why?'

'*They're repositioning in order to rendezvous with the starbridge. Lawrence told me so himself.*'

'For the love of . . .' Harker bit back his words. 'Doesn't that idiot know what he's . . . ?'

'*You think I don't know that?*' Her voice rose sharply, taking on a scolding tone he'd seldom heard before. '*You realize how much more fuel we'll have to burn in order to get back to . . . ?*'

'Calm down. I'm sure you'll be able to work out a new return trajectory.' He let out his breath. 'What do you want to bet that this is why he wanted us off the ship?'

'*I'm not following you. So he could bring* Galileo *closer to the starbridge? He could have done that even while we . . .*'

'I don't know. But this isn't good.' Touching his helmet

again, he reverted the visor back to visible light. A quick check of the direction finder on the heads-up display, then he turned away from the crater until he looked due west. Raising the visor, he peered up at the sky. For a few moments, he saw only familiar stars and constellations – Polaris, Vega, Ursa Majoris, Andromeda – but then he saw a bright spot of light falling toward the horizon.

'*Galileo*'s still there, Hasn't changed orbit yet.' He paused. 'Did you work things out with Arkady?'

'*Affirmative. He's put me on an audivisual patch to the command center.*' A moment passed. '*Not that it will do us much good.*'

'Better to be forewarned. Keep on top of things, all right? Let me know if anything else comes up.'

'*Right* . . .'

'Look, when we've set up the LRC, I'll talk to Lawrence, find out what's going on up there. And once Arkady manages to realign the laser and we've reestablished contact with Mare Muscoviense, they'll get an earful about this.' Harker grinned. 'I'm telling you, after I'm done with the Little Lord Ian, he'll be spending the rest of his days riding the fox around the family estate.'

'*Wouldn't that be grand?*' A short laugh, then a nervous sigh. '*God, I wish you were back here* . . .'

'Want me to scrub the EVA?'

'*No, of course not. You're onto something out there.*' A moment passed. '*I'll keep working at it from my end, and let you know if something turns up.*'

'Sure. Do that.'

'*Please be careful. This place is too weird.*'

'Tell me about it.' He looked back at the nearby crater. 'Have to run now. Keep on the primary channel, right?'

'Sure. Over.'

Harker switched off, then turned toward the two men. 'Sorry, lads. Just a com check, that's all.'

'With the girl he left behind. Of course.' Cruz looked at Ramirez. *'When we get back, I think we're going to be slinging up our hammocks in the aft section.'*

Before Harker could manage a retort, Emily's voice came over the line. *'Keep that up, Jorge, and you'll be sleeping in the airlock. Copy?'*

'Umm . . . well, if you . . .'

'Enough.' Harker bent down to pick up his cases. 'We've got a mystery on our hands. Let's get to it, shall we?'

They set up the LRC at the base of the crater, aligning its dish antenna so that it was oriented with the local ecliptic. There was no point in trying to establish contact with *Galileo*, though; checking his suit chronometer, Harker calculated that the ship was on the other side of Spindrift and therefore out of radio range. *Galileo*'s new trajectory shouldn't put it beyond acquisition, or at least so he hoped.

Once they completed a quick systems check, the three men began their ascent of the crater rim. It was more difficult than they had expected; although the slope wasn't particularly steep, the powdery regolith and the burden of their equipment made the climb particularly treacherous; for every two or three steps they took, their boots slid back a step. They had to stop now and then to wipe dust from their faceplates, and their suits were filthy by the time they reached the top.

Below them lay the broad expanse of the crater. As

they'd seen from Larry's cameras, its floor was covered by a thick blanket of particulate dry ice, resembling snow yet far colder. If Spindrift ever came close to the Sun, solar radiation would gradually evaporate its carbon dioxide deposits, perhaps giving the asteroid a faint corona much like that of a comet. This far from the solar system, though, the snow remained undisturbed. Beautiful, but nonetheless a potential hazard.

They'd come prepared for it, though. Opening one of the cases Ramirez had lugged up the slope, Harker removed three fifty-meter coils of nylon rope and three half-meter titanium-alloy pitons. Using a rock hammer, he drove the pitons through the dust until they were securely planted within bedrock; once he fed the ends of each rope through the loopholes and knotted them, he tossed the coils down to the crater floor. Now they had a safe means of descent, and an easy way to get back out again.

Within one of Cruz's cases was something Jorge and Martin had cobbled together the night before: a battery-powered vacuum cleaner, the type normally used to collect detritus within the ship, only now with its fan reversed so that it would blow instead of suck. Coupled to the unit by a short length of airtight hose was a tank of compressed halon siphoned from *Galileo*'s fire-control system; since the tank was good for only so long, a couple of spares had been included. Because no one knew just how well the improvised snow-blower would work, Cruz's other case contained a pair of collapsible shovels normally used to gather surface samples, yet Harker hoped that the dry-ice layer was as powdery as it appeared. If not, they'd have to dig their way through the crater.

Once the three men used elastic cords to lash the three remaining cases against their backs, they grasped the ropes and, carefully moving backward, rappelled down the crater's steep inner slope. Ramirez was more cautious than the other two, and Harker had to coax him along the first half of the way down, but it wasn't long before he joined him and Cruz at the bottom.

They set out for the crater's center, again following Larry's tracks. At first, it seemed as if the snow wouldn't be an obstacle; as expected, it lay only a few centimeters deep at the outer edge. Yet they were only thirty meters from where they'd left the ropes when they found themselves calf deep in icy particles that, through the soles of their boots, made a dull crunching noise that sounded as if they were walking through rice kernels. Feeling his feet getting numb, Harker glanced at his heads-up display, saw his suit's thermostat was nearing the red line. Time to see whether the snow-blower would work.

Much to his surprise, it did. Holding its nozzle close to the ground and slowly weaving back and forth, Harker whisked away most of the dry ice before them, forming a narrow trench through which they were able to walk in single file. He used the snow-blower sparingly, firing it in short spurts in order to conserve the first tank as long as he could, but because the halon froze instantly, he found that he was able to build embankments that would restrain the powder from cascading back into the trench.

They'd almost reached the crater's center when the first tank finally gave out. By then the trench was almost thigh deep; Ramirez and Cruz followed him, carrying their equipment. 'Still getting a heat signature?' Harker asked as he plugged the second tank into the blower and knocked the nozzle against the ground to clear away the frozen halon that had built up around it.

'*Uh-huh. We're almost on top of it.*' Putting down his case, Cruz raised his visor, then checked his spectrograph. '*Funny, no more* CO_2 *emissions. Like it just shut off.*'

'*If it's an exhaust port of some kind, it may open only periodically, to prevent itself from freezing.*' Ramirez was becoming impatient. '*If we hurry, we might be able to find it before it closes completely.*'

Harker turned to look at him. Through Ramirez's faceplate, he caught an expression of determination. 'You're quite certain of this, aren't you?'

'*Never been more certain of anything in my life.*' Raising his right hand, he took a step forward. '*Allow me, please. With all due respect, I think I know what we're looking for a little better than you do.*'

Harker hesitated, then extended the snow-blower to him. 'Careful. We've only got one tank left.'

'*Thank you. I'll try to be conservative.*' Taking the blower in both hands, Ramirez edged past Harker. He shut his visor, touched the helmet stud to activate the infrared option, then aimed the nozzle low to the ground and fired a short burst to clear away the snow. '*Jorge, get up here with me. Keep an eye on the spectrograph and tell me if you spot anything unusual.*'

Cruz moved around Harker and fell in beside Ramirez. Together, they slowly advanced toward the center of the crater, the geologist aiming his instrument past Ramirez's shoulder as the astrobiologist cleared a path. Harker watched Ramirez for a few moments, then followed them. He seemed to know what he was searching for, even if he didn't care to share his insights with anyone else.

They'd walked only ten more meters when Cruz abruptly came to a halt. '*Metallic trace!*' he yelped, his voice rising in excitement. '*Some sort of ferrous compound, about ten degrees to the right!*'

Ramirez raised his head, looked in that direction. '*Same place as the heat source*,' he said quietly.

Harker quickly lowered his visor and activated the IR. Just as Ramirez said, the translucent column of hot yellow was emerging from the ground less than five meters away. 'Go that way,' he said unnecessarily, because Ramirez and Cruz were already moving toward the source.

The trench was almost deep enough for him to touch its top with his fingertips when Ramirez suddenly came to a halt. '*There it is*,' he said, then he aimed the blower straight down and gave it a prolonged burst. A cloud of crystallized dry ice rose around him like fog. '*Ted! Get up here! I've found it!*'

Ignoring the path the others had blazed, Harker plunged through the waist-deep drifts. All at once, the surface became slippery beneath the soles of his boots, as if he'd just found a hidden layer of ice. He lost his balance for a second and almost plunged face-first into the snow before he managed to recover himself. Taking advantage of the lesser gravity, he resorted to bunny hops much like he'd learned to use during basic training on the Moon; inefficient, but it seemed to give him better traction.

In three short leaps, he was beside Ramirez and Cruz. Ramirez had cleared away a broad patch of snow; both men were staring at it in silence. Looking past them, Harker found himself gazing at a hole in the ground.

No. Not just a hole. Perfectly circular, a little more than a meter and a half in diameter, the edge of the aperture had the unmistakable smooth, dull grey surface of a metallic object. No question about it, this was the mouth of an exhaust shaft.

'I'll be damned,' Harker muttered.

Ramirez looked up at him. '*Believe me now?*'

Harker didn't respond. Instead, he stepped closer to the hole. Raising his visor, he leaned over to peer down into the shaft. Almost at once, his faceplate was fogged over by a blast of warm air but not before the twin beams of his helmet lamps touched upon something deep within the well. He had a fleeting impression of thin lateral bars, like the slats of black window shades, before his faceplate froze up.

Blinded, he hastily backed away, raising his hands to his faceplate to scour away the thin patina of frost. '*Ted! What's going on out there?*' Emily's voice in his headset, and concerned for his safety.

'Nothing.' Then he laughed out loud. 'No . . . it's everything. Jared was right. This isn't a natural vent, it's . . . it's . . .'

'*A radiator shaft.*' Ramirez was oddly detached, almost as if he was describing a normal architectural feature found on any high-rise building. '*The CO_2 exhaust vent should be somewhere nearby, but . . .*'

His voice trailed off. '*But what?*' Cruz demanded. '*Do you realize what we've found?*'

'*Of course I do.*' Distracted, Ramirez regarded the vent for another moment. Then he turned toward Harker. '*When you came over here, you almost fell over. Like you slipped on something.*'

'Yeah, sure.' Harker finished clearing his faceplate. 'I hit some ice beneath the snow . . .'

'*Uh-huh . . . but I don't think it was just ice.*' Stepping away from the vent, Ramirez followed Harker's tracks to the place where he'd slipped. Stopping there, he spread his arms wide. '*All right, now, everyone fan out. Use the shovels, your hands and feet, whatever. Dig out as much snow as you can. It must be here somewhere.*'

'It?' Harker stared at him. 'What are you looking for? The carbon dioxide vent?'

'*Forget the vent,*' he said. '*We're looking for an airlock.*'

Moving in a circular pattern that gradually expanded away from where he'd slipped and almost fallen, Harker and Ramirez used shovels and the snow-blower to clear away as much particulate as they could, while Cruz used the spectrometer to search for more metallic traces hidden beneath the dry ice. Their method soon paid off, for it wasn't long before they located the carbon dioxide vent.

As Ramirez predicted, the vent was shut, sealed by a pie-wedge hatch nearly two meters in diameter. Although they dug out the snow around it, there seemed to be no way to open it from the outside. Cruz took photos of the vent cover, which he transmitted back to the shuttle, then they continued to search for an airlock.

Although Harker had come to realize that Ramirez's theory was correct, he remained unpersuaded that they would find an entrance to Spindrift's interior in the same place where they'd found exhaust ports. Yet Ramirez insisted that this was the most logical place to look. '*Look at it from an engineering point of view,*' he said while they took a break from searching and digging. '*If you've built vents for carbon dioxide and radiators for excess heat, wouldn't it make sense to provide service hatches to maintain them from the surface? Especially when they're spread so far apart?*'

'*Then why haven't they been used?*' Cruz was skeptical. '*The snow is more than a meter thick. There's no sign that anyone . . . or anything, whatever . . . has come out here in ages.*'

'*I don't know . . . I mean, I can't answer that.*' Ramirez let out his breath. '*But that's not to say that it isn't here.*'

'*Well, if they're aliens, then why should we assume that they'd do things we do?*'

'*Why assume that they wouldn't?*'

While the two scientists continued to argue, Harker checked his chronometer. They'd been on EVA for four and a half hours already. Their rebreather units were good for eight hours; he estimated that it would take an hour for them to return to the *Maria Celeste*. An hour and a half if he included a safety factor. That, along with the fact that they were hungry and tired, meant that they couldn't stay outside very much longer.

'All right, okay,' he said. 'That's all well and good, but we've got to head back soon.'

'*Second that.*' Emily came over the comlink. '*You guys need to wrap this up.*'

'Oh, for God's sake!' Ramirez was clearly irritated. '*We're on the verge of one of the greatest discoveries ever made . . .*'

'That's right, and I think we need to sleep on it.' Harker grunted as he bent down to pick up the blower. His back was sore, his eyes itched from reading the heads-up display, and he desperately wanted to scratch his nose. 'We've made good progress, but . . .'

'*Give us another two hours.*' Ramirez's tone became pleading. '*An extra hour, that's all. Then we can set up markers, go back to the shuttle, and return tomorrow to pick up where we left off. Is that too much to ask?*'

Harker was already inclined to order an end to the sortie and return to the shuttle. But if he did that, he'd hear no end of grief from Ramirez. '*I can work for another two hours.*' Cruz sounded just as tired as he was, yet was willing to suck it in. '*I think . . . I mean, we've got enough air left, don't we?*'

Before Harker could answer, Emily stepped in. '*Go ahead, guys. I can hold it down for a while longer.*' She'd been watching the clock just as much as he had. '*Your call, Ted.*'

Harker sighed, then nodded within his helmet. 'All right, then . . . two hours, then we head back.'

In times to come, Harker would reflect upon that fateful decision and wonder whether it had been fortunate or fortuitous. Had he saved lives, or cost them? Had he changed history for better or for worse? If he'd ordered the exploration party to return to the *Maria Celeste*, would all of them have survived, or would they have perished on Spindrift, their demise a mystery to the rest of the human race? Or had this one small, seemingly trivial choice opened the doors to the cosmos?

He could only second-guess the outcome, for the fact remained that, less than a half hour later, they discovered the very thing for which Ramirez had been searching.

'*Holy crap!*' Cruz yelped. '*Hey, guys . . . I think I've found a hatch!*'

By then, Cruz had taken his turn at the snow-blower, and had been using it to clear away a patch of ground at the third point of a triangle whose legs were formed by the locations of the carbon dioxide vent and the radiator shaft. Even though they were down to the last tank of halon, Harker hadn't cared very much by this point who used the snow-blower; all he really wanted to do was make the long hike back to the shuttle, where he could peel off his skinsuit, have a cup of coffee, and fall out in his hammock for a few hours.

Yet it'd become clear, judging from the readings of Cruz's spectrometer, that they were standing on top of a metallic plate about twenty meters in diameter. If Ramirez's hypothesis was correct, then a service hatch should be located somewhere within the proximity.

And so it was. Dropping his shovel, Harker bounded away from the area where he'd been digging to the place that Cruz had used the blower to remove the dry ice. Before he got there, though, Ramirez took the blower away from Cruz. Aiming it at a patch of ground, he blasted away the particulate. A thin white fog rose, then slowly settled, and now they were looking at . . .

'Oh, good heavens,' he murmured.

'*What's there?*' Emily's voice came over the comlink. '*What did you find?*'

Beneath a thin layer of frozen carbon dioxide lay a low, hemispherical bulge, perfectly circular and almost two meters in diameter. Like the vent cover, it had a pie-shape configuration – four triangular segments, sealed together at the apex – except that this one was raised slightly above ground, like a metallic blister.

But that wasn't all. Within each segment, evenly spaced apart from one another, was a small, round plate, no larger than a salad dish. And within each plate, three recessed holes, the two at the top slightly farther apart from the one at the bottom, each no more than a few centimeters deep.

Harker stared at the hatch for a few moments, feeling the last vestiges of skepticism evaporate along with his fatigue. Looking up at Ramirez, he saw the victorious smile upon the scientist's face. Vindication at last . . . and despite himself, Harker felt a surge of wonder.

'Break out the laser,' he said. 'Let's see where this takes us.'

Twelve

JANUARY 8, 2291 – SPINDRIFT

Ramirez helped Harker and Cruz unpack the laser and set it up on its tripod, then stepped back to watch while Harker, who was the only one authorized to use it, adjusted the instrument to low-power level. Once Harker switched on the laser, he carefully guided its ruby beam across the hatch, cutting through the centimeter-thick layer of dry ice that encrusted it.

Even so, breaking through the ice was tough work. Although it melted as soon as the laser touched it, the carbon dioxide refroze almost immediately, making it necessary for Harker to shut down the laser every few minutes so that Ramirez and Cruz could move in with their shovels, digging up fractured slabs of ice and tossing them aside. It took nearly an hour of backbreaking labor, but they finally managed to clear the hatch enough for Ramirez to examine it more closely.

As he'd seen before, the hatch was approximately two meters in diameter, its blisterlike dome rising about twenty-five centimeters above the ground. It was split into four wedge-shaped segments closely joined at the center; the grooves between the segments were only a few millimeters wide. Within each segment, spaced less than fifty centimeters apart from one another, was a circular plate no more than a hand's width in diameter, in which three small holes had been bored. The top two holes were about nine centimeters apart, while the third was centered about seven centimeters below the other two. All four plates had the same pattern, with the top two holes neatly aligned with the center of the hatch.

'*We're running down the clock, gents.*' Harker had moved aside the tripod and was disconnecting the power cable. '*Two and a half hours of air left in our packs. We need to head back soon.*'

'It took us only an hour to get here. We've got enough time.' Ramirez got down on one knee to examine the hatch more closely. Beneath the glare of his helmet lamps, he noticed that the holes weren't perfectly circular, but instead were oval grooves. Extending his right hand, he was able to insert his forefinger within one of them.

'*Maybe so, but we still have to . . .*'

'Will you please . . . ?' Ramirez used his gloves to brush away small chips of ice from the remaining holes. 'We've found the first alien starship, or whatever this thing is, and you're fretting like a little girl.'

'*C'mon, Jared.*' Cruz's voice was as easygoing as always. '*We've got time to come back here. Let's head back to the shuttle, get some rest. It's not going anywhere.*'

'What if the exhaust vent opens again? You want to spend another hour breaking ice?' Settling back on his haunches, he looked up at the other two. 'And what if the captain gets the notion to issue a recall order? Ever think about that?'

'*He wouldn't . . .*' Harker began.

'Yes, he would. You should know that better than anyone.' Ramirez jabbed a finger at the hatch. 'This is important. More important than playing it safe. If having a cup of coffee and a nice little nap is your highest priority, then go on back. I've got work to do.'

For a few moments, Harker didn't respond. '*Emcee?*' he said at last. '*You copy?*'

'*Right here, Ted.*'

'*Think you can move* Maria *a little closer? I mean, is it possible for you to lift off again, then put down near the crater? That way we don't have such a long hike to get to . . .*'

A short laugh. '*I can park her right on top of you, if that's what you want.*'

'*Not that close, thank you,*' Harker replied. '*We just spent the last two hours clearing the site. I don't want to have to shovel aside any snow the thrusters might displace. Home in on the LRC and put it down there, that should be near enough.*'

'*Affirmative. Give me . . .*' A short pause. '*Thirty, forty-five minutes. I'll be there.*'

'*Roger that. Over and out.*' Harker looked back at Ramirez. '*All right, I've just shortened our return trip. That should buy you another hour.*' A pause. '*You can say, "Thank you, Commander Harker. You won't regret this, and I won't give you any more crap."*'

'Thank you, Commander Harker.' Ramirez's faceplate fogged for a moment as he let out his breath. 'You won't regret this, and I won't give you any more crap.'

'*Better not. I was looking forward to that nap.*' Harker stepped a little closer, bent down to study the hatch. '*Right. Now show me what you think is so interesting.*'

Little more than a half hour later, the *Maria Celeste* touched down just outside the crater. Emily had homed in on the LRC's transponder, so she was able to pinpoint her landing within a hundred meters of where the three men had climbed over the rim. By then, Harker had reactivated the laser and used it to evaporate the ice within the hatch panels, including the four round plates that Ramirez had found. The astrobiologist wanted to continue working, but the commander put his foot down. They needed to return to the shuttle, if only to replenish their rebreather packs. So they left the equipment in place and followed the path they'd made through the ice until they reached the ropes and used them to climb out of the crater.

Although he'd been reluctant to leave the site, Ramirez had to admit that it felt good to remove his overgarment, helmet, and gloves. They didn't take off their skinsuits, though; by then, everyone had agreed that all they really needed was a breather. So he sat on the armrest of one of the seats and warmed his hands with a cup of coffee while Emily hooked up their packs to hoses that flushed out the filtration systems and refilled the oxygen tanks.

'The clue is the location of those plates,' Ramirez said, continuing the discussion he'd begun with Harker at the site. 'There's one on each flange, right? And the holes in each one . . .'

'All right. You've convinced me.' Harker walked over to the galley to pour coffee for himself. 'They serve some sort of purpose. No argument there. So what makes you think they're meant as handholds?'

'He's got a point.' Cruz sorted through the selection of food tubes, apparently trying to decide which flavor of paste he wanted to inflict upon himself. 'A lever of some sort, sure. But three little holes . . . I dunno.'

'That's because you're still thinking in human terms.' Shifting his coffee cup to his left hand, Ramirez held up his right hand, palm outward. 'See how evolution has shaped your hands . . . four fingers, with a thumb opposing the others. Look around you, and you can see how nearly everything here is designed to accommodate this arrangement. The control panels, the cabinet doors, the lock-wheels . . .'

'I had biology in school, thank you,' Cruz murmured.

'So you know what I'm talking about. Form follows function. Now imagine . . .' Ramirez folded his little and index fingers into his palm, leaving his ring and middle fingers raised along with his thumb. 'A hand that looks like this, only with the two top fingers spread more widely apart and the thumb placed in the center.'

'That's not a hand,' Emily said. 'That's a claw.'

'Perhaps . . . but capable of manipulation all the same. So wouldn't it follow that a hatch meant to be opened by such a hand . . . or claw, if you will . . . would be shaped to . . .'

'All right, you've got me there.' Harker leaned against a suit locker as he sipped his coffee. 'But there's four plates, one for each flange, each with their holes facing in the same direction.'

'Uh-huh.' Ramirez dropped his hand. 'With the top two oriented toward the center of the hatch and the third facing away. Go on.'

'So . . .' Harker thought about it a moment. 'If all four plates were meant to be turned in order to open the hatch, wouldn't that . . . ?' He shook his head. 'No. That's impossible.'

'Yes, it would be.' Now it was Ramirez's turn to smile. 'If the beings who designed it had only two arms.'

Harker and Cruz glanced at each other, while Emily

turned away from her work to gaze at him. Cruz let out a low whistle. 'Y'know, I'm not sure if I want to meet . . .'

'Hush!' All of a sudden, Emily raised a hand to her headset. She listened intently for a moment, then prodded her mike wand. 'Roger that, *Galileo*, we copy.'

Harker brushed past Ramirez as he hurried into the cockpit. Picking up his headset from where he'd left it in the copilot seat, he pulled it on. Looking around, Ramirez spotted his own headset. He put it on, then found Cruz's headset and tossed it across the cabin to him.

'. . . *establishing rendezvous orbit one hundred kilometers from primary objective*,' Arkady was saying, his voice a static-laced crackle. '*Do you copy?*'

'We read you, *Galileo*. Thanks for the update.' Harker took a deep breath. 'Not sure if the starbridge is still the primary objective, though. We've located the crater vent, and found something quite interesting.'

Ramirez felt his heart freeze. *Not now, you idiot!* He tried to motion to Harker, telling him to be quiet, but the first officer turned his back to him. So he had to sit and listen while Harker delivered a rundown of all that they'd discovered within the crater, up to the point when they came across the hatch leading to Spindrift's interior.

By then, Emily had come forward. While Harker spoke, she reached past him to activate a screen below the com panel. Gazing over her shoulder, Ramirez saw that it displayed an image of *Galileo*'s command center. Although Arkady occasionally glanced up at the camera, no one else seemed to be aware that they were being observed. Lawrence was seated in his chair, with Cole standing beside him, but their attention was focused away from them, upon the forward windows and the screens above them.

Emily looked at Ramirez, silently pointed to the screen, then smiled and touched a finger to her lips. Now he understood. They were spying upon the *Galileo* from the point of view of Arkady's station; so far as everyone else aboard was concerned, they had only voice contact with the *Maria Celeste* team. Ramirez grinned. It wasn't much of an ace, but nonetheless they had it up their sleeve.

Harker was finishing his report when they saw Cole bend down to Lawrence to whisper something in his ear. They couldn't hear what he said, but the captain listened closely; he nodded a couple of times, then he reached up to touch his mike wand.

'Well done, Mr Harker. Pleased to learn that you've made such progress. Your team should be commended for their efforts.'

'Thank you, sir.' Harker gazed at the spy view of the command center. 'I hope Sir Peter is satisfied as well.'

'He's in the observation center, helping Dr Rauchle analyze the data we've received from the probes. I'll pass along your regards when I see them.'

'Of course,' Harker said dryly. 'I'm sure the rest of the science team will be interested to learn what else we find, once we return to the site. We should be able to transmit exact data to you once we conduct a more thorough . . .'

'I'm afraid you won't be able to do that, Commander. I want you to return to Galileo, *as soon as possible.'*

'Bastard.' Ramirez glared at Cole's image on the screen. 'I told you so.'

Clasping his hand around his mike, Harker turned to glare at him. 'Shut up!' he whispered. Then he unclasped the wand. 'Sorry, Captain. Lost you for a second there. Did you say that you want us to return to the ship?'

'*Affirmative,* Maria Celeste.' Lawrence glanced up at

Cole, as if seeking approval. Cole nodded, and Lawrence turned away again. '*Wrap up what you're doing and prepare to come home.*'

'I don't understand, sir,' Harker said. 'Why do you want us to do that?'

On-screen, they watched Lawrence cup his mike as Cole bent forward once more. In the foreground, Arkady glanced at the camera; a brief frown and a furtive shake of his head, then he looked away. Cole stepped back from Lawrence, and the captain uncupped his mike again.

'*Your group has done as much as it can down there,*' Lawrence said. '*I've just conferred with Dr Rauchle, and he'd like to bring down another group to continue the investigation. They'll need to have you along, of course, in order to lead them to the site, but we think it's wise to have your people step aside and let the rest of the science team have a look at what you've found.*'

'He's lying.' Ramirez was barely able to contain his anger. 'Son of a bitch. You know he's lying.'

Harker shot him a warning look. 'Umm . . . yes, sir, that makes sense.' Ramirez started to protest, but he held up a hand. 'However, we still need to go EVA one more time. We left our equipment at the site, and we ought to retrieve it. Dr Ramirez informs me that the CO_2 vent could become active again at any time, and another discharge might bury it beneath new ice.'

Ramirez felt Emily's hand on his arm, gently pushing him aside. Taking her place in the pilot's seat, she quickly typed commands into her keyboard, then silently gestured for Harker to study the data that appeared on her screen. Harker peered closely at the comp, then gave her a knowing wink. 'Ms Collins has just informed me that, given the elements of *Galileo*'s new orbit, our next available launch window won't open until 0300 tomorrow. That's nine and a half hours from now, by our reckoning. Do you copy?'

Lawrence bent forward slightly to address Simone. The helm officer listened, nodded, then typed something into her keyboard. A moment passed while Lawrence studied the display on his lapboard. Cole moved around to stare over his shoulder; he appeared to say something to the captain. A brief nod, then Lawrence sat up straight again.

'*Roger that*, Maria Celeste,' he said. '*You're go for a second EVA. But we need to have you launch by 0400 tomorrow at the latest, and don't conduct any more investigation of the site than necessary. Do you copy?*'

'Affirmative, *Galileo*. Thank you. *Maria Celeste* over.' Harker prodded his mike once more, then let out his breath. 'Nice work, Emcee,' he murmured, laying a fond hand upon her shoulder. 'You certainly pulled a fast one there.'

'What the hell are you talking about?' Aghast, Ramirez stared at both of them. 'Don't you see what happened? Your captain just pulled the plug on . . .'

'I know what he just did.' Yanking off his headset, Harker glared at him. 'You might bother to thank me. If that's not too much trouble, that is . . .'

'Thank you?' Ramirez felt his face grow warm. 'You could have told him . . .'

'What?' Emily removed her headset. 'That we could have launched in five minutes? Or that the equipment you left behind can always be recovered later, even if there's another vent discharge?' Shoving him aside, she stormed down the aisle. 'Ted just put himself on the line for you. You could be a little more grateful.'

'She lied. So did I.' Harker rubbed his eyelids with his fingertips. 'At the very least, we stretched the truth. In any event, we just bought us another eight hours . . . nine if we count the opening of the next launch window for rendezvous with *Galileo*.'

'But the ship comes around every . . . what? Three hours? Four?'

'True.' Harker favored him with a wry smile. 'But it takes a while for us to repack all that equipment and haul it back here, doesn't it? I'm sure there are going to be one or two inconvenient delays. These things take time, don't you know?'

'Time enough for us to return to the site, see if we can open that hatch.' Cruz slurped the rest of his coffee, crumpled the foam cup in his hand. 'They did us a favor, Jared. I think we owe 'em one.'

Ramirez let out his breath. 'I'm sorry. You're right. Thanks, both of you.' Harker nodded, however reluctantly; Emily said nothing as she slipped another cartridge into the coffeemaker. 'But what I don't understand is why . . .'

'They want to recall us?' Harker sat down in the copilot's seat, stared out the cockpit window. 'I can't figure that either. Not after what we've found. Doesn't make any sense.'

'I know.' Cruz leaned against the back of a seat. 'Sir Peter's trying to claim the credit for himself. If he and Rauchle open the hatch, make the first exploration of the interior . . .'

'No.' Ramirez shook his head. 'That doesn't work. Rauchle's the team leader, remember? That means he'll get his name listed at the head of the final report.' He considered this for another moment. 'And Sir Peter doesn't need to come down here. In fact, this isn't his area of expertise. You and me . . . we're the guys who know about this sort of thing, not him and Toby.'

'Besides, it wasn't Toby who suggested that we should be withdrawn,' Cruz added. 'It was Cole . . . we saw that on camera.'

'You got a point.' Emily poured water into the coffeemaker's tank. 'But he didn't put himself forward as being a member of the next landing party.'

'So why would Cole do this?' Ramirez shook his head. 'Believe me, I know him. His idea of exploration is sneaking into the women's dorm.' The others laughed out loud, and he found himself grinning at his own joke. 'All right, maybe he'd take that sort of risk, but anything more dangerous than that . . .'

'Then why . . . ?' Emily began.

'I don't know about the rest of you,' Harker said, 'but I'm not about to look a gift horse in the mouth.' He stood up, moved toward the aft section. 'One hour, gentlemen. Grab a nap, use the facilities, do whatever you need to do. Then we're back on the clock.'

'And what do you want us to do then?' Ramirez asked.

'See if your theory is correct, what else?' A sly grin. 'If anyone's going to make the find of the century, then it's going to be us.'

'All right,' Ramirez said. 'Let's see if we can open this thing.'

Bending down to the hatch, he extended his right hand to one of the plates. Curling his ring and little fingers, he inserted his remaining digits within the oval holes.

He tried to turn the plate clockwise, but it remained inert. When he exerted pressure in the opposite direction, though, it moved ever so slightly. Yet as hard as he tugged, he couldn't rotate the plate more than a couple of millimeters. 'I felt it give,' he said, looking up at Harker and Cruz, 'but it seems to be stuck on something.'

'*But it moved*,' Harker said. '*I saw that, too. Let me give it a try.*' Shuffling over to the adjacent flange, he inserted the fingers of his right hand into the holes of its plate. Ramirez heard him grunt as he tried to twist the plate counterclockwise, but after a couple of seconds he gave up. '*You're right. It turns just a little way, then freezes up.*'

'*My turn.*' Cruz bent down to the third flange, opposite the ones Ramirez and Harker had just tested, and poked his own fingers into the holes of its plate. '*I'm not getting it to . . . oh, wait, there it goes. Just a little bit, though.*' Then he looked up at the other two men. '*Hang on a sec. Did you guys turn right or left?*'

'*To the left*,' Harker said. '*Counterclockwise. Same as he did.*'

'*Mine turned clockwise.*' Cruz moved over to the fourth flange, tested it. '*This one turns to the right, too. No more than an inch or so, then it stops cold.*'

Standing erect, Ramirez studied the orientation of the hatch in relation to its surroundings. As he suspected, the two flanges he and Harker tried to open lay in the direction of the crater's center, toward the carbon dioxide and radiator vents, while the flanges Cruz tested were in the direction of the crater walls. He shut his eyes for a moment, trying to conjure a mental picture. A creature has emerged from the hatch to inspect Spindrift's outer surface . . .

'*Jared?*' Harker's voice broke his concentration. '*What are you . . . ?*'

'Hush. Let me think.' The creature – *no, not a creature; a thinking, rational being* – has shut the hatch behind it. *A wise precaution, if this is an entrance to the interior.* It does whatever it needs to do on the surface, then returns to the hatch. *So how does it get back inside, if it's alone? If it has four hands . . .*

'Jorge, come over here.' Ramirez opened his eyes. 'Stand where I am now. Ted, stay where you are.'

'*What are you . . . ?*' Cruz began.

'Just do as I say, all right?' Stepping away from the hatch, he walked around to where Cruz stood. Jorge hesitated, then walked over to join Harker.

'*You got an idea?*' Harker asked.

'Maybe. Just follow my lead.' Once they traded places, Ramirez got down on his knees, then reached out with both arms until his hands were able to touch the two adjacent flanges. To his relief, he was still able to insert his fingers firmly within the holes of their respective plates. 'Put your fingers in those holes and get a firm grip, but don't try to move them until I tell you. Understand?'

'*What the devil are you guys doing out there?*' Emily's voice came through his headset. '*If this is some sort of . . .*'

'*I think I know what he has in mind.*' Harker got down on his knees, and Cruz did the same. '*You think you can handle both of them at the same time?*'

Ramirez glanced up at him. Harker had caught on. 'Maybe. If it doesn't work, we can always get Emcee . . . Emily, I mean . . . to suit up and join us.'

'*She stays aboard the shuttle, no matter what.*' Harker looked at Cruz. '*Ready?*'

'*Sure, but I still don't know what . . .*'

'On the count of three,' Ramirez said, 'I want both of you to turn your plates counterclockwise, to the left. I'm going to turn mine clockwise, to the right. Understood?'

'*Got it,*' Harker said. '*On three.*'

'All right, then.' Ramirez wiggled his thumbs and fingers as far he could within the holes, making sure that he had a good grip. One last glance to make sure that Harker and Cruz had done the same, then he counted down. 'Three . . . two . . . one and pull!'

He twisted both plates to the right, trying hard to make it a swift, simultaneous motion. For an instant, his hands met the same resistance as before, and he thought he'd failed. Then, all at once, there was a sense of movement beneath his palms, as if tumblers within the door of an old-style bank vault were being released, and the plates revolved freely.

'*They're going!*' Cruz yelled. '*They're . . . !*'

The wedge-shaped panels began to slide apart.

'*It's opening!*' Harker snapped. '*It's . . . !*'

A silent blast of escaping residual atmosphere fogged his helmet faceplate. Startled, Ramirez fell back, his vision obscured.

'*Ted!*' Emily's voice, now frightened. '*What's going on out there?*'

Ramirez raised his hand to his helmet, scraped away the frost, then crawled forward on hands and knees to see what he'd done.

'*Oh my . . .*' Cruz murmured.

The hatch had disappeared, its segments retracted into the ground.

'*We're okay,*' Harker said. '*Just got a scare, that's all.*' The first officer clambered to his feet. '*We've opened the hatch, and we've found . . .*'

He stopped, apparently at a loss for words. Feeling his heart pounding against his ribs, Ramirez managed to stand up. Feeling as if he was at the edge of a precipice, he cautiously approached the pit and looked down.

For an instant, he saw nothing save for a hole in the ground: a deep and seemingly bottomless shaft, dark as the sky above them. Then light began to glimmer along its walls – random patterns of dim luminescence, like veins of radiant copper and silver – that gradually rose in intensity, revealing a curved, ramplike structure that led downward into the depths.

'I'll be damned.' Ramirez felt laughter rising within his chest. 'It's a staircase . . . a spiral staircase.'

'*He's right.*' Cruz's voice was choked with awe. '*If I didn't see it, I wouldn't have believed it.*'

Ramirez tore his gaze from the shaft, looked up at the other two men. 'Gentlemen—' he said, bowing slightly as he extended an arm toward the open hatch '—the way is clear. Let's go make history.'

Part Four

The World, the Flesh, and the Devil

Thirteen

JANUARY 8, 2291 – SPINDRIFT

The ramp leading underground was like none they'd ever seen before. Peering down through the open hatch, they saw that it wasn't as smooth as they had first thought, but appeared instead to be comprised of thin metallic plates, no two exactly alike, that overlapped one another like roof shingles. Although the overall structure resembled a spiral staircase, it was difficult to see how anyone – or anything – could safely use it. The plates were sleek and unevenly distributed, and seemed to grow straight out of the shaft walls, with no other visible means of support. Nor was there a guardrail to prevent one from falling down the empty well that yawned within its center.

One close look at the ramp, and Harker knew that they'd need to rig a safety line before they made their descent. They still had a fifty-meter coil of rope among their supplies, though, and when he aimed a pocket light down the staircase well, he caught a glimpse of a floor no more than thirty meters away. So he hammered a piton into the ground seven meters from the hatch, where there was no underlying metal surface, and once he fed the end of the rope through its loop and tied it off, he wrapped the other end around his chest and shoulders. He'd make the initial descent, and once he reached the bottom of the shaft, he'd unwrap his end of the rope and have Ramirez pull it back up. The other two would descend the same way; Ramirez next, then Cruz. The process would be time-consuming, but he dared not take any chances. And besides, with the rope in place, at least this way they'd have an easy way to ascend the shaft once they were ready to return to the surface.

All that was left, then, was deciding what to carry with them. Opening the last of the cases they'd brought with them from the shuttle, they divided up the equipment – flashlights and lightsticks, a med kit, hand tools, spare batteries and patches for their suits – and tucked it away within the cargo pockets of their overgarments. However, the LRC was too large for them to disassemble and carry down the shaft. Although they had no way of knowing how far their suit radios would continue to transmit once they were underground, and Emily was reluctant to lose contact with the team, in the end they decided that it was a risk they'd just have to take. Otherwise their exploration would be limited to radio range, which might well be no farther than the bottom of the shaft.

'All right, I think we're ready.' Harker yanked twice on the rope, making sure that it was secure, then glanced at the others. 'If I run into any trouble . . .'

'*We'll haul you back up.*' Cruz patted his shoulder. '*Good luck.*'

'*Please be careful.*' There was an anxious quaver in Emily's voice. '*Don't take any unnecessary chances.*'

Harker smiled at this. Everything they'd done so far was an unnecessary chance. 'Wilco,' he said. 'See you soon.' He took a deep breath, then took the first step through the hatch. Extending his arms to maintain his balance and watching where he put his feet, he slowly began to make his way down the ramp.

Although the plates appeared to be unstable, he was surprised to find that they were as solid as rock. Nor were they as slippery as they appeared; the soles of his boots had as much traction as he needed. Yet their uneven shapes and apparently random placement made them treacherous; he had to pause before taking each step to find another shingle large enough for him to plant his feet.

The hatch was designed to be opened by a creature with four hands. What did the ramp tell them about their means of mobility? *No doubt Ramirez will have something to say about this*, Harker thought. At least he didn't have to depend on his helmet lamps; the illumination provided by the radiant, veinlike crevices within the rock walls gave all the light he needed. *And I'm sure he'll have a theory about this, too . . .*

'You're going to love this place, Jared,' he said. 'It's just as weird as you are.'

Cruz laughed out loud. '*Thank you, Commander*,' Ramirez replied. '*I'm glad to know that it wasn't designed by humans. Then I'd be worried.*'

That remark almost stopped him. *Wonder what he meant by that?* He put it out of his mind. He was almost halfway down the ramp. *Focus, man. Focus . . .*

Twenty meters . . . twenty-five . . . thirty . . . and suddenly, he found himself at the bottom. Looking around, he thought for a moment that he'd reached a dead end. Then he looked beneath the final curve of the ramp and caught sight of another circular hatch, identical to the one above except that it was vertical and fitted into the wall.

'All right, I've reached the bottom, and I think I've found

the front door.' Rocking back on his haunches, he turned his helmet faceplate upward. Far above, he could see Ramirez and Cruz, peering down at him. 'You guys ready?'

'*Can't wait*,' Cruz said. '*Doesn't look so hard. Took you only ten minutes.*'

Had it been that quick? He could have sworn that his descent had taken three times as long. 'It isn't, but don't rush,' Harker said as he untied himself from the rope. 'Those steps . . . if you can call 'em that . . . are tougher than they look. Emcee, you copy?'

'*Still here.*' Emily's voice was a little more faint, but at least they had radio reception. '*I had to boost the gain, but you're coming in.*'

'Good to know.' Harker watched as the rope was dragged upward, its end bouncing lightly across the ramp plates. 'Any word from *Galileo*?'

'*Negatory.*' A pause. '*If I hear from them, what do I tell Ian?*'

'That I'm resting and can't be disturbed.' He let out his breath, wishing that he could rub his eyelids. If only that were true. This was his second EVA in less than ten hours; on the Moon or Mars, ESA protocols would've called for a twelve-hour break between excursions. He didn't have that luxury, though. 'When we get back, you and me are going to have some serious bunk time.'

'*Hey, we don't need to hear this.*' Cruz had pulled the line the rest of the way up and was helping Ramirez fasten it around himself. '*Some of us aren't so lucky.*'

'You've got a dirty mind.' Harker grinned. 'I was talking about catching up on my sleep.'

'*Yeah, uh-huh. Sure you were.*'

Harker didn't reply. No sense in rubbing it in. Instead,

he took a moment to walk over to the second hatch. Aside from its orientation, it looked much the same as the one above – four triangular metal sections that met in the center, with circular lockplates in each one, along with their corresponding finger holes – but on closer inspection he noticed something else.

Recessed within the wall to the left of the hatch was a small panel. Located at shoulder height and shaped somewhat like a chevron, it was divided four ways, forming a quartet of four-sided buttons. Something appeared to be inscribed within each button; he peered more closely at them and discerned vertical rows of fluid, almost Arabic-looking, script.

An alien language. Harker felt something run down the back of his neck. No telling what it meant, but he suddenly realized that he was looking at something no other human had ever seen before.

The hell with Lawrence, he thought. *I've got to see what's behind this door.*

'*I'm on the rope*,' Ramirez said. '*Ready down there?*'

'Just a sec. Hold on.' Turning away from the hatch, Harker started to head back to the ramp. Something that made him stop dead caught his eye, something he hadn't noticed before.

A fine layer of dust lay upon the floor. Coal black and powdery, it was obviously regolith that had drifted down from the surface sometime before. His footprints were visible within the dust . . . but among them were scuff marks, broad and oval, between the hatch and the bottom of the ramp.

Harker stared at them for a moment before he finally let out his breath. 'Don't mean to rush you, Jared,' he said, 'but there's something down here you might want to see.'

Ramirez took a few minutes to study the tracks, taking care to avoid disturbing them while he used Cruz's camera to take pictures. '*Hard to say for sure*,' he said at last, '*but my guess is that whoever left them behind wasn't bipedal*.'

'How do you figure that?' Harker gazed down at the alien footprints. 'They all look alike to me.'

'*Not quite. Look closer*.' He pointed to a set of four tracks that lay a little apart from the others, less than a half meter from the bottom of the ramp. '*See? The two up front are a little wider than the ones in back . . . like they carry most of the weight*.' Then he moved over the trail that preceded them, bending over to shine a flashlight on them. '*And look how unevenly these ones are arranged. Left, left . . . right, right . . . left, right . . . left, right . . . like someone came off the ramp, stepped aside for a moment, then walked over to the door*.'

'*Someone?*' Cruz stood on the other side of the footprints. '*You mean* something, *don't you?*'

'*No, I meant* someone.' Ramirez straightened up. '*The sooner you get past the idea that whoever left these behind are some sort of monsters, or whatever else you may think they are . . .*'

'*Don't patronize me*.'

'*Then use your head, and I won't*.' Ramirez turned toward Harker. '*And I wish you'd been a little more cautious. If you hadn't stomped around here so much, I might have been able to tell more. As it is, I can only hypothesize from what little I've found here*.'

'I'll keep that in mind.' Harker held his temper in

check. *Whenever I start to like this guy . . .* 'So what else have you been able to hypothesize? If that's not to much ask, that is.'

His sarcasm was lost on the astrobiologist. '*A little, but not much*,' Ramirez said, turning his light so that its beam slowly traveled from the ramp to the nearby hatch. '*Quadrupedal gait . . . an average distance of about sixty centimeters from one footprint to the next . . . oval impressions, with no clear marks around their edges . . . I'd say whoever came through here moved on four legs and wore a pressure suit of some sort.*'

'How do you figure that?'

'*You think they went outside naked?*' Ramirez walked over to the door to inspect once more. '*Not only that, but he or she . . . perhaps both, if they're asexual . . . is taller than we are. At a guess, I'd say . . . oh, just a little more than two meters.*'

'From the height of the panel, right?'

'*Correct. And from the diameter of this hatch. If it leads to an airlock, then it shouldn't be any larger than it needs to be, in order to conserve internal pressure.*' Ramirez shined his light on the panel. '*Can't read the inscriptions, of course*,' he continued, reaching up to it, '*but if we surmise that this controls the . . .*'

'Hold it!' Harker darted forward to grab his wrist. 'Let's not get carried away here.' He pulled Ramirez away from the panel. 'Emcee, have you been listening to all this?'

'*Roger that, Ted.*'

'Good. Very good.' Feeling his heart hammer at his chest, Harker nervously regarded the panel and the adjacent hatch. *If I had any common sense*, he thought, *I'd quit now, while I'm still ahead*. But his curiosity was greater than his fear. He swallowed, and went on. 'We're about to make an attempt to open the second hatch. If we get cut off, for any reason . . .'

'*Proceed with the mission.*' Emily was more calm than he was. Either that, or she was hiding her anxiety. '*Six hours. If I don't hear from you by then, I'll return to* Galileo *and fetch a rescue party.*'

'That's my lady.' All right, the backup plan was in place. Harker let go of Ramirez's wrist. 'Go on. Give it your best shot.'

'*Thank you.*' Ramirez hesitated, studying the panel for a moment. Then, very deliberately, he laid his right forefinger upon the panel's top left button and pressed it.

Nothing happened. '*All right,*' he said, '*let's try this one.*' He pushed the one to the top right.

Again, no response. '*Maybe this hatch is inactive,*' Cruz said.

'*I doubt it. The vents are still operational. And those footprints look fairly recent.*'

Harker pointed to the hatch lockplates. 'Maybe they're like the ones up top? We have to turn them in the same combination as before . . .'

'*No.*' Ramirez stepped back from the panel, as if to distance himself from the problem in order to solve it. '*This was clearly designed to be opened by one person alone. You can't do that and use the panel at the same time. Those plates are there for . . .*'

His voice trailed off. 'Emergency use?' Harker asked.

'*Yes. Exactly. But if there hasn't been an emergency, then the normal way to use this would be . . .*' He paused. '*Yes, of course. Like this . . .*'

Raising both hands, Ramirez pressed the top two

buttons simultaneously, then immediately pressed the bottom two.

Harker felt a faint vibration beneath the soles of his boots. Startled, he stepped back; the vibration suddenly ceased, and he looked around in time to see the door suddenly open, its flanges smoothly retracting into the wall.

'*Eureka!*' Cruz yelped.

Harker let out his breath. 'Nice trick,' he said. 'How did you figure that out?'

'*The trick is, you've got to think like someone with four hands.*' There was a note of self-satisfaction in Ramirez's voice as he stepped away from the panel. '*Door's open, gents. Let's go see what . . .*'

'*Not so fast.*' Standing a little apart from the others, Cruz stared up at the ceiling far above. '*I think we've got a problem.*'

Harker walked over to join him. Peering up through the well at the center of the spiral ramp, he felt his heart skip a beat. The surface hatch had shut, sealing them inside.

'Oh, hell. I don't like the looks of this. Emcee, do you copy?' No reply; he raised his voice. '*Maria Celeste*, this is the survey team. Please respond.' He waited a moment, but heard only the fuzz of carrier-wave static.

'*Let me try.*' Raising his left wrist, Cruz touched the controls of his suit radio. 'Maria Celeste, *do you copy?*' He waited a moment, then looked at Harker. '*No go. Hatch must be blocking our transmission.*'

'Figured this would happen sooner or later.' Harker noticed that the safety line was still dangling from the ramp where they'd left it. Walking over to it, he gave it an experimental tug, found that it was still firmly attached.

'At least it didn't sever the rope. A little good news. But I'd like to get that hatch open again.'

'*Don't count on it. Least not while this is open.*' While Harker and Cruz were talking, Ramirez walked over to the hatch. '*My guess is that they're set to operate in synchronicity,*' he continued, peering inside. '*The one up there won't open unless this one is shut, and vice versa. At least if this is what I think it is.*'

Harker followed Ramirez to the hatch. Their helmet lamps revealed a darkened chamber, its interior about twice the size of one of the staterooms aboard the *Galileo.* Although its walls, floor, and ceiling were made of the same dull grey metal as the door, otherwise it was featureless, save for gridlike apertures along its ceiling and, on the far wall, another circular hatch identical to the one they'd just opened. As before, a chevron-shaped panel was set within the wall next to the inner hatch.

An airlock, no doubt about it. And if that were so, then Ramirez's conjecture was entirely logical. If it didn't make sense for the airlock to be opened unless the surface hatch was shut, then the control panel would necessarily operate both at once. In that way, internal atmospheric integrity would be preserved.

By much the same token, there had to be some way of opening the airlock while the outer hatch was shut. And Harker wanted to open the surface hatch again before they went any farther; he didn't savor the notion of being trapped down there without any sure way of getting back out again. Besides, Emily was probably in a panic; he needed to let her know that they were all right.

The panel seemed relatively easy to use. All they had to do was figure out the correct combination that would open the surface hatch. Yet when he glanced around, he saw that Ramirez had already ventured into the airlock.

'Hey, get out of there,' Harker said. 'We need to . . .'

As abruptly as it had opened, the airlock's door shut. Harker caught one last glimpse of Ramirez before the flanges closed behind him.

'Jared!' he yelled, as once again he felt the strange tremor beneath his feet. 'Jared, can you hear me?'

For a moment, he caught Ramirez's voice in his headset – '*. . . going down . . .*'– and then his signal faded out.

'*What happened?*' Cruz came up behind him, grabbed his shoulder. '*Where's Ramirez?*'

'In there!' Helpless with frustration, Harker slammed his hand against the closed hatch. 'Goddamn idiot! He walked into that before . . . !'

'*What the hell was he . . . ?*'

'Okay. All right.' Feeling sick at his stomach, Harker reached out to prop himself up against the wall. *Deep breaths. Take deep breaths.* He shut his eyes for a moment, trying to calm down. 'All we have to do is figure out how to open the door, get him back out of there.'

'*I'm not sure, but I think it's more difficult than that.*'

'What do you mean?' Harker looked around; Cruz was standing close to him, his helmet lamps glaring through Harker's faceplate. 'What's more difficult? If it's just a matter of opening the airlock door again . . .'

'*It's not just an airlock. That's what I'm trying to tell you.*' Cruz stared at him, his eyes wide. '*Didn't you feel that vibration?*'

Harker pushed Cruz aside, blinked against the retinal afterimage of his helmet lights. Suddenly, everything fell into place. The tremor he'd felt before the hatch opened, and again after it shut. The interior of the compartment, the way that it was laid out. How Ramirez's last transmission had faded so quickly.

'Oh, God,' he muttered. 'It's an airlock, sure . . . but it's also a lift.'

'*An elevator. That's what I'm thinking, yes.*' Behind his faceplate, Cruz's expression became ashen. '*Then how do . . . how can we . . . ?*'

'Like you said. The same way we got it to open before.' His legs unsteady, Harker walked over to the control panel. This should be easy enough; he'd seen what Ramirez had done before. Push the two top buttons at once, then the two lower buttons. If they were right, and the airlock also functioned as a lift, then they'd know whether he'd made the correct guess when he and Cruz felt the vibration that had tipped them off in the first place.

And yet . . .

His hands wavered in front of the control panel. If he did this, or at least as immediately as his instincts told him that he should, he wouldn't be able to open the surface hatch again. Which meant that he wouldn't be able to resume radio contact with the shuttle. And that meant Emily wouldn't know what had happened to them. Or what he was about to do.

Damn! Although he was half-tempted to let Ramirez fend for himself, the fact of the matter was that, as expedition leader, he was responsible for the safety of his team. And while Captain Lawrence might have abandoned Ramirez, Harker couldn't see himself making that same sort of cold-blooded decision. Jared Ramirez might be a fool, but Harker couldn't simply cut him off.

'Sorry, Emcee,' he whispered. 'You're just going to have

to be patient with me.' And then he touched the buttons in what he hoped was the correct sequence and waited for the door to open again.

Fourteen

JANUARY 8, 2291 – SPINDRIFT

When the hatch closed behind him, Ramirez was caught by surprise. He'd just entered the airlock when Harker started to say something – '*Hey, get out of there, we need to . . .*' – yet as he turned to respond, he felt a sudden jolt . . .

And then the room began to fall.

The descent was so swift, so unexpected, that he lost his balance. Pitching forward, Ramirez barely had time to throw up his hands before he hit the floor. There was a red-hot jab in his left wrist; he yelped and rolled over on his side.

'*Jared!*' Harker's voice in his headset, fading with each passing moment. '*Jared, can you hear me?*'

'I hear you!' he yelled. 'I'm going down!' Clutching his sprained wrist, he struggled to his knees. For the first time, he saw that the hatch had shut. Perhaps he'd tripped a hidden sensor, or maybe the weight of his body on the floor was the reason. Whatever the cause, the result was just the same.

'Ted!' he yelled. 'Can you hear me?'

Nothing within his headset save for static. Yet the room was far from silent. He became aware of a low rumble that seemed to come from all around him. At the same time, it seemed as if he could see a little more clearly – within the metal walls, whorl-shaped patterns of light were slowly glowing to life – even as his faceplate began to fog over. As the rumble grew louder, he raised his right hand to his faceplate; his fingertips left transparent streaks across the surface.

The airlock also served an elevator, pressurizing as it descended. And that wasn't all. Flecks of black dust began to rise from his overgarment; as if caught within a miniature dust devil, they spiraled upward toward the ceiling. Electrostatic scrubbers, just like those at Dolland. Whenever this thing finally came to a halt, his suit would be thoroughly decontaminated . . .

So when was the ride going to end? Ramirez climbed to his feet. The roar gradually subsided; as it did, his faceplate became clear, save for a few smudged fingerprints. The compartment was pressurized, yet he could still feel a vibration beneath the soles of his boots. He was still going down . . . but how much farther? And how deep had he descended already? A few hundred meters? A few thousand? He had no way of knowing.

Ramirez was a lifelong atheist. His adherence to religious beliefs ceased about the same time his mind's eye opened to the enormity of the universe; there was no way any deity could be responsible for everything science had demonstrated was the result of natural forces. Despite his disdain for the supernatural, though, he found himself praying: *Oh, God, please get me out of this one. I don't want to die down here alone . . .*

And then the elevator stopped. Its arrival came as a quick, violent thump that threw him against the wall. He winced as pain shot through his left arm again. Nothing broken, but he'd need to see Jones once he returned to *Galileo*.

If he returned, that is . . . but the abrupt halt seemed enough like an answered prayer that he was able to entertain such a notion, if only for a second. *All right, I'm down*, he thought. *Now let's see if I can get out of* . . .

A hollow rasp from behind him. Turning around, Ramirez watched as the pie wedges of the airlock's aft hatch – forgotten until that moment – slowly retracted into their slots. Light from within the compartment fanned out across a tiled floor, dimly illuminating a wall about two meters away.

Ramirez took a deep breath. Then, having no other place left to go, he stepped into the unknown.

He found himself in a tunnel, black as a moonless night and seemingly without end. When he turned to the left, his helmet lamps revealed only a long cylindrical passageway, apparently excavated from solid rock, that appeared to go on forever. Turning to the right, he saw much the same thing. A barrel ceiling rose a half meter above his head; like the walls, it was segmented as a series of rings, with veinlike grooves forming horizontal patterns between them.

The darkness seemed to swallow the light from his helmet lamps. When he took a few steps, though, the grooves within the walls glowed to life, casting strange shadows across the floor. Looking down, he saw that it was comprised of a mosaic of randomly shaped plates, much like the ramp he'd descended from the outer hatch.

Ramirez realized that he could hear his own footfalls; apparently the tunnel was pressurized. He winced as he raised his left arm; after a minute of fumbling with the buttons on the wrist control unit, he managed to access the suit's atmospheric analysis system. Translucent figures appeared on his heads-up display, revealing the composition of the air around him. As he'd suspected, it was largely oxygen – why else would carbon dioxide be vented from Spindrift's interior? – but there was also a higher than normal concentration of nitrogen, along with trace amounts of argon, helium, and selenium. And the pressure was only 235.6 millibars, rarefied by Earth standards. He might be able to breathe . . . but only until decompression sickness killed him as surely as it would a deep-sea diver who had risen to surface too quickly. Best to leave his helmet shut.

Hearing a rasping sound, he looked around to see the hatch close behind him. Another faint rumble; he hoped the sound meant that the compartment was ascending. Perhaps Harker and Cruz had figured out how to operate the control panel that he'd unwisely ignored before venturing into the airlock. If so, it wouldn't be long before they came down to find him.

And if not . . .

He glanced at the heads-up again. A little more than six hours of air left in his suit. He'd either be rescued well before then, or he'd die down here alone, surrounded by an alien darkness. Despite his fear, Ramirez found himself vaguely amused by the prospect. If that happened, then at least he'd be following the footsteps of many great explorers. *Here lies the body of Jared Ramirez, discoverer of the first alien starship, only to perish in the name of science . . .*

'Hell with *that*,' he muttered. Common sense dictated that he should wait for the others to come to the rescue, but he wasn't inclined simply to stand around like an idiot. The tunnel had to lead somewhere; if he was going to die in this place, then he might as well satisfy his own curiosity.

Since there seemed to be no difference between the ends of the tunnel, he chose to go to the left. Before he went that way, he opened the cargo pockets of his overgarment and rummaged through them until he found a lightstick and a socket-wrench set. He broke the lightstick and placed it on the floor directly in front of the hatch, then carefully arranged the wrench and two of its heads beside the stick so that they formed a crude arrow pointing in the direction he'd decided to take. Not only that, but the stick would also serve as a beacon to lead him back to his starting point.

'Better than breadcrumbs,' he said aloud, trying to assuage his nerves. Then he ventured down the tunnel.

Although the floor was level, its uneven surface made walking difficult; several times, his toe would catch the raised edge of a plate, causing him to stumble. Apparently this suited Spindrift's inhabitants, but it made the going tough for a biped like himself. He'd walked less than ten meters before he realized that the walls within his immediate vicinity were emitting a weak, blood-hued radiance. When he turned to look back, though, he saw the section of the tunnel he'd left behind had gone dark once again; only the soft glow of his lightstick was visible. Whoever had built Spindrift evidently kept energy conservation in mind . . . and yet, the newfound awareness that some mechanism existed that was capable of tracking his movements, footstep by footstep, sent a chill down his spine. One way or another, his intrusion had not gone unobserved.

'Come out, come out, wherever you are,' he said softly, turning to continue down the tunnel. 'Marco . . . Polo. Marco . . . Polo . . .'

Silence, save for the soft hiss of his regulator, the dull tread of his boots upon the floor. Ramirez continued onward, moving his head back and forth so that the twin beams of his helmet lamps could sweep across the walls. Ring sections of the corridor lit up as he entered them, went dark again as soon as he passed through. As before, he was unable to discern an end to the tunnel; it seemed to stretch before him as a limitless passageway. Indeed, he had no idea in which direction he was . . .

'Stupid!' he said aloud, scolding himself. 'Of course you do!' Ramirez stopped to check his heads-up once more. There, in the upper right corner of his visor: the translucent circle of the suit's direction finder, depicting the compass point in which he'd been heading. Its red arrow showed that he was going almost exactly due north.

Seeing this, everything began to make sense. The carbon dioxide emissions *Galileo* had detected from orbit all lay within a central line of longitude, stretching north to south. Since he now understood that one of those emissions came from a hatch leading underground, then it only stood to reason that this tunnel would lead to . . .

Another vent? That would be the most logical conclusion. Yet if that were so, then the next vent would be . . . how far away? A hundred and fifty kilometers. A long march, even for someone with four legs.

No. It stood to reason that there had to be more there than merely a planetwide tunnel connecting one vent to another. They couldn't have been so lucky to have discovered, out of the eight vents *Galileo* mapped from orbit, the only one that also contained a hatch leading underground. Yet why hadn't he found anything else, or at least within this immediate area? Perhaps if he'd gone south instead . . .

Stop second-guessing yourself, he thought, shaking his head. *Go a little farther. If you don't find anything, you can always turn back. And besides, it wouldn't be a good idea to wander too far from the airlock. The others may arrive any minute.*

Or so he hoped. For years, Ramirez had found himself anxious to rejoin the human race. Through all his life, he'd hoped to discover someone better than his own kind. And now that he was on the verge . . .

So he continued down the tunnel, periodically looking back to make sure that he hadn't lost sight of his beacon. The lightstick had become a dim glimmer in the distance when he noticed that the wall to his right had begun to slope outward. The section he'd just entered became illuminated; that was when he found another passageway, its entrance formed by a funnel-like mouth leading to a further tunnel that branched off to the east.

Once again, he was struck by the almost organic design of the place. Save for the random-shaped plates of the floors and ramps, along with the pie-wedge segments of the hatches, he'd seen no right angles; everything else was rounded off and curved, almost biomemetic. He peered down the new passageway. It didn't seem to go very far; the beams of his helmet lamps settled upon its end, less than ten meters away, where another hatch was set within its wall.

Ramirez hesitated. In his haste to explore the tunnel,

he hadn't checked his suit's pedometer. Looking back at the distant lightstick, he estimated that it was little more than a hundred meters from where he was standing. Surely Harker and Cruz would be able to find him if they followed his marker . . . but why take a chance? He broke open another stick, and within his pockets he found a suit-patch kit and a couple of spare batteries. He was reluctant to leave them behind, yet his curiosity was greater than his need to take precautions; he arranged them on the tunnel floor so that they pointed toward the branch, then he entered the new passageway.

Its walls began to glow as soon as he passed the intersection. Now he could see the hatch more clearly. Like the others before, it was cut into four wedges, each with their own finger-hole lockplates. On the wall to the right was a chevron-shaped panel, with four recessed buttons. Another airlock? That didn't make sense; why put a second one so close to the first?

The new hatch had to lead somewhere else entirely. He was fresh out of breadcrumbs, though, and his luck was running thin. Nonetheless, he had to know where it went.

'If it's another airlock,' Ramirez murmured to himself, 'you are not stepping inside.' As he'd done before, he pressed the two top buttons, then the two lower ones.

He wasn't surprised when the flanges slid open, again with the muted, unoiled grind of ancient machinery. This time, though, the ambient light from the walls caught dust motes escaping from the interior, suspended in the air for a moment before slowly settling to the floor. Positive air pressure, he realized. Like a vault door being opened for the first time in ages. Feeling his heart hammering within his chest, he stepped away from the panel. Despite his earlier caution, he found himself compelled to approach the door . . .

'*Jared! Do you copy?*'

Harker's voice within his headset. Ramirez closed his eyes. Despite the relief he felt at having been found, for a moment he was tempted not to respond. The mystery was no longer his and his alone.

'Roger,' he said, 'loud and clear.' He tried to force some levity. 'What took you so long?'

'*For the love of* . . .' There was no mistaking the irritation in Harker's voice. '*Where the hell are you? Why didn't you stay where we could find you!*'

'Sorry. Got carried away there.' Ramirez let out his breath; to his surprise, he found that he was disappointed by the intrusion. 'Did you find my pointer? I left a light-stick on the . . .'

'*We found it, yeah.*' Cruz was only slightly less irate. '*Didn't anyone ever teach you to wait for the other guy if he gets hung up?*'

Turning away from the hatch, Ramirez gazed toward the intersection. Although the other two were still out of sight, he could see faint flashes of light upon the walls of the original tunnel. They were headed his way, all right. In only a few minutes they'd find him.

'Never mind that,' he said. 'Look, I'm pretty close to where you are now. Keep coming this way, then take a right when you find my patch kit. I'll wait here for you.'

'*Whatever you say.*' Harker's vocal tone had shifted to one of awe. '*What is this place? How long have you been down here?*'

'Long enough to find something you may want to see.' Ramirez couldn't help but grin. 'Hurry up. You're just in time.'

They stood just outside the open hatch and peered inside, careful not to cross the threshold until they had a good idea of what lay beyond.

Instead of another airlock, their helmet lamps revealed a circular room, so broad that they could barely discern the opposite wall. Within its center was a large, opaque sphere, positioned upon a slender pedestal and surrounded by a ring-shaped bench that encircled the orb without touching it. Projecting outward from the walls were shelflike structures, each tilted at an angle, that might be control consoles; arranged in front of them were low objects that could be furniture of some sort. To the right, near the far end of the room, lay yet another hatch.

'*And this one opened the same way as the others?*' Harker didn't wait for Ramirez to respond. '*At least they're consistent.*'

'Shouldn't be surprising, really.' Standing between him and Cruz, Ramirez used a flashlight to probe the room's interior. 'Sort of like a doorknob. The first time a small child finds one, he doesn't know what to do with it. After he sees an adult use it a few times, though, he gets the idea . . . and after that, all knobs are the same.' He pointed the light toward the hatch on the other side of the room. 'Bet you that one opens exactly the same way.'

'*Yeah, well, we're not going to find out standing here.*' Cruz started to move forward. '*I don't think this place is going anywhere. Let's . . .*

'Not so fast.' Ramirez pointed his light at the floor. Although it was comprised of the same random mosaic as the tunnels, he saw no indications of footprints. As he suspected, the airlock's electrostatic scrubbers had lifted away any regolith from the outside that would have left traces. There was nothing they could disturb. 'All right . . . after you.'

'*You found it first.*' Harker extended a hand.

Ramirez nodded, then stepped into the room, the others following close behind. As before, capillary-like grooves within the walls slowly glowed to life as soon as they entered, illuminating the interior with an amber radiance no brighter than that of a low-watt bulb.

'*Spooky, the way it does that,*' Cruz murmured. '*Like it knows we're here.*'

'Caused by some sort of motion detection system.' Ramirez pointed his light at the floor. 'Perhaps set off by our footsteps. Whenever you leave a certain area . . .'

'*The lights cut off again. We noticed.*' Harker turned toward the nearest wall. Above the shelflike console were oblong panels of some glassy substance that reflected his helmet lamps. '*Those could be comp screens.*'

Ramirez walked over to study the console. Nearly at the level of his chest, it was about the right place for a being two meters in height and was covered with buttons that had no regular shape but instead appeared to be molded in some random order: circles, ovoids, a few rectangles and hexagons here and there. Leaning closer, he saw that they were inscribed with the same patterns he'd seen before.

'*Don't touch anything,*' Harker said. '*You don't know what it might do.*'

'Oh, really . . .' On impulse, Ramirez reached out and depressed one of the buttons. As he expected, nothing happened. 'Uh-oh. I touched something . . .'

Harker glared at him. '*Don't you think you've caused enough trouble already?*'

'Commander . . .' Ramirez sighed. 'Look around you. It's a control center . . . either the main one or a secondary station. Maybe we can't tell what these instruments are for, but they're probably not all that different than the ones aboard *Galileo*. Not only that, but it's obvious that they've been shut down. We're not going to cause anything to blow up just by . . .'

'*Umm, gentlemen* . . .' Cruz said quietly. '*There's something here you might want to see.*'

He stood nearby, examining one of the low objects they'd spotted earlier. A piece of furniture, or at least it so appeared, considering its vicinity close to one of the consoles, yet unlike any they'd seen before. A narrow couch, elevated about a half meter above the floor, it had no obvious headrest, but instead dipped low in the middle and rose high at either end, its sides slightly folded over. Its shape reminded Ramirez of an enormous Chinese soup spoon.

'*What do you make of this?*' Cruz asked.

Walking closer, Ramirez gave the couch a closer inspection. Its interior was padded with something that, when he gently prodded it with his fingertips, felt like cheap vinyl filled with gelatin. And there seemed to be a narrow indentation within its middle, as if to accommodate some anatomical feature.

'This is how they sit,' he said. 'Belly down, I think, with their legs hanging over the sides.' He pointed to the end closer to the console. 'See? This half is just a little higher, like it's supposed to support the forward part of their bodies . . .'

'Where are you getting all this?' Harker asked. *'You're just guessing, aren't you?'*

'No. Not guessing . . . extrapolating.' He shook his head. 'Trying to piece together everything I've observed so far. Using my imagination a little . . .'

'A little.' Harker was plainly skeptical. *'Right . . .'*

'Yes, right.' Ramirez became irritated. 'And I was doing quite well, thank you, before you two showed up. Now are you going to let me do my job, or are you going to be another know-nothing like your captain?'

Harker stared at him for a moment. *'All right,'* he said at last. *'Do what you've got to do. Have fun. But we've got'* – he paused – *'two hours left before I call this off.'*

'Oh, *c'mon!*' Ramirez glanced at his heads-up. 'My suit says we've got five hours, ten minutes . . .'

'And I'm taking no more chances.' Harker held up two fingers. *'That long, then we head back. Understood?'*

'I'm with Ted,' Cruz said. *'Two hours, max. I don't want to get stuck down here.'*

Ramirez started to argue but realized that it was pointless. Like it or not, Harker had a point. Even though they'd be able to retrace their steps to the airlock, and had a good idea how to operate it, there was no guarantee that they wouldn't encounter more surprises. Even if nothing else went wrong, it would take at least an hour and a half, perhaps longer, to return to the shuttle.

'All right,' he said, surrendering to the inevitable. 'But at least give me a chance to look around some more.'

'Fine.' Harker seemed to relax a little. *'But no more*

wandering off by yourself. From now on, we stick together.'

'Agreed.' So now he was on the clock; two hours to investigate a puzzle that would take a lifetime to solve. Perhaps the next team would find a little more . . . yet he continued to harbor serious doubts whether another team would be sent. Lawrence was much too paranoid about the possibility of encountering hostile aliens, and Cole was more concerned about following instructions from his government than conducting a scientific expedition.

Two hours, he thought. *Make the best of it. You may never see this place again.*

Turning away from the couch, he gazed around the room. Where to start? The hatch they'd just found was an obvious choice, yet he doubted that Harker would agree to going off blindly to explore another underground section. But the sphere . . . there had to be a reason why it occupied a central position in this room.

He walked over to the ring-shaped rail that surrounded it. As he suspected, it was another console; its surface was tilted slightly forward, and was covered with more odd-shaped buttons. Ramirez pushed one at random; nothing happened. *Why a sphere?* So far as he could tell, it served no purpose, unless . . .

'Of course,' he murmured. 'That has to be it.'

'*Has to be what?*' Harker came over to join him. '*Y'know, we're not going to get very far if you don't tell us what you're thinking.*'

'Assume that I'm right, and Spindrift is a spacecraft . . .'

'*You've won that argument.*' Cruz had raised his camera again and was using it to take pictures of the couch and the consoles. '*That's pretty much a given.*'

'Very well, then assume that I'm also correct in

believing that this is some sort of control center.' Ramirez pointed at the sphere. 'If that's so, and given the size of this asteroid, wouldn't it make sense to have some means of displaying vital functions anywhere within the ship? A three-dimensional model of some sort?'

'*I'm having trouble with that idea.*' Harker gazed at the sphere. '*Look, I agree with the general concept, but this looks nothing like what we've seen from orbit. It's all smooth . . . no surface features.*'

'This may control that somehow.' Ramirez looked back down at the ring. As with the console he had examined earlier, the buttons had no obvious function; their inscriptions stood for something, of course, but were meaningless to human eyes. He was tempted to push buttons at random – some stroke of luck might cause him to enter the correct combination – yet he resisted the impulse to stab away at them blindly. 'Look for a pattern. Something that stands out . . .'

'*A pattern?*' Harker was dubious. '*Jared, this place was designed by aliens. I don't . . .*'

'Try to pretend you're one of them.' Ramirez slowly walked around the ring, letting the beams of his helmet lamps drift across the console. 'You're the first officer of a starship, aren't you? Try to put yourself in the mind of someone like you, but not *exactly* like you. You've got four hands, four feet . . .'

'*This one's different.*' Unnoticed by either of them, Cruz had walked around to the other side of the sphere. '*It's round, and pretty large.*'

Ramirez went over to join him. As he indicated, one of the buttons formed a perfect circle. Larger than the others around it, it was positioned in the center of that section of the ring. Reaching forward, Ramirez pushed it.

Harker gasped, and Ramirez looked up to see that the sphere had suddenly become transparent.

Where there had once been an opaque, featureless surface were now layers of some crystalline substance, illuminated by whisker-fine threads of light that revealed the details within its depths. At first he thought it was a holographic projection, until he realized that what he was seeing wasn't an illusion formed by focused light but instead the result of a infinitely precise arrangement of fiber-optic filaments suspended within an immense globe.

'*It's beautiful*,' Harker whispered, clearly awestruck.

It was, indeed: a mammoth sculpture rendered by inhuman hands. Yet it wasn't simply an object to be adored, but rather a tool with a clear and definite purpose. The sphere's outermost shell, tinged reddish brown and riddled with craters and low hills, duplicated the pockmarked surface of Spindrift.

'*Is this what I think it is?*' Cruz asked.

'If you're thinking it represents Spindrift,' Ramirez replied, 'then I'd say you're absolutely correct.'

'*A three-dimensional map*.' Harker slowly walked around the sphere, staring at it with fascination. '*It's like this entire thing has been hollowed out*.'

'That should be obvious by now, shouldn't it?' Ramirez paid little attention to him. He'd spotted the locations of the vent craters, arranged in a vertical band that encircled the sphere from north to south. One of them, located almost precisely at the equator, glowed a little more brightly than the rest; beneath the surface, an orange line descended about a centimeter before it intercepted a horizontal line that traced upward, to the north, until it took a slight bend to the east and stopped at a red spot.

'This must be where we came in,' he said, pointing to the glowing crater and the lines beneath it. 'See, here's the route we took down here . . .'

'*Damn*,' Cruz murmured, looking at it more closely. '*You're right*.' He glanced at Ramirez. '*This thing must have been tracking our movements ever since we came down here. I don't like that very much*.'

Ramirez didn't reply, but he had to agree. Even if Spindrift was a relic of some sort, its instrumentation was less dormant than he'd previously suspected. And if this asteroid – this ship – was aware that intruders were aboard . . .

'*Bugger that*.' Harker was on the opposite side of the globe. '*Look at this over here*.'

Ramirez looked at what caught Harker's attention. Beneath the immense equatorial crater they had seen from orbit, a caldera funneled deep within the sphere until it ended in an enormous, red-tinted cylinder. Surrounding it were vast ovoid cavities, tinted blue-green, with tiny threadlike lines leading to a yellow sphere nestled at the globe's center. The entire structure took up half of the interior, and was separated from the other half by a thick, reddish-brown band he believed to represent solid rock.

'Probably the engine,' Ramirez said. 'Fusion, most likely . . . those blue areas around it may be fuel tanks, with the reactor located at the core.'

Harker tore his eyes away from the globe. '*Since when did you earn a degree in engineering?*'

'To move something this big, you'd have to turn half of it into a colossal engine. Only makes sense.' He returned his attention to the entrance crater and the levels below it. 'Right now, though, I'm less interested in its propulsion system than in what it's supposed to be moving.'

'*For Christ's sakes, guys.*' Cruz slowly walked around the globe, taking pictures from every angle. '*You've found something like this, and you're going to stand around and argue?*'

'*You're right.*' Harker moved back to where Ramirez stood. '*We need to take this one step at a time.*' He pointed to the glowing lines. '*All right, so that's where we are now. Where do we go from here?*'

Ramirez said nothing as he peered into the globe's crystal interior. Beneath the point where their underground route came to an end, there appeared to be a deep shaft, tinted aquamarine, that led almost all the way down to the asteroid's core. Similar shafts lay at fixed locations beneath the other vents. Fanning out from the core, they were separated from one another by dense areas of reddish-brown rock. Taking a few steps to the right, he saw that these vertical shafts formed a pinwheel shape, like a ferris wheel hollowed out within Spindrift's mantle.

'There's something just below us,' he said, pointing to the globe. 'It goes down pretty deep, and there's seven more just like it, each beneath one of the vent craters.' He looked at Harker. 'I'd say they're what we're looking for.'

'*You're sure of this?*' Harker gazed first at the globe, then at the closed hatch on the other side of the room. '*You think that's the way down?*'

'Makes sense that it would be.' Ramirez stepped back from the ring, turned his helmet lamps upon the hatch. 'We've got another hour and a half before your deadline. We can spend it poking around here, or we can see if my guess is correct.' He paused. 'You're in charge, of course. Your decision.'

For a moment, Harker seemed reluctant. Ramirez knew that he was faced with a tough choice: play it safe, or take a chance. He waited, preparing himself to engage in another debate, and finally Harker let out his breath.

'*All right, we'll take a quick look . . . but that's as far as we go.*' He turned to Cruz. '*You agree?*'

'*Turn back now, after all this?*' A short laugh from Cruz as he put away his camera. '*Let me at it. I'll tear the door open with my teeth if I have to.*'

Ramirez found himself smiling. 'Don't think you'll need to go that far. It probably opens just the same way.'

To no one's surprise, he was correct. The panel to the right of the hatch operated exactly like the ones they'd found before; the near-simultaneous depression of four buttons caused the quadrant of wedge-shaped flanges to split apart and retract into the walls. Once again their helmet lamps revealed a spiral stairwell, this one steeper than the one before, leading down into the darkness.

This time, though, they didn't have a rope. Harker was reluctant to make a descent without a safety line, yet he agreed with Ramirez and Cruz that they'd have to take a chance. Now that they knew what to expect, the stairs shouldn't be too hard to handle, so long as they were careful.

Cruz insisted upon going first. '*Hey, I'm tired of being*

the last guy down,' he said. '*You two are getting all the fun*.' Harker was hesitant, but the geologist remained adamant, so he finally agreed to let Cruz lead the way.

That was a fatal error.

Fifteen

JANUARY 9, 2291 – EAS *MARIA CELESTE*

Four . . . three . . . two . . . one . . .

Counting down the seconds, Emily watched the chronometer as it changed from 11:59:59 to 00:00:00. Midnight, at least by shiptime; another day had come to Spindrift. Not that she perceived any difference; beyond the cockpit windows, the asteriod's coal-black surface remained as bleak and lightless as before. No telling how long it had been since the last time this tiny world had experienced a sunrise. Centuries? Millennia?

Who gives a damn? She stared out the windows from where she sat in the pilot's seat. She restlessly crossed her legs, ignoring the ebook she'd been trying to read for the last few hours. *This place can rot for all I care . . . when am I going to hear from Ted again?*

Emily glanced at the mission clock, located on the panel beneath the chronometer. Two sets of digits were displayed; one read 16:39:22 – the hours, minutes, and seconds that had elapsed since the *Maria Celeste* had departed from *Galileo*; and the other read 03:20:24 – the amount of time that had gone by since Ted, Jared, and Jorge left the shuttle for their second EVA. She told herself that she shouldn't be so nervous – after all, they still had four hours and forty minutes of air left in their suits – yet the fact remained that it had been nearly two and a half hours since she'd lost contact with the team, and she had no idea why the loss-of-signal event had lasted so long.

'Damn it, Ted . . . don't do this to me!' In frustration, she threw the datapad at the center window. It made a dull clunk as it bounced off the thick pane and landed, as fate would have it, in the copilot's seat, where Ted had been sitting only a little while ago. Emily stared at it for a minute, absently nibbling at her fingernails before she realized what she was doing and self-consciously removed her hand from her mouth. She'd never wanted to admit to herself that she was in love with him, that their relationship was more than a sly affair among shipmates. Yet now that he was gone . . .

What the hell's going on down there? Once again, she reviewed everything she'd heard over the comlink. They'd managed to open the hatch, found a ramp leading into a deep shaft. They'd descended down it, using a safety line Ted had rigged on the surface. At the bottom of the hatch, they'd discovered what seemed to be alien footprints, along with another hatch with some sort of control panel next to it. Ramirez was trying to figure out how it worked . . .

And then, silence.

It wasn't quiet up here, though. The Mare Crisium Opera's performance of Glass's *Einstein on the Beach*, which she'd put on in an attempt to soothe her nerves, had become irritatingly metronomic. She slapped it off, then, on sudden impulse, bolted from her seat and stalked down the aisle to the aft cabin. Her first thought was to brew another cup of coffee – as if she'd hadn't had enough already – but instead she found herself standing in front of an unopened suit locker, contemplating the helmet strapped to the rack above it. In ten minutes, she could suit up, depressurize the airlock, go outside . . .

No. Ted's orders were strict. By no means was she to leave *Maria*. Even if there was an emergency, she was supposed to remain aboard and report back to *Galileo*. It was Captain Lawrence's decision whether to order a rescue mission; if that were to happen, her prime responsibility as shuttle pilot would be to facilitate the recovery effort.

Emily glanced again at the chronometer – 00:06:21. *Galileo* should be in range, its new orbit once again bringing it above the local horizon. Ted would probably be infuriated with her, of course – after all, Lawrence had told him that he and the others could go EVA again only to retrieve their equipment – but the situation had become critical. Like it or not, she needed to inform the captain that the team had gone missing.

She was halfway back down the aisle, though, when carrier-wave static crackled through her headset. A brief electronic warble, then she heard Arkady's voice: '. . . *to* Maria Celeste, *do you copy?* . . . *Repeat*, Galileo *to* Maria Celeste, *do you copy . . . ?*'

Emily nudged her mike wand. '*Galileo*, this is *Maria Celeste*. Good to hear from you. I was just about to . . .'

A sudden squeal, as if something was interfering with the communication channel. Beneath this, she made out Arkady's voice: '. . . *respond . . . unusual . . . are you . . . ?*'

What the hell? Taking her seat again, Emily reached up to the com panel and boosted the gain. 'Copy, *Galileo*. Reception is faint. Raise your signal, please. I can barely hear you.'

Another sharp squeal, then fuzz. Unintelligible voices, some not belonging to Arkady. A loud, abrupt snap, like a twig being broken, followed by a prolonged hiss. Then Arkady's voice came through again, muted yet distinct. 'Maria Celeste, *this is* Galileo. *If you can hear me, please respond.*'

'We read you, *Galileo.*' Emily clasped the headset against her ears, then reached up to raise the volume as high as she could. 'Is there a problem up there?'

'*Affirmative.*' Arkady sounded tense. '*Going visual. I'll keep this channel open until you've opened the secondary channel.*'

'Copy that.' Emily frowned as she bent forward to switch on the screen. Until now, they'd kept the second comlink channel a secret; if Arkady was speaking of it openly, then there had to be something he felt she needed to see.

For a few moments, the screen revealed nothing but snow. The interference had returned. Arkady said something indistinct; in the background, she could make out voices shouting to one another. For a second, she thought she heard Lawrence – '*. . . aft thrusters . . . !*' – before the rest was lost within the cacophony.

Then the screen cleared, and she saw Arkady in extreme close-up. Although his face was grossly distorted by the fish-eye lens, there was no trace of his characteristic humor; she was startled to see fear in his eyes.

'*Are you getting this?*' he asked. Without waiting for a response, he disappeared from sight, and then she had an unimpeded view of Galileo's command center.

Lawrence had risen from his seat. Grasping the side of his chair for support, he yelled at Simone – '*Back away! Back away!*' – who was hunched over the helm console as if struggling for control. Emily caught a glimpse of Antonia rushing toward the camera; she blocked the view for a moment as she stopped at Arkady's station – '*Try another frequency! Try to get through!*' – then Lawrence turned to shout at her – '*Get back to your station, damn it!*' – and she disappeared.

'Arkady . . .' Emily tried to remain calm, even though it was obvious that havoc was breaking loose up there. 'Arkady, what's going on?'

No response, although she could hear his voice as if he was addressing someone else on another channel: '*This is the EASS* Galileo *. . . repeat, this is the EASS* Galileo. *We're a . . . we're a ship from Earth, engaged in peaceful scientific exploration . . .*'

Who's he trying to talk to? Emily saw Cole move toward Lawrence. He grabbed the captain's arm, started to say something, but Lawrence angrily shoved him aside and continued to yell at Simone, his words incoherent amid the chaos that gripped the bridge.

'Rusic, answer me!' Emily shouted. 'What the hell's going on?'

An instant of static, then Arkady's voice came back online: '*I'm trying to . . . hold on . . .*'

A window opened at the upper right quadrant of the screen: a probe's-eye view through one of Jerry's cameras, probably the same as the flight crew had on their screens at this very instant. In the background, she could make out the silver ring of the starbridge, yet that wasn't what caught her attention, but instead the shape that loomed before it.

An alien starship.

The moment she saw it, Emily knew what it was. Streamlined, almost aquatic in form, the vessel was unquestionably extraterrestrial in origin. Within the front of its tapered bow, light gleamed from dozens of slitted portholes, while an orange radiance emitted from bulges along its flanks. Although it was nearly impossible to put any sense of scale to the thing, nonetheless she had the impression that it was as large as the *Galileo*, if not larger.

On the left side of the screen, Rauchle came into view. Stepping around Cole, he shouted at Lawrence: '*Don't fire! For God's sake, don't fire until we . . . !*'

The captain waved him off, then turned to the right, where Martin sat at his console. '*Mr Cohen, arm the warhead! Ready torpedo for launch on my command!*'

'*Ship continuing approach!*' This from Antonia. '*No reply to . . . !*'

'*Warhead armed, sir!*' Martin's gaze was fixed upon the screens above his station. '*Torpedo ready for launch!*'

Oh, Christ, no! 'Arkady, stop him!' Emily yelled. 'You've got to . . .'

Rauchle grabbed Lawrence by the shoulder. '*Stop! You don't have to . . . !*'

Lawrence pushed him aside. '*Mr Cohen! Launch!*'

'*Aye, sir!*' Martin stabbed at a switch on his panel. '*Torpedo away!*'

'Oh, no . . .' Emily shook her head in disbelief. 'Oh, no . . . God, no. Arkady, tell me this isn't . . .'

'*You goddamn fool!*' Cole came at Lawrence again. He grabbed the captain by his shoulders, flung him into his seat. '*We could have . . . !*'

'*Range to target, ninety-five kilometers.*' Martin's voice was oddly calm, almost as if he was reciting a math equation. '*Ninety kilometers . . . eighty-five . . .*'

'*Abort!*' Rauchle turned to yell at Cohen. '*Abort, damn you! Abort!*'

'*Receiving transmission!*' Arkady snapped. '*I . . .*'

'*Oh, hell, no!*' Martin started to rise from his seat. '*Captain, it's . . .*'

Emily caught a last glimpse of the command center as a white-hot burst of light surged through the windows. She had the impression of Simone – sweet, soft-spoken Simone Monet – throwing her hands across her face as she fell back in her seat, screaming in terror as she was blinded.

Then the screen went blank as an earsplitting screech came through Emily's headset.

An instant later, a false dawn rose upon Spindrift.

Raising her head, Emily stared through the cockpit windows at the miniature supernova that blossomed into existence above the dark horizon. It briefly illuminated distant hills, then quickly faded, snuffed out by the interstellar vacuum.

The *Galileo* was gone.

Emily didn't know how long she sat in the cockpit, trembling with a chill that cut straight to the bone. Even when she shut her eyes, the retinal afterimage remained, just as horrible as the first time she saw it. At some point, she raised a hand to her headset, intending to say what she thought should be said – *do you copy*, Galileo*? this is* Maria Celeste, *please respond* – but when she touched her mike, all that came from her throat was a dry rasp.

Get a grip, a small voice said to her from the depths of her consciousness. *There's nothing you can do for them. You've got to move on.*

But I can't. Tears slipped from the corners of her eyes; she squeezed them tight and let her head fall back against the seat. *All those people . . . Arkady, Nick, Toni, Simone . . . my crewmates, my friends, they're all dead . . .*

Yes, they're dead. The voice was solemn, not without remorse yet nonetheless pragmatic. *Do you want to join them?*

'Yes,' she whispered. 'I mean, I . . .'

No, you don't. The voice became stern. *You know why? Because you've got three more lives depending on you, and if you let them down, then Ted and those other two guys are going to die, too . . .*

'But we're all . . . we're . . .'

Going to die anyway? Maybe, but you're still breathing, aren't you? So suck it in, open your eyes, and do whatever it takes to keep yourself and the others alive.

Emily opened her mouth, filled her lungs with air, slowly let it out. She did it again and again until she finally managed to stop shaking. A little calmer, she opened her eyes and ran the back of her hand across her face, wiping away the tears as best she could.

'All right, Emcee,' she murmured. 'You've had your panic attack. Now let's see about getting out of this pretty little fix you're in.'

First priority was survival. Standing up on legs that still felt unsteady, she hobbled over to the life-support panel above the copilot's seat and checked the readout. Enough air left for another 152 hours at normal rate of consumption for four people; ditto for water, so long as the recycling system remained operational. Eventually shortages would become a problem, but she deliberately pushed what would happen six days from now to the back of her mind. She'd have to worry about that later.

The nuclear batteries were good for an almost indefinite

period – in theory, at least a century – but that was at levels of minimal energy consumption. So it made sense to shut down all nonessential systems, and switch the rest to low-power mode. As a first step, she lowered the thermostat to 18.3°C and made a note to herself to put on a warm-up jacket before too long. The rest would come once she consulted her checklist and made decisions as to what systems were or were not necessary.

All right, so she would live, or at least for another six days or so. Second priority was security. Something up there had destroyed her ship. Although Emily had little doubt that *Galileo*'s own nuclear torpedo was the primary cause – the explosion had occurred too soon after Lawrence had ordered its launch to be mere coincidence – it only stood to reason that the alien vessel had something to do with it. Which meant that she was dealing with a possible – no, make that a *probable* – adversary.

She had no idea what its capabilities were, but she had to consider the fact that it might be able to locate the *Maria Celeste*. Realizing this, she swore under her breath, then reached up to an overhead panel and hastily switched off the floodlights, followed by the red and green formation lights. As an afterthought, she turned down the interior lights, leaving the cockpit and aft section dark save for the wan glow of the comp screens and emergency lamps. There was nothing she could do about emissions from the shuttle's radiators or its carbon dioxide vents; with any luck, though, they would be masked by those from Spindrift itself. Thank heavens she'd moved the shuttle closer to the crater.

Which led to her third, but no less important, priority: the three men on the surface. Or rather, beneath the surface. Once again, Emily gazed through the cockpit windows at the nearby crater, its outer wall discernible only as a blackness rising against the star-flecked horizon. Ted probably had no clue as to what had just happened; if he had, she would've heard from him already. As it stood, though, she had no way of making contact with him, or at least until the outer hatch opened again.

Not only that, she suddenly realized, but it was also possible that any radio transmissions on the surface might be picked up from orbit. If something out there was searching for them, then any attempt to reach the survey team could lead the aliens straight to her. She dared not take that risk.

So now she faced an immediate decision. She could suit up, leave *Maria*, climb over the crater wall, and enter the hatch the others had found. Perhaps even make the perilous descent down the ramp, even though she had little idea of what lay at the bottom of the entrance shaft. Or she could remain where she was, to mind the fort – which, metaphor aside, was exactly what the shuttle had become – and wait for the survey team to reappear.

Every impulse told her to go after them. She didn't want to be left alone, not after this. Standing up again, she started to head aft, where the suit lockers and airlock lay, only to stop before she was halfway across the cockpit. Ted had given her orders to remain aboard, no matter what. *She's our lifeline*, he'd said. *Without her, we're not going home.*

'Oh, God,' she murmured, shutting her eyes and rubbing her temples with her fingers. 'Don't do this to me.'

Don't panic. Once more, the small, calm voice returned.

You won't help Ted if you lose your wits. Just do what he told you to do, and you'll be fine.

She let out her breath, forced herself to sit down again. However much she hated to do so, she'd have to wait, alone and in the dark, if only for a little while longer.

In whatever lonely place her love now walked, he'd have to walk without her.

Sixteen

JANUARY 9, 2291 – SPINDRIFT

The staircase they'd found in the control room was steeper than the one leading down from the entrance hatch, its platelike risers more narrow. At least it wasn't suspended within an empty shaft, though, but instead spiraled down through solid rock. Yet the walls didn't light up as they'd done before; although random-patterned grooves had been cut into the stone, for some reason they remained dark after the three men entered the stairway.

That alone made Harker more wary than before. It was as if whoever had designed Spindrift had deliberately made it more difficult for someone to explore its lower levels. Or perhaps there was another reason why this part of the underground should remain unlit. Either way, he was beginning to think that it might be better to quit while they were ahead and instead begin retracing their steps to the surface. But he didn't want to have another quarrel with Ramirez, and Cruz was equally insistent that they see what lay beneath the control room, or whatever it was.

That wasn't all, though, was there? *Admit it*, he said to himself. *You want to find out what's down here just as much as they do. Turn back now, and you'll regret it for the rest of your life.*

So, against his better judgment, he allowed Cruz to lead the way down the staircase. The geologist took his time, careful to look where he put his feet before he took each step, bracing his hands against the curved walls on either side of them. With Ramirez bringing up the rear, they slowly made their way down the stairs, the beams of their helmet lamps dancing ahead of them.

They'd descended less than thirty meters before the staircase abruptly ended in yet another circular hatch. By then, they'd all become accustomed to operating the control panels that lay to the right of the portals; this time, though, there was no place for two of them to stand while the third person opened the door. Another weird difference. Until then, everything had become relatively familiar, almost repetitious. And now this . . .

But that wasn't enough reason to make them retreat, so Harker remained on the stairs, with Ramirez just behind him, while Cruz simultaneously depressed the four buttons. Again, the door's pie wedges split apart. With a faint grinding noise, they receded into the walls, and before them lay . . .

Darkness. An expanse of fathomless black void, with nothing on the other side that their helmet lamps could reach. The only thing visible was the floor on the other side of the hatch – once again, covered with the same irregular mosaic that they'd found earlier – and even that seemed to come to a sudden end less than three meters away. Beyond its edge lay only empty space.

'*I don't get it*,' Cruz said, standing just outside the hatch. '*There's nothing here but . . . nothing.*'

'*The globe showed that this leads to some sort of shaft.*' Ramirez peered over Harker's shoulder to see what they were seeing. '*I think we're looking at it. If my guess is correct, we should be at the top.*'

The chill that ran up Harker's back was becoming more than he could handle. 'All right, gentlemen,' he said, 'enough is enough. We're heading back.'

'*Like hell.*' Cruz's voice was sharp with excitement. '*Sorry, but I'm not giving up until I find out what this is all about.*'

'Jorge, wait!' Harker snapped. 'Don't . . . !' He raised his hand, but before Harker could stop him, Cruz stepped through the hatch.

Harker had no choice but to follow him. Stepping off the bottom riser, he went through the hatch after Cruz. The geologist was only a couple of meters ahead. He'd come to a halt near the visible edge of the floor, and was bending forward slightly as if to look down at something.

'*Oh, my God,*' he murmured, taking another step forward. '*I don't believe . . .*'

Harker couldn't tell exactly what happened next. Perhaps the toe of Jorge's boot snagged against the edge of the raised plates on the floor's mosaic surface, causing him to stumble. Whatever the reason, Cruz abruptly lost his balance, started to pitch forward.

He yelled as he instinctively raised his hands as if to catch himself. But there was no protective rail for him to fall against; the four-legged denizens of Spindrift were apparently so surefooted that they had no need for that sort of thing. For a moment, his arms pinwheeled as he helplessly flailed at emptiness.

And then Cruz toppled over the edge into darkness.

'Jorge!' Harker started to rush after him. 'Jorge . . . !'

'*Stop!*' Ramirez grabbed him from behind, pulled him back before he could commit the same mistake. Yet this couldn't prevent Harker from hearing Cruz's scream within his headset, a high-pitched cry of pure terror that seemed to last forever.

'Jorge!' Harker fought against Ramirez, struggling to pull free. 'Oh, Christ, Jorge . . . !'

From somewhere far below, he caught the flash of Cruz's helmet lamps, briefly reflecting off the shaft walls, before fading from sight.

'Jorge!' he shouted again.

The scream should have ended. Instead, it went on, and on, and on, a horrible, desperate cry that didn't end until Harker heard an abrupt, sickening crunch within his headset. The light vanished, and he heard only silence.

'Jorge!' He started to lurch forward. 'Oh, my God, no! Jorge . . . !'

'*Stop it!*' Ramirez shook him roughly, not letting him go. '*There's nothing you can do! He's gone!*'

Tears stung the corners of his eyes; Harker reached up to wipe them away, only to rediscover the faceplate in the way of his hand. His breath came as ragged gasps that burned his lungs; acidic bile rose within his throat, and he was barely able to choke it back down. Ramirez gently released him, allowing him to fall to his hands and knees; Harker slumped there for a couple of minutes, struggling to regain control of himself.

At long last, he clambered to his feet and, with great caution, approached the place where Cruz had fallen. He saw what Cruz had glimpsed in his last moments of life: a vast pit, apparently bottomless, that yawned open beyond the platform upon which he and Ramirez were standing. At least sixty meters across; the light from his helmet lamps barely reached the other side.

With trembling hands, Harker pulled out a lightstick. Breaking it, he tossed it over the side. The stick fell past level upon level upon level of ramps that spiraled downward, each without protective railing of any kind; that gradually funneled down toward an invisible floor that lay hundreds, perhaps even thousands, of meters below them. Or at least so it seemed; the stick disappeared from view without ever reaching bottom.

What the hell was this place? Pulling out a flashlight, he aimed its beam straight ahead. Along the walls of the pit, evenly spaced from one another, lozenge-shaped blisters reflected its glow. There seemed to be thousands – no, tens of thousands – of them. Almost as if this was . . .

A hive. That was the only description that came to mind. An enormous hive, as seen from the inside.

'*Look at it*,' Ramirez murmured, quiet awe in his voice. '*The sheer scale of engineering . . . it's magnificent.*'

'Magnificent?' Something in the way Ramirez spoke turned Harker's grief to anger. 'We just lost a man, for the love of . . .' A sudden thought occurred to him. 'We've got to find him. Even if he's dead, we need to . . .'

'*Are you crazy?*' Ramirez stared at him. '*You see how deep this goes . . . maybe even to the core itself. No way we can reach him . . . not with the time we have left, at least.*'

Like it or not, Ramirez was right. A quick glance at his helmet's heads-up display told Harker that they had little more than four hours of air left in their suits. 'Yeah, okay,' he muttered, slowly letting out his breath. 'Nothing we can do for him now.' He turned toward the hatch behind them. 'Better head back . . .'

'*Not so fast.*' Ramirez pointed toward to the left; at the end of the platform lay the top of the ramp they'd seen a moment ago. '*This pit must have been built for some reason. We should try to figure out what it is.*'

'Jared . . .' Harker began, but Ramirez was already walking down the ramp, his helmet lamps illuminating the rock wall on its left side. Harker quickly broke another lightstick and placed it on the floor beside the stairway hatch, then followed him, careful to avoid getting close to the ramp's unprotected edge. 'We don't have time for this. There's nothing we can find that'll make any . . .'

'*I don't agree . . . and I think I just found it.*' Ahead of him, Ramirez came to a halt. His lamps revealed one of the ovoid bulges Harker had glimpsed earlier. '*Come look at this,*' he added, his voice dropping to a near whisper. '*Tell me you're seeing what I'm seeing.*'

Harker cautiously walked down the ramp until he stopped beside him. The blister was nearly three meters in height, and seemed to grow out from the wall itself like an obscene tumor. Composed of some transparent substance, it appeared to be filled with a thick, reddish-orange liquid; tiny lights glowed from panels on either side of it. And suspended within the cell . . .

At first glance, he thought it was an enormous insect. Two meters in height, almost delicate in form, its elongated head resembled that of a cricket or a locust, with two bulbous, lidless eyes – no, there were at least two more, arranged on either side of its slender skull – that seemed to peer back at him from above a narrow snout. The creature's head, which rested on top of a long, thin neck, was tucked in toward its thorax, which appeared to be plated with a chitinous exoskeleton.

'*Biostasis of some sort . . . look, see?*' Ramirez pulled out a flashlight, aimed it into the cell. Rubbery tubes ran from the bottom of the creature's snout to the cell's inner casing. '*A respirator, much like we have aboard* Galileo. *Their bodily functions have been slowed down, but they're still breathing, with carbon dioxide vented to the surface. The fluid . . .*'

'Right. Sure.' Harker was paying more attention to the rest of the alien. Four arms, double-jointed and in two distinct sets – the ones on top slightly longer than the ones beneath them – were folded together across the alien's chest. He wasn't surprised to see that each arm ended in a three-fingered claw. Below the lower set of arms, the creature's thorax tapered to a narrow waist, then expanded once more to form a thick abdomen, shaped somewhat like a chili pepper, that was curled upward and inward. The creature was floating within the cell, weightlessly suspended by the dense fluid, much as he himself had been during *Galileo*'s long journey to this place.

'*Quadrupedal stance . . . see?*' Ramirez aimed his light at the two sets of legs that curled inward from the alien's thorax. '*Notice how the forelegs are backward-jointed, while the hind legs are forward-jointed? That would give them great stability.*' He glanced back at the edge of the ramp. '*No wonder they don't need guardrails. The floors and stairways are designed for four legs, not two.*'

Harker said nothing. Despite everything they'd seen so far, he'd half expected Spindrift's builders to be human-like enough for him to be able to relate to them. This damned thing was a monstrosity, a horror wrenched from his worst nightmare, so far beyond his imagination that he couldn't help but regard it with revulsion. Looking away from the cell, he saw another cell just like this one. Only a few meters away was another, and another, and another, and another . . .

'How many of them are there?' he asked, even though he already knew the answer.

'*Thousands?*' Ramirez shined his light down the ramp. '*Hundreds of thousands? And from what we saw on the globe, this is just one pit . . . there are seven more just like it.*' A nervous laugh. '*There may be millions of them down here. Asleep for who knows how long.*'

Ramirez was aching to continue their exploration. One look at him, and Harker knew that, if he didn't put a stop to this immediately, Ramirez's insatiable curiosity would lead them even farther into Spindrift's depths. 'All right, that's it,' he said, backing away from the blister. 'We're done here. Time to head back.'

'*You can't be serious.*' Through his helmet faceplate, Ramirez's expression registered astonishment. '*Ted, please . . . we've found something no one has seen before. We can't just . . .*'

'We've seen enough . . . and Jorge paid for that.' Harker pointed toward the lightstick a few meters away. 'Cole and Rauchle and the rest of the team can take it from here, for all I care. I just want to get back to the shuttle and . . .' He shook his head within his helmet. 'I don't know. Get sick or something.'

He turned away, heading toward the wan glow of the lightstick. After a moment, Ramirez followed him, if only reluctantly. At that moment, Harker didn't care whether he came along or not. If the price of knowledge was the life of someone as blameless as Jorge Cruz, then perhaps ignorance was a reasonable alternative.

Either way, he just wanted to get out of there.

Harker was surprised to see how easy it was for them to

find their way out of Spindrift and how soon they were able to make their way back to the surface.

The staircase leading up from the pit was the most difficult part. He and Ramirez had to help each other climb the chaotically arranged steps, which they now understood were meant to be used by insectlike creatures with two pairs of legs. But once they reached the room at the top of the stairs – which Ramirez now believed was the control center for this one particular biostasis area – it was a simple matter of following the lightsticks they'd left behind until they found the airlock.

They were careful to enter the compartment at the same time. Once again, unseen sensors registered their presence and automatically shut the hatch behind them. The ascent was just as swift as the descent; the airlock depressurized on the way up, and by the time they reached the entrance shaft, Harker's head-up display told him they'd returned to hard vacuum. Somewhere behind them must be a locker where the aliens stowed their version of EVA suits, but that would be something the next team would have to find. Just then, all he wanted to do was get back to the *Maria Celeste*.

Even so, once the elevator doors opened, Harker deliberately avoided treading upon the alien footprints they'd found on the floor at the bottom of the shaft. If Ramirez was correct, then they'd been left behind uncounted ages ago. Perhaps by the last alien who'd entered Spindrift before the rest of its kind had committed themselves to centuries of hibernation. Gazing down at them, he found himself imagining the scene. One lone alien – perhaps his own counterpart, an extraterrestrial first officer of some kind – whose task it was to close the surface hatch once everyone else had gone below. Perhaps it had taken one last look at the stars before it committed itself to the dreamless oblivion of biostasis, a voyage between the stars that would last centuries, perhaps even . . .

But why would they do something like that if they had hyperspace technology?

The question came to him as he grasped the safety rope and began the long climb up the spiral stairs to the outer hatch. There was a starbridge in orbit around Spindrift. Obviously it was alien in origin. Therefore, it stood to reason that it led somewhere. So why would a race capable of opening wormholes between one point and another, just as humankind had learned to do, undertake the enormous effort to hollow out an asteroid, turn it into a huge ship, then place millions of its kind in biostasis? Why construct something like this when there was no apparent need to do so?

It made no sense . . . and yet, there had to be a reason. Harker considered this as he made his way up the ramp one step at a time, clutching the rope for support. All he'd seen below told him that everything these creatures designed had a clear and very direct sense of purpose. There were no redundancies, no belt-and-suspenders second measures. Hatches that opened the same way every single time. Ramps and staircases that had no guardrails. Control panels, although inscribed with an alien language, were symbolic enough that an intelligent visitor could figure out how to operate them. Everything this race did was simple and straightforward.

So why would they build a vessel meant for a voyage lasting countless years, when they had the ability to make the same journey in only a few seconds?

Harker looked back at Ramirez, struggling up the ramp just behind him. He was tempted to talk to him about this . . . but no, not just yet. For the time being, his primary concern was getting back to the *Maria Celeste* in one piece. After Cruz's hideous death, he wasn't going to feel safe until they'd left Spindrift behind.

It can wait until we're back on the shuttle, he thought as he climbed the last few meters to the surface hatch. *Hell, let it wait until we're aboard* Galileo. *All I want to do is get out of here alive.*

Opening the hatch from the inside was a bit of a trick; now that he knew what the aliens looked like, it was clear that it had been designed by beings whose bodies had a different range of movement. Harker had to squat down on his knees, then reach above his head, in order to reach the panel that lay next to the hatch's underside. Once this was done, though, the flanges peeled apart as they'd done before.

'You doing okay there?' He looked down at Ramirez, still making his way up the stairs. Ramirez raised a hand to give him a silent thumbs-up. Pulling himself back upon his feet, Harker climbed the rest of the way out of the hatch. He gazed up at the cold black sky that lay above Spindrift. The stars had never looked so beautiful.

Thank God, I'm out of there. Time to contact Emily; she was probably worried sick about them. 'Survey team to *Maria Celeste*, do you copy?' He waited a moment, heard nothing. 'Team to shuttle,' he said, 'do you hear me?'

Again, no response. '*I wouldn't worry too much*,' Ramirez said as he emerged from the hatch behind him. '*She's probably sacked out.*'

More likely than not, he was right. Harker glanced at

the chronometer on his heads-up display: 02:11 shiptime. Yet he couldn't help but feel that something was wrong. As if enough hadn't gone wrong already. 'Leave the gear behind,' he said. 'We're heading straight back.'

'*Sure, but first things first.*' Kneeling beside the hatch, Ramirez reached out to close it . . . then jerked back as the panels slid shut by themselves. '*Damn*,' he murmured. '*Guess something must have noticed that we've left the premises.*'

Harker said nothing. Little about this place surprised him anymore. At least the safety line was still in place; the next team would need it. *If* another team came down; after what happened to Cruz, he sure as hell wasn't going to volunteer to lead another survey.

'Let's just get out of here,' he muttered as he turned away from the hatch. 'I never want to see this goddamn place again.'

It took only a few minutes for them to hike back to the spot where they'd left the belay ropes, and only slightly longer to make the climb up the crater wall. Twice more, Harker tried to contact the shuttle, yet all he heard was the low hum of carrier-wave static. By the time they'd reached the crater rim, he'd become seriously concerned; when he discovered that he couldn't see the *Maria Celeste* except as a low form visible only through his visor's ultraviolet function, he abandoned caution and bounded down the slope, making reckless broad jumps that could kill him if he fell face-first upon any one of the dozens of rocks that lay between him and the landing craft.

He didn't care. The shuttle's floodlights were extinguished, its cockpit windows dark. Even the formation lights were out. Something was wrong; he knew that for a fact. 'Survey team to *Maria Celeste*!' he yelled as he charged across the plain, leaving Ramirez far behind. 'Answer if you can! Repeat, survey team to . . . !'

'*Copy.*' Emily's voice came through his headset just as he was within twenty meters of the shuttle. '*Go silent.*'

Startled by her abrupt response, Harker skidded to a halt. Looking up, he saw a faint spot of light within the cockpit. Emily was aiming a flashlight at him. 'Emcee, what are you . . . ?'

'*Airlock's open.*' For an instant, he caught a glimpse of her face, backlit by the flashlight's reflection off the glass. '*Go silent and get aboard, right now.*'

'Emcee, what . . . ?'

Then he heard the low snap of the comlink going dead. Harker looked back at Ramirez; only then was the scientist catching up with him. He started to say something, but realized that if Emily wanted him to go radio-silent, it must be for a good reason. Instead, he pointed to the shuttle's belly ramp. Ramirez raised a hand: he'd heard, and understood.

Harker headed for the ramp. As badly as things had gone beneath the surface of Spindrift, something just as terrible must have occurred topside as well.

Even so, the last thing he expected to hear was that the *Galileo* had been destroyed.

Emily gave him the news as soon as he and Ramirez cycled through the airlock. Even so, it was difficult to understand what had happened; still in a state of shock, what little she was able to tell him came as a rush of disconnected details. An alien vessel coming though the starbridge. Some sort of interference with *Galileo*'s communication system.

Captain Lawrence ordering the torpedo to be launched. The nuke's premature detonation, apparently before it reached its intended target.

Harker took all this in while squatting on the floor of the aft compartment, a cup of lukewarm coffee nestled in his hands. It wasn't until he removed his EVA gear that he realized that the shuttle was colder than when he'd left it; his skinsuit, damp with unrecycled sweat, clung to him like long underwear in which he'd gone for a swim, and he longed to peel out of it. The only interior light was the dim glow of the emergency lamps. Emily had powered down all nonessential systems; although she'd heard him through the comlink as soon as he and Ramirez had emerged from the hatch, she'd dared not respond until they were close enough to the shuttle that she could signal them with a flashlight. In hindsight, he realized that she'd done the right thing. If there was a hostile vessel in orbit . . .

A cold hand closed its fingers around his heart. He found himself beginning to shake. In the space of little less than two hours, twelve lives had been snuffed out: eleven in space and another on the ground.

Only the three of them remained alive.

For a long time, no one said anything. Emily sat cross-legged on the floor, staring at nothing in particular; her last remaining iota of courage seemed to have left her once she'd learned that Cruz was dead. Harker realized that she'd been holding on to the hope that all three of them would return alive. When only he and Ramirez returned . . .

'Well, that's it for us.' Ramirez slowly rose to his feet, sauntered over to the locker where he'd left his clothes. 'We're screwed.'

At first, Harker thought Ramirez only intended to remove his EVA gear. Instead, he pulled out his jumpsuit, unsnapped a pocket, and produced the pipe he'd caught him smoking aboard *Galileo*. Harker had forgotten that he'd given it back to him shortly before they'd left the ship.

'Don't light that,' he said. 'We have only a limited supply of air.'

'Why, does it matter?' Ramirez shook his head. 'Six days, maybe a little more . . . if we don't suffocate first, then we'll starve to death. Or freeze, if we should be so lucky as to last that long.'

'Smoke if you want to.' Emily gave Ramirez a careless wave of her hand. 'I may even join you.'

'Thank you, dear.' Ramirez pulled out a small plastic canister; opening it, he began to stuff the pipe's bowl with cannabis. 'How about you, Ted? Might make you . . .'

'No thanks.' The last thing Harker wanted to do was to try to escape their situation within a cloud of stupor. Even if that form of escape was their only option. 'I'd rather change, if you don't mind,' he added, standing up and walking over to his own locker.

'Suit yourself . . . no pun intended, of course.'

It should have been funny, but Harker was in no mood. He tried to consider the alternatives as he unzipped his skinsuit and realized that there were none that were worth discussion.

Even if the shuttle lifted off from Spindrift, Earth was nearly two light-years away, far beyond *Maria Celeste*'s range, and KX-1 was almost as distant. They could activate the emergency transponder, but its signal wouldn't be received for almost two years, if at all. And even if, by some stroke of luck, its faint radio signal was intercepted by the deep-space antenna at Mare Muscoviense, a rescue mission from Earth wouldn't arrive for at least two and a half years after that . . . by which time Spindrift would have receded even farther from the solar system, once again being lost in the depths of interstellar space.

By then, he thought, *we'll be the stuff of legend.* The notion brought a wan smile to his face. The *Galileo* would soon enter the history books as one more vessel whose fate remained unknown. No one would ever learn what happened to them. And meanwhile, they'd lie here together, joining the dreamless sleep of the dead . . .

Just like the aliens below us, he thought. *They're going somewhere, but they put themselves asleep. Now they're waiting to get to wherever they've got to go . . .*

An idea occurred to him, one so desperate that he wouldn't have taken it into consideration if the only alternative wasn't certain death. Even as Ramirez's pipe began to fill the closed air of the compartment with herb-scented fumes, Harker turned toward the emergency biostasis cells.

There was a chance . . .

'Put out the pipe,' he said. 'No more water, no more coffee. Use the head one last time. Then strip down.'

'What are you . . . ?' Ramirez stared at him, then followed his gaze to the cells. 'Are you crazy? What's that going to . . . ?'

'Yes, he's mad . . . and I'm sorry I didn't think of that earlier.' Emily had caught on. Raising a hand, she let Harker help her stand up. 'Transponder on?'

'Of course. Standard frequency.'

'Sure.' She hesitated. 'You'll have to activate the cells,

though. My only experience with them has been in training.'

'Mine, too. We're just going to have to check each other to make sure we do this right.' He patted her arm, gave her what he hoped was a reassuring smile, then stood aside to let her go forward to the cockpit. Then he reached down to take the pipe from Ramirez's hands. 'No time for that, I'm afraid,' he added. 'Go take a piss, then get naked. We're putting you down first.'

'You can't be serious.' Ramirez regarded him with shock even as he surrendered his precious vice. 'What good is that going to do us?'

'I don't know.' Harker stepped over to the nearest cell. A touch of the control panel, and its lid wheezed open. 'But these things can keep us alive almost indefinitely.'

'Sure, all right.' Ramirez glanced toward the ceiling. 'But what if they . . . ?'

'Find us?' Harker didn't have an answer for this. From the cockpit, Emily looked over her shoulder, silently asking the same question. 'It's a risk we'll have to take. I just know that we don't have anything to lose . . . unless you'd rather die, of course.'

Ramirez said nothing. He took a deep breath, then opened the chest zipper of his skinsuit. Turning away from him, Harker opened the lids of the next two cells. He almost started to open the fourth before he remembered that it wouldn't be needed.

Sorry, Jorge, he thought. *If you'd made it just a little while longer . . .*

'I knew what I was doing,' Ramirez said, very quietly.

Harker looked around at him. 'Pardon me?'

Ramirez had removed his skinsuit. Save for his briefs,

he was almost naked; in the cold of the cabin, he hugged himself. 'When I . . . when I did what I did,' he said, his teeth chattering, 'I knew what I was doing. Because I thought it was the right thing.'

Harker suddenly realized that he was talking about his role in the Savant genocide. Ramirez had always claimed to be a victim of circumstance, an innocent who'd been swept up in a plot with inner dimensions that had not been revealed to him. Now, like a man facing the gallows, he was confessing his sins in hope that the truth would save his soul.

'Why did you do it?' he asked.

'Because I thought . . .' Ramirez looked away. 'Because I thought it was the only way to save the human race. And because . . .'

'Never mind.' Harker glanced toward the cockpit. Emily heard nothing of this. 'You can tell me the rest if . . . when we get through this.'

Ramirez's eyes widened. 'Then you understand . . . ?'

'No. That's a matter between you and . . . well, someone else.' Harker motioned to the nearest cell. 'If we're lucky, then you'll be answering to me first.'

It didn't take long for them to go into hibernation. In fact, Harker was surprised by how easy the entire procedure was once they accessed the tutorial program. Once they administered the proper antibiotics to themselves from the emergency kit, it was a relatively simple matter of inserting rubber lines into major arteries and strapping oxygen masks to faces. They weren't able to shave their body hair, though, but they'd just have to accept the consequences.

He and Emily put Ramirez down first. Once he was safely in hibernation, they had a little more confidence. Harker helped Emily climb into her cell; one last kiss, then the mask went over her face. He shut the hatch, flooded the casing, and waited until its panel lights went green. Then he programmed his cell to repeat the same procedure for him.

Harker closed the hatch behind him, then pulled the air mask over his face. As he laid his arms next to him, he felt consciousness slipping away from him even as warm blue gel began to ooze up around his body.

You're about to die, he thought, and for a moment he felt a surge of panic.

No, you're not going to die. He forced himself to relax. *You're just going away for a while. And when you wake up, you'll be in another place . . .*

Darkness swept in upon him, and he was gone.

Part Five

The Secret of *Shaq-Taaraq*

Seventeen

UNKNOWN

'Wake up, Dr Ramirez. Please, wake up.'

The voice was low and not unpleasant, and also familiar, although Ramirez had trouble placing it. He struggled toward consciousness, eyelids fluttering against the bright nimbus of light that seemed to surround him, lungs aching with every breath he took.

'Dr Ramirez, are you awake?' The voice remained gentle, yet there was an undertone of impatience. 'Please speak if you are able.'

'I . . . I . . .' His mouth was parched, his throat dry. 'Water . . . please, I need . . .'

'Yes, you may have some. There is water in a glass next to you.'

Not making this easy for me, are you? Squinting against the glare, Ramirez tried to sit up. His limbs were weak, though; his entire body felt drained, as if he had run for kilometers without rest. Every impulse told him that he should go back to sleep. Yet his thirst was desperate, and the thought that a cool drink of water awaited him at the end of the ordeal was enough to make him fight against the weariness that threatened to overcome him.

Through sheer force of will, he made himself sit up from the hard surface upon which he lay. He wore a white robe that extended down to his ankles; beneath it, he was naked. His pupils adjusted to the glare; looking down, he saw that he was in a biostasis cell almost identical to the one aboard the *Galileo* . . .

No, no. That couldn't be right. When he'd gone into hibernation, he was aboard the *Maria Celeste*. Yet this cell looked so much like the one aboard the *Galileo* that he . . .

Then he raised his eyes, and realized that his first impression had been correct. He was in the hibernation compartment on Deck B of the *Galileo*. Same antiseptic floor, same windowless bulkheads. Directly across from him was another cell, its coffinlike lid closed, lights gleaming from its instrument panel.

What the hell? The *Galileo* had been destroyed. Or at least so he'd been informed. So how could he be . . .

A rollaway cart was parked beside his cell. Upon it rested a glass of water. Forgetting everything else for the moment, he swung his legs around so that he could sit up straight, then reached over to pick it up. The glass was strangely thick and heavy, almost as if it had been carved from a block of crystal; he nearly dropped it when he picked it up, and had to hold it with both hands. And the water was tepid and flat, warmer than he expected. Yet it was just what he needed; he drank as much as he could without choking, and gasped when he finally pulled the glass away from his lips.

The *Galileo*. He was back aboard the *Galileo*. So Collins had been wrong. The ship must have survived the nuclear detonation she'd witnessed; the *Maria Celeste* had been located, and he and the others had somehow been brought back from Spindrift, where they'd been revived from biostasis.

So where was everyone else? He'd heard a voice when

he woke up, yet so far as he could tell, the hibernation deck was empty. Or had he only imagined that? 'Hello?' he asked as he looked one way, then the other. 'Is anyone there?'

'I am here,' the voice replied, and Ramirez looked around again to see Donald Sinclair.

Ramirez nearly dropped the glass. The last person he expected to see was him. Nick Jones, perhaps, or another crewman, but not Sinclair. Why hadn't he noticed him earlier?

'I apologize.' Sinclair stood a couple of meters away, his arms at his sides. 'I did not mean to' – a pause – 'surprise you. Are you awake now?'

'Um . . . yeah, I'm awake.' Ramirez returned the glass to the table. He noticed now that it was absent of anything else he might've expected to be there; no medical instruments, no drugs, not even a linen cloth to cover its stainless-steel surface. 'Least I think I am. Where's . . . where are the other guys?'

'Guys?' Sinclair stared at him, his gaze unwavering. 'What do you mean?' Then he slowly blinked, almost deliberately, and slowly nodded. 'Yes. Commander Harker and Lieutenant Collins.'

'Uh-huh.' Sinclair's reticence was as unnerving as his stare. 'Ted and Emily.' He glanced at the cell across from him. 'You haven't brought them up yet?'

Sinclair didn't respond for a moment. Now Ramirez began to notice other details that had previously eluded him. The robe he wore wasn't like the one he'd been given when he'd originally emerged from biostasis. This one was thicker, and seemed to have been specially tailored for his own body. Looking down at it, he saw odd designs woven along its sleeves and chest, like none he'd ever seen before. But that wasn't all. As he reached up to touch his face – how odd, no beard stubble – his right sleeve fell back from his forearm, and he saw that the inside of his elbow was unmarked. No puncture wounds where Harker had inserted the feed tubes. Not even a bandage.

Come to think of it, where was the suspension fluid? His body should be covered with slimy blue gel, yet his skin was dry. He looked back at his cell, saw no indication that it had been recently used. Not only that, but the soft pad that lined its bottom was missing, nor could he see any indication of intravenous lines or oxygen tubes.

'They have been revived.' Sinclair spoke as if uncertain of his words. 'They will join us soon. First, I have some questions for you.'

'Uh-huh. I've got a few of my own.' Ramirez gently pushed himself out of the cell. His legs felt weak, yet there was none of the unsteadiness he'd felt before. 'How long have I been . . . ?'

He stopped, not quite understanding at first what he was seeing. Although Sinclair appeared to be standing just a few steps away, he didn't cast a shadow upon the polished metal floor. Yet Ramirez could see him just as clearly as if . . .

'I have no doubt that you do.' Sinclair didn't seem to notice that Ramirez was openly staring at him. 'All will be explained in time if you will only cooperate.'

'Sure . . . whatever you say.' Ramirez glanced at the next cell over. Although its indicators were lit, he couldn't see a face through its window. It was empty. 'Go ahead. Fire away.'

Again, a pause, as if Sinclair was taking a moment to

divine the meaning of his words. 'Why did you come to Spindrift? What did you believe you would find there?'

'You should know this. You're the political officer, aren't you?' Ramirez felt his heart quicken as he gazed around the compartment. Although it superficially resembled *Galileo*'s hibernation deck, it lacked a certain sense of detail. Almost as if it was an elaborate stage set, reconstructed from photos of the actual compartment, yet missing the small, almost unnoticeable things that would have lent verisimilitude to anyone who'd been there before.

'Yes, I am the designated representative of the Western Hemisphere Union.' Sinclair spoke with stiff formality, as if introducing himself to Ramirez for the first time. 'Is there a reason why you do not believe me?'

'I can think of at least one.' Without warning, Ramirez snatched up the water glass. 'Here . . . catch!'

He tossed the glass to Sinclair. He made no effort to catch it, though, and Ramirez watched as it passed through his body and shattered on the floor behind him. Sinclair remained still, his arms at his sides, no emotion on his face.

Ramirez let out his breath. 'This isn't the *Galileo*,' he murmured. 'You're not Donald Sinclair.'

'You are very perceptive. More than we believed you would be.' Sinclair – or rather, the three-dimensional image of Sinclair – slowly raised a hand in a placating gesture. 'You are correct. This is not your ship, nor am I the person you knew. We had hoped that returning you to a familiar environment, along with a representation of a familiar individual in a position of authority, would prompt you to speak candidly.'

An involuntary shudder passed through Ramirez, and he wrapped his arms around himself. If this wasn't where he first thought he was, then there was little doubt where he might be. 'If you'd worked at this a little harder, you might have succeeded. But there're too many . . .' Suddenly, he felt fear being replaced by anger. 'Enough already. You know all about me . . . so who are you? And where have you brought me?'

The fake Sinclair let his hand drop to his side. 'I will tell you these things, but first you have to answer my questions.' A pause. 'I should caution you that the outcome of this is entirely predicated on your honesty. Any attempt to deceive us will be detected at once, and will have consequences.'

'You mean, don't lie or else.' Ramirez regretted losing the water glass; his throat had become dry once more. 'How would you know if I did?'

'Examine the robe you're wearing.' Sinclair pointed to him. 'It is called a *sha*. Among my people, it is considered to be a sacred vestment, worn by our religious caste. You should be honored to be given one, although for this purpose it has been adapted for your form. While dressed in this, a . . . holy person, if you will . . . cannot tell an untruth.'

He paused. 'Try, if you would like. Tell me something that you know to be false and that you believe I might not know to be so.'

Ramirez considered this for a few moments. This entity – he had to assume that it was alien – obviously knew enough about him already that it not only understood his language and was able to speak it, but was also aware of his name and certain details about the *Galileo*. How he'd come across so much information was almost beside the point, at least for now.

'My mother's name is Jean,' he said, 'and my father's name is Douglas.'

From within the patterns on the *sha*, a cool blue radiance. 'This is a true statement,' Sinclair said. 'The *sha* has revealed that. Now, tell me a lie . . .'

'My uncle is a chicken,' Ramirez blurted out. 'He crossed the road so that he could meet my . . .'

Before he could finish, he felt the robe grow uncomfortably warm, almost as if he was swathed in an electric blanket whose thermostat had been turned up too high. When he reached down to pull it open, he saw that the patterns had become an ugly shade of brown.

'Leave it be.' The image didn't raise its voice, but nonetheless there was enough authority in its tone that Ramirez dropped his hands. 'That was a lie . . . we know that now. But if you remove the *sha*, we will assume that is an indication you no longer intend to cooperate with us.'

'And if I don't?'

Sinclair displayed no emotion, yet his voice became colder. 'We will further assume that you intend to deceive us and will respond in an appropriate manner.' The image paused. 'I warn you not to do this. The lives of you and your companions are already in jeopardy. Do not try our patience more than you already have.'

Again, Ramirez felt a chill. Reaching out with his left hand, he braced himself against the side of the biostasis cell. Without being willing to do so, he'd become a player in a game whose rules he barely understood, with an objective that he didn't comprehend. With nothing in his favor, he had no choice but to cooperate.

‘All right,’ he said. ‘I understand. What do you want to know?’

‘My first questions remain the same.’ Sinclair gazed at him with the same implacable eyes. ‘Why did you come to Spindrift? What did you expect to find there?’

Ramirez told him everything.

It took longer than he expected. At least an hour, although there was no way to be certain; the nearest chronometer was perpetually frozen at 07:01:00. Yet the Sinclair-thing listened with endless patience, never interrupting him or revealing any emotion, always regarding him with steady, unwavering eyes that never once blinked or looked away.

More than once as he spoke, Ramirez wondered what lay behind the façade. Was he speaking to a member of the same race that he and Harker had discovered in the lightless depths of Spindrift? Or was the hologram the creation of some sort of machine intelligence, one that could fool even the most advanced Turing test? He had no way of knowing for certain, yet there was no point in lying, or even committing the sin of omission. The *sha* would expose him if he dared to do so. Not only that, but since he had no idea where he was or who was holding him, the only way out was to give his captors what they wanted. So truth was his best defense, even if it might not cast him and the rest of the expedition in the best light.

He finally reached the point in the narrative where he and Harker returned to the *Maria Celeste* only to find that the *Galileo* had been destroyed, at which point the survivors decided to go into biostasis in hope of eventually being rescued. 'And that's it,' he finished. 'Next thing I knew, I'm here.' Sinclair continued to stare at him. 'Wherever or whatever this place is,' he added. 'Perhaps you'd care to tell me?'

'Perhaps.' Again, the pseudo-Sinclair displayed no emotion. 'I still do not understand why the *Galileo* launched a missile at our vessel.'

Our vessel. A small clue there, however minute. 'Nor do I,' Ramirez said. 'My best guess . . . that is, my conjecture . . . is that something occurred that gave our captain reason to believe that his ship was under attack. He may have been trying to defend himself, or . . .' He shrugged. 'I don't know. Your guess is as good as mine.'

The holograph didn't respond for a moment. 'Your captain was afraid of us,' Sinclair's doppelgänger said at last. 'He may have misinterpreted our attempt to contact you as hostile action . . . is that what you believe?'

'Believe, no. I can only speculate . . . but I can't do that without knowing more than I do now.' Ramirez crossed his arms. 'You said you attempted to make contact with us. When was that?'

Another pause, one that lasted a little longer than before. 'When our vessel transmitted a message to the *Galileo*,' Sinclair replied at last. 'Since you were responding to the signal transmitted by our starbridge, we deduced that you had interpreted its meaning, and therefore were capable of interpreting . . .'

'Stop. Wait just a second.' Ramirez raised a hand. 'What signal? You mean the one we . . . I mean, my people . . . picked up when we detected Spindrift?'

'Unless there has been a misunderstanding among our races . . .'

'I think it's safe to say that there's been one, yes.' Ramirez nodded. 'Please, go on.'

'The signal transmitted by our starbridge was a warning to all races that might happen to discover *Shaq-Taaraq* . . . what you call Spindrift. If it had been correctly interpreted, it would have told you that *Shaq-Taaraq* was under the protection of the *Talus* . . .'

'The what?' Ramirez peered more closely at the holo. 'The *Talus*? What's that?'

'That is difficult to explain.' Although Sinclair's expression didn't change, the short pause that followed was as close to any emotion as Ramirez had yet detected during the entire discussion. 'We will return to it later. A message was sent, instructing your people not to attempt rendezvous with *Shaq-Taaraq* . . .'

'Which we didn't understand. We only saw that it was an alien transmission and decided to investigate its source.'

'We understand this . . . but only now.' The holo remained stoical, yet Ramirez detected a tinge of regret in its mimicry of Sinclair's voice. 'If your kind had only taken the time and effort to interpret the message, all this could have been avoided.'

Ramirez let out his breath. 'Perhaps . . . but you have to understand that we've been anxious for so long to make contact with another race. When we detected Spindrift . . . or *Shaq-Taaraq*, as you call it . . . our curiosity compelled us to find out what it was.'

'This may be so.' The ghost of a dead political officer stared at him. 'If that is the case, then we may also share the blame, for failing to realize that emergent races might be so enthusiastic that they would make such a venture without knowing what was there.'

'Look before you leap,' Ramirez said quietly.

'Leap where?'

'Sorry. Old expression among my kind . . . not to be taken literally. Go on, please . . . you were saying that we didn't understand your language.' A new thought occurred to him, one so obvious he was surprised it hadn't occurred to him before. 'You seem to understand ours quite well. Or at least Anglo. Do you also speak Spanish? *Se habla español?*'

'*Sí. Un poco.*' The holo didn't bat an eye. 'This is only because Spanish is among the languages stored in your shuttle's data retrieval system. There are many others. Russian, French, German, Italian . . .'

'So you've been able to gain access to our comps. That means you've also read everything else that was stored there.' Remembering now that *Galileo*'s flight recorder had been automatically backed up by the comps aboard the *Maria Celeste*, he felt uneasy. How much else had the aliens learned about them?

'Correct. Your craft's memory was quite extensive. From our study of it, we were able not only to decipher your languages, but also to construct a facsimile of the *Galileo*'s hibernation facilities.' The holo spread its hands apart. 'As you can see, we were also able to form an image of your political officer, using samples of his voice to duplicate it. Donald Ramon Sinclair, born April 5, 2246, in Mobile, Alabama, Western Hemisphere Union . . .'

'I believe you.' Ramirez shook his head. 'But why go to all the trouble? Why not simply ask me what happened?'

Again another pause. Whoever was controlling this puppet, Ramirez was beginning to realize, was inherently cautious. Indeed, they were probably just as wary of the intruder they were interrogating as he was of them. If not even more so.

'We were unsure of your motives.' Sinclair lowered its hands. 'Try to understand our point of view. Your ship made rendezvous with *Shaq-Taaraq* despite warnings transmitted from our starbridge. You sent an exploration team to its surface, again despite warnings to stay away. When we learned of this incursion and dispatched a vessel to investigate, our efforts to communicate were unsuccessful. Your ship launched a missile at us, which our own commander was forced to detonate by remote means in order to protect his vessel . . .'

'Destroying our ship and crew.' Ramirez couldn't keep the edge from his voice.

'Unfortunate, but not deliberate. We had no way of knowing that it contained a nuclear weapon.' Another pause. 'Indeed, that was the first time in several generations that any of our people encountered such a device. The *hjadd*, along with most other members of the *Talus*, banned such instruments of destruction many years ago. It was only fortunate that our ship was adequately shielded. Otherwise, there would have been no survivors of this incident.'

'Who are the *hjadd*?' Ramirez was confused. 'I thought you said you were the *Talus*.'

'No. The *hjadd* is my race. My race belongs to the *Talus*.'

'All right, then . . . so who or what is the *Talus*? Did you construct Spindrift . . . *Shaq-Taaraq*, I mean?'

Sinclair's ghost became silent. It didn't respond, but simply gazed at him with empty eyes. Again, Ramirez felt thirsty; he regretted having thrown the water glass, for there was no other apparent source of water. Looking around the room, he saw only artifice, nonfunctional and lifeless. How much longer were they going to keep up with this? The interrogation could last for hours, or even days. He had no idea where he was, and no more than a few clues about who his captors were. The *hjadd*? The *Talus*? Little more than words . . .

'Dr Ramirez?' The holograph suddenly spoke, startling him from his reverie. 'Your cooperation in our inquiry has been appreciated. We thank you for your candor.'

'You . . . you're welcome.' Ramirez licked his dry lips. 'I hope that's cleared up a few things.' He hesitated. 'May I see the others now . . . Harker and Collins, I mean?'

'You may, very soon. Yet there is one more question we would like to have answered before you do.'

Relieved, Ramirez let out his breath. 'Sure. By all means . . .'

'According to information stored within your craft's data system, you are a convicted criminal.'

Sinclair's image dissolved, to be replaced by a holographic replica of Ramirez himself. Ramirez recognized the image: it was derived from a full-body scan that had been taken of him when he'd been processed through inmate control at Dolland.

'You were sentenced to life imprisonment in a penal colony on your planet's moon for crimes against humanity,' the pseudo-Ramirez continued, now speaking with his own voice. 'To be more precise, you were found guilty of collaboration with a posthuman species, known as the Savants, in a plot that cost the lives of thirty-five thousand members of your own kind and would have resulted in the genocide of . . .'

'Goddamn you.' Ramirez's voice became a choked whisper. 'I know what I did.'

'Yet you were a respected scientist. A renowned leader in the field of astrobiology.' His mirror image, many years younger than he was now, stared back at him with the angry eyes he'd worn that day when he'd entered prison. 'Why would you, someone who believed that intelligent life existed elsewhere in the galaxy, assist in an effort that would inevitably lead to the deaths of so many of your species?'

Ramirez said nothing for a few minutes. He stared down at the floor, wishing that he could take off the *sha* and, standing naked before his own image, repeat the lies that he'd told not only to attorneys and judges, the jury and the press, but also to his friends and family. Yet this cloak he wore, warm as it was, allowed no such subterfuge; its patterns had faded to pale blue, as if awaiting his response.

'My planet was dying,' he began. 'Every report I read, every scientific study that crossed my desk, told me that Earth was running out of time. All our resources were exhausted, and our climate had turned against us. We could no longer support a population of nearly ten billion people. Someone would have to . . .'

He stopped, swallowed. 'When the Savants came to me in search of access to vital information, I thought their solution was only hypothetical. Kill off one-third of the planetary population in order for the rest to survive. It was just a matter of numbers, statistics . . . almost like I was playing a game.'

'Why did they approach you?'

'Because I wanted to join them. Have my consciousness downloaded into a mechanical body, so that I might live forever. I was scared of . . .' He shook his head. 'Never mind. We reached an agreement, so I conducted research, devised pathways that led to various scenarios, presented it to them . . .'

'And the price for your efforts?' His image stared at him. 'What did you expect to receive for your work?'

'Immortality.' Ramirez coughed against the bile that rose in his throat. 'I never wanted to die.' His breath rattled from him. 'I was so young, so . . . so stupid.'

'And you now regret your choice?'

Ramirez thought about what he'd found within Spindrift – or *Shaq-Taaraq*, as the *hjadd* called it – and suddenly realized that this question was something he couldn't answer now as he had before, even to himself. He took another breath and went on, knowing that the *sha* would forgive no lies.

'I've seen a million or so beings who've sealed themselves inside an asteroid for God knows how long. I don't know why they did this, but it must have been to stay alive, whatever the cost.' Ramirez looked up at his mirror image. 'All my life, I wanted to discover a race out there that was better than my own kind . . . and when I finally did, it's to find that they tried to avoid the only solution I thought possible.' He forced a grim smile. 'So do I have regrets? Yes, I do.'

His image was quiet for a few moments before it finally spoke. 'Thank you, Dr Ramirez. We believe you're ready to continue this conversation with your companions.'

He heard a hollow clunk, and a sigh of escaping air. Glancing to his right, he watched the hatch at the other side of the room. When he looked back, he was startled to find that Sinclair had reappeared.

'If you will follow me, please,' he said, 'I'll take you to them.' The holo turned and began to glide toward the hatch. Although its legs moved, Ramirez noticed that its feet didn't quite touch the floor. 'Your questions will soon be answered.'

Ramirez expected to find the Deck B corridor on the other side of the hatch. Instead, as Sinclair stepped aside to let him pass, he found himself walking straight into a replica of *Galileo*'s library. Apparently the *hjadd* were unaware that the original had been located on another deck entirely; either that, or they simply chose to ignore that detail.

Nonetheless, the resemblance was close enough that, if he'd not known better, he could have sworn that he was back aboard the *Galileo*. Same caged bookshelves, same crystal chandelier, same oak tables and leather chairs. The only differences were that the fireplace was cold, without a simulated fire burning in it, and nothing lay beyond the windows save for dark grey limbo.

Harker was seated in an armchair, peering at a closed book in his hands. He looked up as Ramirez walked in, and quickly rose to his feet. 'Jared! Good grief, man . . . I thought you might be dead!'

'Happy to see you, too.' Ramirez noticed that Harker wore a robe identical to his own; its patterns took on a warm orange hue as *Galileo*'s first officer dropped the book on a table and rushed toward him. 'Don't know why you're so surprised. Sinclair . . . I mean, the holo they made of Sinclair . . . told me you and Emily were here, too, so . . .'

'You saw Sinclair?' Harker stopped short. 'They sent Cole . . . or something like Cole . . . to see me.'

'Yeah, I saw him. He's right over . . .' Ramirez turned

around, only to discover that Sinclair's image had vanished and the hatch had shut. 'Well, he was a second ago,' he murmured. 'Guess they're shy about two of us seeing their puppets at the same time.'

'Either that, or they didn't want us to compare notes.' A grim smile appeared on Harker's face. 'I knew he . . . or it, whatever . . . couldn't be Sir Peter the moment he opened his mouth. Not arrogant enough.'

'Can't blame them for trying. They only had faces and voices to work with.' Ramirez gazed around the room. 'So this is where they've been keeping you? I woke up in the hibernation deck. Close copy, but they missed a few details.'

'You noticed that, too, eh?' Harker walked over to the table, picked up the book he'd been examining. Holding it up by the spine, he shook it a few times. The covers remained shut, its pages unruffled; the book was a solid object. 'Guess the *hjadd* have never seen a book before. They only knew how to duplicate its appearance.'

'The tip-off for me was the biostasis tank I woke up in. Too clean to be real.' Ramirez strode over to the nonfunctional fireplace. 'Been here long?'

'A couple of hours or so. I came to on that couch.' Harker pointed across the room to the one within the study alcove. 'Thought I was dreaming, or at least until Cole showed up and began to ask questions.' Another smile, which quickly vanished. 'Same interrogation? About our mission, and what we were doing on Spindrift? Or perhaps we should call it *Shaq-Taaraq*.'

'That seems to be what they . . .'

A door on the opposite side of the library opened, and they both looked around to see Emily cautiously enter the room, also wearing one of the patterned white cloaks. She halted just inside the door, staring around herself in apparent disbelief, until her gaze fell upon them.

'Oh, thank God!' she yelped, then raced across the library to throw herself into Harker's arms. 'I never thought . . . Ted, you're alive!'

'It's all right. I'm here.' Harker held her close, stroking her hair, whispering into her ear. Embarrassed, Ramirez turned his face away. As much as he once fantasized about having Emily, once again it was clear to whom she belonged. At least he should be grateful that the three of them were still among the living.

'Let me guess,' he said, after giving the couple a few moments to themselves. 'You woke up somewhere aboard *Galileo* and found someone waiting to ask a few questions.'

'You, too?' Emily peeled herself apart from Harker. 'I was in the command deck, all by myself except for Toni.' Her face went pale, and she clutched Ted's hand as tears came to her eyes. 'It was horrid. She showed me what happened . . . everything, right up to the point where we . . . our people, I mean . . . launched the nuke at her . . . I mean, their ship. And then . . .'

'Questions.' Ramirez turned toward her. 'She told you that if you didn't tell the truth and nothing but the truth, then this' – he plucked at the sleeve of his *sha* – 'would expose you as a liar, and the rest of us would die. Right?'

Emily slowly nodded as she pulled Harker close again. 'That's the way it happened with me, too,' Harker said. 'Guess we all received the same treatment, only with a few variations.' He shook his head. 'Awful lot of trouble to go through, just to make sure we'd be honest.'

'Never been arrested, have you?' Ramirez couldn't help but chuckle. 'Standard procedure . . . separate your suspects, tell 'em you'll get the death penalty if you don't talk, then wait to see who sings first and if their stories match.' He sauntered over to the fireplace, idly inspected the pewter model of the *Galileo* upon its mantel. 'Suppose we must have passed the test, or they wouldn't have allowed us to get together.'

'You are correct,' Lawrence said.

Ramirez looked around at the same moment as the others. The image of Ian Lawrence stood behind them, shoulders straight and hands at his sides, wearing his dress uniform. The dead captain didn't look at any one of them, but instead stared directly ahead.

'You have done well,' Lawrence said. 'My kind appreciates your cooperation, as does the *Talus*. Now the time has come for us to reciprocate your candor.' He gestured toward the nearby chairs. 'Be seated, please, and pay close attention. Here is the reason you have been brought to this place and why this encounter is important to the future of your kind.'

Eighteen

UNKNOWN

'First things first.' Harker remained standing after Emily and Ramirez took their seats near the fireplace. 'You said our questions would be answered. Well, then . . . where are we? Why are we here? How long have we been asleep?'

'All this in good time, Mr Harker . . . or do you prefer to be addressed as Commander?' Lawrence's image gestured toward the remaining armchair. 'Please, make yourself comfortable.' He nodded toward a side table, where a pewter decanter and three crystal glasses had been placed. 'There is water, if you so desire. We are still uncertain of what sort of food you consider palatable, however, so . . .'

'I'm not hungry, and I've had it with your pretensions.' Harker's voice rose. 'Are you going to tell us, or . . .'

'Ted.' Emily reached up to grasp his hand. 'Calm down, please.' She looked at the front of his robe. 'Your *sha* . . .'

Harker glanced down at himself. The patterns of his garment had become dark red. She'd apparently discovered the same thing that he had; the *sha* detected emotions as subtle changes in electrodermal response, the ability of the skin to conduct electricity, and displayed them as subtle alterations in the robe's colors. It wasn't difficult to guess that this color scene indicated anger and frustration.

Emcee's right, he thought. *You're in no position to be picking a fight.* Slowly letting out his breath, Harker consciously forced himself to cool off; the patterns gradually faded to neutral grey. 'Sorry,' he said, looking up at the holo again. 'Didn't mean to lose my temper like that. But you've told us nothing of what we should know . . . what we need to know . . . and I think it's time for you to be as honest with us as we've been with you.'

Ramirez nodded. 'I have to agree,' he said quietly. 'If this is as important as you say, then perhaps you should start by telling us what Ted . . . Commander Harker . . . wants to know.'

For a few seconds, Lawrence's ghost didn't respond. Again, Harker had the impression that something was going on that he couldn't see or hear, as if the holo was little more than a projection manipulated by intelligences as yet unseen. 'Very well,' it said at last. 'Since this is obviously of great importance to you, we shall comply.' Turning toward the alcove, it pointed toward its window. 'Look there, and you'll see where you are.'

Harker walked toward the alcove, with Emily and Ramirez rising from their seats to follow him. He stopped, feeling his breath catch. Beyond the mullioned panes of glass lay the darkness of outer space, black as night and speckled by distant stars, save for one that shone nearly as bright as the Sun as seen from Earth's orbit.

Yet that wasn't what caught his attention. In the foreground, stretched out before them, was an immense structure that, at first glance, resembled a magnified image of a snowflake, or perhaps a three-dimensional model of a complex molecule. Dozens, perhaps even hundreds, of forms of all shapes and sizes, some larger than others, connected to one another by a weblike network of threads that seemed flimsy until Harker realized that they were giant cables. Alien spacecraft, many of them larger than *Galileo* yet reduced to the size of insects, floated in and around the spars. A space colony, yet one more vast than anything he'd ever imagined possible, perhaps several hundred kilometers or more in diameter. The largest orbital station yet built by humans would have been little more than one module among countless others.

'This is *Talus qua'spah*,' Lawrence said. 'In Anglo, the closest approximation would be "House of the Talus".'

'Some house.' Harker stared at it in astonishment. 'And this isn't . . . I mean, this isn't another illusion?'

'Only so far as you're seeing a projection of something that lies just a few meters beyond the walls of this room.' Lawrence's image vanished from behind him, reappeared an instant later beside the window. It pointed toward the nearby star. 'This is what your race refers to as HD 143761, also known as Rho Coronae Borealis. A G0V-class star, of slightly lower magnitude than your own sun . . .'

'I know it.' Ramirez moved closer to Harker, stared at it over his shoulder. 'Located in the Corona Borealis constellation, what we call the Northern Crown. We . . . I mean, our telescopes . . . detected terrestrial-size planets there some years ago, but we . . .'

His voice trailed off. Harker looked at him sharply. 'But what?'

Ramirez's face went pale. For a moment, he groped for words. 'It's fifty-four light-years from Earth,' he whispered.

'Fifty-four-point-four, to be exact.' Lawrence's ghost dropped its hands to his sides. 'Farther than anyone else of your race has yet ventured.'

Harker felt his legs become weak. Turning away from the window, he staggered to the nearest chair, eased himself into it. 'What year is this?' he rasped.

'By your calendar, this is the year 2344.' Lawrence remained as placid as before. 'Fifty-three years have elapsed since we found you on *Shaq-Taaraq*.' He paused for a moment, then went on. 'Are you ready to listen now?'

Harker needed a drink. He would have preferred a stiff shot of whiskey, but water would have to do. Trying to ignore the way his hand trembled, he picked up the decanter and poured a glass for himself. The water was tepid, almost lukewarm – apparently the *hjadd* were unaware that humans preferred to drink it cold – but it helped soothe his parched throat. Lawrence patiently waited until everyone returned to their seats by the fireplace, then continued.

'To begin,' it said, standing before the hearth, hands at its sides, 'you must understand that our galaxy is inhabited by many races. Most are separated from one another by vast distances and therefore never meet, even if they suspect the existence of others. Until now, this has probably been the situation with your own kind.'

'It is,' Ramirez said. 'We . . .'

'Please, allow me to continue.' The holo raised a hand, and Ramirez went silent. 'However, upon rare occasion, a race develops the ability not only to leave its own world, but eventually to leave its native system. Even then, however, the chances that they will encounter another intelligent species are remote. Inhabitable worlds are difficult to find, and even more difficult to reach. There are races that have mastered interstellar travel for quite some time and have yet to make contact with another species.'

As Lawrence's ghost spoke, a cylindrical shaft of light glowed to life within the circle formed by their chairs. Translucent, tinted a pale shade of blue, it quickly took shape and form, until Harker found himself gazing at a three-dimensional image of the Milky Way. As it slowly rotated, small sparks flashed here and there among its billions of stars, glowing more brightly than the countless suns around them.

'And yet, despite the odds, a spacefaring race will sometimes take the next step, and reinvent that which only a small handful of like-minded races have invented before . . . the ability to construct what you call starbridges, devices that allow their vessels to leap through hyperspace from one portal to another.'

'Did you say "reinvent?"' Now it was Harker's turn to interrupt. 'Does that mean . . . ?'

'The way by which this is accomplished is always the same, yes.' Lawrence nodded. 'A wheel is always a wheel, no matter who makes it . . . and every tool-making society eventually finds a reason to do this, even if its initial purpose isn't always identical. By much the same token, hyperspace travel by means of artificial wormholes is something that has been accomplished time and again.'

He pointed to the sparks floating within the holo of the galaxy. 'These star systems are those whose dominant species have developed starbridges. Because they have done so, their chances of encountering other intelligent species greatly increased . . . and when they do, they eventually meet the *Talus*.'

Lawrence glided forward, stepping into the light shaft until its image melded with that of the galaxy. 'Again, there is no literal translation for this word into Anglo or any other human language. *Association*, *union*, *society*, *federation*, *conglomerate* . . . none of them adequately describe that which we . . .'

'The galactic club,' Ramirez said softly.

'Hush.' Once again, Harker found himself annoyed by Ramirez's presumptuous attitude. 'Let him . . .'

'No.' Lawrence turned toward Ramirez; as it did, the galaxy faded from view. 'Let him speak. You know of this, Dr Ramirez?'

For a moment, Ramirez seemed mildly surprised, like a lazy student whose lucky guess was the correct answer to a professor's question. 'There's a theory,' he said, sitting up a little straighter in his chair, 'that goes back a couple of centuries, when our kind began to speculate whether intelligent life existed in the galaxy. The hypothesis was that alien races, once they became aware of one another, would eventually form a loose alliance . . . a club, really . . . into which they'd invite other races if they met certain criteria. Ability to communicate with one another, ability to travel, so on and so forth.' He hesitated. 'Is that what the *Talus* is? The galactic club?'

'More or less, yes.' As before, Lawrence's image displayed no emotion, yet its voice seemed to express approval. 'The *Talus* is a . . . club, if you wish to call it that . . . of starfaring races that have chosen to associate with one another. We engage in trade, cultural exchanges, the sharing of information, and so forth, all for peaceful purposes. Otherwise, we leave one another alone. We do not interfere with each other's internal politics or waste energy on conquest. By much the same token, neither do we attempt to bring new starfaring races into our fold.'

'You don't find us,' Harker said. 'We find you.'

'This is one way of expressing it . . . but yes, that is frequently how it happens.'

Emily shifted in her chair. 'So when we discovered Spindrift,' she said, speaking up for the first time, 'that's when we found you. The *hjadd*, I mean . . . and also the *Talus*.'

Once more, Lawrence became silent. Harker glanced over at Emily, raised an eyebrow, and she shrugged; she didn't know what she'd said either. He looked at Ramirez, but he seemed at a loss as well; his left knee jiggled nervously as he waited for a response.

'No,' the holo said at last, 'you still don't understand.'

'Understand what?' Harker asked. 'Come on, now. You've brought us this far . . . what is it about you that you don't want us to know?' Despite his intent to remain calm, he found himself becoming annoyed. 'Look, we've seen the inside of Spindrift or *Shaq* . . . *Shaq*-whatever . . . so there's not much more you can tell us about you that we haven't already seen for ourselves.'

'You proceed from a false assumption.' Lawrence stared back at him. 'You believe we're the ones who built *Shaq-Taaraq*.'

'But . . .' Baffled, Harker shook his head. 'If you didn't, then who . . . ?'

'Listen, and understand.'

Again, the iridescent column appeared. As they watched, another image materialized within it: a spiral-shaped object floating in space, with distant stars visible in the background.

At first, Harker couldn't tell what it was. He thought it might be a globular cluster, perhaps a protostar, until he realized that it was far more complex than either. A brilliant white orb, vaguely resembling a dwarf star, lay within the center of the dense, nebula-like whorl of cosmic dust – magenta, purple, burnt orange – that encircled the nucleus as if it were a vast whirlpool. Yet at the center of the nucleus, barely visible from this angle, was a small black spot, out of which vertical plumes of dense plasma rose from both top and bottom. A thing of great beauty, yet also strangely menacing.

'What is it?' Standing up from her chair, Emily stepped closer to examine the projection. 'It's incredible.'

'Yes, it is. Many have doubtless thought so, in their last moments of existence.' The dead captain slowly walked around the hologram, gazing into its depths. 'The races of the *Talus* have many names for it. *Hu'Mok* . . . *Twarog* . . . *Kasimasta* . . . others that you couldn't easily pronounce. Yet they all mean the same thing . . . the Annihilator.'

'A black hole.' At last, Harker realized what it was. 'It's a black hole.' An unimpressed shrug. 'So? We've known about them for quite a while, although' – he gestured toward the projection – 'this is the best image of one I've ever seen.'

Lawrence turned to regard him with what might have been condescension. 'As much as your kind believes it knows about the universe, believe us when we tell you that your ignorance is far greater than your knowledge. Yes, this is a black hole . . . in much the same way that you are a highly advanced simian.'

'Touché,' Ramirez murmured, mildly amused.

Harker felt his face burn, yet Lawrence ignored the remark. 'The Annihilator is not an ordinary cosmic event. When this image was resolved, it was little more than twice the diameter of the planet you know as Jupiter. That was nearly three hundred years ago, by your reckoning. No doubt it has grown even larger since then, as it makes its way through the galaxy.'

'"As it makes its way . . . ?"' Harker stopped. 'You mean, this thing moves?'

'At a rate of nearly two hundred kilometers per second. Judging from its present course, it appears to be gradually moving toward the galactic center. It has already passed through the outer rim, and it is currently traveling through the spiral arms.'

As Lawrence spoke, the image of the galaxy reappeared. The Annihilator swiftly diminished in size until it became a brilliant point of light suspended three-quarters of the way out from the center of the galaxy. Trailing a luminescent line behind it, it traced a winding course that led from the outermost reaches of the Milky Way, into and through the Perseus Arm, until it finally ended at the spinward edge of the Orion Arm. Harker felt something cold creep down his neck when he realized that the thing was presently traveling through their own sector of the galaxy.

'The Annihilator has been in existence as long as even the oldest starfaring races can remember,' Lawrence continued. 'We believe that it originated beyond our own galaxy, the result of two globular clusters, or perhaps even a pair of dwarf galaxies, coming into collision. Under normal circumstances, the black holes at their cores would coalesce, become as one . . . yet on rare occasion, their opposite spins cause one of the holes to be ejected and thus become a rogue singularity, moving through intergalactic space until it is inevitably drawn toward another galaxy.'

Lawrence pointed to the Annihilator's track. 'This is what has happened here. Countless billions of years ago, the Annihilator entered our own galaxy. It takes millions of years to move from one arm to another, and only lately has it entered our part of the galaxy . . . perhaps as recently as ten thousand years ago. Nonetheless it is unstoppable. It is a force of nature, the most lethal ever discovered.'

Lawrence turned toward Harker. 'The result is always the same. If it happens to pass through a star system, any planet in its path is destroyed. Over time, its accretion belt has grown so large that even a close pass is sufficient to exterminate all life upon a world unfortunate enough to be in its way.' The image of the Annihilator expanded once more, and the ghost pointed to its swirling bands of color. 'What you see here are the remains of worlds . . . perhaps countless in number . . . that have been reduced to little more than dust and rubble. And, yes, some of these have been inhabited.'

'And the survivors?' Harker stared at the image. 'What have they . . . ?'

'No world, no race, has ever survived an encounter with the Annihilator. Save for one, and only one.'

The Annihilator dissolved, to be replaced by a graphic representation of a solar system: six planets orbiting a small yellow star. 'Approximately four hundred years ago, by your reckoning, the Annihilator passed through the Lambda Aurigae system, little more than forty-one light-years from Earth. You should consider yourselves fortunate that your own system was not in its path. Otherwise, you would not be here today. Instead, it came upon the homeworld of another race, known in their own language as the *taaraq*.'

The holo zoomed in upon the second planet orbiting Lambda Aurigae. 'At the time, the *taaraq* had recently achieved the ability to travel from one world to another, though only within their own system. Interstellar travel was beyond their means. Yet they were an industrious and resourceful race, capable of making great technological strides within a short amount of time, and when they detected the Annihilator and realized what it meant for them, they took measures to ensure the survival of their species.'

The view expanded slightly to encompass an asteroid belt near the *taaraq* homeworld. 'Devoting all their energies to the effort, they transformed a nearby asteroid into a starship . . . *Shaq-Taaraq*, or ship of the *taaraq* – and transported as many of their people as they could to the vessel, where they entered a state of long-term hibernation not unlike your own.'

'So that's what it was,' Harker murmured. 'An ark.'

'A goddamn big ark.' Judging from the sound of his voice, Ramirez was similarly humbled. 'There must be millions of them aboard.'

'Two million, five hundred thousand.' The ghost raised a hand, and the holo changed again, this time to display an image they had all seen before: Spindrift, *Shaq-Taraaq*, as a dark and lightless asteroid wandering between the stars. 'At the time of the coming of the Annihilator, there were nearly five billion *taaraq* . . . a race that, until doomsday came upon them, had lived in peace. The majority of their race willingly sacrificed their lives so that only a relative handful would survive. The rest stayed behind and became little more than dust.'

'They fired Spindrift's engines and made their escape.' Emily's voice was choked with sadness. 'Oh, God . . .'

Harker stepped closer to her, wrapped an arm around her shoulders. Five billion dead so that only two and a half million could survive. He knew nothing of the *taaraq* save for what little he'd seen of them within the catacombs of Spindrift, yet he was suddenly ashamed of himself for having thought of them as monsters. Far from that; when doomsday had come to their world, they'd mustered the courage to save some of their kind, even if it meant that the rest would perish, their lives snuffed out by a true horror.

'Where did they intend to go?' Ramirez asked. 'If they've been traveling for four centuries . . .'

'So far as we've been able to determine, their destination is a star system elsewhere in our local arm, one that contains an uninhabited planet suitable for their biological requirements. The *Talus* has decided to keep secret the location of this planet, in order to prevent another race from colonizing it before *Shaq-Taaraq* arrives.'

'Then you've known about *Shaq-Taaraq* for quite some time.' Even as he spoke, Harker realized that he was stating the obvious. 'If that's so, why haven't you helped them?'

'*Shaq-Taaraq* was discovered by a *hjadd* ship about two centuries ago. Like yourselves, its crew decided to explore it. During that time, they were able to access the memory systems, and in time we were able to decipher the *taaraq* language, much as we deciphered your own, and learned the history of their race. When we realized what we'd found, the *hjadd* reported the matter to the *Talus*, where the issue was discussed by the High Councils. In the end, it was decided that the *Talus* should treat the *taaraq* much as they would any intelligent race whom they had discovered that had not yet developed hyperspace technology . . . we would not interfere with their history but allow nature to take its own course.'

Once more, Lawrence turned toward the light shaft. The image changed again, this time to reveal the starbridge orbiting Spindrift. 'However, because the *taaraq* are helpless . . . the *Shaq-Taaraq* has no defensive capabilities, because the race is pacifist by nature and its builders believed there were no other intelligent species in the galaxy . . . the *Talus* decided that it should do what it could to protect the *taaraq* for the duration of their voyage. So a starbridge was established near the asteroid, one equipped with sensors that would alert us to any incursion by an unauthorized vessel . . .'

'And a beacon that was supposed to warn them away.' Harker nodded. 'But what you didn't count on was an alien race . . . us, that is . . . discovering *Shaq-Taaraq* and sending out an expedition before the message could be translated.'

'That is correct . . . and the consequences were unfortunate.' Lawrence gestured toward the light shaft. Now they saw, from an omniscient point of view, the *Galileo* approaching the *Talus* starbridge; Harker suddenly realized that they were viewing video images taken by Jerry, the probe that had been parked in orbit near the starbridge.

An instant later, there was a bright flash of light, then

a strange craft hurtled through the ring. 'That was a *hjadd* ship,' Lawrence said, 'dispatched by the *Talus* to investigate the presence of an alien vessel. An attempt was made to communicate with your ship. However . . .'

As they watched, a small object was launched from *Galileo. That goddamn torpedo*, Harker thought. *Ian, you bloody idiot . . .*

Emily turned away, burying her face against his chest, as the torpedo silently detonated. A white-hot sphere quickly enveloped the *Galileo*, tearing it apart like a plastic toy and scattering debris in all directions, merely buffeting the *hjadd* ship. 'An unfortunate misunderstanding,' Lawrence's specter intoned. 'Had we known better . . .'

'Right.' Despite an instinctive surge of anger, Harker found himself feeling ashamed. Paranoia, distrust, ignorance: all these things had led to the destruction of his ship and its crew. 'If I'd known . . . if I could have stopped this . . .'

'The situation was beyond your control.' The light shaft disappeared, and Lawrence stood before them. 'You are not to blame, nor are any of your companions. As we now understand the circumstances, from our interviews with each of you, it's apparent that you made your best efforts to prevent this incident in the first place.'

For the first time, Harker realized how ironic it was that the *hjadd* had chosen Ian Lawrence's image and voice. 'I'm sorry that it happened this way, too, but . . .'

'Not so fast.' Ramirez stood up. 'We've been asleep for fifty-three years. That's a long time, especially if . . .'

'Yes. I'd like to know that, too.' Pulling herself away from Harker, Emily turned to confront Lawrence's ghost.

'Why keep us asleep for so long? If you found us on Spindrift . . .'

'We discovered your shuttle on *Shaq-Taaraq* shortly after you went into biostasis,' Lawrence said. 'It was recovered by our ship and transported to *Talus qua'spah*, where its memory was probed while your bodies remained in hibernation. As with the *taaraq*, it took many years for us to decipher your language. That is the reason why we're able to communicate with you in your own tongue.'

'Fifty-three years?' Ramirez was skeptical. 'Weren't in any sort of rush, were you?'

Harker realized that he had a point. 'He's right. There's something else going on here.' A new thought occurred to him. 'Why are you still hiding? Aren't you willing to show yourselves?'

Once more, Lawrence went silent for a moment. Emily moved closer to Harker. 'You think you might have pushed it a little?' she murmured. 'I mean . . .'

'What are they afraid of?' Harker didn't bother to lower his voice. 'They're holding all the cards, aren't they? If they want us to trust them, then . . .'

'Quite correct, Commander.' Lawrence's image became active again. 'Perhaps the time has come for us to discard the mask.'

And then Ian Lawrence dissolved, to be replaced by their first sight of a *hjadd*.

The being that materialized before them wasn't as grotesque as a *taaraq*, but it was no less bizarre. A little shorter than Harker, the *hjadd* faintly resembled what he imagined a Galapagos tortoise might look like if it didn't have a shell. Standing erect on two short, thick legs, most of its broad body was concealed beneath a flowing, toga-like garment; only its hands, oddly delicate yet covered by leathery skin the color of dark mud, could be seen, clasped together within the robe's flowing bell sleeves.

Its head, mounted at the end of an elongated neck, was narrow and hairless, its most notable feature a pair of protuberant, heavy-lidded eyes that seemed to move independently of one another. Below a stubby snout was a broad, lipless mouth that seemed to be cast in a perpetual frown. The skin around its face was mottled with colored patterns of stripes and blotches; when it spoke, small membranes on either side of its skull gently pulsed. On occasion a narrow fin, running from the top of its head down the back of its neck, rose ever so slightly.

'Allow me to introduce myself,' the *hjadd* said, its voice a low, almost feminine contralto. 'My name is Mahamatasja Jas Sa-Fhadda. You may call me Jas, for sake of simplicity. I have been designated as Prime Emissary for contact between the *Talus* and your species.' It raised a webbed, six-fingered hand, held it palm outward. 'Greetings and good health to you.'

Uncertain of the proper protocol, Harker hesitantly imitated Jas's gesture. 'Greetings and good health to you as well,' he said as he peered more closely at the *hjadd*. So far as he could tell, it was a holograph, just as Lawrence had been. 'I take it that you're . . . well, unwilling to meet us in person.'

'No insult is intended.' When Jas spoke, the movements of its mouth were out of sync with its words; some sort of translation device was being used. 'Although our atmospheric composition is similar to your own, the nitrogen-oxygen ratio is much different, as is the pressure ratio. You would quickly become ill if exposed to our ambient environment, and vice versa. One of us would have to wear an environment suit in order to meet face-to-face, and since we decided that you should see us for what we are . . .'

'I understand. Thank you, Mamahataja . . .' Harker stumbled over the complex syllables. This was received by a dry, froglike croak; the *hjadd*'s fin rose slightly, and its membranes bulged outward.

'Please, call me Jas,' it said, its voice taking on a terse edge. 'Mispronunciation of clan names is considered an insult among my culture.'

'Jas is your given name?' Ramirez stepped a little closer, obviously intrigued. 'And . . . um, Sa-Fhadda? What does it mean?'

'It designates both my caste and my social status.' The left eye twitched toward Ramirez. 'This would take a long time to explain. For the time being, you need only to know that I am highborn within my society.' Another croak, this one a little more high-pitched, accompanied by a subtle swelling of sacs within the *hjadd*'s throat. 'You should be aware that further inquires would give my clan-mates reasons to challenge you to a duel. I do not believe you would like that.'

'Not at all.' Ramirez hastily stepped back. 'Sorry. No insult intended.'

'None taken, on first offense.' Jas's left eye turned toward Emily. 'Speaking of which . . . Lieutenant Collins? Your marital status is of great interest to our sociologists.'

'It is?' Emily looked surprised. 'Why?'

'You were found aboard a craft with two males. This

indicates that your species has two discrete genders. Since we assume that both males are your mates . . .'

'What?' Emily's face reddened, and Harker had to clasp a hand to his mouth to stifle a laugh, while Ramirez simply turned away. 'No . . . neither of them are my mates,' she said quickly. 'They're simply . . . you know . . . males. And I'm a female. And that's it.'

For a moment, Jas said nothing. It . . . or rather heshe, Harker suddenly realized . . . regarded the three of them with solemn curiosity, hisher eyes shifting back and forth. 'How very curious,' the *hjadd* said at last. 'Two males, one female, and yet no bonding. Your reproductive system is . . .'

'Why were we kept in biostasis for so long?' Harker decided to change the topic. His father had taught him that there were three things one never discussed in polite company: politics, religion, and sex. Now he knew why, although for reasons his father would have never expected. 'You said that we've been asleep for fifty-three years. I understand that you had to learn our language, but even then . . .' He paused. 'I'm sorry, but I don't believe that's the only reason.'

Jas turned toward him again, hisher fin rising slightly from hisher skull. 'Yes,' heshe said, 'you're entirely correct. That was not the only reason. The *Talus* wished to see what else your race intended to do.'

'What else?' Ramirez stared at himher. 'I don't . . .'

'We first became aware of your race when you sent a ship beyond the range of your system two hundred and seventy-three years ago, by your reckoning.'

'The *Alabama*,' Harker said. 'Launched in 2070, on course for 47 Ursae Majoris.' He hesitated. 'That is, a habitable satellite of a superjovian gas giant in orbit around . . .'

'We are aware of the world, yes, and also that particular ship. One of our own vessels spotted it shortly after it left the periphery of your system. This was how the *Talus* learned of the existence of your race.' Jas's eyes wavered between him, Ramirez, and Emily. 'At first, the High Councils considered you to be only a curiosity, and decided not to intervene.'

'Because we hadn't yet developed hyperspace technology?' Ramirez asked.

'Correct. For us, your kind was just one more race that learned to leave its homeworld.' Jas folded hisher hands together within the folds of hisher robe. 'After a time, though, your race sent more ships to that system, and we realized that you were making an effort to colonize. So we decided to wait and watch, to see what you would do. And then you went to *Shaq-Taaraq* . . .'

'That raised your interest.' Harker was beginning to catch on. 'We found the *taaraq* . . .'

'After that, we were unsure of your intentions.' Jas's membranes fluttered. 'Were you destined to be a friend, a foe, or a race best left undisturbed? We didn't know. All we could do was wait to see what you would do.'

'And keep us asleep until then.' Harker tried not to let his temper rise.

'My apologies, Commander. We did not know whether your kind was . . .' Jas hesitated. 'Mature enough to be trusted.'

Harker let out his breath. 'Well, all right then. You've kept us in hibernation for over a half century while you've observed our kind. So what's your judgment?'

The *hjadd* silently regarded him for a long moment. 'We believe the time has come for the *Talus* to make contact with your people. Would you be willing to make the necessary introductions?'

Harker glanced at the others. Seeing no argument, he nodded. 'Very well, then,' Jas said. 'Then we shall proceed with no further delay.'

Heshe stepped back, and the fireplace rumbled lightly as it moved aside, revealing a hexagon-shaped door. As Harker watched, the door split in half. Beyond it lay a long, brightly lit corridor, its paneled walls gleaming like burnished copper. Bowing slightly, Jas extended a webbed hand toward the passageway.

'If you will come this way,' heshe said, 'I will show you how to return to your own kind.'

Nineteen

JANUARY 18, 2344 – *TALUS QUA'SPAH*

Emily felt a twinge of dread as she followed Harker into the corridor. Until now, their surroundings had been familiar; even though the *Galileo* in which she'd awakened was little more than an unconvincing facsimile, at least it was enough of a human environment that she didn't feel threatened. Indeed, that was why the *hjadd* had made the effort in the first place.

This was something new. When the library fireplace turned out to be little more than a façade for a hidden door, she had the urge to grab Ted's arm and cling to it. She hadn't been with him or Jared when they'd explored Spindrift's tunnels, so this was her first exposure to a place that, beyond doubt, had been constructed by alien hands. Perhaps the other two were used to it already, but she wasn't, and it was all that she could do to keep her fear from getting the better of her.

'Where does this . . . ?' she started to ask, pausing to look back only to discover that the door had silently closed behind Ramirez as soon as he'd entered the corridor behind her. Just as startled as she was, Jared turned to inspect the inside of the portal.

'Sorry, guys,' he said after a moment. 'If there's a way to open it, I can't find it.'

'We couldn't be so lucky twice.' Harker gazed at the corridor in which they found themselves. Like the door, it had the same hexagonal configuration, its copper-paneled walls angled outward at shoulder height. 'But we can breathe . . . at least they've accommodated us that much.'

'Our native guide has disappeared.' For the first time, Emily realized that they were alone. No sign of Jas, or even Lawrence's doppelgänger. 'Guess this part isn't equipped for holo imaging.'

'Perhaps it's not important enough.' Harker pointed to the other end of the corridor. Less than fifteen meters away lay another door, identical to the one through which they had just passed. 'Jas clearly wants us to go there. So . . .'

'Sure. Why not?' Emily tried to be nonchalant, yet she took Ted's hand in hers as they continued down the corridor.

They'd just reached the second door when it bisected, revealing what appeared to a small, dimly lit room. Like the corridor, the walls on either side of them were lined with copperlike plates that, as soon as they walked in, glowed to life with a mellow golden radiance. The opposite wall, though, was little more than a floor-to-ceiling plate of black glass. Once again, the door closed as soon as they entered the room. Seeing their reflections in the glass, Emily realized just how helpless they appeared. Three dumb humans who'd stumbled into a place where they had no business.

'This just keeps getting better and better,' Ramirez murmured. 'Maybe next they'll . . .'

'This is only a temporary resting place,' Jas said. 'We hope the surroundings aren't too intimidating.'

Caught by surprise, Emily looked around to see, behind

them to their right, the *hjadd* standing in a shadowed corner of the room. This time, though, the alien wore an outfit that was doubtless an environmental suit of some sort. Light grey and made of some plastic material, it covered himher from feet to neck; hisher head was encased within a cylindrical helmet, with a reflective visor hiding hisher face.

'Please forgive my appearance.' Jas's voice came from a small grille at the base of hisher helmet. 'Your atmosphere is toxic to us, so this suit is necessary. It is more convenient for me to protect myself than it would be for us to manufacture suits for the three of you.'

Yet that wasn't the most startling difference. For the first time, Jas seemed to have form and substance that heshe had lacked earlier. The subdued light from the walls cast shadows from hisher body, giving himher a lifelike quality that had been absent before.

'You . . .' She stumbled for words. 'You're real.'

A sibilant, stuttering hiss; oddly, it sounded like a reptilian sort of laugh. 'If by "real" you mean that I'm not a projection, then yes, I'm a corporeal entity.' Jas raised hisher gloved right hand, palm down. 'You may touch me if you're still uncertain.'

Emily hesitated. 'Go ahead,' Harker whispered. 'Your turn to make history.'

Feeling herself shake with fear, yet nonetheless compelled to do so, Emily stepped closer to Mahamatasja Jas Sa-Fhadda and, extending her hand, gently touched the back of hisher palm. To her surprise, she could feel warmth through the glove; despite appearances, its texture was as fine as cotton gauze.

'See? Not so unalike, you and I.' Jas slowly rotated

hisher wrist, allowing Emily's hand to rest within hisher own. 'We do not clasp hands when we greet one another,' heshe continued, hisher voice quiet and undemanding, 'but we understand the gesture is significant with your kind. May I shake your hand, Lieutenant Collins?'

'Yes . . .' Emily swallowed. 'Yes, you may.'

Ever so gently, the *hjadd* closed hisher hand around her own. Six webbed digits encompassed her five fingers; for a brief moment, she felt a soothing warmth like none she'd ever felt before, sensual and almost erotic, disturbed only by the hard leading edge of hisher talons against the inside of her wrists. If heshe chose to remove the glove, Jas could easily open a vein with those claws, yet she knew that heshe would not do so. This was a gesture of trust, as none she'd experienced before.

'Greetings, Emily Collins,' Jas said. 'I am honored to meet you.'

'Thanks . . . thank you.'

'You are welcome.' Heshe released her hand, then turned to the others. 'Now, let me show you how you will return home.'

The wall became transparent, and they found themselves gazing out at the *Maria Celeste*.

The shuttle rested on its landing gear at the center of a large, hangarlike room. The belly ramp had been lowered, and Emily noticed that the fuselage was clean, the black dust the craft had collected on Spindrift long since cleared away. Indeed, it almost seemed as if *Maria* had been parked there some time ago, and now patiently awaited the return of her crew.

Yet the shuttle wasn't the same as when she'd last seen

it fifty-three years ago. Where there had once been the bell-shaped nozzles of its twin nuclear engines there was now a pair of oblong humps that bulged from the stern. Looking closer, Emily saw that the VTOL engines were missing as well; the underside was smooth, plated over with no sign that the thrusters had ever been there.

'Oh my God!' She stared aghast at *Maria*. 'What have you done to my ship?'

Harker noticed the changes as well. 'You expect her to fly that?' he demanded, the patterns of his robe becoming bright red as he pointed through the window. 'We won't even be able to get off the . . . !'

'Allow me to explain, please.' The *hjadd* hastily backed away from them. Despite her outrage, Emily found a certain dim satisfaction in the realization that these creatures, as superior as they seemed, could nonetheless be intimidated. 'Your ship will still be able to travel. In fact, the alterations have greatly increased its efficiency . . .'

'I don't care about efficiency.' Stepping forward, Emily stared directly at Jas's helmet. She couldn't see hisher face though the visor, only her own reflection, yet nonetheless she knew that the *hjadd* was looking straight at her. 'You never mess with a pilot's craft without her permission. I don't care if . . .'

Jas hissed, more menacingly this time, as heshe raised hisher hands in a gesture that was unmistakably defensive. 'Stand down, Emcee,' Ted murmured, grasping her arm and pulling her back. 'Take it easy. We can work this out.' He moved between her and the *hjadd*. 'No offense intended. We're only . . . surprised . . . by what you've done.'

Jas lowered hisher hands, and heshe assayed a slight

bow. 'My own apologies. Our study of your culture gave us no indication that your kind felt so . . . personally . . . about your craft.'

Now it was Emily's turn to feel humiliated. Less than a minute ago, she'd felt nothing but warmth toward the *hjadd* emissary. Then she'd almost ruined it with a tantrum that she wouldn't have thrown at a spacecraft mechanic back home. 'My fault,' she said quietly, bowing as well. 'Perhaps I should have listened first.'

'Well done,' Ramirez whispered from behind her. 'Now shut up and be nice.'

She didn't look back at him, but made a mental note to herself that she was in the presence of an alien race. So far, this was something only Ramirez seemed to comprehend fully.

'Then I will continue, with your permission.' Calm once more, Jas returned to the window. 'The alterations were necessary for two reasons. When we recovered your craft from *Shaq-Taaraq* and brought it here, we soon discovered that it would be difficult to safely contain the radioactive materials within its engines for a long period of time. The *Talus* has long since ceased relying upon nuclear fission as its primary source of energy for this very reason. So we were forced to dismantle your engines and dispose of them in order to protect ourselves.'

'Quite understandable,' Ramirez said. 'Please, go on.'

'The second reason is that, in order for this craft to travel through our starbridge, we had to install a version of our own drive system.' Jas gestured toward the two bulges. 'Your craft now utilizes a negative-mass means of propulsion far more suitable for hyperspace. You will find that your ship will operate just the same way as it did before. However, of course, the new system will produce a much higher mass-to-thrust ratio, and your internal guidance and navigation system will have a much more limited set of parameters.'

'Limited? I don't understand.' Emily shook her head. 'What do you mean by that?'

Jas's faceplate turned toward her. 'As I explained earlier, the method of hyperspace travel your race developed is nearly identical to those developed by other races in the *Talus*. The basic principles are virtually the same. However, the major difference is that, until very recently, your race had only two starbridges . . . the one in orbit near your world, Earth, and the one you had established at the outermost edge of your solar system.'

'KX-1,' Harker said. 'That was an experimental bridge. We used it to rendezvous with Spindrift . . . *Shaq-Taaraq*, I mean.'

'We are aware of that. Since then, that starbridge has been rendered inactive. The only one that remains beyond your home system is that which was recently established near 47 Ursae Majoris, near the habitable moon of a gas giant in that system.'

'That would be Coyote. You mean to say . . . ?' Emily glanced at Harker, saw the same look of astonishment on his face. 'They've built a starbridge there?'

'During the time you have been asleep, yes.' Jas emitted a hiss that may have expressed either amusement or irritation; Emily was still unsure of how the *hjadd* registered emotion. 'They have used it to achieve hyperspace travel between Earth and its colony. By those same means, you will be able to reach . . . Coyote, you call it? . . . from here.'

'Or Earth,' Emily said.

'No.' The *hjadd*'s helmet swung back and forth upon hisher long neck, an oddly human gesture. 'You will not be permitted to return directly to Earth . . . only 47 Ursae Majoris.'

'"Not be permitted?"' Harker stared at Jas. 'How can you tell us where we will or will not . . . ?'

'Allow me to continue, please.' The *hjadd* raised a hand, admonishing him to be silent. 'As I said, your shuttle's navigation computer has been programmed to function only within a limited set of parameters. This is how all *Talus* hyperspace vehicles operate. In order for a ship successfully to navigate between one starbridge and another, both sets of space-time coordinates must be entered into its guidance system. Otherwise, a wormhole won't be formed, and any ship that attempts to make the jump to hyperspace would be instantly destroyed.'

'This is how our own starbridges work,' Emily said. 'Yes, I understand.'

'Then you understand how such coordinates would be invaluable to both friend and foe alike.' Jas paused. 'A race would be unwise to share such information freely, or at least without knowing the intentions of a newly discovered race.'

'In this case, our own.' Ramirez nodded slowly. 'That would make sense.'

'Pleased to know that you understand, Dr Ramirez.' Jas's head swiveled toward him. 'One of the Precepts . . . the *Talus* constitution, if you wish to call it that . . . states that no member race is required to relinquish the coordinates of its home system's starbridge to another race until both have negotiated agreements regarding security, commerce, and cultural exchange. Furthermore, no newly discovered races will be given coordinates to any member of the *Talus* until that race has been inducted into the *Talus* . . .'

'And we're not ready to join the club yet,' Ramirez said.

'No. Not yet.' Jas hesitated, as if picking hisher words carefully, and once again Emily was struck by how reticent heshe could be. Apparently the *hjadd*, as friendly as they might seem, were guarded about what they shared with other races. 'We know the coordinates of your starbridge at 47 Ursae Majoris. They have been entered into your ship's guidance system. Once your craft makes the jump, the coordinates for the *Talus qua'spah* will be automatically eradicated from its memory, eliminating any chance that humankind will be able to retrace its steps here. In that way, our security will be assured . . . or at least until we are prepared to trust you.'

'But . . .' Emily shook her head. 'Why not Earth? That's our homeworld, after all.'

'To demonstrate that we have no intentions of invading your own planet. Trust should be mutually achieved.' Jas gazed at her with what seemed to be infinite patience. 'This is only the prelude to first contact among our races. Your colony affords us a neutral meeting place. Until then, though, we have much to learn about one another. Which is why we ask you to be our intermediaries.'

An immense weight settled upon Emily's shoulders. She glanced at Ted, then at Jared; even without their saying so, she knew from the expressions on their faces that they felt the impact of hisher words.

'That's . . . you ask much of us,' Harker stammered.

'We barely understand your race, or the *Talus*. You probably don't know much about us, either. We can't . . .'

'Of course not.' Again, a stuttering hiss that may have been a laugh. 'This is why I am making the journey with you.'

'You're . . . ?' Harker's mouth fell open. 'We don't . . . I mean, we can't . . .'

'As I said earlier, I have been designated the Prime Emissary. this is why I have taken the effort personally to introduce myself to you.' Jas waved a hand toward the window. 'As for my accommodations, your craft has already been refurbished to suit my requirements.'

'But . . .' Emily shook her head. 'If you can't return, then how can we . . . ?'

'If your kind wished to join the *Talus*, it will find the ways and means to construct suitable dwellings.' Again, the *hjadd* hesitated. 'The risk is mine to assume. Your race may choose to murder me, just as your Captain Lawrence attempted to destroy our ship . . .'

'That was an accident,' Harker insisted.

'Then I will discover if that is so and not simply the reaction of a hostile and immature species.' Heshe paused. 'Will you accept me and our offer for contact? Or should we simply send you back to your own kind and regard your race as one best left alone?'

Emily started to open her mouth, then realized that she couldn't speak for the others. Instead, she looked around at Ted, then Jared. The three of them studied one another for a few moments; for once, no one argued.

'We accept,' Harker said at last, then he paused. 'But . . .'

'Yes?' Jas's faceplate moved toward him. 'A question?'

'If we're supposed to supply accommodations for you

once we reach Coyote . . . 47 Ursae Majoris, that is . . . then how can we . . . ?' He shook his head. 'How can we feed you, for starters?'

The *hjadd* made a snuffling sound that Emily was at a loss to interpret. 'Our organisms aren't as dissimilar as you might believe,' heshe said. 'When we found your craft, we discovered within it a sample of a vegetable substance that we found quite palatable, even stimulating.' Reaching into a pocket of hisher suit, Jas groped for something. 'In fact, we believe this may prove to be a major source of trade between our races.'

Coffee, Emily thought. *They must have found our coffee supply*. 'I'm sure that can be arranged,' she said. 'It's something that we grow in abundance, so we shouldn't have . . .'

Her voice trailed off as Jas withdrew a familiar plastic canister. Harker's face became almost as red as the patterns of his robe, and Ramirez's robe assumed an aquamarine hue that suited the grin that crept across his face, as the *hjadd* carefully opened the canister and allowed a few precious flakes of cannabis to fall into the palm of hisher glove.

'Delicious,' Jas said. 'May we have more?'

The propulsion and navigation systems weren't the only things different about the *Maria Celeste*. As soon as she walked up the ramp, Emily saw that the entire aft compartment had been rebuilt. Where there had once been four emergency biostasis cells now lay an airtight bulkhead separating the rear of the shuttle from the cockpit, A small hatch, just the right height for a *hjadd* but short enough that an average-size human would have to bend in order to enter it, had been placed in the center of the bulkhead.

'My cabin,' Jas said, as if an explanation was necessary. 'Many apologies for the alterations made by my people, but they were necessary.'

'Understandable. You'll need a place to live, after all.' Emily ducked her head to peer through the open hatch. On the other side of what appeared to be a closet-size airlock lay a small stateroom; she spotted what appeared to be a child-size waterbed, along with a wing chair and a miniature desk. It was even more cramped than her cabin aboard the *Galileo*. 'Rather tight, don't you think?'

'My people are accustomed to close surroundings. Its life-support system will sustain me almost indefinitely, or at least until more satisfactory shelter is provided by your colony.' Heshe hesitated. 'Please refrain from entering my quarters. I consider my privacy to be important to the success of my mission.'

'Of course.' Harker stood off to one side, his arms folded together across his *sha*. 'You're accepting a lot on faith, aren't you? We can't even be sure how they'll react to us, let alone you.'

'Then this will be an interesting journey for all of us.' Turning away from hisher cabin, Jas gestured toward the cockpit. 'My belongings have already been placed aboard. If you are ready, then we will make our departure.'

Startled, Emily stared at himher. 'Now? That's it?'

'Certainly.' The *hjadd*'s helmet rose slightly upon hisher neck. 'Is there a reason why we should not go?'

'Isn't there anyone you need to see before you leave?' Harker glanced toward the ramp. 'A last meeting with your . . . um, High Council, maybe. Farewells to any family and friends.'

The *hjadd* said nothing for a moment. 'No. All my

affairs have already been settled.' A slow hiss. 'My people do not put much ceremony in departures or arrivals. We leave, we are gone for a while, we come back. That is the way of things.'

'But . . .' Ramirez hesitated, as if not quite knowing how to express himself. 'We've only met you. No others of your kind. Don't they wish to meet us as well?'

'No.' This came as a flat statement, almost a dismissal. 'If and when the time comes that further contact with our kind is acceptable, then you will meet other *hjadd*. Until then, I am the Prime Emissary of both my kind and the *Talus*.'

Emily nodded. It wasn't hard to read between the lines. Until Jas established favorable relations with this newly discovered species, the *hjadd*, as well as the rest of the *Talus*, would minimize their contact as much as possible. But just as Mahamatasja Jas Sa-Fhadda was putting himherself at considerable risk, so were they. If something were to happen to himher . . .

'Are you ready?' Jas asked, hisher helmet revolving toward the cockpit. 'My people are waiting to open the starbridge.'

'Of course. By all means.' Trading a wary glance with Harker, Emily turned toward the flight deck.

The cockpit looked much the same as she'd left it, yet upon closer inspection she saw that it had undergone its own modifications. One of the passenger seats had been removed – remembering that this was where Cruz had sat, she felt a surge of remorse – and replaced with a sleek couch contoured to match Jas's broad body and high neck. The left-side console in front of the pilot's seat had been altered as well; the engine control panels and navigation comps were gone, with black, reflective slates in their place. Otherwise, everything else appeared to be untouched.

'Your ship will operate much the same way as it did before,' Jas said, standing behind her in the aisle while she and the others fastened their harnesses. 'The only difference is that you will not need to activate the engines or program your computers. All these requirements have already been preset within the ship's internal control and guidance system.'

'So what do I do?' Emily found her headset dangling from the control yoke. Despite the fact that it was a half century old, the foam pads of the earpieces looked as if they'd been replaced only yesterday. Indeed, except for the alterations, *Maria*'s cockpit had been perfectly preserved, without even a mote of dust to be seen. 'Just . . . take off and fly? Simple as that?'

'Simple as that.' Jas moved to hisher seat, carefully settled into it. 'If you have forgotten how to operate your vehicle, of course, or otherwise lack the confidence . . .'

'Careful.' Harker twisted around in his seat to favor the *hjadd* with a cold stare. 'You're talking to the best pilot the European Space Agency has ever seen.'

'Pardon me.' A slow, stuttering hiss from their passenger. 'I did not mean to insult.'

Keeping a straight face, Ted gave Emily a sly wink. 'That's all right,' she said. 'Just don't let it happen again.' Then she reached forward to the instrument panel and switched it on.

Its lights and screens lit at once, with no trace of a flicker. As an afterthought, she accessed the backup flight recorder; a quick glance at the menu showed her that its memory was intact, with no trace of erasure or core erosion. Apparently the *hjadd*, after probing the system, had decided to leave it alone; the last date registered on the automatic logbook was January 9, 2291, the day the *Galileo* was destroyed and her survivors had gone into emergency biostasis aboard the shuttle.

Emily shared a glance with Ted. Noticing the same thing, he quietly nodded. Whatever else lay before them, at least they had a way to prove their story. She took a deep breath, then pulled on her headset and proceeded with the prelaunch checklist.

She soon discovered that, although the engine ignition sequence was missing, there was no indication that the new propulsion system was active. Yet when she raised the gangway and pressurized the cabin, she glanced through the windows and saw that the hangar ceiling had opened like an enormous clamshell. Above them was a jet-black sky sprinkled with countless stars, the brightest ones forming constellations no human eye had ever seen before.

'We are ready to depart.' Jas was nestled within hisher couch, amorphous flanges holding hisher body secure. 'You may launch whenever you are ready.'

'Thanks.' Emily let out her breath. Then, for no other reason than a stubborn desire to retain tradition, she touched her mike wand. 'This is EAS *Maria Celeste*,' she said to whoever might be listening. 'Requesting permission to lift off.'

She waited a moment. No response. She looked over at Ted, and he shrugged. 'All right, then,' she murmured, then wrapped her hands around the yoke and pulled back.

With only the faintest of hums, and almost no sense of

motion, the shuttle rose from the hangar floor. It almost seemed as if she were flying a simulator, only without the fabricated rocking that a simulator would make to give verisimilitude to the experience. The ascent was smooth, eerie in its almost total silence; the curved walls of the hangar fell away below them, and suddenly she found herself rising into space.

'Ohhh . . .' Harker's voice was little more than a whisper. 'Will you look at that?'

All around them, for nearly as far as they could see, lay the immense structure that they'd glimpsed from *Galileo*'s reconstructed library. Like a vast and measureless molecule of some alien crystal, *Talus qua'spah* stretched out to all sides of them, scintillating in the sunlight reflected from the aquamarine world around which it orbited. Spars and spheres, buttresses and towers, rings and cylinders, all connected to one another by an infinitely complex network of struts and beams.

'Home,' Jas said, gazing out the window beside himher. For a moment, hisher voice sounded forlorn. Glancing over her shoulder at her new passenger, it seemed to Emily as if the *hjadd* was bidding farewell to a familiar place.

'Where to now?' she asked.

'You may release the controls.' Jas looked back at her. 'Your craft will take you there on its own.'

Emily looked at Harker. He silently nodded, and she removed her hands from the yoke. On its own, the shuttle moved away from the giant station, its prow lifting upward and out, until she saw that it was aligned with a tiny silver ring that hovered a short distance away.

Another starbridge, identical to the one *Galileo* had found in orbit above Spindrift. As the *Maria Celeste* hurtled toward it, Emily instinctively grasped the armrests of her seat. 'What do I do now?'

'You do nothing.' The *hjadd*'s voice was calm. 'You'll soon be where you should be.'

She was about to say something when the ring's interior lit with a cold blue fire. Emily had just enough time to grab Ted's hand, then . . .

Twenty

JANUARY 18, 2344 – 47 URSAE MAJORIS

. . . They were through the starbridge.

The second time wasn't nearly as grueling as the first. Although Harker was careful to close his eyes just before the *Maria Celeste* entered hyperspace, nonetheless he caught the brilliant flash of transition. Yet there was none of the violence he had experienced aboard the *Galileo* when it passed through KX-1; a brief moment of vertigo, as if the shuttle were executing a barrel roll, then everything was calm.

Opening his eyes, he took a deep breath. Through the cockpit windows, nothing but stars. *Talus qua'spah* had disappeared, but there was no clear indication of where they'd emerged. Emily was still holding tight to his hand, but already she was beginning to stir. Looking over at him, she gave him a wary smile.

'That's it?' she murmured. 'That's all?'

'Guess so.' He gently released her hand. 'Maybe we're getting used to this.'

'Forgive me for the sin of pride,' Jas said, hisher voice coming to them from behind Emily, 'but our hyperspace technology is more sophisticated than your own.' Another stuttering hiss that Harker had learned to recognize as the *hjadd* equivalent of a chuckle. 'We have been doing this for quite some time now.'

Harker craned his neck to look back at Jas. The *hjadd*

sat calmly in hisher seat; as before, Harker saw only a distorted reflection of himself in hisher helmet visor. For some reason, he found that irritating. 'If you're so confident,' he asked, 'then why . . . ?'

'Hold on,' Emily said. 'Picking up something on the com.'

Clasping her right hand against her headset, she reached up to the communications panel to adjust the frequency. 'Please repeat,' she said. 'Not clear.'

Harker reached up to his own headset, only to find that it had fallen down around his neck. He pulled it back in place in time to hear a male voice, fuzzed slightly by static: '*. . . to unidentified spacecraft, do you copy? Please identify yourself. Repeat, this is Starbridge Coyote to unidentified spacecraft. Please respond and identify yourself.*'

'We copy, Starbridge Coyote.' Emily's eyes widened. 'This is . . .'

'Let me handle this.' Emily gave him an irritated glance, then apparently remembered that, even though she was the pilot, Harker was still the senior officer aboard. She nodded, and Harker touched his headset wand. 'Starbridge Coyote, this is European Alliance shuttle *Maria Celeste*. Do you copy?'

As he spoke, he turned to gaze through the window to his right. Just off the shuttle's starboard wing, he spotted a silver ring: the starbridge through which they had just emerged. About ten kilometers away, he caught a glimpse of a spindle-shaped object that faintly resembled the *Galileo*, although without the torus of its diametric drive. The gatehouse, no doubt.

'They're never going to believe this,' Ramirez murmured behind him.

'Quiet.' Yet Harker exchanged another glance with

Emily. What if he was right? Nothing they could do about it, though, except try to be persuasive. 'Repeat,' Harker said, 'this is EAS *Maria Celeste*, responding to . . .'

'*We copy, unidentified craft.*' A different voice now, older and more authoritative. '*We have no knowledge of any EAS starship called* Maria Celeste. *Supply proper registry number at once.*'

'Told you so,' Ramirez said.

'Oh, for the love of . . .' Impatient, Emily reactivated her mike. 'Starbridge Coyote, this is EAS *Maria Celeste*, registry Alpha Romeo One-One-Nine-Two-Beta, an Ares-class shuttle belonging to EASS *Galileo*, registry Alpha Romeo One-One-Nine-Two-Alpha. Lieutenant Collins, Emily Anne, responding as pilot, with Commander Harker, Theodore Edward, responding as commanding officer. Check your database, or go read a history . . .'

'Cut it out.' Harker reached over to jab the lobe of Emily's headset, rendering it inactive. 'For all they know, this could be some sort of prank. We can't . . .'

'Commander? Lieutenant?' Ramirez was becoming annoyingly persistent. 'Hate to interrupt, but you may want to notice where we are.'

Turning to look back at him, Harker started to tell Ramirez to shut up, but Emily's startled gasp caused him to glance instead at the cockpit windows. And suddenly, everything changed.

While they'd been arguing, the shuttle's prow had slowly drifted of its accord. Where once had been only a starfield lay an immense planet. A gas giant, banded by swatches of light blue and purple, surrounded by a vast and elegant silver-gold ring that cast a dark, narrow shadow upon the cloud layers far below.

47 Ursae Majoris-B, also known as Bear. Harker stared at it in wonder, forgetting his quarrel with Emily. Just beyond the ring, glowing in the mellow light reflected by Bear from the system's distant sun, lay the jovian's family of satellites. Even though he'd never seen them before, he knew their names from the ESA database. Dog, Hawk, Eagle, Snake, Goat . . .

And largest and brightest among them, Coyote.

He was still staring through the cockpit windows when the voice of Starbridge Coyote came through his headset. '*Roger that,* Maria Celeste. *We have you confirmed. We . . .*' A moment passed. '*Never mind. Wherever you've been, welcome home.*'

Emily reactivated her headset. 'Thank you, Starbridge Coyote. We're glad to be back, too.'

Perhaps this wasn't home, not exactly, yet the sound of another human voice was all that mattered. Harker let out his breath, then tapped his mike. 'This is Commander Harker. Please give us proper landing coordinates, if you will.'

Under normal circumstances, the transit to Coyote would have taken at least ten hours. The *hjadd* drive slashed this time to less than two. Yet there was no sensation of acceleration; even as the shuttle hurtled through space, everyone aboard remained comfortable, as if the *Maria Celeste* possessed its own Millis-Clement field generator that negated the tremendous g force they should have been experiencing.

Harker tried to discuss this with Jas, but heshe had become silent since leaving Starbridge Coyote. Sealed within hisher environment suit, heshe refused to answer all but the most obvious questions. Apparently Jas was reluctant to divulge any further details about *hjadd* technology than was absolutely necessary. After a while, Harker gave up; settling back in his seat, he watched as Coyote steadily grew closer.

They were little more than an hour away from touchdown, with Coyote now a planet-size moon whose mottled green surface was crisscrossed with a complex pattern of blue river channels, when the com channel came alive again. 'Maria Celeste, *this is Liberty Communications, Coyote Federation.*' The voice was male, speaking in Anglo. '*Do you copy? Over.*'

Sitting up straight, Harker glanced over at Emily. Her hands remained on the yoke – she'd refused to switch to autopilot, even though Jas had told her that it was safe to do so – yet her eyes met his own. 'Coyote Federation?' she asked. 'Liberty Communications?'

'Damned if I know.' Harker shook his head. They'd learned little from their earlier exchange with the gatehouse. 'Fifty-six years . . . they must have some sort of government going on down there that we . . .'

'Maria Celeste, *this is Liberty Communications, Coyote Federation.*' The voice became more insistent. '*Do you . . . ?*'

Harker touched his mike. 'We copy,' he said. 'With whom am I speaking, please?'

'That's rather rude, don't you think?' Ramirez bent forward from his seat behind them. 'After all, we're . . .'

He was interrupted by a new voice, female this time: 'Maria Celeste, *this is President Wendy Gunther of the Coyote Federation. Would you please identify yourself?*'

'Like you said before,' Emily murmured. 'They've

heard we're coming . . . but they still don't believe us.'

'Hush. Both of you.' Harker tapped his mike again. 'Theodore Harker, first officer of the EAS *Galileo*. Never heard of the Coyote Federation, ma'am, but all the same we're glad to hear you.'

A long pause, during which Harker took a moment to gaze through the window. Coyote lay half in shadow, yet even from this distance he could make out lights here and there. He reached forward to punch up the nav display on the main comp screen; the coordinates they had been given corresponded with a location just north of the equator, near the place where daylight was beginning to fade. Late afternoon down there; he didn't want to land at night if they didn't need to do so.

'I think they're trying to make up their minds about us,' Emily said. 'Ted . . . ?'

'Right.' Time to be a little more persuasive. Harker touched his mike. 'Liberty, do you read?' he asked, and didn't wait for a response. 'We know this must be a surprise to you, but we're coming in fast, and we'd like to know where we can land. Assuming we have your permission, of course.'

Again, no immediate response. 'They must be really confused,' Ramirez said, no longer as sarcastic as he'd been before. 'Don't count on a warm reception.'

Harker nodded reluctantly. Although they'd picked up telemetry from weather and communications satellites during their approach, there was no sign of either the *Alabama* or any of the Union Astronautica starships subsequently sent by the Western Hemisphere Union. Yet the starbridge was a clear indication that the European Alliance already had a presence here. No telling what the political situation was like down there, but if they had to . . .

'*Affirmative, Mr Harker.*' President Gunther's voice came back online. '*You have permission to land. We're dispatching a craft to escort you to a nearby landing site.*'

'It may not be safe for them to do so.' Jas abruptly broke hisher silence. 'The field generated by our drive will cause problems with their vessel if it comes too close to us.'

Now you tell us, Harker thought. On the other hand, he seriously doubted that President Gunther or the Coyote Federation would allow a suspicious craft to enter their airspace unescorted. 'We appreciate that, Liberty,' he replied. 'However, please advise your craft to maintain safe distance. Our drive may interfere with their control systems if they come too close.'

'They're going to love that,' Ramirez said.

'They're going to have to.' The last thing Harker wanted was a crash caused by the *hjadd* drive. He looked back at Jas. 'Thanks for the warning.'

The *hjadd* had barely lifted a hand in acknowledgment when President Gunther's voice returned. '*We copy*, Maria Celeste, *and we'll take that under advisement.*' An uncertain pause. '*Mr Harker, the* Galileo *has been missing for a very long time. Where is it? And where are you coming from?*'

'Here it comes.' Emily's mouth tightened. 'The first of many, many questions.'

'Tell me about it.' Harker sank back in his seat. Simple and obvious questions, yet none with any simple or obvious answers. So much had happened in what subjectively seemed to be a short span of time, and yet he had to remember that fifty-six years had gone by since anyone had heard from the *Galileo*. Sooner or later, he would have to face a board of inquiry, account for not only his actions, but also those of others that were beyond his control.

Damn you, Ian, he thought. *You should have never been in command. If it hadn't been for you* . . .

'Ted?' Emily's quiet voice broke through his reverie. 'You need to say something.'

He sighed, sat up straight again. 'The *Galileo* has been destroyed, along with its crew, including the captain,' he said, prodding his mike. 'Only three survivors, myself included. We made the jump from HD 143761, Rho Coronae Borealis . . .'

Feeling his voice grow tight, he paused to swallow. Suddenly, the last thing he wanted to do was to explain to anyone what he and his crew had just been through. 'We're very tired, and we'd just like to land. We'll explain everything once we're on the ground. ETA' – he glanced at Emily, and she held up a finger – 'um, about an hour or so from now. *Maria Celeste*, over and out.'

Before he had to answer another question, he reached up to snap off the com. 'That was rather abrupt,' Ramirez said. 'What if they . . . ?'

'Jared, I'm getting tired of asking you to do this, but . . .'

'Shut up. Right.' Ramirez withdrew from the space between him and Emily.

Harker rubbed his temples with his fingertips. Beyond the cockpit windows, Coyote lay below them as a vast hemisphere that stretched as far as the eye could see, the outermost edge of its atmosphere appearing as a thin haze that lay above its curved horizon. Somewhere down there was human civilization, the first he'd seen in . . . a little over a week? No, years, really . . . and suddenly he found himself hungry to see his own kind again.

'What about you?' he asked, impulsively twisting about in his seat to look back at Jas. 'You've met three humans . . . ready to meet some more?'

The *hjadd* said nothing for a moment. Within hisher visor, Harker saw only his own face. 'I am prepared,' heshe said at last. 'I have complete confidence that this encounter will be a success.'

'You do?' Harker was mildly astonished. 'We haven't put on our best face, you know.'

'Precisely the reason,' the *hjadd* emissary said. 'Your race does not know I am coming. So they have not pretended to be anything other than what they are.'

It wasn't until heshe said this that Harker realized that he'd neglected to mention the *hjadd* at all.

It was nearly sundown when the *Maria Celeste* made its final approach to Liberty. As the shuttle lost altitude, Harker got a chance to study the settlement from the air, and was surprised to see just how large it was. There were dozens of buildings down there, possibly more than a hundred, ranging from wood-frame homes and log cabins arranged along tidy streets, to larger structures near the middle of town that might be shops or municipal buildings, to vast glass-roofed sheds that appeared to be community greenhouses.

These people haven't wasted any time, he thought. With night falling, lights gleamed within countless windows, He caught a glimpse of children playing softball in a schoolyard; they paused to stare upward at the spacecraft as it soared overhead. At least an entire generation has been born and raised here. Maybe more . . . those could be someone's grandchildren.

'Coming up on the coordinates.' Emily gently pulled back on the yoke. 'Landing field should be just ahead.' She paused, then added, 'Looks like there's more than just one town. I'm seeing more lights.'

As she said, there appeared to be another cluster of houselights, a little smaller than the first, located just beyond several hundred acres of farmland. Two towns so close to one another? There had to be some reason for this; he hoped it wasn't an indication of social division. 'That must be the landing field,' he said, pointing to a broad ring of lights on the outskirts of the second settlement. 'Go ahead and take her down.'

Emily reached forward to click the toggles that lowered the landing gear, then carefully pulled back on her yoke until the shuttle came to a midair standstill. Aside from the whine of the hydraulic systems, the low, steady hum of the *hjadd* drive was the only sound *Maria* made. No roar of engines, no blast of rockets; Harker could almost hear the wind whispering past the panes of the cockpit windows.

Glancing to his right, he caught sight of the spacecraft that had intercepted them just outside Coyote's atmosphere, descending within clouds of dust kicked up by its VTOLs. The CFS *Virginia Dare* was smaller and more streamlined than the older craft, but despite its advanced design, the *Maria Celeste* would have easily outraced it to the ground if Emily hadn't decreased her airspeed to allow the skiff to keep up with them. No doubt its crew was startled, yet they'd maintained radio silence except when absolutely necessary.

'Thirty meters . . . twenty . . . fifteen . . .' Emily kept an eye on the altimeter as she gradually coaxed her craft downward. 'Ten . . . five . . . four . . . three . . . two . . . contact light, one . . .' The lightest of jars, no more than a gentle nudge. 'We're on the ground,' she said, then reached up to kill the engines.

Yet she didn't need to turn off anything. Her console went dark, save for the life-support and communications panels. Red emergency lights glowed to life within the cabin, casting an amber radiance across everything. Harker looked back at Jas. 'What do we do now?' he asked.

'Nothing.' The *hjadd* remained in hisher seat. 'Your craft has safely landed. All you need to do now is disembark.'

'No, he means . . .' Clearly baffled, Emily stared at her instruments. 'The engines. Don't we need to . . . I mean, do something?'

'The drive will remain inactive until I give you the authority to activate it again.' Jas didn't move. 'Please do not attempt to examine or dismantle it in any way. The results would be unfortunate for all concerned.'

Apparently the *hjadd* had taken measures to prevent anyone from reverse-engineering their technology. The drive was, in effect, a sealed box that couldn't be opened without triggering some sort of booby trap. Best to leave it alone. 'Whatever you say,' Harker murmured, then turned to Ramirez. 'Make sense to you?'

'Sure. Fine with me.' Ramirez was staring out his window. 'Getting it through to them, though . . . that's going to be the trick.'

Harker followed his gaze. Three people stood at the edge of the landing field: two women and a man, maintaining an uncertain distance from the shuttle. Behind them were two more men, standing near an open gate within the chain-link fence surrounding the field. Harker couldn't help but notice that, while the first three were dressed formally, the other two wore blue uniforms and carried carbines.

'Our reception committee,' Harker said. 'Bet one of them is President Gunther.'

'Could be. It's the ones with the guns I'm nervous about.' Emily sighed, then unclasped her harness and rose from her seat. 'Well, no time like the present.'

'Sounds good to me.' Harker unfastened his harness and followed her. Ramirez waited for them to leave the forward cockpit, then pushed himself up from his seat. Yet Jas stayed where heshe was. Hisher hands upon hisher seat's armrests, heshe gazed straight ahead, apparently unwilling to move. Harker stopped, turned around to gaze at himher. 'Aren't you coming?' he asked.

'I will remain here.' The *hjadd*'s helmet didn't move in his direction. 'Bring your representatives aboard when you see fit. I will meet with them at that time.'

Harker hesitated, not quite knowing what to say or do next. This was the last thing he expected. After all, it had been the *hjadd* who'd wanted to make contact with humankind. Now that one of their race was there, heshe suddenly become reluctant to leave the shuttle. Perhaps this was normal diplomatic protocol within the *Talus*, and yet . . .

'Pardon me,' he murmured to Ramirez, then gently squeezed past him until he stood beside the Prime Emissary. Bending low, he peered at the silver visor. 'Jas . . . Mahamatasja Jas Sa-Fhadda . . . listen to me. There's no reason to be afraid . . .'

'I do not fear you.'

'No . . . no, I think you do.' Harker sat down on the armrest of Ramirez's seat. 'When we were on *Talus qua'spah*, you were ready and willing to talk to us, but from the moment you stepped aboard our craft, you've been reluctant to speak. I know there are reasons why you can't share everything with us, but . . .' He let out his breath. 'I know fear when I see it.' *Even from an alien*, he added silently.

'We do not fear you.' Jas's hands twitched ever so slightly. 'My race has been from one end of the galaxy to another. We belong to the Elders of the *Talus* High Council. We have seen things that are beyond your imagination. We have beheld the Annihilator . . .'

'All this, and more. Of that, I have no doubt.' Harker hesitated. 'And yet, you're frightened of us. I know this because I've seen it in my own kind. My captain, Ian Lawrence . . . so afraid of the unknown that he panicked when your ship appeared.'

'We have forgiven you . . .'

'You've forgiven us because you know why he did it.' Harker bent closer. 'Fear got the better of him . . . just as fear is getting the better of you.'

The silvered faceplate swiveled toward him. 'You presume too much.'

'Then prove it.' Harker opened his hands. 'You know we're not barbarians. Otherwise, you wouldn't have bothered to revive the three of us. So come meet others of our kind.'

'He's right.' Ramirez came closer. 'We've been waiting for you for a very long time. We have concocted countless stories, folklore, even entire myths and legends about you. Our people have waited centuries, even millennia, for this moment.' He paused. 'I've told you of the mistake I once made,' he went on, speaking more quietly. 'I know now why I was wrong. Life is too rare within the universe for us to waste it.'

'Exactly.' Harker glanced at him and nodded, then looked back at Jas. 'This is our moment. Don't let it pass.'

The *hjadd* didn't respond. Hisher helmet turned away from them, and Jas sat still in hisher seat, staring straight ahead. Harker waited patiently, wondering where this was going to lead. After a few moments, hisher right hand moved slightly upon hisher armrest. The seat restraints folded away into the seat, and the emissary stood up.

'Very well,' heshe said. 'I will accompany you, but only to the hatch. Once I have become convinced that your kind mean no harm . . .'

'We'll bring them aboard. Fair enough.' Harker stood up, turned toward the other two. 'Emily . . . ?'

'On my way.' She was already heading toward the aft compartment. A moment later, he heard the familiar whine of the gangway descending from the shuttle's lower hull.

Harker followed Ramirez down the aisle. Looking back, he saw that Jas was only a few steps behind. Emily patiently waited until everyone was in the aft compartment, then she touched the button that controlled the belly hatch. A hiss of escaping pressure, then the hatch slid open to reveal the lowered ramp.

'You realize, of course, you've got a lot of explaining to do,' Ramirez said.

Harker forced a smile. 'Yes, well . . . so do they.'

The air was thinner than he expected, cool with the advent of early evening, yet nonetheless it was the first air he'd tasted in a week – longer than that, he reminded himself – that hadn't been reprocessed and filtered. At the bottom of the ramp, he stole a moment to take a deep breath, savoring the aroma of tall grass. Beneath the soles of his moccasins, he felt not the hard surface of floor plates, but the coarse, granular texture of dirt. He never thought common soil would ever feel so good.

Yet Coyote wasn't Earth. One glimpse of the ring-plane of the nearby gas giant, just beginning to rise above the western horizon, was sufficient to remind him of that. Even so, it was enough like Earth that he felt like he'd returned to a familiar place. *These people were lucky*, he thought, remembering the cold, barren landscape of Spindrift. *I hope they appreciate this.*

He didn't have long to reflect on that. The three people whom he'd spotted from the cockpit were coming closer. An older couple, both apparently in their fifties, with a younger woman in her thirties close behind. All three were dressed in what looked like homespun clothes that nevertheless were a little more fancy than he would have expected: long dresses for the two ladies, a jacket, vest, and tie for the gentleman. Harker wondered if they'd dressed so formally for this occasion, or if, by some chance, some other matter merited their appearance.

The older of the two women led the others. She strode forward with a sense of purpose that marked her as a leader. Harker had little doubt who she was. He hesitated for a second, then stepped forward. 'President Gunther?' he asked. She nodded. 'Theodore Harker, first officer of the EASS *Galileo* . . .' *Damn!* he thought. *Screwed that up.* 'Or perhaps,' he quickly added, 'former first officer. As I told you earlier, the *Galileo* is no longer with us.'

'I understand.' President Gunther extended her hand. Harker shook it, trying not to show his nervousness. 'This is my husband, former president Carlos Montero, and Commodore Anastasia Tereshkova, former commanding officer of the EASS *Drake* . . .'

'Now the *Robert E. Lee*, under the flag of the Coyote Federation. It was our skiff that intercepted you.' Although Tereshkova came forward, Harker noticed that she didn't offer her own hand. Even in the dim light, there was no mistaking the distrust in her dark eyes. 'I've heard of you, Mr Harker. The disappearance of the *Galileo* has become something of a legend.'

A European Alliance starship that now belonged to an off-world government? There had to be a story behind this. Once again, Harker realized how much things had changed while he'd been away. 'I imagine it has,' he replied, trying to warm her with a smile. 'Fifty-six years ago, or at least so I've been told.'

'You've been told?' Tereshkova raised an eyebrow. 'By whom?'

Perhaps it was only the thin air, or perhaps the dissonance of the moment. Either way, he felt dizzy for a moment. Harker took a deep breath. 'A long story, believe me.' Remembering his companions, he turned to introduce them. 'Jared Ramirez, astrobiologist, and Emily Collins, the *Celeste*'s pilot.'

On sudden impulse, he reached out to take Emily's hand. After all they'd been through, this was the first chance he'd had to express his feelings for her. The patterns of her *sha*, until now a neutral grey, suddenly took on a warm yellow hue. *I intend to marry her*, he wanted to add, but decided that a less intimate introduction was more appropriate just then. 'We owe much to her,' he said instead. 'She's the one who brought us safely here.'

Emily's grasp, tentative at first, became tighter. She understood what he meant, and gave him a smile in return. President Gunther seemed confused, though, not only by what he said, but also by the shift in the colors of their robes. 'Here from where? Mr Harker, you said that you've come from Rho Coronae Borealis. We've checked our star charts . . . that system's over fifty-four light-years from Earth.'

'And fifty l.y.s from 47 Ursae Majoris.' Ramirez spoke up at last. 'We know. We came through a starbridge.'

'But not one built by us, I gather.' Commodore Tereshkova peered more closely at him; there was suspicion in her eyes. 'Haven't I heard of you before, Dr Ramirez?'

Ramirez quickly looked away, yet his *sha* couldn't hide his emotions. It turned purple, the color of shame and embarrassment. 'All in the past,' he murmured. 'A lifetime ago . . .'

He'll never live down what he once did, Harker thought. *Yet we wouldn't be here if it wasn't for him*. Perhaps, once all was said and done, Jared Ramirez would find peace.

'A lifetime, indeed.' President Gunther slowly exhaled, as if frustrated by having no immediate answers to all the questions that nagged her. 'Look, I'm . . . we're pleased you've managed to find your way here, but you must understand . . .'

'What happened to the *Galileo*?' Her husband, silent until then, suddenly became impatient. 'Why were you fifty light-years from here? What . . . ?'

'Did you make first contact?' President Gunther demanded.

Harker didn't know whether to be irate or merely amused. These people wanted explanations for things that he barely understood himself, with no comprehension of what he and his crew had suffered to discover what little they knew. 'Of course,' he said dryly. 'You haven't figured that out already?' He raised his hand before the president, her husband, or the commodore could interrupt him. 'Look, I know you've got a lot of questions, but . . .' He sighed, not knowing where to begin. 'It's a long story, and there's something important you first need to know.'

President Gunther stared at him. 'And that is . . . ?'

Harker opened his mouth to speak, only to find himself suddenly reluctant. At this moment, he abruptly realized, it was in his power to lie. Or, at the very least, not tell everything he and the others had learned. He could concoct a story that would spare humankind the terrible truths they had learned . . . but also the wonders they had seen.

Behind them, aboard the *Maria Celeste*, an emissary from a distant star was listening to their words. Jas knew how to control their craft. Heshe could leave at any time, return to *Talus qua'spah* and inform the High Council that humankind wasn't yet ready to join the more mature races of the galaxy. And his own kind – capable of individual acts of stupidity, yet nonetheless able to travel to the stars – would never know of the chance that it had once been given.

He looked at the others. Emily smiled, and Jared nodded slowly. The time had come.

Harker turned back around, faced President Gunther once more. 'We are not alone,' he said, and so began to tell the tale.

Epilogue

FEBRUARY 1, 2344 – HIGHGATE

Shillinglaw reached the end of Harker's report. He read the closing paragraph, then read it a second time. Staring at the screen, the Director General took a deep breath and slowly let it out; after a couple of minutes, he stood up from the desk where he'd been sitting for the last few hours and walked to the door.

Just down the corridor from the office he'd borrowed was a lift. Shillinglaw noticed that his hand trembled slightly when he pressed the button for the level where the isolation ward was located. He clenched his fists at his sides and sought to keep his temper in check. Whatever else might happen, he had to remain calm. A confrontation wouldn't do him any good.

Yet his resolve weakened the moment a guard opened the door leading to the visitors' booth. On the other side of a thick window, Harker, Ramirez, and Collins were seated in the lounge; Harker and Collins were watching a soccer game on the wallscreen, while Ramirez dozed on a nearby couch. Shillinglaw noted that they no longer wore the *hjadd* robes they had been wearing when they disembarked from the *Lee*; instead, they were dressed in the one-piece jumpsuits supplied by Highgate's doctors to those who'd just gone through the decontamination procedure. With luck, perhaps ESA scientists would have a chance to examine the robes before they were returned to their owners.

Harker looked up as Shillinglaw entered the booth. He murmured something to Collins, and she glanced toward the window as well. Neither made an effort to get up, though; there was an insolent sense of disregard for him, as if they could've cared less whether the Director General had come to see them. As if to rub it in, Ramirez opened an eye, peered at him for a moment, then rolled over on the couch so that his back faced the window.

Enough. Shillinglaw touched the intercom beneath the windowsill. 'Commander Harker? I've read your . . .'

'Don't bother to use my rank.' Harker didn't look away from the game. 'If you've read it all the way to the end, then you know I've tendered my resignation.' Collins smiled, then briefly raised her hand. 'So has she,' he added. 'We're civilians now. And before you say we can't do that, better read the fine print. Our terms of service ended more than fifty years ago.'

'Score!' Collins clapped her hands, then grinned at Harker. 'Told you Liverpool still has it! Edinburgh hasn't put up a good team in . . .'

'Cut it out, both of you.' Shillinglaw turned his attention to Ramirez. 'And you're not getting out of this either, Jared. You're still serving a life sentence for collaboration with . . .'

'You don't have jack on me.' Wide-awake now, Ramirez rolled over again, then sat up straight. 'Political amnesty . . . remember? Received it straight from President Gunther herself. So far as their government is concerned, I'm now a citizen of the Coyote Federation.'

'As are Emily and I.' Harker took Collins's hand in his, lifted it to kiss the back of her palm. 'In fact, we're engaged. Wedding's next Tuesday, after we get back.'

His brow furrowed, and he glanced at Collins in mock-confusion. 'Or is that next Anael? Still getting used to that calendar of theirs.'

'Next Raphael, dear. Two days from now . . . I think. Can't keep it straight either.' Collins giggled, then looked through the window at Shillinglaw. 'Think you'll be able to attend? We haven't had time to send out invitations, but . . .'

'You're not leaving, if that's what you're trying to say.' Shillinglaw glared at all three of them. 'You're no longer aboard the *Lee*. You've passed through quarantine, which means . . .'

'Sorry, but you're wrong.' Harker waved a hand across the wallscreen to silence it, then stood up and sauntered over to the window. 'We're still in quarantine, if you haven't noticed, which means that we still have the right to return to the vessel that brought us here. In fact, all we've been doing is waiting for you to read our reports while Ana . . . pardon me, Commodore Tereshkova . . . off-loads her cargo and takes on passengers. When she's done, we're going to walk right back through that door and board the *Lee* for the ride home.'

'Our new home, that is.' Ramirez stood up, sauntered over to a nearby table to pour himself a glass of water from the bottle resting there. 'Give Warden Torres my warmest regards, will you?' Then he shook his head. 'Or maybe not. He's probably dead by now.'

Shillinglaw tried to ignore him, although it was hard to do so. From the moment he saw that Ramirez was still alive, all he wanted to do was return him to the place where he'd found him. Which had been his intent all along. Instead, he struggled to remain focused on what had brought him here in the first place: the summation of Harker's mission report.

'It wasn't my fault,' he said. 'Whatever happened to you out there, it wasn't my doing.'

Harker stared at him through the window. He said nothing for a few moments, only regarded the Director General with bleak, cold eyes that, Shillinglaw suddenly realized, had seen thing that would have stopped his heart. Shillinglaw started to say something, but suddenly found that his mouth had become dry.

'Perhaps you're right,' Harker said at last. 'It might have been someone else's idea to put a nuke aboard *Galileo*. Beck, maybe, or even Cole. But you had a hand in it, no doubt about it, and that's what I've written in my report. And you'll have to answer to that, one way or another.'

'You can't prove it.' Shillinglaw swallowed what felt like a handful of sand. 'Even if it gets out . . .'

'Oh, but it will.' Ramirez took a sip of water, then put down his glass and ambled over to the window. 'In fact, you should count on it. Right after we docked, Ted and I accessed the local net node through *Maria*'s comlink. When we saw that you were still alive, we downloaded everything.'

Shillinglaw felt his face grow warm. 'Everything? I don't . . . what do you . . . ?'

'Everything you've just read.' Raising her arms above her head and arching her back, Collins stretched luxuriously. 'Final reports, logbooks, flight recorder transcripts . . . all that's on that disk. Sent to every major media source they could find.'

'By now, everyone has the story.' Harker continued to gaze at him through the window. 'The great mystery, revealed at last . . . the disappearance of the EASS *Galileo.* Or maybe first contact with an alien race will be the story that grabs the headlines.' An offhand shrug. 'Either way, it's your problem, not ours.'

'Sorry we won't be attending the press conference.' A fatuous smirk on Ramirez's face. 'We've got a wedding to go to.'

Shillinglaw's legs felt weak. His heart pounding against his chest, he grasped the windowsill for support. Suddenly, he felt like the old man he'd become. And meanwhile, impervious to the years, Theodore Harker gazed at him, not only through a quarter inch of glass, but also from across an abyss of time and space that he could barely comprehend. 'Why . . . ?'

'Why did we come all this way, just to do this to you?' There was no hint of remorse in Harker's face. 'Because I wanted to look you straight in the eye and tell you what I've learned. The most destructive force in the galaxy isn't the Annihilator. It is arrogance and stupidity.'

He paused. 'Good-bye, John. With luck, we'll never meet again.'

Without another word, Harker turned away from the window. Jared and Emily followed him toward the door that would lead them back through the quarantine facility to the airlock. On the other side of the airlock lay the gangway to the *Robert E. Lee*, which would carry them to the starbridge. Coyote lay just beyond, and from there . . .

A galaxy, one whose wonders and terrors he would never know. Shillinglaw watched them leave, then turned to face the consequences of his actions.

Timeline

COYOTE HISTORY

Earth Events

JULY 5, 2070 – URSS *Alabama* departs from Earth for 47 Ursae Majoris and Coyote.

APRIL–DECEMBER, 2096 – United Republic of America falls. Treaty of Havana cedes control of North America to the Western Hemisphere Union.

JUNE 16, 2256 – WHSS *Seeking Glorious Destiny Among the Stars for Greater Good of Social Collectivism* leaves Earth for Coyote.

JANUARY 4, 2258 – WHSS *Traveling Forth to Spread Social Collectivism to New Frontiers* leaves Earth for Coyote.

DECEMBER 10, 2258 – WHSS *Long Journey to the Galaxy in the Spirit of Social Collectivism* leaves Earth for Coyote.

AUGUST 23, 2259 – WHSS *Magnificent Voyage to the Stars in Search of Social Collectivism* leaves Earth for Coyote.

MARCH 4, 2260 – WHSS *Spirit of Social Collectivism Carried to the Stars* leaves Earth for Coyote.

AUGUST 2270–JULY 2279 – The Savant Genocide; 35,000 on Earth killed; mass extermination of Savants, with the survivors fleeing the inner solar system.

APRIL 2288 – First sighting of Spindrift by telescope array on the lunar farside.

JUNE 1, 2288 – EASS *Galileo* leaves Earth for rendezvous with Spindrift; contact lost with Earth soon thereafter.

JANUARY 2291 – EASS *Galileo* reaches Spindrift. First contact.

SEPTEMBER 18, 2291 – EASS *Columbus* leaves for Coyote.

FEBRUARY 1, 2344 – CFSS *Robert E. Lee* returns to Earth, transporting survivors of the *Galileo* expedition.

Coyote Events

AUGUST 5, 2300 – URSS *Alabama* arrives at 47 Ursae Majoris system.

SEPTEMBER 7, 2300/URIEL 47, C.Y. 01 – colonists arrive on Coyote; later known as 'First Landing Day.'.

URIEL 52, C.Y. 02 – First child born on Coyote: Susan Gunther Montero.

GABRIEL 18, C.Y. 03 – WHSS *Glorious Destiny* arrives. Original colonists flee Liberty; Western Hemisphere Union occupation of Coyote begins.

AMBRIEL 32, C.Y. 03 – WHSS *New Frontiers* arrives.

HAMALIEL 2, C.Y. 04 – WHSS *Long Journey* arrives.

BARACHIEL 6, C.Y. 05 – WHSS *Magnificent Voyage* arrives.

BARBIEL 30, C.Y. 05 – Thompson's Ferry Massacre; beginning of the Revolution.

GABRIEL 75, C.Y. 06 – WHSS *Spirit* arrives.

ASMODEL 5, C.Y. 06 – Liberty retaken by colonial rebels, Union forces evicted from Coyote; later known as 'Liberation Day'.

HAMALIEL, C.Y. 13 – WHSS *Columbus* arrives; construction of starbridge begins.

NOVEMBER, 2340/HANAEL, C.Y. 13 – *Columbus* shuttle EAS *Isabella* returns to Earth via Starbridge Coyote; United Nations recognition of Coyote Federation.

MURIEL 45, C.Y. 15 – *Galileo* shuttle EAS *Maria Celeste* returns to Coyote via alien starbridge.

ACKNOWLEDGMENTS

The author wishes to extend his gratitude to his editor, Ginjer Buchanan, and his literary agent, Martha Millard. Many thanks as well to Rob Caswell; Jeff Hecht; Thomas Peters; Dr Horace Marchant, PhD; Terry Kepner; and Sara Schwager for their support and advice; and to the staff of Wilton Park for their hospitality. And, as always, special thanks to Linda Steele for her love and support.

—Whately, Massachusetts
August 2005–April 2006

SOURCES

Arnold, Luc. F. A. 'Transit light-curve signatures of artificial objects'; *Astrophysical Journal*, July 1, 2005.

Bracewell, Ronald N. *The Galactic Club: Intelligent Life in Outer Space*; W.H. Freeman and Company, 1975.

Brown, Michael E., *et al.* 'Discovery of a planetary object in the scattered Kuiper Belt'; *Astrophysical Journal*, August 29, 2005 (submitted).

Burke, Bernard F. 'Astronomical Interferometry on the Moon'; *Lunar Bases and Space Activities of the 21st Century*, edited by W. W. Mendel; Lunar and Planetary Institute, 1985.

Davis, Joel. 'Worlds Enough'; *Analog*, March 2006.

Favata, Marc, *et al.* 'How black holes get their kicks: gravitational radiation recoil revisited'; *The Astrophysical Journal Letters*, April 20, 2004.

Gilster, Paul. *Centauri Dreams: Imagining and Planning Interstellar Exploration*; Copernicus Books, 2004.

Kepner, Terry L. *Extrasolar Planets: A Catalog of Discoveries in Other Star Systems*; McFarland & Company, 2005.

Mallove, Eugene and Gregory Matloff. *The Starflight Handbook: A Pioneer's Guide to Interstellar Travel*; Wiley & Sons, 1989.

Merritt, David, *et al.* 'Consequences of gravitational radiation recoil'; *The Astrophysical Journal Letters*, April 20, 2004.

Nadis, Steve. 'What Happens When Black Holes Collide?'; *Astronomy*, May 2006.

Tarter, Jill. 'One Attempt to Find Where They Are: NASA's High Resolution Microwave Survey'; *Extraterrestrials: Where Are They?*, edited by Ben Zuckerman and Michael S. Hart (second edition); Cambridge University Press, 1995.